A

Regrettable

PROPOSAL

A *Regrettable* PROPOSAL

JENNIE GOUTET

SWEETWATER
BOOKS

An Imprint of Cedar Fort, Inc.
Springville, Utah

ISBN 13: 978-1-4621-4157-9

Published by Sweetwater Books, an imprint of Cedar Fort, Inc.
2373 W. 700 S., Springville, UT 84663
Distributed by Cedar Fort, Inc., www.cedarfort.com

THE LIBRARY OF CONGRESS CATALOGED THE FIRST EDITION AS FOLLOWS:

Names: Goutet, Jennifer, 1969- author.
Title: A regrettable proposal / Jennifer Goutet.
Description: Springville, Utah : Sweetwater Books, An imprint of Cedar Fort, Inc., [2018]
Identifiers: LCCN 2018025566 (print) | LCCN 2018026739 (ebook) | ISBN 9781462129515 (epub, pdf, mobi) | ISBN 9781462123261 (perfect bound : alk. paper)
Subjects: LCSH: Man-woman relationships--Fiction. | Inheritance and succession--Fiction. | LCGFT: Novels. | Romance fiction.
Classification: LCC PS3607.O89525 (ebook) | LCC PS3607.O89525 R44 2018 (print) | DDC 813/.6--dc23
LC record available at https://lccn.loc.gov/2018025566

Cover design by Markie Riley and Jeff Harvey
Cover design © 2019 Cedar Fort, Inc.
Edited by Jessilyn Peaslee and Emily Chambers

Printed in the United States of America

10 9 8 7 6 5 4 3 2 1

Printed on acid-free paper

Dedication

In memory of Frannie Gamber Sadie—
who laughed at the days to come.

Chapter One

*S*tratford Tunstall, former major of the 94th Regiment of Foot and newly appointed Fifth Earl of Worthing, trudged down Oxford Street in a uniform stiff with dirt. One glance down New Bond revealed a street already thinned of the bustling crowds. All the better. It would not do to appear in such attire in fashionable London, but he had no choice if he was going to reach the counting house before it closed. Picking up his pace, he headed toward the stone building housing the bank, its spring flowers poking through the wrought iron gate.

He passed three women at a storefront, inspecting a purchase of embroidered silk, when one broke away from the group with a startled cry. To his dismay, it was Miss Broadmore, the woman who had jilted him before he left for Spain and the last person he wished to see upon his return.

"Stratford! You've come home. When did you arrive in England?" She seemed to check herself upon observing his appearance more closely, but in the end she extended a slender hand encased in calfskin. Her touch was infinitesimal as he bowed over it.

"Only just." Stratford's voice was gruff, and he cleared it. "I've left my effects at the King's Arms and set out immediately. I must transact some business before the counting house is closed."

"The King's Arms?" Miss Broadmore's brow wrinkled in confusion. "I don't know it. Why are you not staying in your house on Upper Seymour Street? Of course, as Lord Worthing, you will have a new house now—"

He gave a curt nod. "Our house has been rented for the upcoming Season, and I did not wish to impose upon the staff at Cavendish Square without having presented myself at the estate first. I leave tomorrow at first light."

"Of course." Miss Broadmore seemed at a loss for words but made no move to end the conversation.

He caught a whiff of her jasmine soap. It had been too long since he'd smelled a woman of gentle breeding, rather than the blowsy laundresses who followed the troops and reeked of lye soap. It had been too long since he'd been near *this* woman.

She peered at him from under her poke bonnet, bringing to mind another day when those same eyes held his as she released him from their engagement. Pain closed about him like a vice, and, as if in sympathy, the tentative late-afternoon sun hid once again behind the clouds.

"I hear congratulations are in order." Stratford forced the words out of his constricted throat. "You are engaged to be wed." *Again*, he thought. This time it was a viscount, and she must regret her haste all those years ago. Had Judith gone on to wed *him*, she would have been a countess. She'd made her mercenary views abundantly clear on the day she jilted him.

Miss Broadmore looked at her feet. "I fear you are under a misapprehension. Lord Garrett sent the announcement after speaking with my father. But he did not address himself to me, and I'm afraid I do not return his regard." Stratford considered her silently, and she continued in a resigned tone. "These weeks have been uncomfortable for me. In public, I'm labeled a jilt by all but my closest friends." Miss Broadmore glanced at her two companions, who had by now examined every inch of the silk in their attempt to appear disinterested. "At home, I must face my father's wrath." Her eyes pooled with tears. "I suppose I deserve it."

Stratford could not remain impervious to this pitiable declaration, though he privately felt she did. "We must be glad our understanding was never made public." It cost him to say as much, but it would be churlish to continue to punish her.

A silence ensued, and Stratford was unable to bring the conversation to a close. He wanted to pull out his pocket watch to see if there was time, but his arms hung heavy at his sides, and the words remained stuck in his chest. Finally, Miss Broadmore broke the silence. "Please accept my condolences for the loss of your father. I had thought you might, perhaps, have had leave to attend his funeral."

"I had it. But we were laying siege to Ciudad Rodrigo in Spain, and officers were in short supply. My father would have preferred me to see the

2

thing through." His throat worked while he chose his next words. "My uncle was not reconciled to my choice to remain, but I felt I must follow where honor led."

"Your father was always proud of you," she assured him. "I'm told he was following every movement in the Peninsula. And then, to miss acceding to the title by only five days . . ."

There was another silence as Stratford clenched his teeth. *The title! Who cares about the title?* He shifted as if to leave, and Miss Broadmore caught the subtle movement. "Will you be in London this Season?"

The street had grown unnaturally quiet, and he noticed that not only were there no other ladies visible, apart from Miss Broadmore and her friends, but also not even the usual bustle of gentlemen gave the street any life. Stratford managed a tight smile. "As little as I can help it. I've a great deal to do at Worthing and must learn where affairs stand."

"I believe your sisters will have their second Season?" she inquired. Her friend signaled to a waiting footman to open the door to the carriage, and Miss Broadmore took a step toward it.

"My aunt is arranging that, yes." Stratford stood, rooted to the spot with the realization that he must indeed return to London and would likely meet her everywhere. He must do what he could to avoid that. "Good day, Miss Broadmore."

Her head dipped at his formal use of her name, but she replied in kind. "Good day, my lord. Our paths will undoubtedly cross when you return to London."

Miss Broadmore's red-haired companion called out, "Judith, my mother will be most unhappy if I'm late to dress for dinner. As it is, we won't have time for Hyde Park."

Miss Broadmore nodded, then faced Stratford. "Be sure to give my regards to your sisters." She curtsied and turned toward the waiting footman, leaving Stratford alone on the street. The driver snapped the reins, and the carriage clattered over the cobblestone pavement.

Now Stratford did pull out his pocket watch as he marched toward his destination, afraid he might be too late. *So, she jilted someone else, did she?* But this time the man had a title, and she refused his hand in marriage, even against her father's will. Why? Had she learned that happiness does not belong to the highest peer in the realm? *Does she regret refusing me?* He remembered her downcast eyes and was tempted to think she missed him.

No. She only regretted his recent acquisition of the title and her precipitous retreat before obtaining the prize. *Now she'll have to jockey with the other eligible damsels who'll be after my coronet.* He'd have to choose one of them in the end, he reminded himself, but on this matter he would remain firm. *It won't be Judith. She must cut her losses and look elsewhere.*

At the broad, wooden door of the bank, young Mr. Brooks had his back to the street as he wrestled with a skeleton key in the unyielding lock. Stratford called out as he rounded the path from the gate. "Hold there."

"The bank is closed. *Oh*—!" Stratford knew from experience that Mr. Brooks did not like to be caught by surprise, be it an unexplained downturn on the 'Change or a client rushing at him like an unbridled colt. However, one glance at the visitor removed the peevishness from his tone.

"My lord. I had despaired of seeing you today." Mr. Brooks turned the key in the lock—a simple matter, it seemed, now that he was not trying to escape to a warm meal. "Won't you come in, my lord? I've readied the papers, and it's just a matter of pulling them out of the safe." He ushered Stratford into the building and closed the door behind them.

"I apologize for keeping you. I've only just arrived in London and leave for the estate first thing in the morning." Stratford followed Mr. Brooks through the narrow corridors into his small, dark office.

"Kindly have a seat while I fetch all that is necessary." Mr. Brooks went into a side-room where he was heard to turn a key in a lock and rummage through papers and objects. He returned carrying a stack of papers, a little velvet box, and a leather envelope. The velvet box he held out. "Here is your signet ring, as requested. I must say it went against the grain with me to hold on to this for you when you might have needed it at any instant. A peer should not be separated from his ring."

"I had no use for it on the Peninsula. It was in much safer hands with you." Stratford slipped the ring on his finger and felt its unfamiliar weight. *My cousin, John, or even Nicholas, should be wearing this—not me. They had been brought up to the role.* "Thank you for sizing it up."

"Not at all. Here is the sum you asked for in notes and coins. Of course, you can draw on the bank at any time, and we await your instructions on the other transactions you wrote about regarding your father's holdings." Mr. Brooks folded his hands on the desk. "Where are you staying? Upper Seymour has been let."

"The King's Arms," Stratford returned with a sheepish grin.

"The King's Arms . . ." Mr. Brooks sat back, stunned. "But why not Cavendish? My lord, may I remind you we have men who will take care of these details for you. You may entrust them to me."

Stratford gave a weak smile and shook his head. "I am much too accustomed to handling my own affairs."

"You must think of your position," the banker pleaded.

"I can hardly avoid it," Stratford murmured. Here he had completed one taxing journey that had not purged his thoughts from the horrors of that last battle. Tomorrow he would embark on a shorter one, but one which would end in no repose. Family members who had not cared to know him before now would descend upon him at Worthing, and his uncle's ward would arrive the day before the reading of the will. *She must be eager to learn of her expectations*, Stratford thought bitterly. This was followed by another reflection: *I am in no mood for entertaining strangers.*

Stratford took a deep breath. "I expect to proceed with joining the two estates once I ascertain where affairs stand at Worthing. The reading of the testament will occur in a week's time. Meanwhile," Stratford stood, bumping the sconce at his right shoulder, "I thank you for your attention to these matters."

Mr. Brooks gestured forward, allowing the earl to precede him. "May I express, on behalf of Brooks and Sons, our pleasure at having you back on English soil."

Stratford nodded and exited through the front door, pulling his cloak about him as he descended the stairs into the evening shadows. Another three steps and he had turned out the gate and down the near-deserted street. A mid-March gale clanged the wooden shutters on the building next door, and he thought of the hot bath and meal awaiting him at the inn. If only this were the end of his journey and nothing further were required of him.

Chapter Two

*E*leanor Daventry's posture was still perfectly erect when at last the carriage turned on the winding road that led to Worthing Estate. "Aunt, we're here."

The older lady gasped and sat up with a start as Eleanor opened the window and leaned out. "There's a rider in the distance headed toward the estate. A gentleman. Perhaps it's the earl come back from the Peninsula early." She pulled her head in and bestowed a mischievous smile upon her aunt. "To find out if he is, indeed, as rich as a nabob."

"Don't be vulgar, Eleanor." Mrs. Daventry tightened her lips, but the admonishment had little effect on her niece. Her next words did. "The former earl was good to you at a time when no one else took up your cause. I wonder that you can speak so flippantly of him or his legacy."

Eleanor studied her hands clasped on her lap. There was no point in trying humor with her aunt. "I should not, I know. It's just that I did not know my guardian as I could've wished. I'm sensible of his every attention, yet I cannot help but feel I would have preferred his company over his benevolence."

Mrs. Daventry's face paled from another jolt in the carriage. "What he did for you is no small thing. He provided for your welfare and your schooling, and he ensured you would have everything you need for your first Season, including an introduction. Under his patronage, you needed not fear being shunned." Her aunt shifted uncomfortably on the hard seat. "Considering your family history . . ."

Eleanor ignored the unspoken words, which she knew very well. Now the fourth earl was dead, there were no such guarantees. She shot her aunt a narrowed glance. "You're unwell. I wish we'd stopped at the inn. The journey would not have been so tedious if we had traveled in easier stages."

Mrs. Daventry closed her eyes and shook her head. "We would have arrived too late, and it would not do to stop in a public inn without a gentleman escort. I don't mind for my own sake. But for you, I *will* do my duty, though I suffer as a result."

"Aunt." Eleanor's voice contained only a trace of exasperation. "I can survive the taint of a public inn. And rest would have done you good. Never mind. We can ask that you're shown straight to your room and that supper is brought to you."

"You'll do no such thing. As your guardian, I'll remain with you throughout supper." Her aunt sniffed and tugged at the folds of her purple wrap. "Even if I doubt I can eat a thing."

Eleanor hid a smile and stared over the meadow at the copse of trees in the distance, which were starting to show hints of green. "I have the barest recollection of this place. I suppose I should be grateful Lord Worthing invited me even once. I had forgotten how . . ." Her voice trailed away as the carriage turned and sped toward the manor, whose rows of windows were filled with the golden iridescence of the late afternoon sun. The beige stones framing them shimmered under the rays, and the effect was breathtaking.

The doors to the manor swung inward before the carriage came to a halt. Two liveried men marched down the steps, and one opened the carriage door; the other stood at attention as Eleanor extended her gloved hand to alight. Her legs were stiff from the journey, and she turned back to lend her aunt a hand, relieved at the reception they'd received.

The happy feeling was short-lived. Eleanor crossed the threshold to where a housekeeper stood, the woman's face set in rigid contours and her voice lending no warmth. "I am Mrs. Bilks. If you'll both come with me, I'll show you to your rooms. We keep country hours here and serve dinner at six o'clock."

Her aunt looked affronted at the curt tone but chose not to heed it as they trailed the housekeeper. "I am glad," Mrs. Daventry said, huffing as they climbed the winding staircase. "I prefer country hours, but this leaves us only an hour to dress. Is there a maid who can assist us? We've brought none. I mentioned in my letter that our mode of travel would not permit it."

"I've hired a girl from the village," Mrs. Bilks replied. "She will see to your needs."

A girl from the village. They would save their trained staff for the more important guests. Eleanor hated that she must give a civil reply. "Thank you. Her help will be most welcome."

At the top of the stairs, Mrs. Bilks led them along the mahogany railing toward the wing that held their accommodations, and Eleanor gave a final glance at the expressionless footmen, rooted in place like statues by the door. She had a flash of sympathy for them. *How boring their days must be and with little choice to do something different. Not*—she reflected—*unlike my life.*

A movement drew her gaze, and she turned to see a gentleman entering the foyer in a black cape that opened to reveal mud-splattered pantaloons. Nearly the height of the tall footmen, his thick blond hair was tied back, revealing heavy brows, an angular nose, and a downturned mouth like a slash across his face. He caught her gaze and froze. When her steps faltered under his scrutiny, his mouth twisted in acknowledgment, and he swiveled back through the door. Eleanor faced forward again to catch Mrs. Bilks' words.

". . . in adjoining rooms. I'll have the scullery maid stoke the fire as soon as she can be spared."

"Would you be so kind as to send tea for my aunt?" Eleanor inquired. Mrs. Daventry frowned and said nothing. Her silence spoke volumes about how unwell she must be feeling.

"The girl from the village is expected at any moment. When she arrives, I'll have her bring some."

Eleanor entered the bedroom assigned to her, having promised she would return straight away to see to her aunt's comfort. The room was likely meant for a nursemaid, with just enough space on either side of the bed to walk around it, and a spindle-backed chair in front of the cold hearth. When the knock came moments later, she opened the door and let the footmen figure out where to stow her trunk. It would just be a tighter squeeze at the foot of her bed.

It was fine, really. Hadn't she already decided she would seek employment once she left her dear Lydia's household? The conditions at her employer's would be no better than this. Eleanor sat on the white patchwork quilt and took a moment to breathe quietly and deeply, appreciating the play of light through the uneven panes of glass.

What would she do for money if she received nothing from the settlement? Her guardian had looked after her in the past, but he had been an indifferent guardian at best. Who's to say he had thought of her at all? She supposed the request for her presence must mean something. But Mrs. Bilks had been unwelcoming. Was it just that she and her aunt fell on the wrong side of poverty? Or did the new earl know of Eleanor's past and disapprove?

Though the answers to these hypothetical questions were elusive, Eleanor was determined to hope. Perhaps the meeting with the solicitor the next day would bring news of independence. She might have a portion that allowed her to set up a small establishment. *If not, I will look for a position at a school where I will* not *be a drudge.* Despite her aunt's hopes she might make a match, and her obvious endeavors to that end, Eleanor had put aside her own dreams of matrimony for the more achievable goal of independence. She had seen firsthand how seldom such a thing came through marriage.

When Eleanor was in better command of her humor, she knocked at her aunt's door. Upon entering, a quick glance told her everything. "Aunt, you really cannot go down," she protested. "You're too ill."

Mrs. Daventry's eyes filled with tears. "But you *must not* miss your dinner with the earl. It is most important you meet him before the other guests arrive."

"The earl. So it *is* him?" Eleanor ignored the urgency of her aunt's insistence, having an idea where that line of reasoning was headed. She would get no support from her aunt for her desired independence.

"Yes. Mrs. Bilks informed me of it after you were shown to your room. Your guardian's successor is here and will be present at the reading of the will." She caught her niece's eye. "It is imperative that you make his acquaintance before he is distracted by others who are more worthy of his notice."

Eleanor moved to stand in front of the fireplace, forgiving the insult by habit. Her aunt prided herself on speaking the whole truth, not appreciating that one could grasp the state of things without having it spelled out *ad nauseam.* "Has anyone brought you tea?"

"No." Her aunt picked at the fringe of the blanket she had pulled over herself. "And they are not likely to, either, this close to dinner."

"I will insist they do," Eleanor said. "And I will go in search of headache powder. You will feel right as a trivet before long." Before her aunt could protest, Eleanor darted out of the room and retraced her steps down the hallway.

At the bottom of the stairs, she looked around. Straight ahead was the main entrance, and there were no longer any footmen in front of it. On the left was the room the gentleman had quit. She wouldn't go there. The double-doors on the right of the hallway must contain the drawing room, and surely the kitchen would be at the end of the hallway, down the stairs?

Indeed, the door at the end opened on a set of worn stone steps that led to the kitchen, and Eleanor followed the sounds of speech—comfortable intonations of a woman who seemed to be in no hurry. Judging by her competent air and white apron, the person speaking was the cook, and she fell silent as soon as Eleanor stepped through the doorway.

The woman's eyes darted to someone beyond Eleanor's sight before returning to settle on her. "Miss, how may I help you?"

Eleanor smiled warmly in an attempt to put the cook at ease, and to mask her own fear of having committed a breach of etiquette. "It is only that I require some headache powder, and I did not know to whom I should address my request."

Once again, the cook glanced beyond her, and there was deference in the look so that Eleanor felt compelled to turn as well. When she did, the blood drained from her face. It was the earl.

He was leaning against the wall, arms crossed, but now he stood upright and gave a slight bow. "Your servant, ma'am," the earl said in a quiet voice. "Is my staff not seeing to your needs?"

Flustered, Eleanor could only repeat herself. "I came in search of headache powder, my lord. I have not seen a servant since Mrs. Bilks showed us to our rooms."

He examined her. *For signs of duplicity, I suppose.* She sighed inwardly. *And no less than I deserve. What guest wanders around a strange house?*

"I will see that Mrs. Bilks provides some for you," the earl said at last. "Is there anything else you require?"

Though the lines around his mouth lent a severity to his expression, Eleanor perceived something like warmth in his eyes that she had not discerned from afar. She met his gaze squarely. "Some tea, if you please."

He glanced at the cook, then returned his regard to her. "As you wish, miss. Someone will be up shortly."

Eleanor gave a brief curtsy and fled the room, feeling the full embarrassment of the situation. She climbed the stairs as quickly as she dared without being accused of running. In her aunt's room, a maid was pulling dresses from the trunk and shaking them out.

"Oh, has she brought you tea?" Eleanor exclaimed, thinking how embarrassing it would be to have pestered the earl for a service already rendered.

"No, she just arrived from the village. You, girl. Assist my niece with her dress and hair. She must be ready to dine in twenty minutes."

Eleanor followed the maid next door in silence. She knew there would be no persuading her aunt to allow her to skip the dinner with the earl. The girl, Betsy, she learned, began to unlace the back of Eleanor's dress. After discarding it, Eleanor slipped on her evening gown—a hand-me-down silk, brown, like her hair and eyes, with ivory lace trim. The girl shook out the travel dress and laid it on the bed. "Miss, if you don't mind, I'll take this downstairs and see to the mud."

"Yes, please do. Now come and lace me up so you'll have time to dress my hair. It won't do to be late to dinner." She remained standing as Betsy pulled her dress tight, and then she sat in front of the vanity table with its small glass and watched the maid weave long, thin braids around the chignon and coax her rather insipid hair into curls that sprang next to her cheeks. The result was pleasing.

In her aunt's room, Mrs. Bilks was setting out the tea tray with pursed lips. Eleanor stood by the door as Mrs. Daventry addressed the housekeeper. "I'm unable to accompany my niece to dinner. Please send my regrets to the earl for my delay in making his acquaintance."

"Yes, ma'am." Mrs. Bilks puckered up even more but opened the adjoining door and summoned Betsy to assist the older woman. To Eleanor, she said, "Miss, will you come with me?"

Eleanor followed the housekeeper out of the candlelit room, whose cozy walls she immediately missed. She was not looking forward to dinner with a man who did not seem prone to comfortable conversation and whose only warmth was hidden somewhere in his eyes. A chilly draft seeped into her bones as she moved through the grim corridor. Its decor hadn't penetrated her senses before, but now she noticed every imposing statue, crossed swords, and frowning portrait, the whole of which left her with a dramatic sense of doom at complete variance with her practical mind. She repressed a nervous giggle. *Like a lamb to the slaughter, there go I.*

Mrs. Bilks ushered Eleanor into a brightly lit drawing room where the Fifth Earl of Worthing stood facing the fire. "My lord, may I present Miss Daventry?"

The earl turned and bowed. "I don't believe Miss Daventry needs an introduction. She has managed that on her own," he said, with a quirk of his lips she had no hope of interpreting. "I hope your headache is better."

Nonplussed by the smile that softened his accusatory words, she could find none of her own with which to respond. Mrs. Bilks continued in a detached voice. "Mrs. Daventry is unwell and cannot join you for dinner. She sends her respects and has asked me to accompany Miss Daventry to the dining room."

The earl nodded and gestured forward. Once they were seated, the footman served the first course and took his place against the wall. Lord Worthing turned to her with a smile that did not reach his eyes. Perhaps she had misread the warmth found there earlier. "I hope your travel was agreeable."

"Apart from my aunt's indisposition, it was very pleasant. I don't travel much and quite enjoyed the new scenery." Eleanor took a breath to continue but knew not what to say next. She fixed her eyes on the centerpiece, an imposing arrangement of evergreens and branches of fuchsia.

She had nearly finished her egg ball soup before the silence grew unbearable. "My lord, I understand you've resigned your commission. Were you still in the Peninsula?" Eleanor felt her face grow warm at the inane question to which she already knew the answer.

Lord Worthing took a moment before responding. "My last battle was in January. The general gave me leave to resign my commission, and I returned to England." She glanced at his face to see what his thoughts were on his change in circumstances but read nothing there.

After another silence, he motioned for the footman to bring the jellies to his dinner companion, saying in a more conversational voice, "Mr. Harrison informed me of your presence at the reading of the will tomorrow. As it will not be read until four o'clock, would you like to have a horse saddled in the morning?"

"That would be kind of you. I do not often have this pleasure."

"I can lend you my groom. Unfortunately, I have a meeting with the bailiff, which will last the morning, and I'm unable to accompany you." The earl glanced at her, then resumed eating.

"Thank you," Eleanor said, unsure of what to say further. She was not an experienced conversationalist, and this was only the second course.

When the silence stretched too long, Lord Worthing broke it. "You're situated in Surrey I believe?"

"For the past ten years, I've resided at school or with my aunt, Mrs. Martha Daventry, who lives in Camberley. My guardian—the former Earl of Worthing—consigned me to her care when I lost my parents." Her composed voice hid the inner turmoil. "My father's friendship with your uncle, as you might know, was of long date."

"I'm afraid I've not yet had time to apprehend this branch of the family's genealogy or acquaintances. I was unable to return home in the two months before my uncle's illness had reached a critical juncture. I was made aware of my succession to the land and title only when my cousin fell at Badajoz." For the first time, his eyes met hers squarely, but he looked away again before she could register her thudding heart over what felt like a frontal attack.

"I . . . I see. So you were not raised with the expectation." The answering silence was so overwhelming, she dared not mar it by clinking silverware and laid her fork on the tablecloth.

"No," he responded finally. "I was not." He looked as if he would say more, but in the end his gaze settled on her, and his green eyes pierced in the most uncomfortable way.

Eleanor wanted to inquire what occupied his thoughts when he stared at her in such a penetrating way, but instead she cast about for a more suitable question. "Were you well acquainted with your uncle?"

His frown was back in place. "I met him but once when I was thirteen. He didn't think he would be passing anything on to me, you see, and I was therefore beneath his notice." Lord Worthing twirled the stem of the glass in his fingers while his meat grew cold.

Oh. Her mouth formed the word. She had been impertinent with her personal questions. She had better done to stick to the weather.

At last the earl seemed to remember the meal in front of him and picked up his fork so that Eleanor was encouraged to do the same. He chewed his beef thoughtfully and stared at the emerald green curtains that shut the view of the darkening sky from the dining room.

Eleanor ate mechanically and attempted no more conversation until Lord Worthing finally stood, signaling the end of the meal. He turned toward her then, and when she raised her eyes to his, he held her gaze and his expression softened. "Miss Daventry, tomorrow our house will be filled with guests, but I've spoken to Mrs. Bilks to ensure there will always be someone dedicated to your comfort. If you want anything, you need only ask."

Feeling the urge to blink back tears at this unexpected show of kindness, Eleanor inclined her head. "Thank you, my lord," she said, and then she followed the housekeeper into the hallway. The candle threatened to extinguish in the cool, drafty hallway, but the door to the dining room remained open, spilling light into the corridor. She felt the presence of the earl's regard until they turned to go up the stairwell.

Chapter Three

*S*tratford walked alongside his bailiff, both leading their horses as they approached the Munroe hamlet. The silence between them was brooding on one side and respectful on the other.

Images of his return filtered through Stratford's thoughts. He'd had a full year to adjust to his mother's death before he left for the war, and though he expected his homecoming to be strange without his father there to welcome him either, the reality of the double loss filled every corner of his life. The weight of new responsibility on top of it was nearly crippling. If only his father had been alive to inherit the title first, giving Stratford time to adjust to their change in fortune, it might have eased the transition. Moreover, yesterday's post brought a letter from his sister, reminding him that caring for the family now fell squarely on his shoulders.

He feared those burdens would include Miss Daventry. As the former earl's ward, surely she would receive a small portion to live on. Unless her guardianship was foisted on him. *Was such a thing possible?* Apart from her wandering his house unescorted, she seemed a timid little thing in want of protection, and he hoped her aunt was generally more visible than she had been last night. He was certainly not interested in taking on the role, having more than enough to worry him.

Despite his unease concerning his potential role in Miss Daventry's future, Stratford had noticed from their first encounter in the kitchen the pleasing profile she presented when she spoke to the cook. After dinner, there had been something in her look when she raised her eyes to his as they bid goodnight. He'd thought her conversation commonplace enough, but when he turned to face her at the end of the evening, he beheld an understanding in her eyes that arrested his attention. It made him regret not having paid more attention during dinner. What else had he missed?

What had occupied his thoughts over dinner, however, was that chance meeting with Judith on his way to the bank. What were the odds? That unlucky encounter had given Judith the boldness to contact him again, for yesterday's post also brought an invitation from the Broadmore residence, even if it was just for a party they were hosting in London and contained no other personal words than to welcome him back. He, however, was not ready to return the gesture and invite *her* back into his life.

They had not yet announced their betrothal before she claimed to have changed her mind, spurring his determination to leave for the Peninsula. There had been no scandal; they had only been suspected of sharing a *tendre*, but if his heart had leapt at the sight of her in London last week, the haunting words of her refusal forced him to harden his heart.

I was too hasty in my promise . . . nothing more than an infatuation . . . don't wish my children to mingle with the shop. It was the last bit that stung more than all else because it revealed at once a ton prejudice against his mother he had refused to acknowledge and his own failure to recognize shallowness in the fairer sex. He had been thoroughly taken in.

What galled him was how hard it was to reconcile Judith's smiling greeting, her hand placed intimately on his, with those stark words from three years earlier. It was as if, in her mind, that conversation had been wiped clean from their history. *For someone who grew up surrounded by women*, he thought grimly, *I know nothing of them.*

The bailiff—a Mr. Grund—gestured to the meadow on their left. "The tenants who live here work this plot of land. It's the most lucrative of the Worthing property on account of that stream over there that feeds it. It's not entailed, but that should not signify as it was your great-uncle's prize purchase during his days of expansion. He considered the acquisition his greatest coup." Mr. Grund leaned in. "You'll not mind my familiarity, my lord? I believe you wished to know every detail I can think of." Stratford nodded.

"See here—" Mr. Grund took a clump of earth and crumbled it in his fingers. "It's the richest soil I've seen in this part of the county. This portion of the land alone brings in three thousand pounds per annum."

Letting out a quiet whistle, Stratford said, "Good news indeed. The estate is in better condition than I was led to believe." He looked toward the horizon, appreciating the pale sunbeams so different from the Peninsular glare he had learned to live with. His horse shuffled impatiently, breath steaming in the early spring air. "How did the tenants view the former earl?"

"Oh . . ." Mr. Grund stroked his chin. "They liked him well enough. They held him in esteem and observed all the signs of mourning when he left this world."

Stratford absently touched his own black armband serving double duty, even though the six months were nearly up. "And how do they look upon the new earl?" He glanced at the bailiff out of the corner of his lashes, wearing the hint of a smile.

Mr. Grund eyed him speculatively. "They are full of confidence in the new earl's condescension and hope to see his children grace the house before long."

Stratford let out an unwilling laugh. "So we're there already, are we?" He shook his head, but his frown returned, as did the unwilling image of blonde curls and a smile he did not trust. "There is no prospective Lady Worthing at present, but I do not intend to remain a bachelor like my predecessor. It is yet another affair I must see to in my new role."

The bailiff furrowed his brows but let the comment pass. "Now, my lord, if you'll just ride with me to the east, I'll show you the part of the estate that needs the most work. I believe the former earl's illness had weakened him some time before he let on because he stopped caring about this less visible portion of the estate."

Stratford swung into the saddle and spent the next hour and a half taking mental note of how he would prioritize the repairs. He and Mr. Grund promised to meet two days hence.

On his return, the horse's hooves struck out a soothing beat, and Stratford began to relax for what seemed like the first time since he set foot on English soil. He may have been new to the title, but he was already familiar with how to turn an estate to profit. And this one showed great promise. Now if only he could acquire the necessary grace to interact with his tenants so they might be on good terms . . .

"Ho, Tunstall!" A voice from behind made him jolt upright in the saddle. The earl swiveled on his horse and looked down the path to see a familiar face.

"Amesbury," Stratford replied, his eyes lit with surprise. Though John Amesbury could hardly be considered above an acquaintance, he had frequented their circle of friends in school and was part of the young bucks in London in the short years before Stratford had left for the war. He was also the first of old acquaintances Stratford had met upon his return. "What brings you to these parts?"

Amesbury rode alongside, leaned from his horse, and stuck out his hand. "*The devil.* You're *Worthing* now. Old habits die hard. I just heard news you'd arrived, and I came to see you. Some were laying bets you'd resign your commission as soon as you got your title."

"With the struggle we had after Ciudad Rodrigo, I didn't like to. They could ill spare me, but in the end, the general himself gave the order. He was tight with the old earl before his death. Sent his condolences when my cousin Nicholas fell. But you, *here*! Is this the part of Sussex you're from?"

"I'm your neighbor. My property borders yours on the southwest. I used to get into all sorts of mischief with your cousins growing up, and we both went after the same Miss Hamilton—now Mrs. Cranford—and lost out. Obviously."

"You said not a word of this when we were at Cambridge together." Stratford reined in to keep pace with Amesbury.

"Faith, I'd forgotten you were even related. You didn't come from the same parts, and they never breathed a word of you."

"We were not intimately acquainted. We shared blood only." Stratford shot a considering look at his neighbor. "My father married a Cit, and that was the end of that."

Amesbury gave a negligent wave. "People put too fine a point on it. It's the way to go if one needs funds and the chits making their come-out are none too plump in the pocket. *And* as long as she don't squint." Amesbury continued. "By the by—I'll have you know, Miss Broadmore will be married. You might not've heard the news since you were away. Word had it you and she had thought to make a match of it at one time."

"She will not marry," Lord Worthing said, shortly.

" 'Twas in the papers. Saw the announcement myself," Amesbury protested. "You're not still holding out for her! You can do better now with your title."

"I'm not holding out for her," Stratford said, his unconscious stiffening urging the horse a pace forward. "I had a chance meeting with Miss Broadmore in London, and she informed me herself of having just broken the engagement. Said they should not suit."

Amesbury eyed him keenly. "She was wearing the willow, then. Pity the affair didn't take off four years ago. I lost a bet on it—" He fell silent when he realized to whom he was speaking, then continued weakly, "Wish you happy."

"Please." Stratford's voice was dry. "Save your felicitations. You are mistaken." In an effort to divert him, he spoke without thinking, and without any real enthusiasm. "I'm meeting the stagecoach to see that the solicitor is properly welcomed, then we lunch at one o'clock. Will you join us?"

"You'll have to give up these notions of welcoming people yourself now that you're the earl. It's just not done, Tunstall—Worthing, I mean. People expect a man of consequence, not one who does what any footman can do."

"Never mind what they expect. In the end, they'll get me. I've told James to meet me there so we'll welcome Mr. Harrison and then go to Worthing. The reading of the will is not until four, so a one o'clock luncheon will suit. You'll need to put off your more colorful stories as we'll be sharing the meal with some of my uncles—what? Why are you laughing?"

Amesbury shook his head. "Are you trying to draw back your invitation?"

"Of course not." Stratford gestured to a fork on the right. "This way."

Eleanor, returning from her morning ride, found the manor in a livelier state than the previous night. She spotted three carriages unloading passengers in front of the circular stone staircase and paused to watch the ensuing bustle. A gentleman, encased in a padded coat in jaundiced yellow, called out in stringent accents, "You there! Take Lady Keyes's portmanteau. You'll need to remove these two trunks first. Take care what you're about, man."

Hiding a smile, Eleanor turned and rode toward the stables and allowed the groom to assist her in dismounting. In the dim interior of the far end, his back to her, the rather shabbily dressed earl teased a gentleman whose spine was as stiff as his collar. "I see you still don't trust anyone but your own groom—"

"Or myself—" the earl's friend inserted.

"—or yourself, which is a ridiculous notion. Are you still racing Thunder?"

"He's retired from the lists. Shame. He brought me a fair profit. I had high hopes for Salamander—you ain't seen her yet—but she's foaling and won't be racing again." The gentleman flicked his riding crop against the stall and turned when Eleanor's horse blocked the light pouring into the stable. He threw a surprised look at the earl.

Lord Worthing moved forward when he saw his groom trailing Eleanor. "Jesse, Mr. Harrison will be returning to Salisbury after our meeting, and you'll need to have the carriage ready any time from six o'clock." Jesse gave a nod and led the horse into the first stall on his left.

Flicking a glance her way, the earl said, "Mr. Amesbury, allow me to present Miss Daventry. She was my uncle's ward and is here to attend the meeting with the solicitor. Miss Daventry, this is Mr. Amesbury." She sank into what she hoped was a graceful curtsy as he executed a correct bow.

"It's a pleasure." Mr. Amesbury spoke in a bored voice, but his eyes missed nothing as the groom rubbed down Eleanor's mount. "She's short in the hind legs, you know."

"I know," said Lord Worthing. "She was my uncle's."

Eleanor's brows snapped together—*what?*—as the earl addressed her. "Jesse will care for the horse. We sit down to lunch at one o'clock."

Dismissed, Eleanor nodded and turned on her heel, head held high. Skirting the groom, she picked her way across the stable floor and had reached the sun-filled opening before she realized they had been talking about the horse. *Horses* have hind legs. Girls do not. She grinned weakly at her own foolishness and prepared to go on, but the next remark stopped her in her tracks.

"Little dab of a thing, ain't she?"—words she knew she was not meant to hear.

The anger returned and this time with cause. *Yes, Mr. Amesbury*, she thought, resuming her march toward the house. *I know I'm a dab of a thing. Not at all to your liking. It's fortunate I'm not out to catch a husband or I would be quite out.* She took in a lungful of fresh air and blinked against the sting in her eyes.

The short strip of grass beyond the stables led to the stone path and circular driveway, which was empty now with all newcomers indoors. The manor looked as it did the day before. *For all its beauty and pleasing layout, this place does seem to bleed the life from one.* Eleanor walked with purpose up the stone staircase, squinting in the darkness that enveloped her as soon as the footmen gave her entrance. Making her way directly to her aunt's room, she scratched at the door.

"You're looking well, Aunt." Eleanor bent over and gave her a dutiful kiss. "I didn't want to disturb you before I took the horse out this morning. Will you spare Betsy when your toilette is complete? Lord Worthing told me we lunch at one."

Mrs. Daventry examined her niece in the glass. "Have a seat, my dear. I'm told we will be quite numerous. How was your dinner with the earl?"

Eleanor perched on the edge of the chair and gave a rueful shake of the head. "Torturous. He couldn't bear to make conversation. I understand I am not yet nineteen and, and . . . perhaps not much to look at, but were he more of a gentleman, I should not have known it."

Mrs. Daventry frowned. "Perhaps you will grow on him with time. It's quite possible those years in the Peninsula affected him. I understand soldiers can suffer from melancholy."

Eleanor shook her head. "He seemed at ease with the friend who will be joining us for lunch. Do you know who is here? I saw no less than three carriages when I rode in."

Her aunt shrugged as Betsy clipped a gold chain in place around her neck. "Will that be all, ma'am?" the girl asked.

"Yes, you may attend to my niece." Mrs. Daventry frowned. "Eleanor, you'd best wear your blue muslin. That brown you make such a habit of wearing does nothing for your complexion."

"Yes, Aunt." Eleanor gave a quiet sigh and caught Betsy looking at her with sympathy. The maid bobbed a curtsy. "Miss, if you please? I will go and fetch some hot water."

"Thank you, Betsy." When the door closed softly behind her, Eleanor came and stood before her aunt. "How soon may we leave after the will is read?"

"My dear, it depends largely on what the will contains." Mrs. Daventry swiveled in her seat. "And the procedure for carrying it out. *And* how well the earl takes to you. In any event, it was kind of your guardian to make known his intention to provide for your Season. At the very least, you need not be ashamed to present yourself to The Lady Ingram."

"How well he takes to me?" Eleanor said. "I hope you aren't scheming because I assure you any efforts you or I might make are wasted. He has no interest in me."

Her aunt's face fell. "What a pity. Well," she patted one of her curls, "maybe one of the other gentleman will." She caught Eleanor's scowl before it could be whisked away. "Take care, my dear, or you'll get wrinkles."

"Yes, ma'am," Eleanor replied, turning to the window so her aunt wouldn't comment on her slumped shoulders as well.

Lunch was spent only slightly more tolerably than the previous night's dinner, with Eleanor seated between Mr. Amesbury and Sir Ambrose Keyes. Mr. Amesbury, who had decided she lacked looks, address, and a portion, did not put himself out to please, but performed his part punctiliously. When all other subjects had been exhausted, he forged ahead with the battle-weary pluck of a hardened conversationalist. "Miss Daventry, I understand from the earl that your father succumbed to illness from battle wounds when you were still quite young."

"Yes. I was nearly six when he died."

"And your mother?" Mr. Amesbury was busy attacking his steak and did not see her tense.

"My mother gave up all claims to natural affection when she remarried. Her husband is a French count, and they moved to the Continent in 1802." Eleanor's voice was firm, and she bore her glass steadily to her mouth, despite the alarming look her aunt shot her from across the table. She continued as if she hadn't seen. "The former Lord Worthing was a great friend of my father's and showed his kindness in taking me on as his ward."

Before Mr. Amesbury could respond, Eleanor was called upon to listen to Sir Ambrose's condescending oratory on the subjects that interested him. She was grateful for the reprieve and that little time remained that required her to converse with Mr. Amesbury, whose fixed gaze on the plate in front of him told her he felt no duty to continue the conversation.

Stratford did not learn of Amesbury's views on Miss Daventry until the meal had been shared and Amesbury was ready to leave. He announced that he would take himself off immediately rather than rejoin the ladies in the drawing room, not wishing to encroach on a family party. Stratford accompanied him to the stables, where Amesbury confronted him.

"I say, old friend. I'm surprised you have Miss Daventry residing here. Her family is too smoky by half." Amesbury's mouth twisted with indignation. "I'll not thank you to have placed her next to me."

"What the deuce do you mean?" True, Miss Daventry had had little to say when he dined with her, but she'd uttered nothing that could be called objectionable. Stratford frowned, realizing that the failure of their dinner together might not lie entirely with her. *I did not behave as a gentleman ought. I was in no humor to dine with anyone, much less a young lady who was a perfect stranger . . .*

"Do you not know?" Amesbury replied. "Her mother abandoned her daughter and eloped with a Frenchman, and they now live on the Continent. The devil only knows whether she was yet a widow. That your uncle recognized the girl baffles me, but my advice to you, dear fellow, is to let her collect her share of the pot—whatever that may be—and send her packing. Your connection is not widely known, and it may not be too late if you give her the cut direct as soon as you are able."

"Surely, someone whose consequence is as great as mine cannot be hurt in any way by a connection I choose to form." Stratford's voice was mild, but had his neighbor chanced to look at his face, he would have seen his lip curl.

Amesbury missed the irony. "No, no, you have it all wrong. You can never be too careful—" He did not finish his thought because the groom came forward leading his horse. "Ah, you had him saddled, did you? I'll just check the straps myself. No, you see they're too tight here, don't you?"

Stratford's thoughts went to Miss Daventry for a second time that day. It seemed it would not prove an easy thing for his uncle's ward to find a suitable match, and unlike Amesbury, it was not in his nature to cast off an object of ill-repute—or pity, since she was not the cause of it. He hoped for her sake she'd receive something to live on so she was not dependent on society—most particularly, his.

"I'm for London on Friday." Amesbury, now mounted, was ready to be off. "Come play billiards with me this evening. I've found the most excellent brandy buried in my father's cellar. I've been kicking my heels in this cursed place for too long and am in need of some diversion."

Stratford smiled to himself, having learned in as little as two hours that—far from being a "cursed place"—Amesbury's estate was his pride and joy. "I cannot escape my duties of playing host at dinner," he replied.

"Come afterward. No one can have a thing to say about that." When he saw Stratford start to shake his head, he drawled, "Come, and I'll tell you what really happened with Mack and the hog when they went to the prizefight."

Stratford laughed at the unexpected memory. Years fell away, and he was back in school, where there was no disappointment in love, no bloody war, no title and estate to uphold. "Mackery always did kick up the best larks. I thought you swore to secrecy. Word of a gentleman and all that."

"He spilled the story himself at White's. It was the talk of the town. You were away though." Amesbury's horse sidled impatiently, and he gripped the reins. "So I can count on you to come?"

"I'll come as soon as I'm able." Stratford gave a wave, and Amesbury rode off.

Chapter Four

*T*he reading of the will took place in the library at four o'clock. The chairs were arranged in two rows of semicircles with an aisle in the middle. Stratford sat in the front with Mrs. Hester Tunstall, sister-in-law to the former earl, who had been more gracious to him at their first meeting in twenty years than he'd expected. Her two sons had been destined for the earldom were it not for their untimely deaths in the war, but there was no trace of acrimony in her conversation or tone.

Behind them in the last row, the old earl's steward and his wife took seats, shifting uncomfortably in their chairs. Stratford knew if their presence were requested, it meant they would be receiving something. He was glad for their sakes but had been prepared to show his uncle's respect on their behalf.

On the other side of the aisle were two more of his aunts, sisters to the former earl, neither of whom he had met more than once. Aunt Lucretia and her husband, Sir Ambrose, sat at an angle in order to converse with Aunt Gertrude behind them, who was flanked by her husband and three daughters. In the last row were four people whom Stratford had met only minutes before entering the drawing room. He gathered these to be distant relatives or recipients of the earl's generosity.

Miss Daventry and her aunt took up the two seats directly behind Stratford, and the urge was strong to turn and see what Miss Daventry's face revealed. What was she anticipating from the bequests? Stratford couldn't shake the disquieting feeling he would end up with her as his charge. What impoverished female wouldn't call upon any connection she might have to gain introduction to the ton? He could hardly turn her away since she had been a guest in his home.

At the same time, he couldn't help but be intrigued by the secret glimpses into what he thought was her true nature. A girl who was not afraid to wander a strange house in search of headache powder and tea. As to that, his staff's lapse in seeing to Miss Daventry's needs did not do him any credit, and he had been obliged to take Mrs. Bilks to task.

Miss Daventry had also accepted to dine with him, a strange man, with only the footmen in attendance and had not shown any discomfiture over his lack of warmth. Stratford was determined, when they next spoke, to pay her every courtesy to make up for that evening. And just this morning, she had agreed to ride with only a groom in attendance, where Jesse said she had acquitted herself well on horseback—no small compliment coming from him. Overall, Miss Daventry was showing herself to be quite intrepid.

Just as the solicitor called the meeting to order, the door opened and a young man in a pink-and-teal-striped waistcoat entered. "You'll have to pardon my tardiness," he announced. "I had a near run with a cow-handed stagecoach driver and had to pull over to calm my leaders . . ."

"Come in, come in," Sir Ambrose fretted. "Let's not waste any more of this good man's time."

The solicitor looked up from his documents and gestured the gentleman to the remaining seat. "Ladies and gentlemen, we will now commence with the reading of the Last Will and Testament of Everard Miles Sherborne Gerard Tunstall, Fourth Earl of Worthing. We begin with the entailed property left to the Fifth Earl of Worthing, detailed with precision, as you see here in this map."

The solicitor traced his finger along the document until he found the coordinates he was looking for and began the demarcation. "This is the border of the southeastern part of the estate, situated near Amesbury. The entailed portion does not include this stream here or these acres touching it. The eastern portion of the territory includes this section of forest and the hunting box within it."

Mr. Harrison continued to demonstrate the extent of the entailed property that would fall into the hands of the fifth earl before ending the foreseen details of entailment and beginning the list of bequests. A general stir in the room accompanied this change, with Sir Ambrose leaning over to whisper to his wife, and Gertrude's husband patting her hand.

Hester Tunstall, widow of the fourth earl's brother, received the apartment in Bath the former earl had purchased independently of the estate. Lady Keyes, sister of the deceased, was given that portion of the library she had requested for her husband's use, and his nephew Philip, a gold fob left by the third earl.

Gertrude Halsey, second sister of the deceased, received the grandfather clock and extra set of chinaware in Cavendish Square, since, "as the earl stipulated"—the solicitor peering above his spectacles to quote—"you were forever pestering me about them."

The young gentleman in the pink coat—Stratford discovered—was Richard Crenshaw, another of the earl's wards. In addition to his small independence of 500£ per annum, he was to receive the prized mare in the stables, but, "he must stable her himself now that he is of age."

At last, the solicitor came to Miss Daventry. Stratford's heartbeat sped a notch, and he leaned forward. "For Miss Eleanor Camilla Daventry, the Fourth Earl of Worthing has left a sum of three hundred pounds for her London Season, which should be enough to secure a trousseau, a court presentation, her hand, etcetera." *Good*, thought the earl. *That should launch her. I wonder where her aunt has lodgings . . .*

"The earl has also bequeathed Miss Daventry a dowry of fifty acres of unentailed land on the southeastern edge of the property, bordering the stream to Amesbury, known as Munroe hamlet and its surrounding . . ."

The rest of the words were lost as Stratford spun around in his chair. Miss Daventry was so still she looked to be barely breathing. He turned back in time to hear the solicitor give the crowning touch. ". . . of which the income—apart from the sum set aside for the London Season—will be bestowed on her upon marriage."

Stratford's mind raced furiously. He'd lost the most lucrative part of his estate—to a girl who wouldn't benefit from it. At least not until she married, and then the land would pass straight into her husband's hands. So then Miss Daventry was no better off than before, except that she would be hounded by every fortune hunter on this side of London. He ground his teeth. *Of all the fool things.*

The solicitor stacked his papers neatly and slid them into the stiff leather bag. He removed his spectacles and gave a nod to the earl. Stratford, rooted to his chair, felt all eyes on Miss Daventry as the buzz of conversation in the room increased. Crenshaw, in particular, leered at her in the most repulsive way. Finally, the earl stood and turned as Mrs. Daventry, a gloating smile in place, pulled Miss Daventry's arm. *Of course she would be smug*, he thought angrily. *What a coup she has made.* Then one glance at Miss Daventry's stricken face gave Stratford pause.

The Daventrys had not yet exited the room when Sir Ambrose put his hand on Stratford's arm. "It's utterly preposterous. A young girl of that stock inheriting such a large share of the estate. Can't you do something?"

Stratford looked from the hand on his arm to the florid face of his distant relative, his voice icy. "I will do what needs to be done, of course."

At this, Sir Ambrose pulled his arm back. "Well, well," he muttered.

Stratford turned away. Honestly, what *could* he do? He would inquire, but these testaments could not, in general, be overturned. He'd have to make the best of it and hope for no more spurious remarks from greedy or overly sympathetic relatives. These people may be relations, but they'd had nothing to say to him before he inherited. How he hated such affectation. Now he'd have to endure dinner and an evening's insipid entertainment. *What I need*, thought the earl, *is a stiff drink.*

He didn't get it. In the short interval before dinner, a delegation of sympathizers came to bemoan his uncle's stupidity. And if he thought Miss Daventry and her aunt might not appear at dinner, he was wrong. Mrs. Daventry showed either good breeding or an utter lack of sensibility by appearing as if nothing were wrong. He suspected the latter.

The same couldn't be said for Miss Daventry, who was pale and quiet. At least she wasn't flaunting her success. He wanted to know what she was thinking, what she planned to do now that she had this inheritance. Did she have any designs on him? He should just steer clear, but the less she spoke the more curious he became.

It was not until after dinner in the drawing room that he was able to get a word alone with her. Her aunt, the Keyeses, and Gertrude's husband were engaged in whist, and he suspected only a play for points could resign the baronet to mingling with Mrs. Daventry. Crenshaw took off after mumbling about a prizefight not three miles distant, and both Gertrude and Hester had pleaded a headache.

Poised on the edge of the settee was Miss Daventry, book in hand.

Stratford approached, and when Miss Daventry lifted her face to his, he was again struck by the look of intelligence in her eyes, which he now saw were light brown in color with specks of gold. He reached across her to turn the cover of her book, baring the title.

"*Romance of the Forest,*" he said. "A fan of the gothic novels, are you?"

"I cannot say. It's my first one. I found it in your library." Miss Daventry put her finger in the place where she'd been reading and gave him her full attention.

"Hopefully from the section of the library that will go to my aunt. May I sit?"

Once beside her, it was harder to find something to say. He rested his hand on one knee and faced her. "Your mother is on the Continent."

Miss Daventry nodded. "I understand it to be so. I've not had word from her since she left, and I was but seven when that occurred."

"Likely communication was interrupted by the war." Stratford gave her a searching glance.

"Perhaps." She returned his gaze, and he caught the flicker of a rueful smile. "But I would not wager on it. She has not once shown, to my recollection, a single display of maternal affection." Miss Daventry did not appear disconcerted by the admission.

"So your aunt raised you then?" He looked ahead to the lady in question but could not find in her the author of such quiet character as Miss Daventry appeared to possess.

"My aunt has been most attentive, but it was my former nurse who deserves the credit. Or the blame." She laughed, and the musical sound lifted the corners of his mouth, rusty from disuse. "Prisca was not intimidated by the late earl, and she persuaded him to allow me to attend Miss Spencer's Academy, which was highly recommended by the rector. And so I was given the benefit of a real education."

This was the longest speech from her yet, and he wanted more. "You were fortunate in your protectors," he said. "Not many nurses would be willing to brave conversation with an earl to gain an advantage for their charge."

"I was most fortunate," she agreed. "And Prisca was not an ordinary nurse. Her consideration for others was equally given, be it to a duke or a chimney sweep." Miss Daventry's lips twitched in humor. "However, I've sometimes wondered if, in speaking to the earl, she was merely attempting to relieve herself of my charge."

"Oh, yes. A burdensome one, to be sure," he teased. Her answering smile deepened the perfect dimples on each cheek and transformed her demure look to one of mischief.

Stratford's own smile lingered. "Where does your aunt reside when she's in London?"

"My aunt rents a lodging in Bedford Square when she's in town." The words sat between them before silence reigned over both. Stratford fixed his eyes on the party of four playing cards on the other end of the room, a sense of foreboding lodged in his chest. A rented lodging in Bedford Square did not bode well for Miss Daventry's London Season. Surely she would expect something from him, and more than he was capable of offering. *What am I doing getting mixed up in affairs that are not my own?*

Too uncomfortable to pursue the matter further and conscious that he was ending the conversation in haste, Stratford bid her good night. He felt her eyes on him as he made the rounds, speaking to each of the guests, all the while reasoning to himself that she would likely launch into society just fine under her aunt's chaperonage now that she had something of an inheritance.

Still, he cursed his uncle's folly. This piece of land would be of little worth to anyone but himself or—now he thought of it—Amesbury, who also bordered the property. Left in the charge of her silly aunt, Miss Daventry would probably end up marrying some fool content with the land's income when it had the potential for so much more. *Whoever it is will have a blasted piece of luck. They'll get income from a parcel of land that means nothing to them. And,* Stratford admitted to himself begrudgingly, *they'll get a snug little armful as well. Ah, I've been away too long.*

Late that night at Amesbury's house, and far from the prying eyes of his relatives, Stratford finally had the drink he had been waiting for. It did not take long for the excellent brandy to have an effect. *I've grown soft,* Stratford thought as he accepted two more fingers of the spirit . . . or four. The flickering fire had the most amazing, mellowing effect after his brisk ride in the cold, and were it not for the irritation that the best part of his unentailed property had been willed to someone else, he would have felt quite content. He didn't need the income, he reminded himself. *I just hate to see an innocent like that snapped up by fortune-hunters.*

"Come, ole man; drink up. You're positively blue-deviled," said Amesbury. "Although why is anyone's guess. You've just become heir to the largest estate in West Sussex with a title to boot! Were I in your shoes, there's not a thing that could keep me from celebrating."

Stratford frowned, his eyes fixed on the fire. "The land bordering Bailey Stream from the Munroe hamlet to the turnpike road has been bequeathed to Miss Daventry."

"What?" Amesbury stood, knocking the decanter on the floor, where it smashed. "That's impossible!"

"Careful," Stratford said in a listless voice. "The brandy is leaking toward the fire."

"*Blast!*" Amesbury jumped and dropped his handkerchief to block the stream of liquid. "I only have four of these bottles left." He rang the bell, and the door to the library sprang open. "Get someone in here to clean this, and bring me another bottle."

When a second footman had made away with the broken pieces of glass, and the new bottle of brandy had been uncorked, Amesbury sat down. "Start from the beginning," he said.

"My uncle, the Fourth Earl of Worthing," Stratford enunciated, jaw clenched, "was moved to bequeath the most prosperous portion of the unentailed property to a penniless maiden, wholly unrelated to our family." He took a long draught. When the fire had slid down his throat and he could speak, he added, "I don't know why, but I intend to find out. Perhaps she is not a Daventry." As soon as the words left his mouth he regretted them. This was not worthy of her. Or him.

"There must be a loophole. This is madness. How long has that property been tied to your estate?" Amesbury so forgot himself as to fill his friend's glass to the brim with the precious liquid.

"There is never a loophole. And this is tied up in her dowry. The man who marries her will get it." Worthing drank the entire glass in one shot. "Ah," he said, when he had blinked away the tears. "If I'm not careful, I might find myself on the go."

"Nonsense," Amesbury replied, absently. He stood again and went over to the fire, then paced back to his seat, took the glass and swirled its contents thoughtfully. "Tied up in her dowry, you say? Marry her! And get the land back. She's not a bad-looking chit, and with her family past, she'll throw herself at your feet."

Stratford shook his head, trying to clear the fumes that must be interfering with his hearing. "You're telling me to marry her. You, who wanted me to send her away as soon as the will was read because of her questionable past. A girl out of the schoolroom?"

"Well this inheritance puts everything in a new light, of course. It appears she is not without a portion, and that makes her a more palatable choice." Amesbury mumbled, "I'd marry her . . ."

"What?" snapped Worthing.

"I said, 'I'd marry her.' Why let someone else walk off with the inheritance when it only serves those connected to the land. Unless you wanted her . . ."

"I will not offer for a young lady who is under my protection, even temporarily, for such mercenary reasons as this. She will have to find some other suitor."

"Oh, she will." Amesbury walked over to the billiard table and spilled the weighted ivory balls onto the felt cloth. "I wager her dance card will be full, the wastrels will vie with the sharks, and she'll have a proposal from some fellow punting on the River Tick before summer. No reason we shouldn't try our luck first. Come. I'll give you the first shot."

Stratford stood and felt the world spin. If he could spend some time focusing on the game, it would clear his head and he would be none the worse for wear in the morning. However, his friend poured more brandy in his glass, and he was obliged to take a swallow. He looked at it strangely, the liquid spinning in the most beautiful shades of amber. Not . . . unlike Miss Daventry's eyes.

He took another sip, caught by the superior taste, the recollection that many years had passed since he had no battles to fight and nothing to do but seek his own pleasure, and the niggling irritation that Miss Daventry would indeed be hounded by every gentleman, young and old, who had run through his fortune. Stratford leaned against the billiard table, cue in hand, forgetting for an instant what he was meant to do with it.

Her pale face and soft amber eyes wavered before him, and he had an odd notion that those intelligent eyes were pleading with him to do something to protect her. He shook his head.

I have enough worries without adding the burden of a woman I barely know. But as he rubbed chalk on the end of his cue and took aim, the thought persisted.

Chapter Five

Sleep would not come. Eleanor lit a candle on her bedside table and carried it to the clock on the wall. Five o'clock. Well, she could continue to toss and turn and worry, or she could take a walk and see if it cleared her head.

Donning woolen stockings and a heavy day dress, she quickly brushed her teeth and tied up her hair. With a pelisse over one arm, she crept into the hallway where all was quiet and dark. Trailing her fingers on the wall to guide her, she tiptoed past shadowed frames of indistinguishable ancestors marking her progress, reminding herself they were long deceased. She was alone.

The black forms of trees loomed in the distance beyond the tall glass patio doors, and she hesitated at the entrance to the library before setting out to reach them. At least the curtains weren't closed, and she could see what was outdoors before she turned the handle. She almost turned back, though. Who knew what those trees could be hiding, what dangers might be lurking. *No. I'm not so hen-hearted*, she thought, impatient with herself. *There's nothing there.* The pink sky heralding dawn would not be long in appearing.

In a few short steps she had left the house behind her, its façade cold and unwelcoming, and she moved across the meadow, swinging her arms to stave off fear and cold. The trek to the edge of the woods was farther than it appeared—farther than it had seemed when racing over the meadow on horseback. By the time she neared the other side, the sky had started to lighten, revealing a stone wall and a bench tucked on its edge. The perfect place to think.

Once seated, Eleanor couldn't help but dwell on the problem at the forefront of her mind. *What* would she do following the London Season? It seemed as urgent a business as it was elusive. There was one thing of which she was certain. She would not marry this Season. She could not accept an offer when she was this young and knew as little of her own heart as she did of men. Those who had their London Season aspired high. They aspired to a title. She . . . well, she hoped for deeper sentiments than a marriage of convenience could provide.

Dinner last night was a foray into acute discomfort as her aunt flaunted her satisfaction at Eleanor's success. Of course, no one else viewed it as success. More like thievery. At one point she found Lord Worthing staring at her, but when their gazes met, he broke it first and turned away. Then he came into the drawing room, revealing more of that warmth and humor she suspected was tucked away, until he abruptly left her after she divulged the details of her aunt's less-than-modish address in London. Eleanor sighed. He needn't have put himself to the trouble of conversing with her if he thought she was so far beneath him.

Although she hoped her Season in London would be a comfortable one, she did not harbor false expectations. It would be necessary at the Ingram house, where Eleanor would be staying for the Season, to entertain any suitors Lady Ingram put forth for her benefit. When none came up to scratch—as they surely would not, particularly after witnessing Mr. Amesbury's reaction—she might be free to seek employment, a necessity since she had been denied any kind of useful inheritance. *And what will happen to the land if I don't marry? I shall have to ask.*

"What's this I see—"

Shocked out of her reverie, Eleanor sat bolt upright at the slurring, taunting voice that was clearly addressing her. Her neck tingled with fear as her gaze darted back and forth.

"A Bird of Paradise? Here in England," the voice continued.

The edge of the meadow had begun to take shape, and the lumpy form she had thought to be a bush moved. She took a deep breath and blew it out in a cloud before deciding to investigate.

The mystery cleared when she grew near, as she discerned the gentleman sprawled across another stone bench. She recognized the face, the form, the well-built shoulders, but the cool poise was gone. He was clumsy, disheveled, entirely different. "My lord," she said, unable to keep the irony from her voice.

He grunted and, peering up at her, let his head drop back down. "*Not a Bird of Paradise.*" He shook with silent laughter. "A game pullet."

When Eleanor didn't answer, he opened one eye and stared at her until he was able to focus. "Miss Daventry," he slurred. "What are you doing on the grounds late at night? It will not do."

Suddenly, any intimidation she had felt before in his presence was gone, and she lifted her chin. "It is not late at night, my lord, but early in the morning."

Lord Worthing sat up slowly and opened both eyes. "Morning, you say? Yes, I suppose it could be morning." His voice was thick, but intelligible.

"The two blend together, I suppose, when one has dipped rather deep," Eleanor said, dryly.

He waved his hand. "I'm nothing more than a trifle disguised." Then, squinting at her, said, "What do you know about dipping deep?"

She sniffed. "The stable hand in Camberley tells me things so I will not be quite so green."

"Not so green, eh? For all that, green is what you'll remain until you . . . well, never mind." Lord Worthing put a hand to his head. "So, Miss Daventry. What will you do next?" He shot her a glance under heavily lidded eyes. "Now that your inheritance depends on catching a husband?"

Eleanor felt her back stiffen. "*Not* that it's any of your concern, but I don't intend to marry. Inheritance or no, I will not put myself out to please so that some gentleman I don't care a snap of my fingers for can line his pockets."

The earl appeared to mull this over. Then, whether from forgetfulness or doggedness, he asked again. "So what will you do?"

The wind went out of her sails. There was no easy answer. "I'll have my London Season. And while I'm there, I'll search out genteel opportunities to become a governess or teach at a girl's school." She stared at the edge of the black pond between the meadow and the estate and tied a weight to her dream of falling in love and having a family of her own. *Palunk.* She dropped the secret desire and watched it sink to the bottom.

"Why not marry?" There was again that sardonic curl to his lip. How could she have ever thought there was warmth to this man? "Assuming, of course, you can distinguish yourself from the other bird-witted debutantes clamoring for a matrimonial prize."

"I'm not . . ." She fumed for a moment before answering. "I don't think I'll marry this young, if I marry at all." *And you are only proving the soundness of my objections. What have I to look forward to in marriage but a drunken lout who thinks he can ring a peal over me whenever it pleases him? I thank you, no.*

Lord Worthing snorted. "All young women want to marry. You'll change your mind soon enough." He kicked the earth at his feet, missing the clump of grass and losing his balance in the process. "And you'll jostle one candidate against another until you get the best fool to come up to scratch." He closed his eyes as if in pain.

Eleanor swiveled abruptly. "My lord, I wish you good day. I must return to my room."

With unexpected agility, he grabbed her arm and pulled her next to him on the bench. "No, stay." He waved his hand in a tipsy salute. "Some men like brown hair."

What is that supposed to mean? Eleanor pulled her arm away and glared at him. "My lord?" she said, torn between confusion and anger.

He blinked, as if coming to himself. And though she wanted to leave, his sudden, direct gaze rooted her to the spot. "Miss Daventry, I have a proposition to make, and I ask you to accord me a few minutes of your time." Now her heart was in her throat. Gone was the slurring. He was focused.

Lord Worthing shifted on his seat, pulling away from her to draw breath and, she feared, to combat a wave of nausea. "I also must do the London Season, but unlike you, mine comes with the weight of responsibility. I must find a wife." He leaned forward on his elbows and shook his head. "What maggot got into my uncle's head to will away the unentailed estate that way. He must know it's only useful to Worthing. And I don't like having my hand forced in marriage." Eleanor tapped her foot, waiting.

With a sideways glance, he went on. "This is what I propose. Marry me, Miss Daventry. You're young enough to be trained as a peeress and not likely to be an exacting wife, which is just what I should choose. In return,

I'll be an undemanding husband. Then, you get a title, and I'll get the land that should've come with the estate. I imagine the benefit will be mutual."

Having thus laid his heart bare, Lord Worthing loosened his limp necktie, and Eleanor was afraid he would truly be ill. He did not notice her concern—or her disgust—but went blindly on. "It will save us both from a Season that is unlikely to be pleasant or brought to a satisfactory conclusion."

Eleanor leapt to her feet, quivering with rage. How dare he insult her in such a manner. Not even to accord her the barest courtesy of a gentleman? Oh *ho,* and he thought she might be tempted to accept his proposal? Not if her life depended on it! She struggled for mastery over her emotions and cast about for the perfect retort, her fists clenched at her sides.

"So, Miss Daventry? What's it to be?"

Eleanor lifted her gaze to the windows of the manor, which now reflected the pink hues of sunrise. He may not act the gentleman, but she could still be a lady.

The noble thought died quickly when the earl made an impatient gesture, assaulting her senses with the overpowering smell of spirits. *Never mind being a lady,* she thought. *He won't remember this conversation anyway.* With cloying sweetness, she replied, "I am sure, my lord, to be just the sort of undemanding wife that would please you"—she took a step back, this time cautiously lest he reach for her arm again—"however, I'm sorry to disappoint. My answer is 'no.' "

Lord Worthing's voice was harsh. "Miss Daventry, on what grounds do you refuse me?"

"On the grounds that I do not love you, my lord," Eleanor blushed at the vulnerability of her words, but turned to face him fully, "and that you clearly have no love for me."

"No one marries for love! You have no great fortune, beauty, or prospects apart from this parcel of land that's of use only to me. It's unpardonably mawkish of you"—he spat out the word—"to refuse me for such a paltry reason."

"And yet, my lord, I remain steadfast." Hugging her arms inside her pelisse, she faced Lord Worthing, her eyes narrowed. "Were love not possible in a match, I should at least demand respect. You have shown me by your proposal the impossibility of such a thing."

"You're being unreasonable," he called out, swaying now from effort.

"It appears you and I are alike in one thing, my lord." She turned to leave. "Neither one of us wants our hand forced in marriage."

Eleanor walked away, her dark brown skirt heavy with moisture from the frozen grass. "You are not *a trifle disguised*," she muttered, her words floating back on the breeze.

"You, sir, are foxed!"

Chapter Six

osiah Benchly strode across the room and ripped the curtains across their iron rod, allowing the bright sunlight to force its way across Stratford's face. That the valet was displeased with his master was obvious, and that he dared show it revealed he had been in Stratford's employ since before the earl had reached manhood. The shaving cream was mixed vigorously, and the brush whapped against the coat with loud thumps.

When the valet picked up a boot, Stratford said, "Enough. Benchly, I implore you. Have a care for my head. What o'clock is it? Am I to hurry for lunch?"

Benchly let the brush fall loosely to his side. "Lunch, my lord? The ladies will be sitting down to tea before long. Billings asked Mr. Grund to lead the company on a tour of the grounds in your stead. We let your guests understand you were laid up with a megrim."

Stratford groaned. He sat up quickly, but his stomach revolted, forcing him to lie back down. "That's a woman's complaint. Could you not have been more inventive?" When Benchly did not respond, Stratford sat up again, this time more gingerly. "You said it's tea time? The sun is too bright for that. It cannot be much past midday."

"I believe you are not yet accustomed to the manor, my lord," Benchly replied. "I am told the sun reflects off the windows on the side of the estate that juts out, and it appears to be overhead. But, I assure you, it's three o'clock. Now, my lord," the valet coaxed, "if you'll just make your way over to the bath, I shall see that you are properly turned out."

"Blast you," Stratford barked. "I'm not a milksop. Just get on with it."

Seeing his valet reduced to sniveling silence, Stratford stood, giving a cross between a groan and a laugh. "I'm a beast, Josiah. I don't know how you put up with me."

"Well, you are not yourself, if I may make the observation." Benchly picked up the bar of soap and set it on the stand near the copper tub. His features seemed less glacial.

"Yes, well, I don't know whatever possessed me to get so bosky like a regular greenhorn." Three o'clock, and his guests must soon return from the tour. It would be too cold and damp for them to remain out of doors for long. He would have to . . .

Damp! How had he known it was damp? After spending most of the night drinking Amesbury's brandy, he'd spent the remaining hours outdoors, and, aye . . . Who was it he'd met there? A vision floated before his eyes of a fresh face peering at him against the grey sky. *Miss Daventry.*

He drew in a sharp breath, this time his mind revolting as much as his stomach. He'd *proposed* to the girl! And, if his hazy memory was correct, in the most insulting terms imaginable. He was not a sensitive creature, but this was obtuse even for him. What in the world had possessed him to do such a thing?

Pity, most likely. No wonder she'd given him the right-about. Stratford sank into the water, as boiling hot as he could stand it. His stomach lurched, and he almost lost it into the basin the valet had provided for the purpose, but he held back. Instead, he quietly took the sponge, eyes fixed on the copper rim of the deep tub. His hand holding the sponge sank down to his leg and remained there. He was horrified.

His own words came back to him. *You're not likely to be an exacting wife, and I will be an undemanding husband* . . . That alone would not have been so bad, but then when she'd refused him: *You have no great fortune, beauty, or prospects.*

Why did she refuse him again? Oh, yes. Love. *And perhaps my mode of address,* Stratford thought wryly. He applied soap to the sponge and started to wash, but the almond scent did nothing for his conscience. Ducking under water, he allowed the hot liquid to fill his eardrums and block everything else out.

The last thing he remembered with any sort of clarity from his evening debauch, after his befuddled mind had grappled with Miss Daventry's plight, was how little he wanted to see Judith in London—how tempted he was by her still, and how he'd do anything to resist her spell. The brandy had muddled the two situations until one became a means of escaping the other. What a fiasco.

The more he thought about it, the worse it became. He was going to have to apologize. That much was clear. Three years in the Peninsula had obviously been enough to erode his manners. Now, if he had any hopes of still calling himself a gentleman, he needed to rectify the situation. No one could behave like he had to Miss Daventry and still deserve that title.

"Benchly!" At a word, his valet came in with a plush towel and handed it to his master, who had stood, letting the water splash over the sides of the tub. Stratford took the towel and buried his face in it. Apologies did not come easily, but he was not a man to shirk his duty. He must own his fault and face up to it as soon as possible.

The party following the tour had just entered the hall when Stratford descended the stairs. The guests, stamping their feet and removing wraps, turned as one when he came into view.

"I beg your pardon for not joining you earlier. I had . . ." he scanned the crowd, searching for Miss Daventry's face and catching her gaze, ". . . the headache." He couldn't speak to Miss Daventry now. It would cause too much talk to pull her away from the crowd. Besides, it would be a simpler task when he'd got something in his stomach.

Stratford retreated into the library, trying to summon the energy to ring for something to eat though he wasn't sure it would help. He opened his ledger and let the numbers swim before his eyes until he finally turned to stare out the window, willing the pounding headache and bouts of nausea to fade. *Oh lord, I deserve my punishment.*

Eleanor watched the earl enter the library and turned to face the window so no one would witness her confusion. How uncomfortable it was to see him again. Worse than she'd feared. What had she expected? An apology? For him to look contrite? *It appears only I am to suffer from embarrassment.*

When the butler brought her aunt's attention to a letter she'd received, Eleanor was finally ready to show her face. "Who's it from, Aunt?" Eleanor went to her, guessing it might be from her aunt's sister. Perhaps Mrs. Renly would invite them to stay. Now that the will had been read, nothing prevented them from leaving, and she had no desire to spend another night in this house.

"It's from Matilda." Mrs. Daventry noticed the butler still standing there, and she turned the letter over. "Ah, it's not been franked." She reached into her reticule and pulled out two small coins. "Thank you."

Silently, Eleanor trailed her aunt up the stairs and into her room where she walked over to the window. Goodness! Those were snowflakes falling, and at this time of year. Her aunt had not been mistaken in insisting they all return because the weather was getting colder.

It would only be a light dusting, she decided, as she watched the flakes fall. Not enough to keep her here with Lord Worthing. He had appeared only partially recovered this afternoon. Clean, upright, and freshly shaven, but he looked almost as if he were in pain. Maybe he did regret it. Or better yet, perhaps he had forgotten about the whole incident. That would be fortuitous. Since she was neither his inferior to take by force nor someone he would pursue seriously while sober, much better he forget about the entire thing than embarrass her by bringing it up.

You have no great fortune, beauty, or prospects. So she had no fortune, did she? She would bet he'd not have made her a proposal had she not inherited that parcel of land. He was trying to downplay it, but she knew it was no paltry inheritance. This morning, the bailiff had taken her to view it on the solicitor's instructions, and she was stunned to find out how much she was now worth. A small fortune, and unfortunately one she would never fully own.

Eleanor had never seen what a marriage based on love looked like. She had no role model for it nor would anyone of her acquaintance consider it a worthy ambition to marry for love. Yet she knew with all her heart the only thing that could induce her to enter the state of matrimony was that she loved a man and was loved in return. With such conditions, there was little hope of marriage, but she could show Lord Worthing that even a girl with no very great beauty could receive a more worthy proposal than his.

Her aunt folded the cream-colored paper, and Eleanor turned to her. "Are we invited to stay? When may we go? Does she mean to come to London this Season?"

"Not so many questions, Eleanor." Mrs. Daventry placed the letter on the dressing table. "We are invited to go, but I fear it won't be a pleasant stay. My sister is sick. It seems quite sick because I've never seen her write such a short letter. I'm concerned and think we should remove from here as early as tomorrow if a conveyance can be found."

"Of course," Eleanor said. She clasped her hands together. "Let us go at an early hour. I will pack my things. Or would you like me to speak to a footman about hiring a carriage?"

Mrs. Daventry held up a finger. "First, I must speak to the earl. He will see to it that arrangements are made." Her aunt sighed. "It's really a shame you cannot spend more time with him, secure a proposal, and enjoy the Season with a marriage contract in hand. But I suppose it can't be helped." She sighed again, as if to say that if only Eleanor had done what she was bid, this might have been arranged.

"A great pity," Eleanor replied. She went to her room, relieved her aunt could not read the turmoil in her mind. *Good!* She would soon be removed from the source of embarrassment. If she could avoid Lord Worthing at dinner tonight, she need only risk his improbable attendance at breakfast and then contrive to avoid him were he to come to London. He did not seem to be keen on the idea, and men had more power to direct their paths. In any case, Lord Worthing and she would not move in the same circles.

Time was running out. Informed by her aunt of Miss Daventry's departure on the morrow, Stratford knew he could not let her go until he'd said his piece. He owed her an apology, and once delivered, he could put her from his mind once and for all. Dressing with care, Stratford rehearsed until the apology came out smooth and sincere.

Fortune was not on his side. At dinner, Stratford was seated next to Mrs. Daventry instead of her niece, and he spent the meal explaining there was no need to worry. He'd found a conveyance to Reading, the roads would be in good condition, and he'd given Miss Daventry's forwarding direction to the solicitor. They would be perfectly comfortable.

Stratford rose from the table, hoping at last to corner Miss Daventry in the drawing room, but found himself instead losing a cat-and-mouse chase. Miss Daventry was deep in conversation with that coxcomb, Crenshaw, who unfortunately hadn't given any kind of notice about when *he* would take himself off. She kept him engaged in chatter before turning to young Keyes, who'd finally made his appearance a day after the reading of the will, provoking his father to a fit of apoplectic proportions.

"Philip, you've arrived at last," Stratford called out, hoping that by entering the conversation with his cousin, he could find a way to single out Miss Daventry.

Miss Daventry gifted Keyes with a smile. "The two of you will have much to discuss, of course." Then she turned her back on Stratford.

His aunt Hester chose that moment to prevail upon Miss Daventry to play piano. If Stratford hoped to have his chance with her after she played (prettily, he thought), he was doomed to disappointment. Keyes still had him cornered as the ladies bid the party goodnight.

Stratford ground his teeth in frustration. The next day he had arranged an appointment with the bailiff from early morning to discuss how to adjust production without access to the stream that ran along the Munroe hamlet, and he would not be present to see them off.

Confound it. He could not bring himself to put this apology in writing. He would have to meet her in London.

Chapter Seven

Eleanor barely registered that the journey to Mrs. Renly's house had ended, though the last mile was over uneven roads. What a difference Lord Worthing's well-sprung carriage had made. She hadn't realized he'd lent his own until they stopped at the first posting house and a ray of sun illuminated the crest as she was handed back into it. *It was kind of him*, she thought, begrudgingly.

The housekeeper was out the door before the carriage came to a complete halt. "Mrs. Renly is expecting you, ma'am. If you'll follow me, I'll see that Foster brings in your trunks."

In the darkened sitting room, Mrs. Matilda Renly reclined, eyes closed, face framed by a lace cap. "Oh, Tilly, is it really as bad as that?" Mrs. Daventry chided, but her brows were pinched, for as much as Eleanor's aunt didn't have any great affection for anyone, she had some for her sister.

"Apparently not," Mrs. Renly replied, weak but tart. "I was at death's door when the letter went out, but my firm constitution—or so declares my doctor—has allowed me an unexpected recovery. I'm glad of your company, however," she said as her sister leaned down and planted a kiss on her cheek. "Eleanor, you've grown into a passable young woman. Let us hope your intelligence has survived."

"According to the headmistress, I fill my head with nonsense," Eleanor replied with a winning smile, "but she says I have enough sense to *know* it's nonsense."

"You'll do." Mrs. Renly struggled to sit up but soon gave up the fight and surrendered to the pillows. "Every bit of effort exhausts me. How long will you stay?"

Mrs. Daventry pulled a spindle chair next to her sister's bedside and sat down. "As long as you need me. Unfortunately, we weren't at Worthing long enough for the earl to fix his interest. But Eleanor has been invited to spend the Season in The Dowager Lady Ingram's household and is expected there next week. Perhaps she will *take* in London. Since I'm not needed to chaperone, this places me entirely at your disposal, Tilly."

Mrs. Renly glanced at Eleanor. "How do you know the viscountess, my dear?"

Eleanor approached the bed and rested her hands on the round post. "Her daughter, Lydia, was my closest friend at school."

"It's kind of her mother to sponsor a young girl with no prospects—to bring her out in the same season as her own daughter." Mrs. Renly sought her sister's gaze. "Unusual."

"Oh, but you don't know," Mrs. Daventry replied with satisfaction. "Eleanor now has a portion. Her guardian was generous in his bequeathment and left her an entire parcel of land that will bring in an income of three thousand pounds a year."

"Well that changes everything." Mrs. Renly looked at Eleanor shrewdly. "But Lady Ingram didn't know that before she invited you."

Since Eleanor had no intention of divulging why Lydia had made her a favorite with her mother, she kept silent. However, the reminder of it brought forth the memory of the night she came to Lydia's aid all those years ago. Young, impressionable, and reeling from her father's death, Lydia had been on the brink of running off with her Latin teacher had Eleanor not intervened.

If only Eleanor had been able to do it without risking her own reputation, but she'd had the ill luck of getting caught returning after hours by Harriet Price—the one person who delighted in tormenting her for her lack of fortune, and who never ceased to remind her she did not belong to their set. How one unfortunate episode could turn Harriet's unpleasantness into something worse—thinly veiled innuendos that it needed only the right moment before she exposed Eleanor publicly to censure . . .

Eleanor shook her head. She had been glad enough to leave her school years behind, and with any luck, Harriet would not attend the Season in London. Although that was, perhaps, too much to hope for.

The conversation had passed to a spirited discussion on whether the two sisters should remove to Bath for the season, with Mrs. Daventry cataloguing its virtues and Mrs. Renly dashing each one. In the end, plans were made for Bath, and letters were sent to inquire of suitable lodging. Mrs. Renly, recovering her constitution in record time, sped the house-maids into a frenzy of packing. Once decided, Mrs. Renly was not one to waste time.

The week passed with Eleanor swept along in the tide of domestic industry until finally her trunks were loaded onto the carriage, and she settled next to a maid who would accompany her to the Ingrams, then visit family in London. Mrs. Daventry called out last-minute instructions on how Eleanor might reach her in Bath, reminding her, for heaven's sake, not to forget to smile at the gentlemen suitors if she didn't want to remain on the shelf, since really it was her only attribute besides a passable figure. "You positively frowned at the earl, and it's no wonder he did not seek to further your acquaintance."

"I declare," Eleanor murmured, waving her handkerchief as the carriage lurched forward, "the whirlwind of routs and balls Lydia has told me about will be quite restful after this week."

Major Thomas Fitzwilliam of the 11th Regiment of Foot stared at the brass knocker in the form of a sphinx. He reached into his breast pocket and fingered the rigid seal on the felted paper he was carrying. The paper felt innocent enough, but the message inside was not one that could fall into the wrong hands, and it had been entrusted to him. The door opened. Taking one look at his dress uniform, the butler opened the door wider.

"I've come to speak with Lord Ingram," the major said. "Here's my card. He won't be expecting me, but I'm carrying a correspondence addressed to him."

The butler ushered him in, and after requesting him to wait, went through the first door on the right, leaving the major to kick his heels. The wallpaper was dark green damask, and the black bust of some family member, placed on a pedestal in the hallway, presided over the dim corridor. *Ingram is not married*, he thought. This was not the modern decor of a wife.

He saw a flash of color at the end of the hallway of someone exiting a room. This was followed by the profile of a young woman with alluring features, who did not perceive him standing there in the gloom of the hallway. "Mama," she said, "if I'm to have a court presentation it will be with Eleanor. We're sponsoring her this Season, and I will not go without her."

He couldn't hear the muffled, angry response before she continued. "Besides, you can gain her access anywhere you please. I will not have her treated like an impoverished companion."

An older woman followed the younger one into the hallway. "Lydia, don't try my patience. The girl may now have a portion, but she was hardly left with enough for her Season without the court dress, and I will not put your brother out to the tune of one hundred pounds to provide it. Besides, what with her mother—"

"You yourself said her mother need not be a consideration with the ton when she comes with an inheritance. I don't see why Carlton House should be any different," the girl replied, her foot making a staccato on the wood floor.

"My dear girl, imagine if Princess Charlotte were to object. We would all be turned out of the royal house. I was perfectly willing to humor you in this invitation, but don't think for a minute you can have your way in everything. You will attend every assembly of the haut ton, and your friend will attend what she can. And," her mother threatened, "I expect you to accept the first eligible offer for your hand." The major, embarrassed to have interrupted a domestic scene, was grateful his presence was hidden behind the stairwell.

"I will marry when and whom I please, Mama," the girl shot back. "With my inheritance, I can set up my own establishment if it comes to that, and Freddy will support me in it too. You know that to be true. I'm no longer a small girl who'll come running when you order it."

"Headstrong child—" her mother snapped. The rest was lost when the dark-haired beauty entered the far room and her mother followed, closing the door behind them. Major Fitzwilliam shook his head, a reluctant smile on his face. *A formidable opponent*, he thought.

The butler returned and indicated that Major Fitzwilliam follow him to the first room on the right. Inside, Lord Ingram sat behind an imposing oak desk, writing furiously on a sheet of paper, a lock of black hair falling over his face. *The young lady's brother.*

Lord Ingram set his quill down when the major entered. "Good afternoon, major." He stood, tall and in civilian clothes. "You've traveled some way, I apprehend. You're carrying news from Spain?"

"That is correct," Major Fitzwilliam answered. "I've a letter from Badajoz that I was to give only to you." He pulled the envelope from his coat.

"Let's have it then." Lord Ingram held out his hand and broke the seal with a quick swipe of the penknife. Lifting the paper to the sunlight streaming through the window, he perused its contents. He then sat at his desk and read the paper again more slowly, his gaze narrowed.

"Major-General Le Marchant has sent you," he observed.

"Yes." Major Fitzwilliam offered nothing further.

Lord Ingram considered the major for a minute and then dropped the letter on the desk. "How much do you know of its contents?" he asked.

"I was made privy to its entirety," Major Fitzwilliam answered. "I carried Lord Wellington's instructions to the major-general and waited for him to formulate this request. The general would like each officer to be given a detailed report on the supplies and troops they can expect to arrive in the next three months. He has not always found his demands are met in a satisfactory manner." With the ghost of a smile, the major added, "He said I could pass that information on. Le Marchant wants regular reports about the progress to be sent through a messenger chain. A rider will meet you south of Hyde Park at seven in the morning every Friday to receive your missive. The first will be in two weeks' time. Le Marchant preferred to leave the details of the rendezvous out of the correspondence." Major Fitzwilliam folded his hands behind his back.

Lord Ingram tapped the corner of the folded paper on the desk. "He said he wants to get to the bottom of the leaked intelligence regarding the deployment schedule of troops."

Major Fitzwilliam nodded. "Efforts are being made to expose the traitor at the battle lines, but there's some indication that there's at least one traitor here at headquarters. I believe he thought it would be more effective to bring me in as an outsider."

Lord Ingram frowned. "With all due respect to the major-general, he takes much upon himself. I'm not sure the gentlemen at headquarters will take kindly to his offer to help."

"You are right, of course," Major Fitzwilliam said. "And he himself spoke almost identical words. I think this is where you come in. He said he knew your father, and I think he trusts you to handle the thing with diplomacy."

Elbows on his desk, Lord Ingram steepled his fingers and appeared lost in thought. At last, he looked up with a smile. "He did know my father."

Leaning back in his chair, he continued. "We're aware of the leak at headquarters. I agree that sending the troop deployment through your rider, rather than using our traditional channels, will be more to the purpose if we're to have any hope of the enemy remaining ignorant of where our forces are concentrated. I assume Le Marchant wants you implicated in the search?"

Major Fitzwilliam gave a nod. "I'm to assist you in whatever is needed, whether surveillance or communication, paying special attention to the soldiers recently returned to England or those on the point of departure. I myself won't return to the Peninsula before July."

"Meanwhile, you are commanded to attend every rout, ball, and soirée, are you not?" The corner of Lord Ingrams's mouth twitched.

"I see you are familiar with the way the general operates," Major Fitzwilliam said with an answering smile. "Yes. I'm to be everywhere and to relay to you what I see. I am also . . ."—he looked at his hands and wiped a speck off his glove—" 'commanded to find some amusement and stop being so demmed serious.' "

Lord Ingram threw back his head and laughed. "That sounds like the Beau. You must know how things are done in Welly's inner circle. Or, at least if you didn't before, you do now. He won't promote an incompetent or a jaw-me-dead. You'll do just fine."

When the mirth died down in his eyes, Lord Ingram continued. "Have you any contacts in London?"

"I came with Jonathon Braxsen, who's recovering from a minor injury that has earned him some furlough."

"I know him," said Lord Ingram. "We were at school together and spent time on the hunting field during the holidays. Good. You'll have someone to enter society with." He pulled a sheet of paper and picked up his pen. "I'll put your name up at White's and the other clubs and mention you to Lady Sefton for Almack's. And you can show this letter at Jackson's on New Bond Street if you want to throw a few punches." He finished scribbling something and sprinkled some sand over it. "Are you set for rooms and banking?"

Major Fitzwilliam pulled himself up stiffly. "You need not put yourself out, my lord. I have everything I need."

Lord Ingram gave him a shrewd look, his smile lurking. "Don't come the ugly. I have no wish to intrude, major, but we will be working closely together, and I want to make sure you're comfortable." He added in a mild tone, "And do call me Ingram. If we're to be working together, I will soon tire of 'my lord.' "

Major Fitzwilliam felt his ears burn. "Yes, of course, my l—Ingram. Thank you for your assistance. And please. Call me Fitz."

Ingram met his gaze and gave a nod. "All right, Fitz. Here, take this letter. Where are you staying?"

"At Steven's on Bond Street."

"Excellent. I'll expect to see you soon at one of these routs, balls, or soirées." He gave a wink and gestured forward. "Come. Hartsmith will see you out."

If the major expected another glimpse of the dark beauty on his way out, he was disappointed. Tucking the letter into his coat pocket, he stepped into the sunlight and breathed in the scent of hyacinths poking through the ground in the small patches of earth. He had liked Ingram much better than he'd expected.

Chapter Eight

Ushered into her host's drawing room at last, Eleanor would have sighed with relief that her journey was at an end were she not so nervous to meet Lady Ingram. Lydia, whose lustrous black hair was hanging in loose curls in the back, in what must have been a new style, threw her embroidery aside and ran to hug her. "I've been waiting for you for ages! The Season couldn't properly begin until you'd arrived." She took Eleanor by both hands and stepped back, studying her from bonnet to toes. "And apparently the Season cannot begin until we go shopping."

"Lydia, allow Eleanor some refreshment before you begin planning wardrobes." Lady Ingram stood, dwarfing even her daughter whom Eleanor had thought tall, and gave a placid signal to the footman. "Will you ring for tea, James?" Crossing the room, she examined Eleanor with dark blue eyes. "Welcome," Lady Ingram said. "I hope you've had a pleasant journey."

"It was quite comfortable, thank you, my lady." Eleanor sank into a curtsy. "My aunt insisted I convey her thanks as well. She thinks it excessively kind of you to sponsor me when we are not related, and regrets that accompanying her invalid sister to Bath did not permit her to make your acquaintance."

Lady Ingram waved this aside. "Yes, well, I've had her letters and sent her my best. Please, don't give it another thought. We are quite obliged to you for your friendship with Lydia these past four years." She shot an indulgent glance at her daughter. "As you know, her father's death affected her profoundly, and the tone of her mind was not what it should have been. She has spoken of how valuable your friendship was during those years."

The footman brought the tray in just then, and Lady Ingram gestured for Eleanor to sit as she poured a cup of tea. Lydia took up the fashion plates and began to flip through them. "Eleanor, I've seen just the dress for you in here. I'll find it. Thank you, no, Mama. I don't care for tea just now."

"Your aunt informed me in her most recent letter you've just received an inheritance," Lady Ingram said with a raised eyebrow. "I expect our house to be overrun with fortune-hunters when I launch you both. I shall have my hands quite full chasing them off." She laughed without mirth.

Eleanor sipped her tea while gathering her thoughts, but the subject must be brought up from the start. "Did my aunt also tell you about my mother?"

"I was aware of your somewhat irregular situation," Lady Ingram said. "I insisted upon learning everything there was to know before inviting you to stay. True"—she set her cup down with an elegant clink on its saucer—"an elopement taints the whole family. But in your case, your former guardian saw fit to take you up, and his condescension has paved the way so well you won't even be denied vouchers for Almack's. He was a most kind benefactor. Although, I must own that it was also through my influence you received those vouchers. Lady Sefton is a particular friend."

"I am indebted to my guardian. And I thank you, indeed," Eleanor said.

"Your inheritance is the crowning touch, my dear. The ton does not lightly dismiss a gentleman's daughter who has a portion. When possible they will overlook the less savory details." Lady Ingram signaled for the footman to remove the tea tray.

Eleanor chewed her lip as the words sank in. She was desirable because she had a portion. That particular truth stung. "While I'm thankful to have an inheritance, I must be clear that it's not an independence. The bequest is tied up in a strange way, and I'm to be married before I can touch it."

Lady Ingram shrugged. "Well, there's nothing unusual in that. You will make a match—a considerably better match than what I'd hoped for when I invited you to stay—and you shall benefit from your own income at that time as well as his."

"I should have liked to have had the choice—" Eleanor began.

"Choice is one thing women do not generally have," Lady Ingram said, "except the choice to show to advantage and marry the first acceptable candidate that comes forward." She looked at Eleanor critically. "With the money your guardian has set aside for you, you will do very well. Your figure is good. We can change that hairstyle. But you mustn't attempt Rifle Green; you haven't the complexion for it. Lydia will guide you in the choice of colors."

"Eleanor! Only consider—" Lydia held up a fashion plate. "These ostrich feathers are dyed the boldest pink imaginable. I'm glad this is no longer *à la mode*! But come, I've found the pages I want to show you. We can head to the modiste tomorrow morning, and you'll have at least one dress before Mrs. Jenkins's soirée."

Eleanor set her teacup on the table. "Excuse me, ma'am, while I see what it is Lydia insists I must have." Her attempt at levity fell short, and Lady Ingram dismissed her with a nod. Eleanor felt her measuring stare while she walked over to the settee. She would not have an ally in Lydia's mother.

Lady Ingram left after tea, saying she must speak to the cook, and Lydia and Eleanor were not alone for long before the door opened again.

"Occupied are you? Lydia, who's this?" A handsome gentleman, a male version of Lydia who moved with easy grace, came up to the two ladies on the settee. Eleanor stood.

"Oh, Freddy, you know very well this is Eleanor Daventry, who is to stay with us for the Season. I've talked about her countless times. Eleanor, this is my brother, Ingram."

"Miss Daventry. Why of course." Lord Ingram gave a deep bow to Eleanor while still addressing his sister. "And I agreed to your scheme to invite Miss Daventry knowing you would cut up my peace with your gabbing if you didn't have someone else to talk to."

Eleanor couldn't resist a grin when Lord Ingram winked at her. He seemed much more like his sister than his mother. "Good afternoon, my lord," she said. "I'm pleased to make your acquaintance. You must know how highly your sister thinks of you. She was forever telling me stories when we were at school."

"You must not believe any of them," he said promptly. "She is prone to exaggerate. Lydia—" he turned to Eleanor, "forgive me for discussing family affairs, but I think we must put aside some formality if you are to live here for three months, do you not agree?" When Eleanor nodded, he continued. "Hand over your bills, and see that you don't forget any that you've stuffed in some drawer. It won't do to be dunned and refused by the milliner, will it? I'm headed to the counting house and will draw out your quarter pay."

"Oh, it's time you thought of that. I've not had two coins to rub together." Lydia's skirts rustled as she moved across the room. "I'll be two minutes, Eleanor."

"Please sit, Miss Daventry," Lord Ingram said when they were alone. Taking a seat on an Egyptian chair, he gave her a smile. "It's not your first time in London, I take it?"

"Only if you count a visit when I was two," she answered. "I'm eager to take in all the sights if Lydia can spare me during the day."

"Refreshing," said Ingram with an appreciative gleam. "I'm glad you did not try for boredom."

"Bored! In London?" She shook her head.

"At least you know Lydia well enough not to expect her to accompany you. I daresay you will be pulled to pieces with plans every evening, and you will soon be taking your chocolate abed in the mornings."

"I am indefatigable," Eleanor said, the corners of her mouth lifting.

Lydia swung back into the room holding a fistful of papers. "Here they are, Fred." She leaned down and pecked his cheek, depositing the slips in his lap so that half the papers slid to the floor. Lord Ingram rolled his eyes and leaned over to pick them up, then stood.

"I bid you both good day. Stratford is back in town, you know, and I haven't seen him since his last furlough. I'm off to his new house."

"Oh, Stratford," Lydia said. "Do say hallo to Anna and Phoebe if you see them, won't you?" She turned back to Eleanor, her brother forgotten. "On our way to the dressmaker, we can pop into a store on New Bond that has the most darling furbelows in the window. Shall we?"

Eleanor nodded as she watched Lord Ingram disappear through the door, her cheeks drained of color. *Stratford. Here. And friends with the Ingrams?* She had spoken so little of her guardian, she was sure Lydia hadn't made the connection. But wouldn't Lady Ingram have spoken of it when she read Mrs. Daventry's letter?

Could there be two with such a name in London?

Lord Ingram whistled as he strode toward Cavendish Square. Despite the summons he had received that day from headquarters, he couldn't be immune to the sun making its appearance after what seemed an interminable winter. He was also glad his oldest friend had made it back from the Peninsula. Stratford's sisters needed him after the loss of their father and, well, *there's no one I trust more,* he thought.

The knocker was in place at the Worthing residence, and Ingram could see signs of the house being brought to life through the windows—flashes of white as the holland covers were removed, a maid leaning out the window to dust the shutters on the third floor. Stratford's butler informed him that the earl had gone off to Jackson's for a bit of sparring, and Ingram turned his steps in that direction.

Stratford had just buttoned his shirt when Ingram walked into the changing room at Jackson's and gave a lazy salute. "Just finished, have ye? None of your usual bruises to show for the effort?"

Stratford laughed. "Ingram! It's mighty good to see you." They shook hands, warmly. "Thanks for the reminder, old friend, but that happened once." He selected a cravat from a waiting servant and turned toward the glass.

Ingram gave an answering grin. "What would old friends serve if not to remind you where you come from?" While Stratford turned his attention to the serious matter of tying a *trône d'amour*, he looked around the empty changing room. The Season was not yet in full swing. "One neckcloth and you have it. I'd have thought you lost your touch in the Peninsula."

"The conditions may have been rude at times, but an officer must look the gentleman. I heard you were at Lisbon with Wellington. When'd you come back?" Stratford shrugged on his close-fitting coat, spurning the help of the servant who had leapt forward.

"I was there, but briefly," Ingram replied. "I carried the plans for building Torres Vedras but left as soon as the construction started." Ingram waited until the servant retired from the vestiaire. "There was some strange business going on. We ran across a platoon of Boney's men, and one could almost say they knew where we were headed."

Stratford met Ingram's eyes in the glass before turning. "I'm unsurprised. We also got heavy fire at Talavera, and Donkin had us retreat. Anson was cleared of blame, though it was never determined what intelligence caused him to pull back, leaving us exposed. Not a friendly one, I daresay."

Ingram gave a noncommittal grunt and asked, "Where are you headed now? I'll accompany you."

"Back to the new house. My sisters are expected within the hour, but I needed to get away. I couldn't stand any more housekeeping questions."

"I should say so," Ingram said. "All right, I'll go with you. That direction is as good as any." They stepped outside into weather that had become overcast in the short while he had been inside Jackson's and walked down the street in silence, dodging the few pedestrians. Ingram waited until they turned the corner and there was nobody else about. "I need your help with something."

"I figured as much," Stratford said. "You're only quiet when you're stewing over the best way to ask me for a favor. And it usually involves trouble."

Ingram smiled and shook his head but still didn't speak. Stratford shot him a sideways glance. "That serious then? Tell me. If it's within my power to help, I'll do it."

"I know you will," Ingram said, but they walked in silence some more before he finally spoke. "You flushed out one spy in your regiment and another in the sixty-second."

"You know of that, do you?" Stratford was only mildly surprised. He knew his friend was connected, at least in part, to the war intelligence unit. "It was sheer luck, though. I stumbled on one traitor meeting with the French near where we camped at Almeida. He didn't see me in the trees, and the creek kept me from being heard. I figured the odds were against me, so I waited before confronting him. When I followed him, he led me directly to his accomplice in my regiment. It was a piece of luck, really."

"Hmm. For all that, it took some instinct to know how to bring him in." Ingram turned as a carriage clattered down the nearly empty street. "Not surprisingly, there *is* espionage on the campaign trail, but what's more worrisome is that there's a new leak coming from headquarters. It's likely to be someone higher up since the lower staff don't have access to information concerning the movement of troops. Where they're being sent, when, how many." He stopped and looked at Stratford. "I've been put in charge of uncovering it."

"A gentleman traitor," Stratford mused. "I can see your concern. Why involve me?"

"I should think that would be obvious." Ingram shot his friend a wry glance, then warned, "This conversation doesn't go further than us."

Stratford retorted, "Do you find me so changed in the past three years?"

"No, which is why I need you. The thing is, with this new leak, I can't be everywhere at once, and I want to be sure of whom I trust. In short, I need your help."

"You have it. But doing what, exactly?" Stratford asked.

"We're looking at people who have a reason to spy. Bitterness toward the army, sympathy for the French, stuck in dun territory . . . Anything that could get them to question their loyalty. It'll be an officer with access to all the social functions. I don't need to tell you it'll have catastrophic implications if the traitor gets information on troop movement, especially with what's going on in the Americas. We risk getting spread thin."

Stratford nodded. "Any leads?"

"We have three who might be bought," Ingram said, "but only two valid ones. Lord François de Delacroix—he's dropped the prefix—Robert Conolly, and Giles Cooke. All three will be coming to the end of their resources if their luck doesn't change soon."

"Giles Cooke is no surprise," Stratford replied. "I think everyone in London must know except, perhaps, his wife."

"Yes," said Ingram, "and he has no connection to the military. But Lord Delacroix and Conolly do . . . Or at least Conolly is on leave, and Delacroix runs with a military crowd. I'm having them followed. Major Fitzwilliam—I'll introduce you—is handling that, but you'll be the better man for gaining information from conversations. People watch their tongue around me, knowing I'm at headquarters, but with you they'll let down their guard because you've sold out. They'll think you have no particular military loyalty."

"They don't know me then," Stratford replied, his face grim.

"That they don't. Which helps the cause. And is another reason I asked you. And Stratford—" Ingram clapped his shoulder. "I'm glad you're back."

"I can see that. Barely a hallo, and you're putting me to work," Stratford retorted.

"It's no less than what you wish. You can't bear to be idle," Ingram said.

"Idle! I will not have the luxury of idleness for some years, I predict." They had arrived at Stratford's residence. "Come inside and have a drink. Phoebe and Anna will be here at any moment."

"You'll have to pass on my greetings," Ingram replied. "I must be off. Oh, and Lydia sends her love to all of you as well."

"Lydia's home from school, then. She has her come out soon, does she not?" Stratford asked.

"This year. I've heard about nothing else for the past six months. Fortunately, she has a friend staying with her, so she can chew *her* ear off with how fetching she looks in each dress she's had made up. A Miss Eleanor Daventry will be spending the Season with us."

Stratford turned to his friend, sharply. "Miss Daventry? How are you acquainted with her?"

Ingram stopped, his attention arrested. "She's Lydia's classmate from school. You know her?"

Stratford gave a short nod. "Only the barest acquaintance. She was my uncle's ward, and she spent three days at Worthing for the reading of the will." He glanced at the front door then back to Ingram, clearly uncomfortable. With a forced laugh, he said, "I must go in and face more questions about where this flower arrangement or that chair should go. Phoebe cannot arrive soon enough."

"Well, I'll let you get to it then." They shook hands, and Ingram watched Stratford enter the house, his mind busy even after the door closed. *The barest acquaintance, hmm?*

Chapter Nine

"$\mathcal{S}$tratford! We're here." The sound of a young lady's footsteps flying up the stone stairway echoed through the rooms. "It's grander than our last house, and in a better location, but it doesn't feel quite like home. However, you'll be able to hold your coronet ball here. We shall be so distinguished."

"Anna, slow down, my dear. You're running and shouting like a *gamine*, and a not very elegant one at that. What will your suitors think?" Their aunt's affectionate but indolent voice had no power to check her niece, and it was over Anna's breathless perusal of the cascading stairwell that the aunt intoned, "Stratford, would you ring the footman for some tea? We've had a most fatiguing journey across town." She turned a soft, plump cheek for him to kiss.

Phoebe, nineteen, and a facsimile of her sister but with more grace than Stratford remembered her possessing, came to the rescue. "Would you like to sit down, Aunt Shae? I believe the morning room must be this way."

Stratford opened the door and gestured them in. "It is. James, bring the tea tray for my aunt and sisters." Turning to Phoebe, "Are your dresses ready at last then? If I didn't know better, I'd almost think you were trying to escape having to visit Worthing."

"Only Anna was," the more demure twin replied. "I've been quite impatient to see the estate, but she kept finding fault with her dresses."

Anna stuck out her tongue. *Apparently*, thought Stratford, *it hasn't registered to Anna that she's nineteen as well.* "It was not the moment for retiring to the country," Anna said. "It takes ages to prepare for one's Season, and we were lucky to stay with the Jervils until the house was ready." She skirted the room as her aunt and sister found places to sit. "Who is the gentleman in this painting? He looks disapproving and therefore must go."

"That is the third earl, and I was intending to replace the painting, but perhaps he will stay. You need someone disapproving to keep you in line, and it will save me the trouble. Ah, thank you, James." Stratford gestured toward the table nearest his sister. "Aunt, as soon as you've had your tea, I'll show you the house." His gaze shifted to the ruby-red felted wallpaper. "We will need to redecorate, but that might best be left to the countess."

"The countess!" Anna smiled at him with false innocence. "Who is she? Will you be having your Season too?"

"See to your own affairs," Stratford bit back mildly. "You have enough to occupy you. Like learning to curb your tongue." All he got in return was a smirk.

"Stratford, you haven't answered a single question in my letters about this ball we're to have." Phoebe reached over and poured a cup of tea for her aunt and handed it to her. "We want to organize it early enough in the Season that people will not have a load of invitations to choose from, but not so early that no one is here."

"I suppose we shall have to discuss it, but pester me only about the spending decisions, if you please," Stratford replied. "The rest you must sort out without my help."

Anna turned. "May I see the ballroom? Where is it?"

"Drink your tea first, Anna," Stratford said, as he accepted a cup from his sister. Anna rolled her eyes at his patronizing tone but obeyed the summons.

Pouring her sister and then herself a cup of tea, Phoebe stirred a spoonful of sugar in each. "What news is there of the estate? You told us nothing of the reading of the will in your letter, only that you would arrive in town Tuesday."

"After your sharp reminder that my presence was required immediately to escort you to every societal gathering, I cut to the essentials." Stratford leaned on the mantel.

"One would almost think you didn't know your duty, Stratford." His younger sister's words were laced with humor, but her blue eyes penetrated uncomfortably. "Aunt Shae can chaperone us, but we need a male presence. Had you forgotten everything in your three years overseas?"

Stratford shifted to the other foot. "I cannot forget what I don't know. I am . . . unaccustomed to our father's absence." He stopped suddenly and swirled the tea in his cup.

Phoebe's eyes shimmered. "We're glad you're home, Stratford." After a pause, she said, "Tell us of Worthing."

"Yes, is the estate falling to rack and ruin?" Anna, flipping the pages of *La Belle Assemblée*, allowed her tea to grow cold. "Aunt, I told you we should've chosen the white rosebud overlay. Look here how fine it is over the Damascene sarcenet."

Phoebe waited while her brother sipped his tea. "There were no surprises," he admitted. "Well, but for one. The former earl's ward will inherit the most promising piece of land, and I shall be obliged to use my own resources to bring parts of Worthing back to their former glory."

Phoebe's brow creased. "Was not the entire estate entailed?"

"All but this and some property bequeathed to the old earl's sisters." He reached down with the iron poker and jabbed at one of the logs that had fallen too close to the grate.

"What will the young man do with the land? Is he willing to sell it to you?" Phoebe glanced at her sister to see if she were following, but Anna was still engrossed in the magazine.

"It was a Miss Eleanor Daventry who inherited the property." Stratford couldn't resist a look to see how his sisters took this surprising news.

"A Miss Eleanor Daventry! But she's not even in the family." Anna's gaze flew to her sister, then Stratford. She had been listening. "Who is she? Why was she his ward?"

"I don't have the particulars, but I believe her father and our uncle were friends. She was in need of a portion, but why she was given this piece of land I cannot fathom." Stratford put the iron poker back in the ring with unnecessary force. "Would you like to look over the house?"

Phoebe helped their aunt to her feet while Anna sidled up to her brother. "You have only to marry her, Stratford. That will solve all the problems, and you can keep our family's property intact." She tiptoed to peer at his face with an impish smile that was too perceptive for his comfort. He turned away before she could divine his thoughts.

"Is she a Homely Joan, then?" Anna called after him at his abrupt departure. Her aunt and twin sister followed Stratford through the door, but Anna was still rooted to the spot. "That's it then? She's pudding-faced?"

"She's tolerable," Stratford said over his shoulder, knowing his face was flushed now in earnest—and knowing, too, he was a liar. *It will seem strange if I don't tell them she's staying with Lydia.* With a bluster he didn't feel, he added, "You will meet her soon enough. She's Lydia's friend from school and is staying at the Ingram house for the Season."

"Is she now," Anna said, with an arrested expression.

Stratford knew dodging Anna's questions for any length of time when she had *that look* on her face was an impossibility. As soon as they had toured the house, he made a strategic retreat, informing the ladies he intended to visit White's.

Phoebe called out. "I'll have that list of questions pertaining to the ball by tomorrow."

"I'll have some too," Anna added with a mischievous gleam.

Lydia tied her bonnet securely under her chin then pulled Eleanor's arm, sending her own ribbons askew. "I've heard from Madame Baillot, and they expect us at two. I cannot wait to outfit you in something more suitable. If I have to look at such a drab-colored dress another day, I shall be tempted to take my scissors to it."

Eleanor chuckled and pulled her arm away to retie her chip hat. "There's no rush. I won't have my dresses in under a week, so I don't see the need to race about—" she took the voice of their former schoolmistress, "'like a hoyden.'"

Lydia smirked. "I'm quite certain there will be a dress that someone has ordered and has not taken, and that we will walk out of the store with a new dress for you today. Then we can both attend Mrs. Jenkins's soirée tomorrow night."

"Perhaps," Eleanor said, not yet ready to enter the lists.

Lydia was right. Madame Baillot had a dress ready-made in the perfect size for *mademoiselle*, a forgotten article among a large trousseau for a lady who had already removed to Norfolk. Though the dress was suitable, Lydia employed her good taste in choosing fabrics to drape over Eleanor that would have a more striking effect for her remaining wardrobe. The gold Apollo *crèpe* was something Eleanor would not have chosen for herself, but the transformation when she stood before the glass was heartening.

"I knew it. Eleanor, this color is perfect for you." Lydia hugged Eleanor from behind before going over to examine more bolts of fabric in shades of lavender. "We will certainly need one in Stifled Sigh for after the come-out ball. And one in ivory, of course."

Madame Baillot encouraged Lydia's planned expenditures with murmured approval while examining Eleanor from head to toe. "We take off some length from ze bottom, and we bring to you zees afternoon." Turning to Lydia, she added, "*Oui, je suis d'accord.* Miss Maxwell will take ze measurements for riding habit, day dress, walking dress . . ."

"I think two walking dresses to begin with," Lydia stated. "Where is the fabric for the evening gowns? I have some fashion plates with ideas . . ."

Eleanor, bemused, gave full rein to Lydia in deciding the number of dresses she would need, stopping her only to say she would not take the pink—(*vous avez raison, mademoiselle, zat color will never do*)—and allowed Miss Maxwell to wind the cord around her waist, her arms, and her bust, and write down the measurements.

After two hours of this, the first step outdoors felt like freedom, and Eleanor wanted to laugh. "I was afraid I'd be buried under fabric and they wouldn't find me for three days."

"Well, it's only because you needed so many," Lydia said. She paused on the side of the road to tell the driver, "One more stop before we head home, but we can walk to the carriage from there. We won't be but a minute."

"Haven't you had enough?" Eleanor groaned, as Lydia pulled her forward.

"No. I promised you a turn in the store on New Bond, and we shall have it. There's likely to be a crowd if we come tomorrow morning, and you will need accessories for your new gown. I saw *just* the gloves with pearl buttons . . ." She stopped and pulled Eleanor close to whisper, "Do you see that woman there? With the blonde hair?"

Eleanor couldn't miss her. She was dressed in the first stare of fashion with a white muslin draped gown and a pale-blue spencer that matched the color of her eyes. She was laughing at a gentleman's remark—he, a Pink of the Ton if ever there were one—showing her perfect teeth set in pearly white rows. *I must always be a dowd next to a woman like that,* Eleanor thought dismally.

"*That,*" disclosed Lydia, "is one of London's terrible jilts, Judith Broadmore. She threw off our friend Stratford, though no one outside the family knew they had an understanding. I'm sure that's what caused him to leave his father's business and go off and join the regiment."

Eleanor felt a queer pain in her chest. She knew to whom Lydia was referring but couldn't bring herself to remind Lydia of the connection. She would have to say his name. Instead she asked, "Would that not ruin her?"

"You forget that no one knew. Stratford was a gentleman and kept their understanding secret at her request. Then she changed her mind because he didn't have a title. At least, that's what Anna told me. I'll bet Judith is regretting her haste now. He inherited an earldom." Lydia lifted an eyebrow at that choice morsel of gossip.

Eleanor had only time to think, *She doesn't remember that I have met him,* before Lydia prattled on. "If you ask me, she will try her luck with him again, counting on their former attachment. He was simply pining away with love for her. And look at her now. She's positively on the shelf! I fear our Stratford is just nice enough to be taken in again."

Oh. Eleanor's mouth formed the word, but she had no chance to respond before a nondescript, bony gentleman sporting a pink waistcoat and a bored expression was bowing before Lydia. "Miss Ingram," he said. "You're looking very grown up."

"Mr. Braxsen," Lydia exclaimed, her whispered disclosures forgotten. "I haven't seen you in years. Had my brother not thought you fit for my company, or is there another reason for your absence?"

"Only going off to Spain would keep me from your charm," Mr. Braxsen said, with more practiced flirtation than sincerity. "I've been with the regiment at war these past two years."

"Well, in that case, I hope we shall be seeing more of you while you're in town." Eleanor heard the sincerity in Lydia's light reply. The late Lord Ingram had been a major-general, and Lydia respected those in service.

"I imagine there's not a party you will miss this Season," Mr. Braxsen said, "now that you're out."

"As to that, I'm not out just yet. In fact, let me introduce you to Miss Eleanor Daventry, who will be staying with me. We'll have our come-out together in a week's time, and I'll see that you receive an invitation. However, not officially being out won't stop us from attending Mrs. Jenkins's assembly tomorrow night. Will we see you there?"

"If you'll promise me the first dance, I'll come," Mr. Braxsen rejoined. Beyond him, a red-headed military gentleman, whose arresting features were not quite handsome but made one wish to look twice, descended the steps of the imposing stone building. He looked surprised to see Mr. Braxsen there. However, after the initial start, he stared, not at Mr. Braxsen, but at Lydia. Eleanor wondered if Lydia knew him, but her friend seemed unconscious of his gaze.

With the dance promised, Mr. Braxsen turned to join the other gentleman, and Eleanor linked her arm through Lydia's. Lord Worthing's—*Stratford's*—jilt had, by now, been joined by another admirer, and Eleanor was transfixed by her smile.

"So we shall attend Mrs. Jenkins's, hmm?" Eleanor said, but she wasn't listening for Lydia's answer. She was busy thinking of an earl who had once loved (*still loved?*) this woman enough to be engaged to her. He had then proposed to Eleanor, but *not* for love. And although his could not truly be called a proposal, it was enough of one to signify that Lord Worthing had been rejected in marriage twice.

Stratford walked briskly toward the club, saluting a surprised acquaintance on his way, but he did not stop. His entrance at White's provoked no small reaction once his presence was made known. It needed only hailing a gawky fellow with a cowlick, who went by "Finch" and another gentleman in colors who answered to "Gerry" for everyone to return with handshakes and slaps on the back.

He shook Gerry's hand, congratulated him on his marriage, and asked how he had left the Peninsula. It didn't take long for them to come to the story that brought them together: their successful maneuver against the French army at Bussaco. They laughed at Masséna's confusion when Hill's brigade came over the ridge and, as Gerry said, wiping his eyes, "discovered there were more of us on the other side!" After that battle, their brigades had gone separate ways, and it was the last time they'd seen each other.

"So I heard you inherited a pretty estate. Now we shall not only put up with your presence at White's, but actually welcome it." Gerry's cynical words were belied by the amusement in his expression.

"If the fellows at White's are this fickle, I'd better make my way to Brooke's." It was an old joke. No one could explain Stratford's acceptance by the peerage when his father had no title and his mother's family was in trade, but from his early days at Eton, then at Cambridge, everyone liked him, and no one contested the invitation. He was sure his long-standing friendship with Ingram helped matters, but if he thought his addition to the peerage changed anything to those who counted, he would have turned his affections elsewhere.

At that moment, Mr. Braxsen spotted him and came over, his expression mocking. "Is this Lord Worthing? And to think I'd hoped to outrank you in the military. I'd no idea you were in line for a peerage."

His tone was playful, but Stratford felt there was some truth to his words. "With an uncle and two cousins in line ahead of me, it was too far removed a possibility for me to speak of it. And you? You've sold out?"

"I'm on furlough," Braxsen replied. He turned his head toward a laughing, impeccably attired Corinthian verbally sparring with only the faintest of accents. "Look over there," he said with a sneer. "How did one of Boney's men push his way in?"

"Oh, I suppose he came over in eighty-nine with his family." Stratford fingered his pocket watch and looked over the crowd.

"Don't it bother you, then? I, for one, can't bear to see 'em here," Braxsen said.

The dark leather walls and the sounds of the club faded away as Stratford remembered his first close encounter with the enemy. A white-faced boy, who could not have been more than seventeen, trembling alone in a cow shed, his breeches wet from terror. The boy put his arms up to shield his face from the sunlight streaming through the spaces in the wooden lath-board.

"*Vas-y. Caches-toi. On sera parti avant l'aube,*" Stratford had told him. Hide. We'll be gone by dawn. On the battlefield, en masse, the French were the enemy. As individuals, they bled red like he did.

"No." Stratford answered Braxsen firmly. "They're pawns under Boney and Murat. If he—" Stratford jerked his head toward the Frenchman, "has gained acceptance at White's, his loyalties must be unexceptionable."

"Worthing," Amesbury called from his table, interrupting a conversation Stratford was increasingly glad to leave. "You've come so soon." Stratford nodded a farewell to Braxsen and took a seat next to Amesbury.

"I did, indeed. It's my sisters' second Season, and as much as I'd have liked to stay at the estate, I'm responsible for opening the house and launching their ball."

Amesbury nodded, and a short silence ensued before he drew a breath. "I say." He paused to take a drink and leaned back with studied nonchalance. "Have you seen Miss Daventry in London yet?"

"No, I've only just arrived. Why do you ask?" Stratford looked out the window as a sudden rainstorm sent figures scurrying for cover outside.

"I say," Amesbury repeated, absently. There was another pause as he tapped the edge of his lorgnette on the table.

"I wish you would," Stratford said. Amesbury shot him a look of confusion, and he clarified: "*Say it*, that is."

Amesbury sucked in his breath and said, "I was thinking I might try my hand at Miss Daventry."

Stratford's brows shot up. "I thought you disliked her parentage, and just about everything else. You found it hard to sit next to her at lunch."

"Yes, but I've been thinking." Gathering steam, his friend refilled his glass. "Her lineage cannot be that questionable if your uncle accepted to be her guardian. And her owning the Munroe hamlet would be an asset to my property. If I lent her my credibility, I'm sure she would be received." Stratford felt bile rise in his throat.

Amesbury went on, "Unless, of course, you . . ." His voice trailed away as he looked a question at Stratford.

"No, no, of course not," Stratford declared. "As you've reminded me, I cannot be too careful in choosing a countess."

Amesbury missed the sarcastic tone. "You're right about that. I, however, need look no further than a gentleman's daughter with a good portion." Amesbury straightened the neckcloth around his skinny neck.

"You can take your chances with her in a week's time," Stratford said, in a clipped tone. "I have it on authority from Ingram that she'll be presented at Lady Ingram's ball when she brings Lydia out."

"Miss Lydia Ingram. Now she would make a suitable wife to an earl," Amesbury mused.

"Lydia's a scamp," Stratford said roundly. "She'll marry someone she can bring 'round her thumb." Dismissing Ingram's little sister, his thoughts drifted to the brown-eyed woman who was staying at her house.

Amesbury stared ahead unseeing, already, it seemed, planning his assault on Lydia or Miss Daventry or anyone who would have him. Stratford looked around the club to see what other long-lost face might bring relief. He was feeling out of sorts.

Chapter Ten

Eleanor did not expect her first *soirée* to be a success, and therefore she was not disappointed. Lady Ingram had made no objection to the girls attending a small gathering—quite a private affair—with no more than fifteen partners standing up to dance in Mrs. Jenkins's ballroom, saying it would give them practice for their own come-out ball in a week's time.

Her first peek into the room confirmed her suspicion that even an intimate London gathering was an intimidating affair. Mrs. Jenkins had grossly underestimated the number of people who would reply in the affirmative. There were nearly seventy people present, with the younger generation camped at the refreshment table and the adults closer to the fire. The warmth was welcome, coming out of the cold, but the room would soon become stifling.

Returning Lydia's bolstering smile, Eleanor straightened her shoulders and followed her into the room. There was no formal announcement, and no one noticed her, although she spotted more than a few pairs of eyes drawn to her friend—the men with interest and the girls with envy. Eleanor tugged at her gloves and fought to keep her expression neutral. *At the very least, the numbers are evened so I needn't fear I'll lack for partners.*

Lydia leaned in to whisper. "I know some of the gentlemen here since I cut my first teeth. Do you see the dashing one there in the dark blue coat?" Eleanor nodded. "That's Lord Carlton, and he has his eye on politics, besides being an earl. He spent his first year out of Oxford caring for his mother at their country estate. Everyone will be setting her cap at him now that he's in London, but *I* shall introduce you, for he is friends with my cousin. He's pleasing to look at, is he not?"

"He is indeed, but young to be on the catch for a wife, don't you think?" Eleanor knew Lord Carlton could not possibly notice her with Lydia nearby. She watched him make the rounds. He seemed to know everyone and pay particular attention to the older women, giving wide berth to the women his age.

Lydia shrugged. "Perhaps. But securing his notice will be a feather in your cap."

Eleanor attempted a smile, her clammy hands betraying her nervousness. She was grateful for the gloves. Mr. Braxsen chose that moment to approach, his copper-headed military companion in tow. "Miss Ingram," Mr. Braxsen said, "may I claim your hand for the first dance? You'd promised it to me, remember?"

"Certainly, Mr. Braxsen. It's fortunate I keep my word. I could have given that dance away several times over."

"A woman who keeps her word. Now that is something." Mr. Braxsen took the dance card Lydia slipped off her wrist.

Lydia's frown disappeared as fast as it came, and she took Eleanor by the elbow. "Eleanor, you remember Mr. Braxsen, and this is . . ." She tilted her face to his friend like an inquisitive bird. *No wonder men love her.*

"Excuse me," Mr. Braxsen said, "This is Major Fitzwilliam. Fitz—allow me to present Miss Lydia Ingram and her companion, Miss Daventry."

When the introductions were made, Major Fitzwilliam pulled his eyes off Lydia and bowed to Eleanor. "Have you been claimed for the second dance? I am not free for the first, but I should very much like to dance with you if you care to."

Eleanor gave the major a friendly smile and handed him her card. "Already the musicians are warming up, and my dance card is still empty. So you see, you are saving me from complete humiliation."

He scribbled his name and returned it, creases appearing in his square jaw. "I'm at your service, Miss Daventry." Turning to Lydia, he pinned her with his gaze. "Miss Ingram, have you any dance for me?"

Lydia had been scanning the room and was about to whisper in Eleanor's ear, but she was checked by the frank regard settled on her. "I'd be delighted, Major Fitzwilliam. If only to do my duty in encouraging the men who serve the king."

Major Fitzwilliam responded, "And if only it were not done solely out of duty, we poor soldiers might dare hope." There was a playful intensity to his gaze that Eleanor privately felt was irresistible. This man might not have a title, but he had no shortage of charm. If he turned it on Lydia, a hardened flirt, even she might not be immune.

Lydia laughed then, a bright tinkling sound. "You shall have your dance, major." She appraised him more closely. "And not solely out of duty."

The major bowed, and Mr. Braxsen clapped him on the back as the two men walked away. "You're trying to steal a march on me, Fitz."

"Lydia," Eleanor said in a low voice, "it seems you've found favor with one at least. Is not Major Fitzwilliam distinguished in his colors? He must be on furlough."

Lydia glanced after him. "Red does not suit him," was all she would say. Her lingering gaze betrayed her.

To cover an excess of nerves, Eleanor fanned herself and murmured, "It appears I'll not be obliged to sit on the sidelines *all* evening."

"Gudgeon." Lydia poked her side, then leaned in to whisper, "Look here. Stratford Tunstall is headed our way. I told you he got jilted? Except now he's an earl—"

He was here. Eleanor wanted to interrupt, but Lydia rushed on. "He's an old family friend from back when he was a mere son of a gentleman and tradesman's daughter. Even my mother likes him, though she couldn't extend an invitation to his mother, of course."

As Lydia spoke, Lord Worthing strode toward them, his gaze unwavering as he held Eleanor's. Her heart beat unsteadily, and she could barely find the strength to respond. "Lydia, did you not remember that my guardian was the former Earl of Worthing? I was at Worthing for the reading of the will. He and I have met, of course. No introduction is needed." *Nor desired.*

"No, indeed! *I* am the gudgeon for forgetting *that*. But you did not often speak of your guardian, so I didn't make the connection. Still, how foolish of me."

Having exchanged a word with the hostess, the earl now advanced again, his face set in a frown. "He doesn't look best pleased to see us," Eleanor said.

"Oh, that's just Stratford," Lydia whispered. "He's so severe. He probably thinks my dress is cut too low." Before Eleanor could reply, the earl was upon them.

"Lydia." He bowed over Miss Ingram's hand. "I see you're acquainted with Miss Daventry." His gaze held Eleanor's, and she forced herself to return it.

"Indeed I am, my lord," Lydia drawled. "How kind of you to grace us with your presence now that you're an earl."

Lord Worthing cut her short with a look. "Don't be arch, Lydia."

Lydia rolled her eyes. "That's not being arch, Stratford. That is funning, which you have forgotten how to do. Very well. Eleanor is spending the London Season with me."

"Good evening, Miss Daventry." Lord Worthing bowed. "May I inquire after your aunt's ailing sister?"

"I thank you. She is on the mend. They have taken a house in Bath so she may recuperate fully. I'm grateful to Lady Ingram for sponsoring me this Season." *I'm rambling like a ninny!* Eleanor attempted to herd her disordered thoughts as the earl, after that first searing regard, seemed to look everywhere but at her.

"You cannot do better than Lady Ingram for gaining access anywhere you might wish to go." Lord Worthing turned to nod at an acquaintance. There was a silence until the first strains of a violin filtered through the room. "Will you both do me the honor of a dance?" He held out his hand for Lydia's dance card.

"Why, certainly." Lydia handed the card still attached to her wrist and peered above his head as he leaned to write his name in one of the few remaining lines. "Look, Eleanor. There's the Duke of Marlborough. Oh! And Mr. Braxsen is coming to claim his dance."

Eleanor's eyes were on Lord Worthing's dark blond locks as he bent over Lydia's card. It gave her time to still her jumpy nerves and realize he was just a man who need not have any significance over another, proposal notwithstanding, even if his strong jaw and broad shoulders were pleasing to look at. Lord Worthing straightened and stepped aside to allow an approaching servant to present a tray of assorted drinks. Eleanor shook her head, but the earl accepted a glass.

At his choice, Eleanor's eyes widened in surprise, and a smile quivered on her lips. "Lemonade, Lord Worthing?"

She thought to have perceived a faint blush. "I'm thirsty," he said. He drank it in one go and then set the glass back on the tray. "Miss Daventry, your card?" Her breath caught when their gaze met again. *He is just a man, like any other man.* She held out her card, looking away as he wrote his name for the quadrille. It would provide a better chance to talk than the first two dances, which were both a reel.

There was only one other name on Miss Daventry's dance card, Stratford saw, now that he'd turned his attention to it instead of her hastily averted face. Her profile was appealing with a decided chin that matched a pert nose and a tendril of light-brown hair next to her cheek. With only one name, it seemed he need not be afraid she would be hounded by fortune hunters. He dropped Miss Daventry's card and let it dangle from her wrist.

"Worthing!" Lord Carlton came to his side, a young chub who'd regularly come up to London during school leave. "When I saw you at Tatt's, you'd not mentioned you'd be attending."

Stratford coughed, darting a surreptitious look at the man, who, though likable, had never possessed an ounce of discretion. "I hadn't made up my mind then to come, but there were some people I wished to speak to this evening." He shot a hopeful look at Miss Daventry, but she was studiously watching the dancing couples. It wasn't going to be easy after so many weeks, but honor demanded he make an apology, and the promised dance would be his best chance.

With a natural address, Lord Carlton put his hand on his heart and bowed to the ladies. "Miss Ingram, grant my heart's desire and introduce me to your friend?"

Lydia, flirting at her finest, gave a delicate snort. "Pay him no heed, Eleanor. Lord Carlton led my cousin into all manner of mischief during their years at Cambridge, I'm told. It seems he has at last turned respectable. Very well, Lord Carlton, I present my dearest friend, Miss Daventry."

Lord Carlton's eyes widened in mock affront. "You malign me, Miss Ingram. That was two full years ago and is now a thing of the past." He nodded to Mr. Braxsen, who had come to claim Lydia's hand, and then said, "Miss Daventry, would you do me the honor of according me a dance this evening?"

"Of course, Lord Carlton." Miss Daventry's voice was soft as she handed him her dance card. Stratford was surprised by Carlton's interest, and he scrutinized Miss Daventry. Perhaps it was because she was so petite and it made one wish to protect her, or because she met one's gaze frankly, without being coy.

Stratford frowned. He might have judged her safe from fortune hunters too soon. If Carlton, who had no need of her money, were interested, there was no telling how many others would come forward. The man would have her all the rage before long.

Continuing with his conquest as if Stratford didn't even exist, Carlton bent his head toward hers. "Miss Daventry, this next dance is a reel and no one has put his name down for it. I hope you will not be shocked, but I claimed this dance as well as the last one of the party."

She answered with a smile of her own, eyes dancing, and Stratford was bewitched. He didn't know her face could light up that way. "Thank you for sparing me the disgrace of sitting this first dance out, Lord Carlton." The musicians began the prelude, and Miss Daventry put her hand on Carlton's arm to join the other couples in the set, leaving Stratford prey to the looks of more than one hopeful mama whose daughter lacked a partner.

When Stratford was finally able to claim his dance with Miss Daventry, he nearly lost his courage. Only a dogged sense of determination to right a wrong led him to continue. They took their places in the set, and while waiting for the music to start, he leaned down, knowing the loud buzz of conversation would make his words private. "Miss Daventry, please allow me to apologize for proposing to you."

A smile was whisked away before he caught it—he was sure of it. Why would she find humor in words that were so difficult for him to utter? Then, after a minute's reflection, *Ah. I apologized for proposing, not for the manner in which I proposed.*

The dance had begun and as they circled each other, hands clasped, she answered. "You need not, my lord. As I imagine it won't happen again, we can both pretend it hadn't happened at all."

They changed partners, and when the dance brought them back together, Stratford blundered on, hoping to dispel Miss Daventry's frown. "I don't make a habit of proposing to ladies almost at first sight. My only other experience with proposing was done after two years' acquaintance." He paused. "Of course it didn't end well either." His whole body felt hot with embarrassment, a regular pattern around her, it seemed. He hadn't meant to say that.

"Did you propose to her while you were in your cups, my lord?" A shock went through him as the dance separated them again. He took the hand of another lady in the set and wondered what was behind that tone. Miss Daventry was a schoolgirl miss—*his sisters' age*—but her words whipped his already smarting conscience.

They were brought back together by the music, and he tugged at his dignity. "Please accept my sincere regrets for proposing to you in such an unworthy manner. As you said, it shan't happen again."

The dance separated them once more. *Impossible to talk this way. What had possessed him to try?* He was barely conscious of his own partner as he watched Miss Daventry in animated conversation. *Why was she so silent around him?* When they were joined after the promenade, her words were subdued. "I thank you for your apology. Of course it won't. We need say nothing more."

He looked at her downturned eyes, and something compelled him to insist. "Pardon me, Miss Daventry, but . . . do I have your forgiveness for my ungentlemanly behavior? It is important to me."

The music had stopped, and she removed her suddenly trembling hand from his arm. "My lord—" Her husky voice was difficult to hear over the crowd. He leaned in and felt the warmth of her face, her breath tickling his cheek, his unexpected desire to put his arm around her waist. Perhaps with the air between them cleared, they might share some future dances. A Season in London could possibly be enjoyable.

She seemed to struggle within herself, finally biting her lip before raising her eyes to his. "Perhaps this is not very Christian of me, but I should like to see your repentance before returning an answer."

The gleam in her eye provoked him into a startled laugh. "Was the lemonade not repentance enough?" he asked, a smile still playing on his lips. Then he grew serious. "I see I shall have to labor to earn your good opinion of me." The couples dancing cleared the floor to make room for new ones, and he took her arm, conscious of her nearness.

At that instant, the voices grew in volume, and he looked up. A vision of loveliness had entered the room in pale green, crowned with golden curls and a delicate tiara of emeralds. Judith Broadmore. So she, too, had been invited to this *intimate* gathering of people. Stratford would not trust that descriptor again when attached to a London assembly. He would not have come, even for the apology, had he known he would be thrown in such close quarters with Judith.

Miss Daventry was studying him with a crease between her brows. He had to say something. "I'm afraid I must leave. I promised to meet a friend for dinner and am past due."

Other couples were joining up for the next set, and Lydia, mercifully, was still on the sidelines, rapping a gentleman's sleeve with her fan. "I will bring you to Lydia," he said.

At Miss Broadmore's entrance, Eleanor felt a stab of dismay. In a day dress, Miss Broadmore was beautiful enough to turn eyes, but in an evening gown she was nothing short of stunning. Never had Eleanor been so chagrined at her own curves, short stature, and plain brown hair.

The dance was over, and the brief glimpse she had behind Lord Worthing's facade now seemed imagined. They were once again at Lydia's side, and his face was a mask as he turned to leave.

"Well, if that isn't like Stratford," Lydia huffed. "Not even a proper farewell."

Eleanor's gaze trailed Lord Worthing as he bid the hostess good night and left without turning back. He did not speak to Miss Broadmore as he passed, but Eleanor saw his profile as he acknowledged the woman. She was sure the look he cast at this Venus was one of longing.

Miss Broadmore also watched him leave. Then, with swaying hips, she followed.

Chapter Eleven

"Lord Worthing, wait."

Stratford had retrieved his cloak and was on the steps leading to the street when he turned to see Judith hurry after him. He did not relish having this conversation, but better it be now at the beginning of the Season so there was no ambiguity between the two of them.

"Miss Broadmore." He completed the last three steps to the street and waited for her to reach his side before giving her a short bow.

She seemed to be breathless as she curtsied, and he wondered if she was nervous. He had never seen her other than entirely sure of herself, but perhaps some of the confidence that came with being a young, beautiful woman disappeared after a few Seasons and no successful matches.

That errant thought disappeared as Judith smiled at Stratford and slid her hand into his arm. No, it seemed her confidence was still in place. Her touch was painful, as much for the memories it evoked as for his certainty she was not the one he wished to be holding.

"I am delighted to see you have not only arrived in London at the start of the Season but are also out socializing. I did not have such high hopes for you." Judith gave his arm a playful squeeze as she spoke, and Stratford did not respond right away. Knowing what one must say did not make the words any easier to get out.

"Have you none of your witty replies then?" Judith breathed in deeply and looked at the stars. "Do you remember when we were caught in the rain on our way back from Hyde Park? It was right around this time of year. We stopped in the baker's, and you bought me a strawberry tart to eat while it poured outside." She looked at him, a coy smile on her face. "That was the day you proposed to me."

Stratford pulled her arm out from his and turned to face her. "Miss Broadmore, it is better for us to be clear before the Season begins so there might be no ambiguity." After only a moment's hesitation, he drove his words home. "Any hope for us is over."

Judith's lips trembled into a smile. "How like you to come straight to the point, Stratford. You might simply have humored me, treating me as an old friend to spare me the embarrassment of a confrontation."

Whatever friendship we might have had is long gone. Judith was still tempting, but it was all the more reason to set limits and expectations. He knew keeping possibilities open with her laid a path to more heartache— *his.* Stratford shook his head. "It is my furthest wish to embarrass you, but you must know where things stand."

Judith seemed to be waiting for him to say more, but anything else would only be belaboring the point. He gave a brief bow and turned to go. "I bid you good night."

The drawing room held a modest display of flowers sent every day by admirers since Mrs. Jenkins's party. Eleanor and Lydia had barely had time to sit for the morning callers when Mr. Braxsen and Major Fitzwilliam were announced. Eleanor whispered to Lydia with a roguish smile. "They're here bright and early, though they'll see you tonight at the ball. I believe they wish to beat the others out with an advance attack."

"Unless they're here for you," Lydia replied without conviction, but also without malice. "And it's *our* come-out ball."

Eleanor gave a tiny shrug but favored her friend with a smile, which grew broader when the door opened and Major Fitzwilliam strode toward Lydia with a single focus.

"Mr. Braxsen, Major Fitzwilliam." Lydia gave them each her hand. "I trust we will see you both at our ball tonight?"

"We came to see if we might help you prepare." Major Fitzwilliam maneuvered next to her on the settee, showing more address than he had yet shown in her presence. Or more determination.

Lydia, not indifferent to the major's attention, sat straighter. "I believe everything is looked after. We've been fortunate that Frederick is here to oversee the details with Mama." After a small pause, Lydia patted her glove. "Of course, he is more than usually busy."

Mr. Braxsen took the chair near Eleanor and drawled, "Yes, I spotted your brother at Brooke's laying bets on Milford's mare against Dalton's. I can see he is entirely devoted to the success of your ball."

Eleanor stifled a giggle and studied Mr. Braxsen's face, wondering what brought him to visit. It was clear he had no marked partiality for Lydia, but he didn't seem generous enough to come simply because his friend was enamored.

"And will you come this evening, Mr. Braxsen?" Eleanor asked, bent on being amiable.

"Undoubtedly," was his reply. He toyed with the fob attached to his waistcoat as Lydia and the major bent their heads in conversation that left little room for anyone else. Eleanor folded her hands on her lap and waited, but Mr. Braxsen was content to look around the room in silence.

She sighed. Was there no man in London capable of conversation? Lydia made conquests of every gentleman she met. With Eleanor, men seemed bored. *As if I'm not worth the effort.*

But there was one. For all his faults, Lord Worthing, at least, did not ignore her.

Lydia's maid slipped Eleanor's dress over her outstretched arms. The pale gold underdress would have been lost beneath the white overlay had it not been for the gold rosebuds that caught the sheer fabric in dozens of tiny gathers. The gold silk made up the bodice of the dress, with a white gauze fichu providing slightly more modest cover. *Not enough though*, Eleanor thought. She felt exposed.

Still, although she knew she would pale next to Lydia, she was quite pleased with her appearance. She hooked the gold pendant diamonds that her mother had left behind in her haste into her ears, and the maid clasped the tiny pearl necklace with a matching gold pendant around her neck.

As expected, Lydia eclipsed her friend in beauty when she entered the drawing room in pale pink with a spray of flowers in her hair. Her cheeks held a natural rosy glow, unlike Eleanor's more sallow complexion, and her hair was nearer to black, which would always outshine Eleanor's mousy brown. *I'm happy Lydia looks so well*, Eleanor told herself, desiring to be generous.

Lord Ingram, dressed to the nines in a crisp black jacket and snowy white cravat, stepped away from his mother by the fireplace and moved toward them, greeting his sister with a kiss on the cheek and then bowing over Eleanor's hand. "Brunettes are in fashion this year, and I see our household will be the center of the ton with two such beauties as this." Despite his smile, Lord Ingram had a tiny frown line between his eyes, and Eleanor wondered if it could possibly be the stress of hosting. Apart from the brief snatch of conversation they'd had upon her arrival, she had only seen him in passing since.

Lydia stuck out her bottom lip. "How can you say so? You know Mary Wexby has enamored all of London with her flaxen hair until no one has eyes for anyone else."

"All the better to set you apart, my dear," Lord Ingram said sincerely. *What a lucky thing to have family.*

Lydia gasped. "I almost forgot my posy." She darted over to the side table where the small arrangement was waiting.

"Will you have some sherry, Mama, before we take our positions in the hall?" Lord Ingram was determined to do everything correctly, it seemed, now that he was actually here.

Lady Ingram accepted a tiny glass of sherry. "Better to have a cake with your cordial, girls. We will be greeting guests for hours, and I do not wish for you to faint."

The lady of the house had spoken no less than the truth. After two hours of greeting guests in the hall by the front door, Eleanor was beginning to force her smile. At least she was near the entrance where more fresh air poured into the stifling residence that boasted crackling fires in every chimney. She breathed in the fresh air now and felt a frisson of nerves. Lord Worthing had not shown up, and she had been sure he would, given his close ties with the family. Eleanor wasn't sure why she wished for him and could only conclude it was because she knew so few people. She wouldn't admit to herself that everything seemed more interesting when he was near.

"Mr. Amesbury, Mr. Ashton," the footman announced. He appeared never to grow tired of giving each name with relish.

Lydia curtsied as Mr. Amesbury bowed over her hand and kissed the air above it. "How do you do? Mr. Amesbury, may I present my friend—"

"We've met," he said. "Miss Daventry, I regret we did not have more time at dinner to converse."

The nerve! They'd had plenty of opportunity. He was just too disgusted then with Eleanor's lineage to act the part of a gentleman. She could guess what prompted the change. "Good evening, Mr. Amesbury."

Oblivious to her lack of enthusiasm, Mr. Amesbury inclined his head toward the card around her wrist. "Allow me to claim a dance."

"I believe my card is full, sir—" She was not able to finish before he slipped the dance card off her wrist and examined it.

"No, see here. There's one dance left, even if it's only a reel. I dare not claim your hand for one of the waltzes, for I'm sure Lady Ingram would not permit it." *Thank heavens for that.* He penciled his name in the last slot.

"You honor me, sir." The words had only just left her lips when the footman announced, "Lord Worthing."

Despite herself, Eleanor's heart leapt. *I must learn to be less transparent,* she thought. It would be humiliating if Lord Worthing were to guess her pleasure at his arrival, an emotion that did no credit to her dignity.

"My lady, you outshine everyone here"—words that seemed too glib for Lord Worthing, but it was he bowing over Lady Ingram's hand and then reaching out to shake Ingram's. "Frederick. Magnificent turnout."

"Stratford," Lady Ingram said, disapproval apparent in her voice, "we had quite given you up. How unlike you to be so late for a party." In an instant, her demeanor changed. "Ah, I see you are not quite alone in your delinquency. Mr. Brummel, you've come at last."

"As you see." Mr. Brummel shot a glance at Lydia. "And perhaps I shall stay." The exquisitely attired gentleman was flanked by a small satellite of Corinthians, nattily attired but falling short of his magnificent elegance. Feigning boredom, the four men looked to the Beau, who responded to a sign from within. With only the slightest bow to Lydia, they vanished into the salon without paying heed to Eleanor.

Lady Ingram followed them with her gaze, her lips pursed. "The most deplorable manners, I know. But Mr. Brummel's attendance assures your ball is hailed a success, girls."

Eleanor arched a brow. "*He* is the famous Beau Brummel? I expected someone more impressive."

The earl caught her words and laughed, eyes crinkling. "Don't let him hear you say so, Miss Daventry. You'll be snubbed out of town." Eleanor felt the corners of her mouth lift as his laughter warmed her like a caress. *Here* was someone who did not find her boring.

Lord Worthing then turned to Lydia with a rueful smile. "I, alas, have less license than he does and had to let him go first. I'm sorry, Lydia."

She was having none of it. "Stratford. We expected you hours ago."

Ignoring her scolding, he gave a chaste kiss on her cheek. "Phoebe bid me to thank you for your reply to her note. She and Anna are still laid up with a cold and regret very much having to miss this evening."

All signs of petulance vanished, and Lydia's face showed concern. "It's more important your sisters are *en forme* for their ball next week. If they are well enough to receive before then, I'll visit." Lord Worthing nodded and moved in front of Eleanor.

"Miss Daventry, you look lovely." His gaze lingered on her exposed bosom, then shot up to her face.

Eleanor took a breath but had trouble getting the air into her lungs. "Lord Worthing," she replied in a composed voice, but her trembling lips gave her away.

He peeled his gaze from hers when the doors to the manor were closed, and Lady Ingram relaxed her posture. "I believe we may join our guests now. Frederick, you will take Lydia." Her sharp eyes scanned the earl. "Stratford, your arrival is timely. You may escort Miss Daventry into the assembly."

There was a stir when the party made its way into the ballroom. Eleanor, unaccustomed to such attention, only noticed she had gripped the earl's arm when he patted her hand reassuringly. She forced herself to relax. Thankfully, all eyes were on Lydia as her friend descended the stairs on the arm of her brother.

Lord Worthing leaned down to speak, and Eleanor felt the warmth of his cheek next to hers. "It's only natural that I should escort you into the ballroom," he said. "My friendship with the Ingram family is of long date. We were neighbors before I inherited Worthing."

Eleanor nodded. There were now only a few curious stares directed her way as the people in the room geared up for the first dance. "I find I don't like a great deal of attention," she said.

"Which you could hardly hope to avoid at your own come-out ball."

She gave a prim smile. "Even so."

"Lady Ingram was right about you both being a success. I felicitate you. But tell me, your intimacy with the Ingram family intrigues me. How did you come to know Lydia?"

"We became friends at school. It was as simple as that," Eleanor said.

"As simple as that. Yet you are not very alike. You are not two in whom one would expect any affection to grow." Lord Worthing guided her to the side to let people pass. "Lydia is only concerned with fripperies and conquests, and you seem of a more serious nature." Pausing, he added, "If you'll permit my saying so."

"For all you know Lydia, I believe you have misjudged her in this," Eleanor said. Her lips grew more prim. "If you'll permit my saying so."

"Perhaps. That Lydia would wish to invite you is one thing, but for her mother to accept is quite another. It's a mystery, really. The late Lord Ingram was a generous man, but Lady Ingram is slow to foster acquaintances and even slower to invite one into her home." He drew his brows together, trying to puzzle it out. "I suspect she felt you posed no real threat to Lydia's chances."

Eleanor jerked and Lord Worthing looked at her, his startled eyes betraying too late the unintentional insult and the regret that followed. Before either could speak, Frederick Ingram was in front of Eleanor. "Miss Daventry, I believe this honor is mine."

Eleanor, still stunned from the blow, grasped at her unruly thoughts and tried to put them in order. *So, my lord. You wish to remind me of my dearth of fortune, beauty, and prospects. This is hardly repentance.* She placed her hand on Lord Ingram's arm and dismissed Lord Worthing in a cool voice. "I thank you for escorting me into the ball."

Before she and Lord Ingram moved away, Eleanor had the satisfaction of seeing Lord Worthing speechless.

Chapter Twelve

Lord Ingram was an accomplished dance partner and didn't show the distraction he must be feeling as host of the ball. His ease in keeping Eleanor engaged in conversation, even making her laugh, allowed her to forget the insulting words uttered by Lord Worthing. Her next partner, Mr. Weatherby, did not afford this luxury as he was too nervous to make any conversation at all.

Mr. Weatherby, whose burnished cheeks and apple-shaped face were crowned by a halo of blond hair, bowed before her and gulped as she rested her hand on his arm. In silence, they took a place in the set and waited for the music to begin. *Where is Lord Worthing now?* she mused. Nowhere to be seen, though there was Mr. Amesbury staring at her as if she were prey. *Small wonder he and the earl are friends*, she thought with spite.

Eleanor forced herself to focus on her silent partner and gave him an encouraging smile, which he returned. Here was a promising beginning. "Mr. Weatherby, how well you dance," she said.

"Thank you," he returned and offered nothing further. *How could Lord Worthing insult me by comparing me unfavorably to Lydia? Surely he cannot be so obtuse as to have done it accidentally. But he looked remorseful . . .* She and her partner turned to face the orchestra, continuing their dance in silence. If only Mr. Weatherby would make conversation, she would have an easier time focusing on the dance and not on a frustrating gentleman just out of sight.

She made another attempt. "Lydia tells me you've just completed your studies at Edinburgh. Will you be making your stay in London?"

"If my father permits it. He wishes me to learn the management of the estate, and I had to petition him for at least one Season in London." Mr. Weatherby nearly turned the wrong way but caught himself before he did any damage.

There was Lord Worthing. Not leading anyone in a dance but talking to Lord Ingram. How comfortable for him. She refused to give him any more of her notice. Turning to her partner, Eleanor said, "I understand having a London Season is *de rigeur*, particularly since there are no Grand Tours to the Continent anymore. It's natural you should wish it." They moved to the side to allow the next set to finish their figures.

"I've grown up on the estate and trailed my father and his bailiff since I could walk. In Edinburgh, I learned new farming techniques and business practices that I will never be permitted to implement as long as my father has the run of the place." He shrugged. "*I* feel my greater need is to acquire a bit of town bronze." His ears turned red, and he added, "Somehow I don't feel awkward saying that to *you*."

She warmed to him. "You needn't feel awkward saying *anything* to me. I confess to sympathizing with your wish. I'm trying to look as if this is all natural to me, but the truth is I've led a rather secluded life. This," she used her free hand to encompass the throng of people, "is quite besides what I am used to."

"Miss Daventry," he said, gaining confidence, "I would never have guessed you were not born and bred in London."

She leaned back to look at him, eyes wide. "That is a bald-faced lie, and you know it, Mr. Weatherby," and she laughed at his answering grin.

By the time the dance ended, Mr. Weatherby was perfectly at ease, even loquacious. She was glad she had danced with him rather than a rude and incomprehensible earl. Mr. Weatherby voiced his own pleasure with his parting words. "Now that I've been bolstered by Miss Daventry, I need have no fear of presenting myself to more intimidating partners."

"Indeed not!" she replied. "I should think any lady present would be delighted to be asked by you."

Eleanor's dance card was full, which took away some of the sting of Lord Worthing's barb. Aside from Mr. Amesbury, who claimed his dance and made stilted, desultory conversation, she was asked by Mr. Braxsen, who could be humorous when he chose; Lord Carlton, a perfectly amiable gentleman who seemed ready to be pleased with any of his partners; and even Major Fitzwilliam, whom, she suspected, wished for the dance as an excuse to inquire after Lydia.

She looked into the latter's frank, smiling brown eyes and contrasted them with Lord Worthing's green ones, which always seemed to be shadowed by irritation, or—when she was being fair—worry. As Major Fitzwilliam led her down the promenade, she followed his gaze over to Lydia, who was partnered with an elegantly clad gentleman on the other end of the room.

"Don't you think Miss Ingram looks perfect tonight?" Eleanor peeped at him with a mischievous smile. "She couldn't have made a lovelier picture for her come-out ball."

"Miss Daventry." The major's steps almost faltered, and he shook his head with a rueful smile. "You have caught my wandering eye, I fear—and which is most unfair. *You* are a picture of loveliness, and may I remind you it is your come-out ball as well."

"It was gracious of the Ingrams to include me this Season, but it was never my intention to draw any notice to myself." She added simply, "Lydia is my dearest friend."

"She is lucky to have you." Major Fitzwilliam seemed to wrestle with himself for a moment. "Miss Daventry, might I . . . would it not be too forward if I . . ." He stopped short with a wrinkled brow.

Eleanor stepped into the pause. "You may safely confide in me, Major Fitzwilliam, if that's what you're asking."

His shoulders slumped in relief. "I should just like to know whether Miss Ingram's heart is previously engaged and, perhaps, what sort of things she likes."

Eleanor remembered how her friend's eyes sparkled as she bantered with the major in the drawing room and had formed her own opinion, but it was not one in which she was at liberty to share. "Miss Ingram has not confided in me any prior attachment. She likes to dance, is an excellent horsewoman, and adores strawberry ices and white peonies."

Major Fitzwilliam's grave reply was belied by his wink. "Your intelligence has provided me with my next strategic move. I fear I don't show to advantage on horseback—not alongside a bruising rider—but dancing, peonies, and Gunters I can do. I'm lucky to have had my intelligence from someone who is so close at hand."

She nodded, reflecting that this had been her second most pleasing dance. If only the others might be as friendly.

Eleanor caught glimpses of Lord Worthing. Here he was talking to Lydia and Lady Ingram. There he was heading into the card room with Major Fitzwilliam. There again he was dancing with a pretty debutante, and he did not so much as glance Eleanor's way when he passed her in the dance figures. Eleanor then threw herself into the evening—reveling in the new sensation of being in the spotlight, dancing the lively reels with abandon, and laughing more brightly at each sally—all out of a desperation she could not explain to herself.

Lord Worthing remained at the ball nearly as long as the hosts, and although he could not have known Eleanor's dance card was full, he stayed on the sidelines most of the night. Eleanor, reckless and sparkling, danced until the wee hours of the morning, never once having been solicited by the earl.

A week later, Lord Worthing held his coronet ball, disguised, it seemed, as a ball for his sisters. "Stratford will not draw attention to himself," Lydia explained.

Eleanor was invited, of course, because she accompanied the Ingram family. It would be her first formal outing since the come-out ball, and she was relieved to attend an event where she would not be a prominent feature. Lydia thought of it as sharing the spotlight with childhood friends, for it was inconceivable she should disappear completely into the backdrop.

When their party came in from the brisk outdoors, Lord Worthing was at the head of the receiving line. He shifted when she came into view, and his gaze searched hers, but she couldn't read his thoughts. Eleanor stood apart as the two parties greeted one another as old acquaintances.

When Eleanor was before Lord Worthing, he looked as though he wished to address the lingering awkwardness. Instead he gestured to his right and said, "May I present my aunt, Mrs. Shae, and my two sisters, the Misses Phoebe and Anna Tunstall."

Mrs. Shae acknowledged Eleanor's curtsy with a gracious nod before returning her focus to the door, apparently tired and ready for this part of the evening to be over. Eleanor then found herself staring at two curious, identical faces with smooth blonde hair, eyes so blue they bordered on violet, and smiles—one demure, one mischievous. She noticed Lord Worthing watching the exchange.

One of the twins spoke. "Stratford mentioned we are to be neighbors. You've inherited a portion of our property." Eleanor couldn't discern any malice, though the words themselves sounded cutting. What must they think of the circumstances surrounding her inheritance?

She couldn't imagine how to respond to the question and only nodded. Grasping for conversation, she asked, "Will you tell me again, please, which one of you is Miss Anna Tunstall and which one is Miss Phoebe?" Tonight, at least, one wore a white dress with blue accents and one wore a white dress with red.

The one who had spoken answered first. "I'm Phoebe." She gestured to the other in red accents. "And this is Anna."

Eleanor smiled. "I will remember now. I'm pleased to make your acquaintance." Risking another look at Lord Worthing, she attempted to move on, but he stayed her with one hand.

"Miss Daventry—" He stopped short when he saw that Anna's attention was on him, and Eleanor wondered what he was about to say. She was quite certain it was not what came next. "I fear I may be preoccupied tonight with the duties of a host and unable to see to your personal comfort, but it is my sincere wish that you should enjoy yourself."

Eleanor nodded and followed the Ingrams down the stairwell to the ballroom. That meant Lord Worthing would not ask her to dance tonight. Suddenly the prospect of the evening felt flat. It was incomprehensible that she should care for him after his disastrous proposal and blundering speech at every turn. Yet, she couldn't shake the feeling that deep down there was something redeeming in him, something likeable, even.

Then she remembered his words. *I suspect Lady Ingram felt you posed no real threat to Lydia's chances.*

Lord Ingram, looking as if he wished to be elsewhere, escorted his mother to the sidelines, leaving Eleanor and Lydia near the circle of dancing couples. Major Fitzwilliam was not long in making his appearance at their side. "Good evening, Miss Ingram, Miss Daventry. I came to solicit a dance, and to beg your company for a ride in Hyde Park Tuesday."

Eleanor wondered at Major Fitzwilliam's choosing to ride when he'd said he didn't show to advantage but murmured a response that she was free. She looked a question at Lydia, who was scanning the ballroom, and her heart sank for the major. It would take a miracle for his suit to prosper.

Lydia was too accustomed to adoration from men more handsome and titled than he. Furthermore, whether Lady Ingram would countenance such a match was more than Eleanor could say, despite the familiarity in discourse between the major and Lord Ingram that suggested they had campaigned together. Perhaps he might find a champion in that quarter.

Just when Eleanor thought Lydia wouldn't answer the question, she turned to the major. "What vehicle do you drive, Major Fitzwilliam?"

"An ordinary phaeton," he replied. "But I propose we ride. Shall I come for you at eleven?" Major Fitzwilliam clasped his hands behind his back, his eyes alight, and Eleanor chuckled to herself. He, at least, had not suffered any doubt over her eventual reply.

"Why, Major Fitzwilliam, that is not the hour to be seen in Hyde Park." Lydia raised her eyes to his in astonishment.

"I don't wish to be seen," he replied promptly. "I only wish to see you." He gave a friendly nod to Eleanor. "And Miss Daventry, of course."

"You are bold, major," Lydia returned, not without some degree of admiration. "Is it your habit to lay siege to young ladies in this way?"

"I cannot say. This is the first time I've been tempted to. But my furlough is over in June, and now is not the time to retrench. Come, what say you?" His smile included both women, and Eleanor hid her own. Lydia would have to be made of sterner stuff than she was to resist.

Behind Lydia, Lord Worthing descended the stairs in the wake of his sisters and aunt. He caught her glance before she could look away and held it, his mouth forming the beginning of a smile. He lifted his hand as if to wave but stopped when he saw Lord Carlton approaching her.

"Miss Daventry, you look . . ." Lord Carlton followed her gaze to Lord Worthing, then paused until she pulled it away. Her thoughts were not so obedient. *I wish it were Lord Worthing asking me to dance, though I would rather die than admit it, infuriating man.*

". . . lovely," finished Lord Carlton, his intent expression insisting upon her notice, his gloved hand tugging hers when her gaze had wandered back to the staircase.

Then he released her, stood back, and said with an arch look, "Have mercy on us lesser men, Miss Daventry. We can't all have Lord Worthing's address."

"Nonsense," Eleanor replied, the shock at being discovered sharpening her wit. "For myself, I prefer a man with more amiable conversation."

After Lord Carlton had claimed his dance, Eleanor sat on the sidelines fanning her neck. Almost immediately, Lord Worthing wound his way through the crowds, pausing only long enough to return a greeting, and came to Eleanor's chair.

"Miss Daventry, may I sit beside you?" he asked.

When she nodded, he took his seat. Grasping his ruby and gold fob, he passed it from hand to hand and seemed unsure how to proceed. Eleanor bit her lip and looked over the crowd of dancing couples.

"I wished to say earlier . . . that is, with my sisters there, I couldn't . . ." His words came out in a rush. "I did not consider my words before I spoke at the Ingrams'. I'm sorry."

Eleanor, though suffering some compassion for his chagrin, was unable to resist delivering her own riposte. "Perhaps we may end with apologies from here on in. *You* shall undertake to choose your words with more care, and I—" She turned to him, a smile hovering on her lips, "I shall endeavor to disregard them. By doing so, we shall both be in perfect charity."

Lord Worthing's look of surprise gave way to a quiet chuckle. "I deserved that, Miss Daventry." He reached over to clasp her gloved hand, his expression serious. "Yet I harbor some hope that I might learn to utter words that are worthy of your regard."

He stood and turned toward the card room, and Eleanor could hear her heart beating in her chest.

Chapter Thirteen

$\mathcal{A}$t an early hour the next morning, Stratford met Ingram at Jackson's saloon. They were well-matched in a fight, and Stratford felt the need to exert his body in an attempt to exorcise his mind. Despite the light banter with Miss Daventry, following his apology last night, he knew he'd done her less than justice from the moment he'd met her, and the thought left him with a restlessness he couldn't shake. Was it because he acted so out of character whenever she was near?

True, his acquaintance with her had started innocently enough. They'd shared an uninspiring dinner, followed by two brief meetings, with nothing to distinguish her from another woman—that is, until he had seen fit to throw away twenty-nine years of steady character and make a cake of himself by proposing. Drunk.

Ingram pulled his cuffs through the sleeves of his coat. "I admit, Stratford. You haven't lost your touch these three years. You almost had me winded."

"High praise, indeed." Stratford was too tired to offer anything further.

"White's?" Ingram said, as they quit the boxing saloon, and Stratford nodded, turning south.

"So what do you think of Fitzwilliam? Has Le Marchant sent us someone who can aid in our efforts?" Ingram asked, though Stratford knew he had already formed his opinion.

"He's not addicted to gambling, that much I've discerned," Stratford replied.

"No, he's not. I've asked him to attend the games at Watier's but so far he's come up with nothing."

Stratford thought it over. "I think he can be trusted. He appears to be a man of good sense and is a likeable fellow."

"I'm glad to hear it. Make good use of him, if you will. I think fleshing out the traitor will require our combined efforts," Ingram said. "Braxsen has already befriended him, and if everyone knows you and I have also taken him up, it will open the doors he needs. From there, he's astute enough to follow the right leads."

"He seems to have become a favorite of Lydia and Miss Daventry." Stratford tapped his cane in studied nonchalance. "How is Miss Daventry faring in your household? I'm surprised your mother would welcome her into it."

"My mother must've felt she could do a charitable deed without giving any threat to Lydia's success or any danger to my heart." Ingram smiled ironically.

Exactly! "That's what I thought too," Stratford said. He couldn't have erred so badly if Ingram was thinking the same thing. And yet, there had been a bite behind Miss Daventry's teasing reply to his apology, and he felt he had much to do to redeem himself in her eyes.

"Judging by appearances alone, Miss Daventry does not possess any great beauty, apart from an engaging smile and a trim figure," Ingram observed. "Men have fallen for less."

Stratford privately felt her beauty lay in a pair of speaking eyes, but he returned nothing except to ask, "She's going on well enough then? She and your sister, that is—are they able to withstand the fatigue of the Season?"

"Oh, they're young enough. Miss Daventry can even outshine my sister in stamina, but I don't think she takes any real pleasure in society. I think it's because she wants to be a support to Lydia."

"Is that so?"

"She would make a capital wife for Fitzwilliam," Ingram added, and reverting to their former topic, "Ours is not the only good opinion of Fitz, you know. The Beau recommended him to Le Marchant."

Stratford frowned. "Wellington keeps only men from the best families on staff. I own to being surprised at his taking up Major Fitzwilliam."

"He's not a peer, if that's what you mean. He's a gentleman, though, on both his parents' sides, but with no title he can inherit. He's not on staff, precisely. Not on Wellington's. Perhaps he's on mine." Ingram flashed a grin. "Le Marchant just told me to keep him close and employ him when needed, and that we'd see our next move more clearly when he returns this summer."

Stratford was tempted to ask on what business but knew it would be an impertinence since it was not merely his friend before him but a rising official in headquarters. He changed tack. "Major Fitzwilliam is not interested in Miss Daventry. His eyes are on Lydia."

Ingram laughed. "So he told me, to his credit, but she'll never have him. Even if she did, she's not the wife for him. She can't bear to be deprived of her little pleasures, and even if he has the successful career I think he'll have, she's not made to follow the drum."

Stratford nodded. "I can see that."

"But Miss Daventry," Ingram persisted, "shirks at nothing. Like I said, she'd make Fitz a capital wife."

Stratford tipped his hat to an acquaintance on the street, and being sure they were once again alone, said, "I see your heart is untouched. Your mother calculated well."

"My heart is intact concerning Miss Daventry." Ingram gave a rueful smile. "Perhaps it wouldn't be had it not been taken some years ago."

There had been more than one mention of a Miss Georgiana Audley in Ingram's brief missives to Stratford, and he assumed it might be she who'd laid claim to Ingram's heart. Stratford raised his eyebrows, but knew better than to ask questions that would only earn him a rebuff.

Handing his cane to the servant in attendance at White's, Ingram said, "I thought we'd see more of you at Grosvenor this past week, but I suppose your sisters keep you busy. Unless it's because you and Lydia are again at daggers—"

Stratford shook his head. That wasn't it. "I feared I'd offended Miss Daventry. I made the mistake of thinking aloud at the ball the other night. I said Lady Ingram wouldn't see her as a threat to your sister's success—" and seeing the look of shock pass over his friend's features, added, "the same thought you expressed just a minute ago, let me remind you."

Ingram stared for a long moment, then began to laugh. "Yes, but I'm not such a jackanapes as to say it to her. I expect all the ladies of my acquaintance know of it by now. Our friendship's finished, Stratford. I'm amazed Lydia hasn't descended on me with orders to call you out."

Stratford stiffened. "I've apologized. Although—" he paused uncomfortably, "she did say she would endeavor to disregard my words in the future. She was teasing, mind you."

"Teasing, you say? My dear fellow, you leave me in some doubt. After a cut like that?"

Stratford, aware the servants were listening and, he feared, secretly laughing at him, kept silent until they had taken a table. "Perhaps if I sent over some flowers to show my sincerity . . ."

"It's the least you can do," agreed Ingram, trying, it seemed, to keep a straight face.

Stratford took the decanter that had been brought and poured a glass for each of them. He drank and then lowered his glass with a frown. "You know I'm not at ease with ladies."

"Excepting your sisters and mine. I'll never forgive Miss Broadmore for that. Well, I hope you aren't too enamored of Miss Daventry's engaging smile and trim figure, because in my mind, you haven't a hope after a blunder like that." Ingram set his glass down and leaned in, a lurking smile. "Stratford?"

"What?" It came out sharper than he'd meant.

"You're looking ill."

Stratford glared at his friend's perfect nose, wishing they could go another round in gloves. Or without. "I'll send flowers," he said.

Perhaps Miss Daventry's light words masked a deeper hurt. Stratford decided he could not let things stand and should deliver a more formal apology. He must leave her in no doubt of his sincere regard, particularly since the two households were so close. Besides, her inheritance inevitably meant they could never escape each other for long. If nothing else, he and Miss Daventry—and, presumably, the doltish husband she'd shortly acquire—would always be neighbors.

"Flowers," said Ingram. "Very good."

One suitor left and another arrived bearing flowers and compliments for the sparkling Lydia while Eleanor stifled a yawn. She would have been surprised to learn that some of them came for her and what they deemed 'Miss Daventry's comfortable conversation.'

The only one Eleanor suspected of forming an attachment to her was Lord Carlton and, astonishingly enough, Mr. Amesbury, though she was certain his sudden address was due to the land she'd inherited that lay adjacent to his. His suit didn't count, of course. Her repugnance at a marriage of convenience, particularly one so blatantly pecuniary, drove her to avoid him wherever possible.

Lord Carlton, however, bore consideration. He had invited her to dance at the very first opportunity, though that might have had more to do with his generous nature than any sudden *tendre* he'd felt for her.

The second time they met he was squiring his younger sister to the Pantheon Bazaar, and Eleanor was quietly impressed he didn't try to excuse his presence in such a feminine and common setting as he performed the introductions. Then, at Eleanor's come-out ball he'd requested two dances with her, adroitly assuring Lydia he wouldn't dare deprive Miss Ingram from her crowd of admirers for more than one dance. He behaved just as he ought, entertaining Eleanor in conversation and offering to bring her a lemonade before restoring her to Lady Ingram.

It was only when their paths crossed at Hyde Park that she began to suspect he might feel something more. With a hasty promise to return, Lydia flagged down an acquaintance while Eleanor chose to continue, her gaze on the bucolic scene.

"Miss Daventry," cried Lord Carlton. "I'd hoped I might meet with you here. And Miss Ingram is deep in conversation with the Billinghams. Excellent. I shall have you to myself. Are you headed toward the lake?"

"Yes. It's an afternoon that begs to be enjoyed." Eleanor smiled at him, shading her eyes with her hand. It was a crisp day, and she turned to let the sun warm her face as the wind made the wisps of her hair dance next to her cheeks.

"It is indeed. And I could add that the flowers pale when compared to your beauty, but I suspect you don't care for flattery." Lord Carlton glanced at her sideways.

Eleanor laughed. "Am I so transparent? No, my lord, I abhor it. It serves only to gratify the speaker of his eloquence or the listener of attributes she's already convinced she has."

Lord Carlton's brow went up in mild protest. "I will not embarrass a lady by unwanted attention, nor will I contradict one who contests the truth. Even if truth is not subjective. It's only true."

She sighed. "Such glib words. Are you destined for politics, Lord Carlton?"

"Would you care for a man in politics?" His smile vanished when he saw the frown his words produced. "Now I have teased you beyond what is pleasing. Do forgive me, Miss Daventry."

"Readily. If only we will limit our conversation to something innocuous. Like the weather."

"Whether the cook will find strawberries in season for her tarts." He swiped at a flock of ducks intercepting their path.

Eleanor followed the turn of discourse willingly. "How many of these milkmaids are indeed from dairy farms." She indicated the women distributing fresh milk for a few coins from the small herd of cows on the meadow.

"That is indeed a subject for profound thought." Lord Carlton waved to his sister, who stood at the lakeside throwing bread crumbs to the swans, and the uncomfortable moment was brushed aside.

At home, Eleanor puzzled over their conversation, wondering if Lord Carlton had been deliberate in his line of questioning and, if so, whether she could return his regard. When she thought of her conversations with Lord Worthing, which produced such an array of emotions, she was convinced that the steady, pleasant attention from Lord Carlton was what she longed for. At other times, when she remembered the earl's apologies, his laughter and intent regard, the way she was conscious of him the moment he stepped into a room, she was sure she couldn't accept something so complacent as her feelings for Lord Carlton.

However, when the butler announced Lord Carlton's arrival at the Ingram residence after a stream of admirers for Lydia, Eleanor was glad to see him. It was a nice change that someone would come for her, and surely Lord Carlton deserved his chance. She met his smile with her own as he made his way to exchange greetings with Lydia. Before he could bow over Eleanor's hand, the butler had returned, announcing Mr. Amesbury. Custom dictated Lord Carlton not sit until he had first greeted Mr. Amesbury, and before he could claim his spot, Lydia called out to him to settle whether there would indeed be a card room at Mrs. Buxley's ball.

Meanwhile, Mr. Amesbury had taken the chair next to Eleanor so that when Lord Carlton returned, he had to take a more distant seat and listen to Mr. Amesbury's discourse about the horse he had just gotten for a song from a young fellow in a hurry to gain some funds after a run of poor luck.

"It's a bad thing when a gentleman is forced to sell," Lord Carlton interjected. "It's not something I would wish on anyone. Miss Daventry," he said before Amesbury could respond, "have you visited Bullock's Museum, which is newly opened? It's something one must see if you are to be *au courant* in London."

Eleanor eagerly latched onto this new thread. "We've spoken of it, but I've been unable to tempt Lydia with the idea." She shot an affectionate glance at her friend, and Mr. Amesbury jumped in.

"If you wish to see the Egyptian exhibit, it will take only the small part of one afternoon. Once you've seen the thing, you can add your mite in the conversations when people talk about it." Mr. Amesbury crossed one leg over the other, displaying a shiny Hessian boot that sported a large tassel in the middle. "I daresay I can find time to squire you there."

Eleanor opened her mouth and then shut it, and a silence ensued. Just as Lord Carlton was about to speak, she found her words. "That's excessively kind of you, Mr. Amesbury, but I had planned to visit it in the morning when the rooms are less likely to be crowded."

"Before lunch!" Mr. Amesbury shuddered. "Nothing could induce me to leave my lodgings before noon."

"I will be happy to take you there." Lord Carlton caught Eleanor's gaze with a mischievous smile. "I'm an early riser myself, and visiting the museum while it's quiet before the grand public descends is just the way the exhibit should be seen. If Miss Ingram does not care to rise early, I'll bring my sister with me."

"I would be delighted." Eleanor beamed with pleasure, which was only enhanced when Mr. Amesbury took his leave shortly afterward, muttering something about people not adhering to decent hours for civil society. She was careful not to catch Lord Carlton's gaze for fear she might betray herself.

"I'm sorry," murmured Lord Carlton. "I have scared off your swain."

"Heavens, no," said Eleanor. "You have performed a rescue. I'm grateful." She looked up as the door opened, and the butler brought in an arrangement of flowers that was the biggest one yet to arrive in the Ingram drawing room. The vase was filled with white lilies, dewy pink roses, and black tulips, the entirety interspersed with purple violets.

"Oh, who could have sent this?" Lydia jumped up and grabbed the card as Eleanor and Lord Carlton shared a conspiratorial smile. One of

Lydia's admirers was certainly determined. Envelope in hand, Lydia looked at Eleanor, shocked. "It's for you," she said in disbelief. "From Stratford!"

Taking the card from Lydia, Eleanor opened it, conscious of her shaking fingers.

Miss Daventry, it said. *As per your request last night, please consider this missive to be the last of its nature. However, I could not let things stand without assuring you in a more formal manner of my heartfelt apology for ill-advised words in the past and my earnest desire that my words do you justice in the future. Yours, Lord Worthing.*

Lydia's gaze was intent, but she wisely did not ask her what the note said. Lord Carlton also looked at her, his friendly face showing the closest Eleanor had ever seen to a scowl. "Miss Daventry, I must take my leave. I promise to secure tickets for Friday morning." He bowed. "Miss Ingram."

No sooner had he exited than Lydia came to sit by Eleanor, eyes wide. "Stratford has never sent anyone I know flowers. Except perhaps that Miss Broadmore. Eleanor," she breathed. "He has a *tendre* for you."

"No, Lydia—"

"No, he does. He does. I can see it all now. He will be so perfect for you. And our families are such *friends*." Lydia grasped her hands until Eleanor could do only one thing. She handed Lydia the note.

Lydia read it, her brows furrowed. She looked up. "An apology? What did he say to you?"

"Nothing of import—"

"It must have been significant for him to realize he'd done something wrong and send *flowers*. He's the most difficult, arrogant—although really he's loyal and such a good friend . . . it's just sometimes he's so dense." Lydia gave a sharp look. "He would never dishonor you . . ."

"No, no, nothing like that." Eleanor smoothed the card Lydia had returned to her. "He merely hinted I was invited here as a companion because I was too plain to pose any threat to your chances." She smiled at Lydia, "which we both know to be true."

Lydia stood abruptly. "It is *not* true. When did he say this? You should have told me. I'll have his hide. How dare he insult my best friend."

Eleanor stood and gave Lydia a hug. "You are the very best of friends, but please do not say anything to him." She turned Lydia to face her. "Promise me. You will only embarrass us both."

Lydia rolled her eyes. "I suppose you're right. Though I really want to take him down a peg. He's too arrogant for his own good." Hands on hips, she examined the flower arrangement. "At least he did this one thing right. I shall only compliment him on his choice of flowers."

Eleanor, preferring the matter never to be mentioned, knew her friend could not be persuaded to say nothing at all and had to be content with that.

Chapter Fourteen

*S*tratford's sisters rode with their friend, Miss Emmett, in the newly crested carriage in Hyde Park, and he rode alongside on horseback. They were slightly earlier than was fashionable and the crowds were thin, so when their path intersected that of Judith Broadmore's, Stratford found he could not avoid her without giving the cut direct.

Miss Broadmore was accompanied by the same friend as when Stratford had first chanced upon her in London and the French gentleman from the club—Lord Delacroix, whom Ingram had spoken of as a man to watch. Her companions had pulled over to greet a newcomer, but Miss Broadmore brought her horse directly to Stratford's side, her gaze fixed on him.

"Good day, Miss Broadmore." He gave a civil nod and pulled his horse forward, attempting to cut the conversation short.

"Stratford," she called out in a throaty voice. "How delightful to see you about. We've not met recently at any society gatherings."

"I'm accompanying my sisters," Stratford replied, shooting a glance at the carriage as it moved forward.

"I trust you've not forgotten how to entertain *yourself* in London?" Miss Broadmore gave an inviting smile. It was as if Stratford hadn't made himself perfectly clear at their last meeting. *What was she playing at?*

In the distance, Stratford thought he saw Ingram's carriage, and he focused on discerning the crest. Would Miss Daventry be in it? Anna said Lydia always rode at this hour. Eyes forward, he murmured, "Where there is good conversation, I must always find amusement."

The carriage came fully into view, but it was not the Ingram crest. He turned to Miss Broadmore in time to see a calculating look to her eyes.

"Well, you shall have to do without mine for the next two weeks. I've promised to go on a repairing lease with my friend Miss Redgrave." She nodded at the elegantly dressed redhead, who was in conversation with Lord Delacroix. "Miss Redgrave's father has ordered her to their country estate while he sorts out some business there. She begged me to come and keep her company so she wouldn't go out of her mind with boredom."

Determined to leave the conversation at all possible speed, he called out to Mr. Braxsen, who was riding by at a slow trot. When Braxsen reached them, Stratford turned to Judith. "I hope you can contrive to be entertained while you're there. Good d—"

She did not give him a chance to finish. "How do you do, Mr. Braxsen?" Miss Broadmore held out her hand, and keeping both men captive, she went on, "Yes, it will be vastly entertaining. We have little card parties planned, and there promises to be enough young people to form a set for a dance. But Christine is happier in London and will be most anxious to return. She's collecting riddles from some of the ton and is planning on hosting a *soirée pour les plus malins* on her return. Everyone is to guess not only the answer to the riddle but also who wrote it. You must tell her you'll participate."

"I shall have to think of a clever riddle first," Stratford answered. He caught Anna signaling to him from the carriage. "I must go. Shall you join us, Braxsen?"

Mr. Braxsen shook his head. "No, I would find out more about this soirée." With a practiced air, he waved to Miss Redgrave and pulled his horse alongside Judith's. "Whom have you invited to attend?"

Breathing a sigh of relief, Stratford left them and rode to join the carriage. If he didn't see the Ingrams today, he would have to pay them a visit tomorrow. What did he expect, that Miss Daventry would send him a thank-you note for the flowers? No. If he wanted to see her, he was going to have to seek her out. He hoped she would be glad to receive him.

As he rode up behind his sisters, he was in time to hear Anna lean over to Phoebe while their friend was in conversation with the occupants of an adjacent carriage. Her voice carried. "Did you see Stratford smiling at Judith Broadmore? *Ugh*. I wish she might break out in spots."

Phoebe leaned in. "She was horrid, but perhaps she has changed. You know she pulled out of an engagement to Lord Garrett. It can't have been easy. And to be so pretty and still on the shelf. Perhaps she truly desires a love match."

Stratford made himself visible before Anna could retort with some cutting remark that their companion might overhear. He gave a bland smile to the three women who turned toward him, and it grew broader at his sisters' consternation when they realized they had been overheard. He rode on, but not before he was made privy to the raptures of Miss Caroline Emmett, who had heretofore thought "Lord Worthing the most severe gentleman I'd ever met" and was now sending the pronouncement to the other end of the trajectory. It was turning out to be an eventful day, one that would have been much improved had he crossed paths with Miss Daventry.

A sharp clatter erupted outside Cavendish Square, and Stratford was awake. He sat up, perspiring, his gaze darting back and forth until he remembered he was in London. The house was still unfamiliar, but he made out his coat, brushed and ready at the foot of the bed, and his empty trunk next to a spindle-backed chair. He leaned over in the dim light and turned his pocket watch face upward. Six o'clock in the morning.

No sooner had he walked across the room to the washing stand than the valet rushed into the room, dressed and sleepy. "My lord, allow me. I will ring for some hot water."

"Very well," Stratford said. Then, turning to him in surprise, "Don't you sleep?"

"I had a restful night, my lord. I always sleep in my clothes. It will not do to be resting while you are needing help in the morning."

"But I don't need your help. I was very able to care for myself in Portugal, you know."

Benchly was not deterred. "My lord, if you will permit my saying, dressing for the field of battle is not the same as dressing for a London outing, although," he muttered, "I'm sure your batman did his very best."

Stratford's mouth quirked upward. "Well, I don't expect to have to perform any social niceties at six in the morning. I'm just going for a ride." The valet had, by this time, rung for hot water and was laying out the white neckcloths in case Stratford should care to attempt something more complicated.

Stratford submitted to Benchly's ministrations, waiting for the hot water to arrive and his valet to shave him. He allowed help with his coat, which now fit tightly across his broad shoulders, having gained back some of the weight he lost during his time on the Continent. When the valet was done pulling on the boots—"the navy blue Hessians with a white band on top, my lord, which will suit your navy coat and cream pantaloons to perfection"—Stratford went downstairs to breakfast, thinking how foolish he'd been to submit to Benchly when he was sure to come home mud-spattered and in need of a complete change of clothes.

The butler didn't show any surprise at the earl's appearing at sunrise and directed the footmen to fill the sideboard with ham and kippers, saying, "I will have the coffee brought in directly, my lord."

"Very good." Stratford set about to reading the previous day's correspondence, which he'd not had time to peruse, and was finished with breakfast just as Phoebe walked in.

She must have seen his confusion because she gave a weak smile. "Do not ask. I've not slept well and saw no sense in remaining in bed." She poured a cup of coffee from the white china coffeepot on the sideboard and sat across from him. "I've not had occasion to speak to you of Miss Daventry."

"What is there to speak of?" he asked, wondering what she knew, as he attacked the thick slice of ham on his plate.

Phoebe raised her eyebrow at his abrupt tone. "I only meant that she is quite the success and already has her pick of suitors if our ball was any indication. Perhaps you can inch one her way that you would deem acceptable as our neighbor."

Stratford grunted. It was too early for the gleam of mischief he heard in his sister's tone, besides the fact that it hit entirely too close to home. He cut the herring and put a piece in his mouth. When he didn't respond, Phoebe took a sip of coffee and set her cup on the saucer. "Her inheritance is not to be despised, so of course there is that to tempt one."

Provoked, Stratford stood. "A desirable piece of land," he said, impatient to be off for his ride. "However, I hope it's not the only reason for her success. I trust any suitor who has made her his ambition will realize that between the land she's inherited and her hand, *she* is the greater prize."

Without pausing to reflect whether his hastily uttered words revealed more than he intended, he took his hat and went to call for his horse.

When the mare was brought round to the door, he swung up in the saddle and clicked his teeth.

His horse started forward, and he let her go at an easy pace. A few streets from his quiet residential square, there was already a bustle as men unloaded crates of carrots, parsnips, and beets to the marketplace. He picked his way around the deliveries and continued another mile beyond Mary-le-Bone where he could let his horse run. A good gallop cleared his mind, allowing him to appreciate how much he'd needed the escape from escorting his sisters and aunt to parties, and now apparently early morning breakfasts too, God bless them. He couldn't live a bachelor's life all these years without feeling his loss of freedom.

Stratford's horse began to tire, breath steaming in the brisk air, and he allowed her to slow to a trot, still discovering the unfamiliar routes leading from his new house. The well-kept roads and bright morning sunshine brought him pleasure, and he began to feel almost complacent. The feeling did not last, however, as his thoughts turned again to the ball, his apology, the flowers. He had not seen Miss Daventry since.

Apart from their brief conversation, he'd been too occupied to do anything but watch her dance with other men. First, it was Lord Carlton. They stood very near one another, and when she turned her face to his, Stratford saw the effect it had on the man. He ground his teeth at the memory. Fortunately, another gentleman had come to claim his dance at that moment, and Miss Daventry was whisked into a lively cotillion, where her red cheeks and sparkling eyes drew him from across the room and made him long to invite her for a turn. Since he wasn't dancing that evening, he hadn't dared single her out.

Stratford conjured up Miss Daventry's teasing response to his apology and then her laughing, dancing eyes as she whirled through the steps with Mr. Berrymore. Stratford wanted those eyes turned to *him*. Perhaps they had lit up when they saw the flowers he'd sent. He'd give anything to know. It was time. He would call on her today. Whistling, Stratford nudged his horse into a canter.

At Grosvenor Square, Lydia stood in the morning room to greet him, but she was alone. "Stratford," she said, brows raised. "Who have you come to see?"

There was something in her look. *She knew.* Wondering how much she knew, he decided not to dissemble. "I've come to see Miss Daventry . . . if she will receive me."

Lydia pursed her lips, gazing steadily at him, punishing him with her silence, he was sure of it. "Eleanor's not here," she said at last. "She's gone out with Lord Carlton."

Stratford folded his arms. Again Lord Carlton. The man was everywhere. He did seem a sincere suitor, but he was too young to be thinking seriously of marriage. Although, if Stratford were honest with himself, he was not an impartial judge where Miss Daventry's suitors were concerned.

Lydia gestured toward the bouquet he'd sent, which dwarfed every other arrangement in the room. Perhaps he had been too enthusiastic. "Well done," she said, "even if the gesture was a necessary one." She knew, then, but mercifully didn't tease. "Do take care what you're about, Stratford. Eleanor is a woman of noble character, and I do not care to see her hurt."

"Nor I," he said, vexed at her tone. Surely Miss Daventry had shown him more grace than Lydia and Ingram thought he deserved, old friends that they were. If only he could see her for himself.

Chapter Fifteen

*B*ullock's Museum was empty of all but governesses and children not yet out of the schoolroom. Eleanor breathed in the mingled odors of stuffed elephants and other wildlife she'd never heard of, her gaze transfixed by jeweled carriages, mummies, and the foreign characters written on tablets of stone and the adjacent columns. That a people could live an existence so foreign to her own, some long dead and others still living and breathing on the other side of the world, seemed incredible.

Lord Carlton followed, hands behind his back, providing what answers he could to her questions and supplementing his knowledge with a guidebook he had brought for the purpose. His sister, Cecily, seemed content to follow Eleanor's lead and exclaim over whatever she found to marvel at.

"Do you see the suit on the wall?" Eleanor puzzled at it, her face lifted. "I cannot fathom how it's secured on a person. Is it meant for a man or a woman?"

"I . . . I don't perfectly know," Cecily answered. "It's too broad for a woman. But it has a skirt."

"It's the native dress from Captain Cook's voyage to the Australias," Lord Carlton said, looking up from his guidebook. "That is the chief's wardrobe. And that over there," he pointed to the opposite wall, "is his headdress."

Eleanor's gaze followed where he indicated. "I shall never again complain of the folly of having added fruit to my bonnet," she said, eyes twinkling. "I now see I am but an amateur and have not added nearly enough."

"Oh no, I think it's enough," Cecily said earnestly.

Lord Carlton was also quick to reassure. "Your bonnet is very becoming. I've been meaning to say so since I first laid eyes on it."

Eleanor glided to the next exhibit with a quiet sigh.

Upon completing their tour of the lower level, they began the climb upstairs, where Eleanor spotted a familiar profile. "Why, Miss Tunstall," she called out. The woman turned and took in the party at a glance, encompassing them with her smile.

"Miss Daventry, how wonderful to meet you here. I didn't expect to see anyone of my acquaintance at such an early hour. I'm here with my young cousins, who cannot be far." Miss Tunstall glanced around, then signaled to a boy a few feet away.

"I confess it was my own inclination to come at an early hour, and Lord Carlton was kind enough to accompany me, and this"—Eleanor, having given Lord Carlton time to bow, turned to Cecily—"is Miss Cecily Carlton, Lord Carlton's sister."

"It's a pleasure to meet you." Phoebe Tunstall glossed over Cecily's youthful blushes and brought her cousins to her side to perform the introductions. "Amelia and John live in Canterbury and are visiting London on their way to Norfolk."

Lord Carlton addressed the young man. "Confess. It was you who dragged your sister and cousin up the stairs to see the stuffed snake eating a woman, was it not?"

The boy laughed. "Yes, but truly, where else will you find such a thing? I could not leave London without seeing it. I shall have such stories to tell my friends when we're home."

"Come then," Lord Carlton called out, marching forward. "Let's see the thing. The ladies can decide whether they have the stomach for it."

"Are you and your cousins here alone, Miss Tunstall?" Eleanor fell in step with Lord Worthing's sister as Cecily followed her brother and the two new acquaintances.

"Yes, Anna would never rise this early. Oh, and do call me Phoebe, will you? We're not strangers because you're staying with one of my childhood friends, and I understand from Stratford you had made his acquaintance at the estate."

"Then you must call me Eleanor," she responded warmly. "Yes, we met in Sussex, but I didn't know then his connection to the Ingrams."

"I'm sure had he known you were to stay with Lydia, he would have introduced us as soon as we arrived in London. He has always had so many friends staying at our house on holiday, but Frederick is his closest."

"I didn't imagine him to be someone who'd have a stream of friends over—" Eleanor stopped short as her cheeks grew warm. "Forgive me. Of course, I cannot claim any knowledge of what he is likely to do."

"Ah." Phoebe looked at her keenly. "You're thinking, of course, that he's too somber to have many friends."

Eleanor hesitated over how honest she should be with the earl's sister and finally settled for the truth. She chose her words carefully. "Although he is at ease with Lord Ingram, he seems to be a man who is not prone to gaiety. But perhaps with the war . . ."

Phoebe exhaled. "My brother was different growing up," she said, her eyes fixed on a distant memory. "My father was very jolly, and . . . capable. Stratford was never forced to endure the pressure that eldest sons are sometimes made to feel." She looked again at Eleanor. "I believe he suffered his broken engagement very deeply, even if he never spoke of it. It was not made public, but I think Lydia will have told you . . ." She paused, and Eleanor nodded for her to continue.

"He left immediately for the Peninsula. I can only imagine what horrors he faced there. The men hide it from us women, but I've caught scraps of conversation. And then . . ." She sniffed and turned bright eyes toward the group making its way back down the aisle.

"And then we lost my father, which no one expected. He was thought to be too hearty to expire from an attack of influenza, but the doctors believe there was something else, and that he had been suffering for a while without telling us. I think Stratford stepping into my father's shoes at the same moment he inherited a title was indeed a strain." Phoebe concluded, "He's not as light-hearted as he once was. But I hope one day to see my brother's old humor return."

Eleanor nodded. "Of course." She did not know how else to respond. That was a heavy burden, indeed.

Phoebe moved alongside Eleanor, taking her arm. "I'm sure my brother did not show to advantage at Worthing, having just arrived in England." She smiled. "But he does think highly of you. Just this morning, he said,"—Phoebe paused in her steps, pulling Eleanor back as Lord Carlton was almost upon them—"He said he hoped your suitors would realize between your inheritance and your hand, you are the greater prize of the two."

Eleanor's breath froze in her chest.

"We've seen it all," Lord Carlton announced, flanked by the younger set, still arguing whether the detail of the half-eaten woman was realistic or exaggerated. "And it's just as I predicted. You two have no interest in the reptiles."

Phoebe laughed. "You have judged correctly, my lord. Our meeting was most fortuitous, for you've saved me from any nightmares I'm sure to have suffered by the sight."

Eleanor summoned a smile. "I believe I shall have enough conversation from the curiosities we've visited below for my purposes."

As the two groups converged on their way to the awaiting carriages, Eleanor wondered at all she'd learned of Lord Worthing. Those rare glimpses of kindness and humor were buried under a serious and unyielding disposition. Yet his sister spoke of Lord Worthing's pain and her hope of seeing the return to his former self.

And if his sister is to be believed, the thought churned through Eleanor's mind with delight and surprise in equal measure, *Lord Worthing holds me in esteem.*

Eleanor saw Phoebe again the following afternoon in the company of Lord Worthing and their sister, Anna. It was the hour to be seen at Hyde Park, and it was not an opportune time for private conversation or testing theories about whether the earl was burdened and reticent, as Phoebe had seemed to suggest, or simply uninterested. Did he really admire her? Impossible to say, especially when he bowed over her hand with a solemn, "Miss Daventry," and then greeted Lydia more informally.

Lydia linked arms with both twins, leaving Eleanor to fall back on the path beside Lord Worthing. Carriages drove by, and the men and women on horseback *clip-clopped* on the fenced-in path to her right while a stiff wind in the leaves overhead caused the sunlight to dance in her eyes. At last she said, "Thank you for the bouquet of flowers, my lord."

He sought her gaze before turning to face ahead. "I wanted to show my repentance."

She remembered her implacable words after his first apology and laughed quietly. "When I said I would withhold my forgiveness until I could be certain of your sincerity, I had no idea you were so adept at apologies."

Lord Worthing smiled. "I don't believe I've ever had to offer so many."

They walked in silence as Eleanor thought up and rejected a series of things she could say, and finally settled on, "Phoebe told me you brought home many of the gentlemen I am now becoming acquainted with when you were still at school. So, apart from Lord Ingram, you knew Mr. Braxsen?"

"Not as intimately as Ingram, although in a sense, everyone knows Braxsen. We grew up with him. He was part of Ingram's hunting party, so we spent at least one week a year together, besides seeing each other in London."

"He does seem to be a favorite. And Lord Carlton?" Eleanor turned to him. "I imagine he was not one of your guests since Phoebe did not seem to know him."

The firm set to Lord Worthing's mouth reminded her of their first meeting, and she wondered at it. He seemed to choose his words. "Lord Carlton is several years my junior, and I can only claim the barest acquaintance. We're both members of White's."

"Oh."

The earl tapped his cane against a tree trunk in passing. In the ensuing silence, it dawned on Eleanor that perhaps she'd not been wise to have brought up Lord Carlton's name since he was showing himself to be a suitor. Before she had time to dwell on the thought, Lord Worthing asked, "Will you be presented at Almack's?"

Eleanor nodded. "Wednesday hence. Lydia's mother prevailed upon Lady Jersey to lend her support to Lady Sefton, though I am virtually unknown. She was successful in securing the vouchers. So I'll go." Eleanor knew she should exalt at such a victory, but in truth, she dreaded it. She'd heard that not even when presented at court were women put so on display. She longed for quiet conversation and small assemblies where she could dance with people who were comfortable. Here, walking with Lord Worthing, she had it. Yet she longed for something else as well and couldn't put her finger on it.

"I will accompany my sisters there," Lord Worthing said. "Will you do me the honor of saving me a dance?" She peered at him from the corner of her lashes and noticed his flush. With his cane, he took a swipe at the grass, and something blossomed in her heart. She wasn't the only one who felt unsure.

"I'd be delighted, Lord Worthing," she answered, and was rewarded with one of his rare smiles.

Chapter Sixteen

Stratford and Major Fitzwilliam left the treasury building at a brisk pace and were about to part ways as the major headed toward the war offices. They were using this time to compare notes on the people they'd deemed, along with Ingram, worth watching. Fitz was studying the activity of the soldiers who had just returned, and Stratford was listening in the clubs for any *tête à tête* that could be considered suspect. So far, neither had come up with much.

Their path required some side-stepping through the teaming streets. Idle young men contemplated their next lark, mothers hurried their daughters along before someone else took that last bit of lace in just the color yellow needed, older gentlemen made steady strides toward parliament for the session that was to open.

"Fitz!" To his left, Mr. Braxsen disengaged from a crowd of brightly plumed young men and came forward, hand extended. "I'd not thought to see you here. I expected you'd be buried in running messages for Lord Ingram." He seemed to notice Stratford then. "Oh, hallo, Worthing. You two together?"

"As you see." Stratford gave a nod, not wishing to say too much in case Mr. Braxsen should guess their objective. With access to every social circle, the man was a known gossip. Fitz answered more fully, turning the conversation with practiced ease.

"I am indeed on my way to the Ingram residence. And you—" Fitz grinned disarmingly. "I'm sure to find you on any street corner where there are people to watch. How did you ever keep up with the rigors of the campaign?"

"One does what is required. But I'm enjoying the slower pace for once. In Portugal, it was nothing but bad rations, joints stiff from the cold ground, and getting fired at, which is a deuced nuisance." He brushed a falling blossom from his sleeve and affected unconcern, but Stratford knew better.

The major looked at him sideways, a sympathetic grin lurking. "You'd sell out in a heartbeat, wouldn't you?"

"I don't see why you don't. Worthing, here, did." Braxsen jerked his head toward Stratford. "You're not in straightened circumstances, and there are other ways to serve the country than going off to fight."

Fitz patted Braxsen's shoulder. "But someone does have to fight, and I'm a career soldier, so who better than me? Let me run this up to the person who's waiting for it, and you can join me at Colonel Ingram's house."

Mr. Braxsen gave a sly smile. "Are you going for military intelligence or to see his fair sister?"

"What makes you think I tell people my business?" Fitz retorted good-naturedly. "I'll be back in ten minutes if you want to wait."

When he was gone, Stratford tapped his cane on the ground. "What will you do if you leave off soldiering? One day you most certainly will since your heart's not in it. Have you something to fall back on?"

Braxsen met Stratford's eyes briefly. "I have some income from my mother's estate, even if my father lost most of it. Perhaps I will hold out for a wealthy debutante."

Stratford shrugged. "You could, I suppose. As for me, I don't like to be doing nothing. If trade doesn't suit you, and you won't enter the church—" He laughed when Mr. Braxsen shuddered, "You might try politics. You know enough people."

Mr. Braxsen gave a considering look. "I'd thought of it. If you and Ingram will take me up, perhaps I will try my hand."

"Let us first meet to see if we are in accord on the issues. But why not?" Stratford replied. When Fitz returned, Stratford left them to their visit. Though he was tempted to haunt Ingram's drawing room in hopes of having conversation with Miss Daventry, he had a meeting with his solicitor that could not wait.

Fitz hailed a hansom cab and swung into it, laughing at Braxsen's grumbling over their mode of travel. He continued to complain until they pulled up at Grosvenor Square, but it was in such a comical way, Fitz could not take offense. Lord Ingram was out, but the ladies would receive them. For once, Miss Ingram was not surrounded by suitors, but was sitting next to Miss Daventry, embroidering with more determination than skill. She set aside her needlework with relief.

"I'm very glad to see both of you. Eleanor, didn't I tell you Major Fitzwilliam and Mr. Braxsen are our most faithful friends and would not fail us today?"

"You are indeed a welcome diversion," Miss Daventry said. "Lydia insisted on staying in because she says I have been running her ragged with all these places in London I wish to visit."

She quirked her brow, adding, "However, I daresay it's only the description of these wonders that fatigues her, as I've yet to convince her to come with me." Miss Daventry shifted her gaze. "Mr. Braxsen, you are from London, I believe, so the sights must not enchant you. But Major Fitzwilliam, have you not been tempted to take every available moment to visit the places you won't find elsewhere?"

Fitz raised his eyebrows in surprise. "I fear I will only disappoint you, Miss Daventry. I have not given any thought to visiting London, apart from the places I must go to conduct business." Turning to the hostess, he said, "Miss Ingram, if you're not touring London, how do you spend your days? Unless you simply pass your time resting from the balls the night before." He shared a complicit look with Miss Daventry that pleaded indulgence. Though she'd told him how Lydia passed her time, he was a man bent on a mission.

Lydia bridled at the implication she was indolent. "Well, major, contrary to what Eleanor said—" she shot her friend a look, "I do not like to be idle. And I don't like embroidery." She tucked the frame from sight. "I like to ride, and I like to dance. I'm not overly tired after the *soirées*, though I do take my morning chocolate later than when we keep country hours. Otherwise, I like to go for long runs, and the idea of sitting in a carriage while we traipse from one boring exhibit to another does not tempt me."

"That sounds like the very thing. Perhaps—"

The butler's entrance, announcing the unwelcome arrival of Mr. Amesbury, interrupted Fitz's proposal. By way of greeting, Miss Ingram quizzed Mr. Amesbury on his absence at the card party the night before, but Miss Daventry merely inclined her head. Fitz noticed a slight frown as she looked out the window.

"Becoming quite the family party, aren't we? Good to see you again, Braxsen." Amesbury included Fitz with his nod. "What a pleasure it is always to be meeting here," he added in a tone that showed anything but.

Mr. Braxsen and Fitz exchanged an amused glance as Amesbury bowed over Lydia's hand, then Eleanor's, holding her gloved fingers longer than was necessary. *So that's the lay of it*, thought the major.

"Major Fitzwilliam comes to see my brother, I'm sure. They're military friends." Lydia gave an arch look at Mr. Braxsen. "Mr. Braxsen has no such excuse. I believe he's here simply because he likes our company."

"I'm here because you're always invited to the best parties of the Season. I learn of them here, and if I'm not invited, I waylay the hostess to secure an invitation of my own."

"And it is, of course, because you're ready to settle down and wish to find the most eligible young lady," Lydia teased, giving him a sideways glance.

Mr. Braxsen threw his arms outward. "I can hide nothing from you, my fair lady. If I ever hope to sell out, I must always be in search of the woman whose charm enslaves me."

Amesbury looked at him, then Miss Daventry in turn. "My advice to you, Braxsen, is to go about it with a more practical mindset. Charm will not keep the coffers full."

The major's voice was sharp. "I think you forget your company, sir." Before Mr. Amesbury could attempt a biting reply, the major changed tack. "Miss Ingram, speaking of going on long runs, you had promised to ride with me, but I have not yet had this pleasure. I must leave London for a week on official business, but upon my return, I hope you will do me the honor of joining me for an excursion the morning of Friday next—both of you, in fact. Mr. Braxsen has promised to join us as well."

This falsehood was met with a lift of the eyebrows, but Mr. Braxsen answered faithfully. "Indeed I did. I hope both of you will come."

"We shall be delighted," Lydia said. Mr. Amesbury scowled into his hat perched on his lap, and like that Mr. Braxsen and Fitz closed ranks.

Eleanor cherished the quiet of the drawing room. Weak beams of sunlight lit the golden silk rug in the middle of the floor, and she watched the cherry blossoms dance on the branches outside the window. She sighed in contentment. Perhaps she was only going through the motions of having a Season rather than plunging into the gaiety, and perhaps she didn't measure up to Lady Ingram's expectations of a pleasing young woman, but for a few brief months, she could forget her future was uncertain and pretend her greatest concern was what to wear for that evening's party.

The bell rang, and Eleanor sat quietly, expecting Hartsmith to turn the visitor aside as Lydia had not yet made an appearance. To her alarm, the door opened, and Mr. Amesbury entered right on the heels of the butler.

"Miss Daventry, I apologize." Hartsmith looked pained as he glanced at the visitor. "I did not know anyone was in this room. Miss Ingram has gone back upstairs for her shawl and bade me to show any visitors to the drawing room until she arrives."

Eleanor stood. "It's all right. I expect Miss Ingram will be here momentarily. Will you take a seat? Hartsmith, please tell Lydia that Mr. Amebsury is here."

When the butler had closed the door behind them, she took a seat. "Mr. Amebsury, I hope you've had a pleasant—"

"Miss Daventry," he began, claiming a seat so close his leg touched hers. "Hear what I've come to say. I've not much time before Miss Ingram arrives, and there's something I've been meaning to say to you, but *dash it all* if I can get you alone for even a minute."

Eleanor's eyes widened in alarm. "I assure you, there's no need to—"

He continued as if she'd not spoken. "As you may have guessed, when I first made your acquaintance I found your background objectionable. First your father dies under the hatches with only the shirt on his back. Now *there* was a loose screw, even if he was granted a military funeral. Then your mama goes off and elopes with a Frenchman. Who knows if she did the deed when she was yet a widow. Even if we disregard your family, it's not as if there's a pretty face to tempt a fellow into making a foolish match. Thank heavens for that, I say, because I cannot think of anything more insufferable. One needs to go about these things after great deliberation." *On that point, we are quite in agreement, sir,* Eleanor fumed, eyes snapping dangerously.

Sounds of Lydia's descent made their way to the drawing room, but she was speaking to one of the servants, and Amesbury rushed on. "Then you inherited that piece of land that is just what my estate needs to double its value. That stream there . . . it's not merely the income from the property that adds value. You'll be happy to know that the stream can be diverted to irrigate a dry bit of land that has so far produced too little to be of value. With the stream pouring into it, those fields will be filled with crops, and I can convert the land closer to the estate as training grounds for my horses."

Mr. Amesbury had a gleam in his eye as he contemplated this delicious vision, and Eleanor opened her mouth to cut short his effusions. He must have seen the necessity of coming quickly to point because he gave her no chance to speak.

"It won't do to spend too many Seasons in London. You'll be an ape-leader before you know it and lucky to get any offer that comes your way. I don't like to go about the thing rushed like this, but Miss Ingram might arrive this moment, and I don't want to spend any more time in London. I aim to have the affair settled so I can return to my estate. I'm offering to marry you. You'll have a comfortable home, and my name is good enough to protect you from any embarrassment should your family history come out. Shouldn't though. I don't plan to spend much time in London, so you needn't worry about that."

Humiliated and enraged, Eleanor answered him at once. "Mr. Amesbury, I thank you for your offer, but it is impossible for me to accept. I wish you happiness for your future."

"Cannot accept? But this is madness." Mr. Amesbury took both her hands in his. "Surely you do not mean to refuse."

Eleanor yanked her hands back. "I'm sorry. I must. I wish you will not bring this subject up again, which will surely be painful to both of us." Her cheeks burned, and she began to long for Lydia's arrival.

"But you have no other engagement. Why should you not wish to spare yourself the humiliation of sitting on the shelf? Be reasonable."

Eleanor turned to him in fury. "By insulting me in such a manner do you think to win my hand? I would much rather be 'on the shelf,' as you term it, than yoked to a man who holds me in so small esteem."

Not to be deterred, Mr. Amesbury said, "You will change your mind before you are very much older." He stood. "Listen my gel, I am naturally of a generous nature and will give you some time to rethink your answer, which will, without a doubt, change upon reflection."

Lydia was almost at the door, and Eleanor was nearly bereft of words. But there could be no room for doubt that might enable Mr. Amesbury to attempt another suit. In a flash of inspiration, she silenced the ardency of her suitor with a falsehood. "Mr. Amesbury, I can never marry you. My heart is otherwise engaged." Mr. Amesbury's mouth fell open, just as the handle of the door turned.

Chapter Seventeen

When Lydia entered the room, she stumbled upon a scene of great confusion. Mr. Amesbury stood, his thundering expression illuminated by a beet-red face, and Eleanor sat, poised but equally red, in her usual spot in the drawing room.

"Oh!" said Lydia. And, lacking imagination, she offered nothing further to dispel the tension.

The three of them stayed frozen for what seemed an eternity before Mr. Amesbury grabbed his hat from the settee and forced it low over his brow. "Miss Ingram, I came to bid you *adieu* as my presence is required immediately at my estate. I will be leaving London today."

Lydia opened her mouth to speak but was not able to utter a word before he was gone. She went, at an unhurried pace, to occupy the spot the rejected suitor had just quit. Eleanor, still struggling to keep her composure, and despite feelings of outrage, nearly laughed at the sudden reflection: *Mr. Amesbury has managed the impossible. He made even Lord Worthing's proposal seem romantic.*

Tucking her skirt under the chair, Lydia turned a steady gaze her way. "Eleanor, we are friends. You cannot tell me I haven't just interrupted a scene. Was there a declaration?"

Eleanor shook her head and turned pleading eyes to her friend. "You know I cannot tell. It's bad form to reveal what a gentleman has disclosed in confidence."

"Hmm. I figured you'd say as much. Oh, if you aren't the most annoyingly discreet creature ever to have as a best friend. How can I find entertainment if you won't share anything with me?" Lydia sniffed and turned her nose in the air.

"In anyone but you," Eleanor replied, "I might say it's because you see it as entertainment rather than cause for compassion. Because it *is* you, I've come to know your words don't always reflect your heart. You're making light of a situation you worry might have troubled me." Eleanor smiled warmly at her. "You're a dear friend."

Lydia gave a *harrumph*. "Still. I know Mr. Amesbury declared himself. He's been showing marked attention to you, though his heart has never been touched by anything but money and property. You represent both, and I assume by his stormy expression he has been met with rebuff. I'm glad, dear Eleanor. The man who deserves you is the man who recognizes all your excellent traits and loves you for them."

Eleanor flushed and looked down. "You are good to me. But you look at me through the lens of a friend. I assure you, a gentleman does not have such generous filters."

"Perhaps not any gentleman," Lydia hinted, "but a man in love . . ."

Eleanor retorted, "Well as to that, Mr. Amesbury is certainly not in love. Trust me. When the proposal contains irrigation and crop yields . . ." Eyes twinkling, she held Lydia's stunned gaze until they both collapsed in laughter.

"Of all the foolish men," said Lydia, wiping tears of mirth from her eyes. "Bravo, Eleanor, for opening the budget with me. A man who abounds in idiocy does not deserve your confidence." Sighing, she shook her head. "Oh, my poor friend. I shall never be civil to him again."

Still laughing, Eleanor replied, "I daresay he is too puffed up in his own conceit to notice the cut."

Stratford was the last to see Amesbury before he left London, but that was quite by chance. He'd had an appointment at Angelo's to try to see whether anyone at that worthy school of arms could stand up against what maneuvers he'd learned from the French prisoner on the Peninsula. Bent on his destination, Stratford almost missed Amesbury, who, in a black humor, was directing his trunks to be put up on the traveling chaise.

"Amesbury, you're off then?" Stratford held out his hand.

"She wouldn't have me," Amesbury said, ignoring the hand.

Stratford nodded, guessing to whom Amesbury was referring, but not wishing to say her name in the hearing of the groom. *Of course she wouldn't have you, you lump,* he thought. *You made no efforts to win her.* Then he wondered if perhaps Amesbury had been more assiduous in their private dealings. "Did she say why?"

"Says her heart's previously engaged." He turned to the footman. "Put the portmanteau inside the chaise, not on the back."

Stratford felt cold. Her heart engaged? To *whom*? What a fool he'd be to think *he* was the object of her affection when all he'd done was to blunder and insult. Hadn't she asked if he were well-acquainted with Carlton when they walked together? It could only be him.

Stratford was standing there, quite stupidly, as the footman and groom finished equipping the carriage, and his reverie was broken only when Amesbury turned to him. "I'm not in such a hurry as all that to get leg-shackled. Not enough to keep spending twenty-five pounds a week to stay in London at any rate."

At this point, Amesbury had already climbed up, whip in hand. "Send word when you're back at Worthing." With a nod he was off, leaving Stratford to finish his walk and enumerate the times he saw Miss Daventry and Lord Carlton together and wonder if her heart were indeed taken.

At the opera that night, Stratford escorted his aunt and sisters to their seats in the center row. He sought out Ingram's box to see who was present. *Only so I can invite Ingram to Boodle's tomorrow night,* he told himself.

Miss Daventry sat in the center of Ingram's box, her eyes sparkling in the candlelight that emanated from the chandeliers. She wore her hair in curls, brushed to the side and secured with jeweled pins, which softened a pointed chin. Her delicate collarbones lay exposed between tiny puff sleeves, flanking the bodice that covered her generous bosom. She and Lydia were laughing, and although Stratford had long abandoned his first impression of her being a dull creature, he had never seen her wear such a merry expression. He wished it were something he'd said to make her look that way.

When her gaze met his, the smile still in place, she raised an eyebrow, and his heart thudded in his chest. *I will have to go say hello to Frederick and Lydia*, he thought. *They will expect it.*

Miss Daventry did not turn toward him again during the first act, and he was only dimly conscious of Madame Catalani's aria. At the first intermission, Stratford turned to his sisters and aunt. "Shall we visit Ingram's box before we take some refreshment?"

"By all means." Phoebe stood, shaking out her skirts.

"Where is our new neighbor, Mr. Amesbury?" Anna interpolated. "I fear he's not here this evening. I haven't seen him, though I don't know where he has his box."

Having left their aunt with Mrs. Wyndham for company, Stratford replied to Anna as they entered the corridor. "Mr. Amesbury has gone to Sussex. I saw him earlier today on the point of departure. Besides," he looked at her strangely, "why should you care about seeing Mr. Amesbury?"

"I find him fascinating," Anna replied, with a sardonic look Stratford knew well. "I've never met anyone so transparent." She nodded at a passing acquaintance, and Phoebe shared an amused glance with her brother.

Stratford went ahead of his sisters, thinking of Amesbury's assertion that Miss Daventry's heart was engaged. Stratford might deplore Mr. Amesbury's superficiality, but at least he understood that the man's determination to marry well stemmed from his father's having to pull his estate back from the peril of moneylenders. Amesbury's thrifty habits were engrained young.

Carlton, on the other hand, posed a threat if Miss Daventry's heart were indeed taken. Even Stratford was hard-pressed to find fault with the man. He remembered Phoebe's disturbing report that Carlton and Miss Daventry had visited the museum together. What bothered him was that, unlike Mr. Amesbury, Lord Carlton had natural address.

Not two steps out of the box, Stratford crossed paths with Judith Broadmore, and his sudden stop caused his sisters to bump into him from behind.

"Good evening, my lord." Miss Broadmore's pale blonde hair and fitted silver dress were a stark contrast to the glimpse of warmth and comeliness he had seen in Miss Daventry.

In such a public place, he could not ignore her greeting without causing remark. "Good evening, Miss Broadmore. You remember my sisters, I believe. Miss Phoebe and Miss Anna Tunstall."

"Of course." Miss Broadmore inclined her head with a gracious smile. "I see you are all grown now. I hope you're enjoying your Season. I'm sure you've already made so many conquests."

Phoebe smiled politely at the condescending tone, but Anna tilted her nose and said, "Oh yes. I'm sure it's *vastly* more entertaining to be in one's second Season with leagues of conquests than it is to go through Season after Season for *ages*."

Miss Broadmore's smile grew brittle. "My lord," She turned back to her quarry, "I haven't seen you at any assembly this past week. Will you be at Almack's on Wednesday night?"

The tension between Miss Broadmore and his sisters increased Stratford's desire to move on. He gave a curt nod. "Yes. I will be escorting my sisters."

"I must own that it will be good to meet again in more exalted company." Miss Broadmore gave a sideways glance to where the Ingrams' box was just visible through the opening. "Only at Almack's can you be sure to meet the most select of the ton"—she turned back to Stratford and gave her hand—"unlike here where anybody may attend."

Stratford ignored what seemed to be a slight toward Miss Daventry. Perhaps Judith suspected some interest for Miss Daventry on his side. "Yes, well . . . good evening," he said.

"Until Wednesday," Anna cooed, wiggling her fingers. She rolled her eyes as soon as Judith left.

They came across Ingram as he was escorting his mother to the hall. "Ah, just the thing," he said, as their party came into view. "Stratford, I rely on you to attend to these two young ladies while I bring my mother for some air. There's only one of me, and I'm frequently reminded it's not enough."

"How well do I know it," Stratford replied with a good-natured laugh. "Do not forget I have two sisters and an aunt, and my odds are usually worse than yours."

"Well then." Ingram clapped his hand on Stratford's shoulder. "Our year of sacrifice has come upon us. It must happen to every man, I suppose. May they marry quickly and well so we can go about our business again." His voice rang out cheerfully, but he was somewhat quelled under the look his mother gave him. "No, no, Mother, I shall not continue in this vulgar strain. Come, let us have a bit of refreshment."

When Stratford and his sisters arrived at Ingram's box, Lydia moved to the back row and called Phoebe and Anna to her, exclaiming at their dresses, one in a demure rosy sheen, and the other in a deep lilac. "Are you never tempted to dress exactly alike? Think how you could fool everyone."

"Anna has tried," Phoebe said, with a gleam of mischief in her eyes. "She wants nothing more than to have fun at other people's expense. I, however, thwart her plans by choosing dresses she would not be caught wearing."

"It's so vexing," Anna exclaimed. "I know the styles that become you, and you refuse to acknowledge my superior taste." She began to fan herself. "Have you seen Lord Delacroix? He's come to town just before we did, but some of Stratford's old friends say they knew him before and that he left under suspicious circumstances. They won't say what."

"No!" Lydia's face lit up. "Do you not know anything more?"

Stratford had made a pretense of listening to the beginning of the conversation, but partly from fear of being applied to and partly from desire, he addressed Miss Daventry. "Are you as taken with Madame Catalani's singing as everyone else?"

"It's the fashionable thing to be, is it not?" Miss Daventry replied. "I fear I'm too green to give her only the temperate praise the world expects of me. I must be enthusiastic."

"Must you?" Stratford smiled. "Feigning boredom is outmoded." Eyes on Miss Daventry, he willed her to turn and look at him, but she remained facing forward, and he wondered if it were out of shyness or if she were thinking about Lord Carlton.

"I am modish then, quite by chance." Miss Daventry shot him a smile then turned to watch the throngs of people milling in and out of boxes and into the corridors. Stratford continued to study her profile, enjoying the sensation of being at rest while the opera house buzzed with activity.

For no other reason than to see her face turned to his again, he asked, "What are your plans after the London Season?"

"Oh." Miss Daventry gave him a startled glance. "I'm planning to seek out employment. I would prefer to teach at a school rather than accepting a post as governess, though. At a school, I might find girls like me who have no parents, and I think I could be of real use to them."

He could picture her speaking to her young charges, her lips moving as she guided them with that gentle but firm voice. That image swiftly changed to one where he kissed those lips, and the answering shock that went through him forced him to look straight ahead. Before he could reply, Lord Carlton appeared at the entrance to the box. *That man is always where he is not wanted.*

Confronted with the crowd assembled, Lord Carlton sighed, his gaze glued to Miss Daventry at Stratford's side. "Ah. Miss Ingram, I see I'm too late to gain the favor of conversation with you. I suppose it's unsurprising your box is always full."

"We were just leaving, were we not, Phoebe?" Anna stood and beckoned to her brother. "Stratford, I'm parched. We were to go in search of refreshment before the second act. Goodbye, Lydia. Miss Daventry."

Phoebe stood as well and reached over to clasp Eleanor's hand. "We will see you at Almack's then." She gave a warm smile and, with a glance at her brother, followed Anna into the hallway.

Stratford had no choice but to leave, hating that he hadn't finished his conversation with Eleanor Daventry, and hating the feeling of having lost ground to Lord Carlton.

Miss Daventry employed? Surely that was not the sum of her ambition. She might look much higher. In the natural order of things, he would have courted her properly, from the beginning, as she deserved. Of course, this was now unthinkable after such an inauspicious start. One time he drank too much. *One* time.

Anna turned at the entrance of the box and looked back. "Oh, do stop scowling, Stratford, will you?"

Chapter Eighteen

$\mathcal{E}$leanor's thoughts were disordered as Lord Carlton took his place at her side. Instead of attending to him, she found herself reliving her encounter with Lord Worthing. He had regarded her in a strangely intense way for a moment, and it had almost looked like . . . desire. But then he ripped his gaze away, and she wondered if she had imagined it.

"—Basilio's part was supposed to be played by Frangini, but the stand-in is quite good."

Eleanor snapped to attention. "Yes, I've been enthralled." She turned to give Lord Carlton her full consideration. "Are you here with your sister?"

"No, I've come with Miss St. Clair and her family. We're sitting in the middle of that row there." He indicated the box where Miss St. Clair had been watching them, and now looked away. Next to her, in the adjoining box, was a dark-haired gentleman, who stared at Eleanor in the most peculiar manner and did not look away when caught. It was an intent, questioning gaze, which made the hairs on the back of her neck stand up.

"Lord Carlton—" Eleanor hesitated, fearful of calling more attention to herself.

When she didn't speak again, he prompted, "What is it?"

"I wonder if I might ask you to look at the gentleman sitting in the box to the right of Miss St. Clair—if it is indeed Miss St. Clair wearing the yellow dress—and tell me who he is. Please—" She stayed Lord Carlton with her hand. "Do not let it be known you are looking at him."

Lord Carlton obeyed by turning his face to the stage, then sweeping the entire audience with a glance, pausing at the gentleman in question.

"I'm afraid I was not very subtle. But that is *le Vicomte* Delacroix. He is received everywhere in society, even Almack's I am told, though we've never crossed paths there. His family came over during the Great Terror."

Eleanor chewed her lip as she pondered this information, and Lord Carlton leaned in. "May I ask why? Need I feel threatened?"

Eleanor returned a look of mild exasperation. "My lord, please do not tease." She risked a glance at the box again and saw that Lord Delacroix was still staring. He lifted his hand slightly as if to wave, but she averted her gaze before he could. "It is only that he seems to stare at me so, and we've not been introduced."

"He must have heard your praises sung, Miss Daventry. I can think of no other reason." The bell chimed, signaling the curtain was about to rise. Lord Carlton stood partway, then sat down again and murmured, "He didn't hear it from me, though. I know better than to show the Babylonians all the treasures in the temple." He stood again and bowed over her hand. "Good evening, Miss Daventry. Miss Ingram, your obedient servant." Turning to the friend who had come into the box with him, he added, "Bower, shall we go?"

As soon as they left, Frederick Ingram appeared and looked around. "Is Mother not back yet? She will expect me to escort her." He did an about-face, and returned minutes later accompanied by his mother as the final movement of the audience settled to a quiet hum. The curtain opened.

The rest of the opera was lost on Eleanor, who was busy thinking of the drama that played out in her own life. Lord Carlton's interest was too marked for her comfort. It's not that there was anything wrong with him. In fact, from what she could see, he seemed genuinely attached to his mother and sister. He had displayed to advantage at the museum with Phoebe's younger cousins. Handsome enough—not that it mattered. Illogical as it might be, her hesitation was based only on feelings, and the fact that he did not seem to ignite very remarkable feelings in her.

As for Lord Worthing, his interest seemed more friendly than particular, and so she was wrong to set any store by it. It was just that . . . she felt *interesting* when he was near. For just a moment she allowed herself to remember the sensation of his arm touching hers, his coaxing gaze and the awareness in his look. And when Madame Catalani sang her celebrated aria, Eleanor's heart soared with the notes.

At Hookham's the next day, Eleanor perused the newest titles, deaf to Lydia's entreaties to make her choice and be done with it. She'd already chosen the Ann Radcliffe novel she'd not had time to finish at Worthing estate and was now looking for a second book. The Ingram library was centuries old and seemed to hold little more than Latin prose and ancient farming manuals. She would not waste this opportunity to choose from a greater selection.

"I need a new bonnet with coquelicot trim, Eleanor. And you need one in white, might I remind you. We have only this very short while before we must return—"

"You go then," Eleanor said, pulling out one of the titles and flipping it open. *Ah, this one has plenty of dialogue. It's sure to be good.*

Lydia scrutinized her, then looked around the empty aisle before launching her attack. "Stratford came to see Ingram this morning while you were out walking, and he said you wished to be a governess. Eleanor, what kind of nonsense is this?"

Eleanor looked up in surprise. "I've told you I wouldn't marry for anything less than true attachment. Why should you be surprised?"

Lydia leaned in to catch Eleanor's gaze. "I'm surprised because you seem to think such a thing so out of your reach. You have plenty of beaux."

"I need only one, Lydia." Two women entered the aisle, discussing the merits of Belgian lace, and Eleanor stepped aside to let them pass.

"You shall have only one then," Lydia retorted. "You have your pick. Why should you think about taking a hired position?"

"I must make my life on my own terms," Eleanor said. "If I do not find someone who will suit this Season, I'll have employment to fall back on until I find someone who does."

Lydia shook her head with such adamancy, Eleanor was surprised. "No. You will only take yourself away from London, where such opportunities might be found. And even if you find a position in London, you will place yourself so far removed from society, it cannot be breached. Do not do it, Eleanor."

Eleanor met Lydia's look with one of her own. She would not say anything to try to dissuade her, but Lydia had no financial concerns to worry her. What in heaven's name did she imagine Eleanor would be doing while she waited for this elusive offer of marriage? Despondency threatened to wrap around Eleanor like a damp blanket, but she refused to give into it. "I will think on it," she said.

Lydia hugged her. "Do. I'll just run over to the milliner's across the street. I won't be but a few moments. Shall you wait for me here?"

Eleanor knew that Lydia, in search of a new hat, would not be content until she'd seen at least twenty. "Go on. I shall be perfectly content here."

When Lydia left the library, Eleanor continued her perusal, wondering if Lord Worthing would remember to solicit her hand at Almack's as he'd promised. He didn't seem the type to forget. She reminded herself to dampen any hopes where Lord Worthing was concerned until he had given her more cause to raise them.

Ah. Here was *The Absentee*—a book only just come out. Running her fingers over the blue leather binding, she decided to borrow the library's only remaining copy while she had the chance.

Taking it with her, Eleanor found a seat and opened, not the Radcliffe novel she needed to finish, but the new one by Ms. Edgeworth. She turned to page one and allowed the bustle of the library to fade away as she read the opening page, then the first two chapters.

"Miss Daventry." Eleanor was yanked out of the deeply engrossing story and looked up until the pink face of Mr. Weatherby came into focus. "Miss Daventry, I say, it's a pleasure to run into you. First time we meet out of a ballroom. Choosing a book, are you?"

He seemed to be trying on personalities for size because gone was the confiding, nervous young man who was counting dance steps. In its place was a garishly dressed fop affecting indifference. "Do all young ladies love to read?" he asked.

"Not all young ladies," Eleanor said with a smile, thinking of Lydia. She stood to greet him. "But this one does, at least. You must, too, if you are here."

Mr. Weatherby's hand flew to his chest. "I cannot lie to you, Miss Daventry. I'm not bookish. It's only that my friend saw you through the window and desired an introduction. Do you know Lord Delacroix?"

Before she could register her surprise, the same gentleman from the opera, whose broad features were at odds with his slender limbs, stepped around Mr. Weatherby and made a low bow. Mr. Weatherby went on. "Will you allow me to make the introduction?"

"Of course," she murmured, assessing Lord Delacroix's face for clues as to why he would seek her out.

"Miss Daventry," the gentleman said, "I'm delighted to make your acquaintance. I've heard so much about you."

"Have you?" she asked, not quite pleased. "I am not generally thought to garner much interest."

"Oh, the person who spoke of you was *quite* interested," he said with a mysterious grin. "Quite interested, indeed." He paused to see if she would question him further, and when she did not, he cleared his throat. "Will you attend the rout at Mrs. Maxwell's house?"

Eleanor replied, "We've received the invitation, but Lady Ingram did not think it quite the thing as we are both of us in our first Season."

Lord Delacroix answered with an arch smile. "Is it? You seem so experienced, one would hardly guess it was your first."

Eleanor frowned and was saved from answering by Mr. Weatherby, who retorted, "Miss Daventry is the picture of modesty. Don't make me regret having introduced you."

Lord Delacroix was momentarily silenced and said, "My levity carries me too far. I beg your pardon. We shall meet again at Almack's, I daresay. Now that we have been properly introduced, may I claim a dance with you there?" He performed another elegant bow at this request.

Eleanor's heart sank at the thought of conversing with him for the entirety of a dance, but she didn't know how to refuse. With relief, she spotted Lydia entering the library and waving, two parcels in hand. "The hats are not yet ready," Lydia announced, "but I found just the gloves I will need for my riding habit, and I had them for a song. I would take you there, but James is waiting. Are you ready?" Only then did she perceive Mr. Weatherby and Lord Delacroix standing in the aisle of books.

"I'm ready," Eleanor said, and moved toward Lydia.

"And my dance?" Lord Delacroix called out.

Eleanor paused. "If there is still room on my card," she replied. Lydia nodded to the two gentlemen and led the way outdoors. Eleanor wasn't able to breathe again until she was seated out of sight against the squabs of Lydia's carriage.

Before the door was shut, Lydia began. "Goodness, have you met Lord Delacroix then? *Who* introduced you? If it was Mr. Weatherby, he shouldn't have done it. Lord Delacroix is not thought to be quite the thing, you know. He's welcome at Almack's through his connection with Princess Lieven, and because of that, no one dares cut him. But he has a reputation for being rather fast. No mother is keen to let him dance with her daughter, even if his fortune appears to be intact, and *that* despite his love of all games of chance."

Lydia paused to take a breath after this galloping monologue, but Eleanor remained silent. "He made you promise him a dance, has he?" she continued. "He is handsome."

Eleanor looked up in alarm. "Lydia. No—"

"How can I help it? You know I favor Byronesque men, with dark curls and melting brown eyes." Lydia grinned mischievously and, when Eleanor continued to peer at her in reproach, finally retracted with a laugh. "But I'm grown now. I will surely end up with someone respectable, like Major Fitzwilliam."

Eleanor softened. "Oh, do you like him? He's so reliable, and . . . and good."

Lydia retorted, "No, I do not like him. Or—he's nice enough, but he doesn't catch my fancy. He will make someone a respectable, if stodgy, husband."

"Do you think so?" Eleanor asked in amazement. Lydia was saying this now, but Eleanor had seen the way she looked at Major Fitzwilliam and was certain she was not unaffected. "Don't you see that he is someone whose attention will never wander, whose household will never suffer from ill-management, whose children will never have to endure bouts of disagreeable temper?"

"Oh, if you like him so much, *you* marry him," Lydia said, crossly. Eleanor wisely kept her thoughts to herself.

The night of Almack's, Eleanor was sent a pink posy from Lord Carlton and Lydia was sent three flowers: a white peony from Major Fitzwilliam, a yellow posy from Lord Carmichael, and a red one from a new suitor Eleanor had not yet met.

"Oh, I shall have to wear Major Fitzwilliam's peony," Lydia said, disgruntled. "It's the only one that matches my dress. How did he know I would be wearing purple? You would think he had sent out spies to follow me to the dressmaker."

"You love peonies. Anyway, you told him what you'd be wearing when he last paid a morning call," Eleanor reminded her cheerfully. "He didn't need spies, only a good attention span, for how a man can listen to a woman talk so much about fashion and still retain the essential information, I do *not* know." She couldn't resist a chuckle. "Perhaps that is why

Lord Ingram says he shows so much promise. He's not distracted by any of the feints the enemy troops put in his way. He presses on to lay siege to the stronghold."

"Are you speaking metaphorically to me, Eleanor?" Lydia turned to her, arms akimbo. "Am I supposed to be the feint or the stronghold?"

"You are both," Eleanor assured her. "Your feint is boring your audience with things like clothes that are sure to hold no interest in all but the most superficial of men. And your stronghold is your heart and what truly matters to you if only someone can break down the walls to reach it."

"*Harrumph.*" Lydia frowned. "A bunch of nonsense if I've ever heard it."

Chapter Nineteen

Eleanor's first impression of Almack's was one of disappointment. The rooms were less gilded than anticipated and shabby, she noted when the last of the fresh air from outdoors had dissipated and she was enclosed in the sweltering mass. A sip of the orgeat lemonade drink Lord Ingram brought her was unreviving, and the swirling couples on the dance floor overwhelmed her.

A beacon of promise came in the form of Lord Worthing, who sighted her and broke away from his sisters, inching his way across the room. He addressed her gravely with a "Miss Daventry" and a bow, but his eyes didn't leave her face. Only when Lydia nudged him did he turn to her.

"Eleanor and I do not have our dance cards full yet, Stratford. You must request one."

Lord Worthing looked up as a noisy group of young bucks entered, causing Lady Castlereagh to frown and rush to the door. He seemed deaf to Lydia's hint as he waved to an acquaintance, and Lydia, request forgotten as quickly as it was made, moved to greet a friend.

Eleanor, alone with Lord Worthing, found herself holding her breath—*he will not ask*—until he turned his smiling focus on her, and she felt the full force of its warmth. "Miss Daventry, since Lydia has not stayed to receive my invitation to dance, will you come and greet my sisters? My aunt has pleaded unwell, and I'm their sole chaperone this evening."

Eleanor took his arm, and they made the slow circuit of the room. "Your sisters are fortunate to have you. When I think of how you had no interest in coming to London . . ." She smiled at him mischievously.

"I could hardly have escaped it." He chuckled. "I was so newly returned from the Peninsula and in full denial of my duties to family."

"That is understandable, my lord." Eleanor followed Lord Worthing through a break in the throng of people and exhaled in relief as he led her to an area that was less crowded.

He pulled her to the side and bent his head close to hers to ask, "What is your opinion of Almack's?"

"That the slightest excitement would turn into a charge, and that after the crowd had dispersed, I would have to be peeled from the floor."

Lord Worthing laughed aloud. "You *are* rather petite," he said.

"It is seldom I am not reminded of the fact," she replied, demurely, but her mouth twitched.

"I shall take care that you are sheltered," he said. "You may leave that to me."

Eleanor was conscious of the happiness that bubbled up inside her, and she strove to keep it in check. He had not said anything more than common chivalry required, and she would not read anything into it. In an effort to keep her hopes grounded, she steered the conversation to him.

"Now that you've returned to England and have got acquainted with the estate," she said, "are you more at your ease as Earl of Worthing?"

He surprised her by laughing, however, and sent her efforts awry by turning the focus back on her. "Am I better-mannered, do you mean? The verdict is out. You and I are now on friendly terms, but I don't remember getting a pardon. When you have forgiven me, I'll dare answer in the affirmative."

She joined him in his laughter, but as he brought her to his sisters, she feared she was more in danger than ever of losing her heart.

François Delacroix had arrived before Eleanor Daventry and was looking for an opportunity to speak with her. He saw Worthing escorting Eleanor to his family party before going to speak to Lady Sefton. Even a fool knew what that meant, and he was no fool. If Worthing were introducing Miss Daventry to a patroness, it was so the young lady would gain permission to waltz with him. Well, Delacroix, too, knew a patroness, and perhaps he could out-jockey the earl for the first dance. He spotted Princess Lieven and judged she would not be inconvenienced if he requested speech with her just now.

"*Bonsoir*, Princess," he said, bowing over her hand.

"*Oui, bonsoir. Qu'est ce que vous voulez.*" Her eyes narrowed as she inspected the crowd.

It was not a promising beginning, and he decided to come straight to the point. "Princess, will you introduce me to the Miss Daventry, who is standing near Lord Worthing? I wish to waltz with her, and I dare not ask without first having your permission."

"Delacroix, I'm not pleased with you," the princess replied in her blunt way. She threw a brittle smile at Dunhill, who was dancing the scotch reel with such enthusiasm as to be almost absurd. He was saluting her on the sidelines, oblivious to the spectacle he was making. Lord Delacroix knew it cost her to allow the man admittance simply because the other women liked him, and it gave him a perverse satisfaction that she didn't have her way in everything.

"Princess, *mais qu'est ce que j'ai fait?*" he said. "What have I done to displease you? You know I take your good opinion very much to heart."

She turned a bony shoulder to him. "Word has come of your *déroute* at the gaming hell Wednesday night, and there were even rumors of cheating. I did not introduce you to society *pour ce genre de choses.*"

He turned pleading eyes to her. "Princess, *en toute franchise*, I've had a run of bad luck. The very worst." He tugged at his gloves. "But if there had been cheating, it would have been found out. All the charges have come to nothing, and I am not yet run off my legs. I am still . . . *honorable.*"

"It is bad ton to be much addicted to dice, and people look to us to dictate matters of the ton. Soon I shall regret having taken you up." Princess Lieven lifted her chin, and her eyes held his in a challenge.

"I will not disgrace you, *je le promets.*" Delacroix looked at her rigid countenance and decided to go for broke. "Will you present me to Miss Daventry?"

"I do not know a Miss Daventry, nor did I extend a voucher to her. *Bonne soirée*, my lord."

Lord Carlton had also noticed Worthing making the rounds with Miss Daventry, and his pause at Lady Sefton's station. He saw an opportunity with Lady Jersey, who had just bid farewell to the Speaker of the House.

"Good evening, Lady Jersey," he said with a bow. "Are you gathering wisdom this time or imparting it?"

Lady Jersey gave an indulgent smile and an evasive answer. "Lord Carlton, you were born for politics if ever a man was. Shall I take you up?"

"Most readily. With you to champion me, I'm sure to succeed." Carlton answered cheerfully, but Lady Jersey gave him a calculated look.

"You're young for politics, but there have been others who started at your age. Some younger. Is your mother not pleased then? No soldiering for you? No politics?" Her tone held enough teasing to make the question conspiratorial without insulting Lady Carlton.

"She doesn't like either. It's true." Carlton sighed, watching the whirling couples in front of him. "But of course, I will choose my own path when the way is clear." He glanced at Miss Daventry, who was now talking with Lord Worthing's sisters, and he saw Worthing was no longer with them.

"Of course you will, young man." Lady Jersey accepted a glass of lemonade from a passing tray. "I believe you'd do well to marry young before embarking on politics. Not every man is ready to choose a wife at such a young age, but you were born for responsibility. And you were like that before you were out of short coats. Your wife must be gracious enough to move in the first circles and intelligent enough to guide them." She followed his gaze, and her eyes narrowed shrewdly as she picked through the group and settled on Miss Daventry. "And who is this woman you've picked? For I assume that is why you've come to speak to me tonight."

"She is Miss Daventry, an heiress of a moderate income, and a possessor of grace and intelligence." His eyes gleamed.

"Ah. Lord Worthing's ward." Carlton shot her a surprised look, but Lady Jersey went on. "I believe your case to be serious. Her fortune is not to be despised, but then you are not in need of it. She does not possess the beauty of some of the other debutantes. And yet, you choose her."

"Is she not considered beautiful? I had not noticed." He looked toward the musicians who were striking up a waltz. "I was hoping you could perform a small service and present me to her so I might claim her hand for this dance."

Lady Jersey opened her fan. "In politics, there is a time to make rousing speeches, and there's a time to work behind the scenes if you wish your mission to succeed. This is something you must learn. I believe you are too late." She motioned with her fan to where Lady Sefton was speaking to Miss Daventry, then putting Miss Daventry's hand on Worthing's arm with a gracious smile to both. Carlton grit his teeth as Lord Worthing led Miss Daventry to the dance floor.

Ingram had been deep in thought since he entered Almack's. He'd be meeting Le Marchant's rider a week from Friday for the first time, and he had to sort through the various bits of intelligence to be sent. It might be wise to make a duplicate, though that would be a cursed lot of work, and not something he could pass off to anyone else. A loud voice at his ear jostled him out of his contemplation, and he became aware of his surroundings.

Noticing Anna Tunstall was not dancing, he approached her. As well her as any other. "Anna, will you do me the honor of this waltz?"

"Why, yes. It would be most unfair if Miss Daventry were the only one of us to dance the very first waltz of the evening. She's only here on special invitation because she knows your family. It's not as if she were a long-standing member of the ton."

"Do you not like her?" Ingram put his arm around Anna's waist but frowned at her words. "I'd have thought you would have more compassion on her. She has no protectors."

"Apart from you," Anna corrected. "It's not *her*, per se. I don't like that she was foisted on our family by the old earl. And that she inherited the part of the estate that will be most inconveniently situated in someone else's hands. Unless, I suppose, the person in question is Mr. Amesbury. But I would not wish him on her."

"Nor I." Ingram gave an absent smile as he led her around the room, his mind elsewhere.

They'd turned around the room twice without conversation, and he was made aware of his lapse when Anna smiled and lifted her eyes to his in what he recognized as pure mischief. "Well, Ingram. Have you the most recent *crim. con.* to share with me, or shall I delight you with what I know? Gilly has cast off his bird of paradise at last, and she has demanded a sum that's likely to run him off his legs—"

"Anna!" Ingram's steps faltered. "This speech is not becoming. I'll thank you not to enter into these sorts of conversations with my sister."

Anna raised a haughty eyebrow, but her eyes were merry. "Very well, my lord." She followed his turns twice before adding, "But I had my news from her."

Chapter Twenty

Lord Worthing led Eleanor to a place in the center of the room, and she faced him, filled with the awareness of his solid presence as he bent his head toward hers. The pressure of his hand on her back was light, and every nerve tingled at his proximity. Then the music began. She knew how to waltz—had learned in school—but this was nothing like waltzing with the thick-waisted dancing teacher who smelled like sausage. This was magic.

The lights and sounds whirled by, the colors of other couples spinning, the music compelling their movements, and Lord Worthing holding her, grounded, as they moved. She spun in his arms, and their eyes met as he guided her across the floor. She knew she should speak. A good dancing partner should say something, but she could find nothing to say that was not so utterly mundane as to break the spell. He didn't speak either, but only pulled her closer until their heartbeats pulsed in concert, their steps intertwined.

Too soon, the music finished, and the room stopped spinning. Eleanor returned her gaze to Lord Worthing, who remained frozen, his eyes examining every inch of her face. The corners of his mouth turned up, though it looked like it cost him. "Thank you, Miss Daventry."

She answered with a dip of her head, and in silence, Lord Worthing led her off the dance floor. They stood on the sidelines for a full minute before he turned to her and smiled. How could a man with such rigid, stern features have such a warm smile?

"Miss Daventry, you dance very well. If you were not staying with Lydia, who must have taught you by now, I would not have dared ask Lady Sefton's permission to invite you to waltz."

She matched his light tone. "Miss Spencer's Academy was quite progressive, I'll have you know. She hired a dance teacher who instructed us in everything, including the waltz. Miss Spencer knew it would become the rage before the local matrons did and didn't want one of her students bringing her shame."

"And who was your teacher?" He frowned, and she allowed herself the luxury of wondering if it was from jealousy.

"Oh, an older gentleman with a paunch. His feet were nimble though." She grinned as Lord Worthing let out a laugh.

On the edge of the room, Miss Broadmore was threading her way through the crowd, and Eleanor felt a flash of irritation. *She will be wishing for a dance too, I'm sure.* Focusing again on Lord Worthing, she said, "Thank you for honoring me with your invitation. I know there are some who are still waiting for partners."

"The honor is mine," he returned, with a bow. "Let me lead you over to the refreshment table. I believe Lydia said you've no other dances lined up as yet."

"As a matter of fact, Lord Carlton has requested the first quadrille, and Mr. Braxsen and Major Fitzwilliam both promised they would ask. Mr. Weatherby was kind enough to offer as well. It has not been as difficult a thing as I imagined to secure a partner." Eleanor accepted the drink he handed her and then confided, "I'm not so naive to think that my inheritance does not play a part, though you once hinted even that would not be enough." Her prim mouth was belied by the mischief dancing in her eyes.

Lord Worthing met her sally with a weak smile, but his words were serious. "Miss Daventry, I did not do you justice. It's not simply that I behaved wretchedly to you. I didn't then see your worth."

Warmth unfurled in her heart at his words. Eleanor turned to answer, but Lord Worthing's gaze was fixed on Lord Carlton, who was headed their way. She let out a quiet sigh of disappointment.

The earl must have felt the mood shift too, because when he spoke, his voice held a hint of steel. "It would be a waste of your admirable qualities to let you go to some fortune hunter, or to someone who is too inexperienced to fully grasp your value. It behooves me to care for you the way I care for my sisters. Or for Lydia. I feel responsible to see you well-situated."

Eleanor's eyes widened at the indifferent words that had come on the heels of such praise, but she was in sufficient command of her voice to give a light reply. "My lord, what makes you think I require your aid? I am under the auspices of Lady Ingram, and by association, Lord Ingram. He will deter anyone who is unsuitable." She gave a bland smile, then noticing that Lord Carlton had been waylaid, signaled Lydia, who had just returned to the sidelines.

"Lydia, who did you find to partner you for the waltz?" She turned her shoulder on Lord Worthing. *Let him reflect now on whether he has chosen his words with care.*

"The Duke of Roxburgh," Lydia said in triumph. "He asked Mrs. Drummond-Burrell to present me. And now I'm at liberty to accept other invitations. Stratford? If you see I'm sitting out, you will come and spare me, will you not?"

"Hmm?" Lord Worthing was not attending, and Lydia's question brought his gaze back to Eleanor's. "Yes, yes of course. If you're not dancing, and I'm at liberty, I will ask you. Now, if you'll excuse me. I see Anna is still talking to Ingram, and though it's harmless enough, *le beau monde* might not see it that way." He strode off, his gaze fixed on his sister.

Lydia looked at Eleanor, who had begun to scan the room for a source of fresh air. "I'm glad you were able to waltz with Stratford. He did you *such* a service. Now anyone may ask you." She squeezed Eleanor's hand.

"I wish he'd saved his kind offices for someone else." Eleanor lifted her chin, torn between feelings of irritation and a sense of the ridiculous. For all his more amiable qualities, it could not be said of the earl that he was a paragon of tact. Well, she *had* said she would endeavor to disregard his words. "I do not need a champion in Lord Worthing. Come, it's feeling so warm here. May we not go to the alcove and find fresh air?"

Lydia, who was wearing a most becoming dress, had to sacrifice her own inclination at the altar of friendship and trail behind her friend. They were not halfway to the door when Miss Broadmore blocked their path.

"How lovely you both look this evening," said Miss Broadmore in a soft voice. "Miss Daventry, is it? You were fortunate to secure the notice of a peer in your first Season. Now you need not fear for partners."

Lydia returned the glittering smile for one of her own. "Oh, she's had no lack of partners, I assure you."

"No—is it so?" Miss Broadmore fanned herself slowly, her gaze never leaving Eleanor's. "I suppose an inheritance will make anyone appealing to the ton. Where was it you hail from?" Her lips parted, showing tiny pearl teeth.

"From 28 Grosvenor Square." Lydia gave a smug smile. "The Ingram residence. Now, if you'll excuse us, we were on our way to get some air."

Five minutes spent away from the bustle, breathing in the fresh air that poured into the windows Lydia had wrenched open, and Eleanor began to find an inner calm. She examined dispassionately everything Lord Worthing had said, ignoring her unruly feelings from when they'd danced together, and chastised herself for thinking he had begun to seek out her company because he appreciated it.

She could find humor in his having spoken, once again, without thinking, because she was certain he would eventually realize it, and that when he did, he would feel chagrined. He would wrestle over the decision of which course to follow. *Give Miss Daventry the apology she deserves or obey her directive to cease with the apologies all together.*

Find humor she must, however, because she could not allow herself to dream about a future with Lord Worthing when it was clear he had not made up his mind about a future with her. She suspected he felt some degree of attraction. The way the air snapped between them was difficult to ignore. But this was not the conversation of a man decided.

"Eleanor, you're so quiet. Are you feeling more the thing?" Eleanor knew Lydia was making an heroic effort to wait patiently for her to recover when, all the while, gentlemen were probably searching for Lydia in vain.

"I am recovered. Thank you for coming with me." Eleanor reached over and shut the window, wishing to leave everything as she had found it, and linked her arm through Lydia's. They entered the swarming mass of people, and Eleanor followed in Lydia's wake. If only she could find someone comfortable, she might take refuge there for the remainder of the evening.

Lord Delacroix intercepted them both. "Good evening, Miss Daventry. I was just coming to request your hand for the next waltz. Will you do me the honor?"

Eleanor could think of no reason to refuse, though she wished to. "I've not filled my dance card yet," she said, and handed it over to him. He wrote his name for the next waltz.

"*A toute à l'heure,*" he said, with a wink, and took his leave without requesting an introduction to Lydia. She didn't offer.

"Hmm," said Lydia. "A *vicomte*, is he not? He has such . . . continental features, which is not in fashion just now. Still, I find him pleasing to look at. And he seems to be interested in you. My dear friend, I knew you would be all the rage in London."

"Oh, Lydia," said Eleanor, dispirited. "You knew no such thing. It's that cursed inheritance."

"Cursed? You will make a brilliant match because of it." Lydia squeezed her friend's arm.

"Yes," Eleanor said sadly, "but it won't be for love."

Stratford was not good company. His sisters were well in hand, with one dance after another. Lydia seemed to have disappeared, along with Miss Daventry—the two of them sought out for every dance. He had not liked the way he'd left things with Miss Daventry. Perhaps he had spoken without giving weight to his words, but when Carlton headed her way, he'd felt the full force of how wrong such a match would be. Wrong in every way . . . except, perhaps, what logic dictated when an eligible man sought out an equally eligible young woman for matrimony. It was only his own feelings that revolted at the thought of Carlton and Miss Daventry together.

Marriage. He couldn't consider such a prospect himself until he had his own life in order. His foolish proposal to Miss Daventry at Worthing had only happened because he was reeling from having seen Judith so soon upon his return, was doubly crushed under the weight of a peerage and the unexpected twist in inheritance that involved Miss Daventry— and because he'd been dead drunk. Until he was fully ready to pursue the thought of taking a wife, it was not fair to Miss Daventry to present himself as a serious suitor. Surely she must appreciate his disinterest and protection of her feelings and her future.

He had barred his heart securely after his disappointment with Judith, and no one had come close to breaching its gate. Until now. Stratford thought of Miss Daventry in his arms as they waltzed, sweet-smelling, her eyes closing each time they spun, and the look of pure joy on her face that melted his defenses. The vision did not quit his senses for some time.

Lord Delacroix was on time to claim his waltz, and Eleanor knew no pleasure from being held so closely. When Lord Worthing held her, it felt intimate without compromising her. When Lord Delacroix took her in his arms, she felt ill. Any attempt to create distance only caused them to dance more awkwardly. It was not the sensation of flying she had experienced with . . .

"I was perhaps forward in seeking an introduction," Lord Delacroix began, "but I was desirous of making your acquaintance after hearing your praises sung in the most unusual quarter."

Eleanor looked desperately to the sidelines to see if there were no one she could stand with when the dance was over. There was more than one young lady eyeing her with something akin to envy. It seemed not every debutante had high aspirations for marriage. Some, like Lydia, were attracted to her partner's Byronesque looks.

"Will you not ask me who it is that sings your praises?" he teased.

Her gaze snapped to his. "I do not care to hear that my name is bandied about in any crowd. I don't wish to know more."

"You wrong me, Miss Daventry. The praises came from one person who can have no harm in singing them. I was in Paris. Was it . . . oh, it appears to have been ten years ago. I was a greenhorn then." He looked at her, but she revealed no signs of comprehension.

"And I saw a woman who must have been ten years my senior—a woman whose name had once been Daventry. She was in the company of *le Comte* de Chambourd." He leaned down as if to impart secret knowledge. "He was a particular friend of my family's, the count, and although I won't call him a fool for choosing to return to France when anyone can see his standing there was not the most secure, I will say he was *un bon vivant*. Shame I've not heard from him since."

Eleanor's pulse beat erratically in her throat. Blackness threatened to cloud her vision, but she forced it away by sheer will. Lips clamped together, she made herself look at him.

"Your mother was exquisite." He whispered the last word, turning and sweeping her with him. "Men received her favor as a benediction, though I own she was most devoted to her count."

Eleanor willed the song to end and could no more cause a scene than she could free herself from his grasp.

"You don't favor her," he said reflectively. "Not in looks. But perhaps you favor her in temperament?" He smiled. "As I said, I was most desirous of making your acquaintance."

Eleanor did not speak until the waltz was over, which was less than a minute later. Lord Delacroix bowed before her, and she curtsied, keeping up the pretense until the end. She'd had her share of insults and rebuffs as a young girl and knew how to bear it. Fortunately, her guardian's decision to put her in school in a distant county spared her from further recriminations. It had been some time since Eleanor had to mask any fear, anger, or sadness from faces eager to drink in her downfall.

She took his arm as they made their way to the sidelines and spoke in the space of the short steps until they reached it. "Lord Delacroix, I was not raised by my mother. I was raised by my aunt and my nurse, and the teachers in a select academy for young women, all of whom were carefully chosen by my guardian, the Fourth Earl of Worthing. You are mistaken in the reading of my character, and I will be most obliged if you do not solicit conversation with me in the future. Good evening."

Chapter Twenty-One

Stratford stared at the spot of sunlight on the table next to his seat at White's. Usually the room needed candles in the sconces, even in daylight, but today the sun pierced the room's gloomy interior. It couldn't reach his spirits, however, as he continued to wrestle with what he was coming to identify as *the dilemma*. Was he willing to hold on to his freedom as a bachelor at the risk of losing Miss Daventry forever?

Surely she could wait until he was more certain of his heart? In the meantime, his attention to her was patent enough to show interest without giving undue cause for hope. It was not every young lady he treated with the care he gave his own sisters. And they were, in some way, connected after all. His uncle obviously felt the need to continue his guardianship from the grave. Why else would he give her such a lucrative piece of his property? Stratford paused. *Why indeed?* He would have to see if Billings knew any more to the story. The butler had been in his uncle's employ since he was a boy.

A vision passed before his eyes of Miss Daventry last night wearing a dress in a cream color so pale it looked as if the fabric were a continuation of her skin. Miss Daventry looked elegant until she smiled. Then her crinkly eyes, and her white, uneven teeth that stretched between two perfect dimples transformed her look to mischievous. Kittenish. Odd that the memories he had of her in his home, wearing a simple brown dress, delighted him just as much as those of her wearing her finest. He pictured her in the kitchen, asking the cook for headache powder, and a reluctant smile came to his face. Nervous though she'd been, she had seemed to belong there.

The door opened, and Stratford looked up, giving a mechanical salute in response to Mr. Braxsen's greeting. The latter indicated the empty chair with a lift of his eyebrows, and Stratford replied, "No, it's not taken. Have a seat."

Mr. Braxsen set down his high crown hat and rested his cane against the table. "Are you going to the cockfight Friday?"

"No," Stratford said shortly. "I don't care for them. You?"

"I abhor watching bloodshed, even if it's just animals. I seem to be alone in my disdain, however. You're the first I've met who will miss it. Will Ingram attend?" Mr. Braxsen fiddled with the edge of the discarded newspaper on the dark wood table.

Stratford shrugged and signaled the waiter to bring another glass. He leaned forward. "Braxsen, do you think about the Peninsula? Are you able to forget it while you're here?"

Mr. Braxsen drummed his fingers on the table, looking bored, but he paused before answering. "I think about it enough that I don't have any immediate desire to return."

The waiter appeared, and Stratford leaned back as he poured a glass for him and then for Mr. Braxsen. "I lost track of you while you were over there. Where were you stationed?"

"I arrived in oh-nine and followed the trail from there. Was in every significant battle, except for Badajoz, when I was sent with a couple of fellows as a rear guard that was not needed."

"Oh, that was a bad one. I was there." Stratford took a sip of his drink, eyes downcast. "You missed a bloody mess. I'm glad you were not there to see it."

"No," Mr. Braxsen said, shoving the newspaper away and leaning back. "But my brother fell there. Came across his body when we rode the trail back to the regiment. It didn't appear to be near the fighting, and I can't think how he came to be there."

"I'm sorry," Stratford said, setting his glass down.

"What division did you lead?" Mr. Braxsen asked when the silence stretched long enough.

"I led the Ninety-Fourth Foot. I was with them right until I left. I'd be with them still if I were going back. What about you?"

Mr. Braxsen shrugged. "I'll go to the same regiment I left off. My father did not leave me with what one might call a fortune, so I have little alternative. But for now, I'll spend time contemplating the choice food and drink at the clubs and the feeling of clean breeches." He attempted a smile, which to Stratford looked resigned.

"So you're done then," Mr. Braxsen added. "With the inheritance and the title . . ."

"I sold out," Stratford said. "I like to see a job well done and would have seen it through to the end of the war. But in my case, there's no one left to inherit. It's time I settled down and produced an heir." He leaned back, lip curled, and he knew his face revealed more than he wished.

"Duty calls for each of us in different ways," Mr. Braxsen said, his voice heavy with irony. He pushed his chair back as if to go, but Stratford detained him.

"I think this is the first I've seen you without Major Fitzwilliam. It was good of you to take him up in London. How came you to be friends with him? He's from Norfolk, is he not?"

Mr. Braxsen fingered the silver handle to his cane. "He chanced upon that rear guard envoy of ours while he was on mission. And though we didn't see any action from where we expected, we were fired upon from the trees on the hillside. Fitz went out into the gunfire to pull me to the rock that shielded us from Boney's men. I got leave because I was wounded, and he came at the same time with intelligence to bring back to London. At least that's what I suppose to be true." He shrugged. "I guess he still feels responsible for me."

Stratford accepted this with a nod. It was unsurprising. He had seen a good amount of courage shown by ordinary men, and Major Fitzwilliam was born to lead. The door opened, and Lord Delacroix entered in the company of the Marquess of Egerton.

Mr. Braxsen lowered his voice. "You will think me old-fashioned, but I still don't understand how he came to gain acceptance at White's. With the war going on, I, for one, don't trust the French, even one who was raised on English soil."

"You're not the only one who feels that way. But the greatest danger lies not with the Frenchmen who've made their home in England. They are sometimes more loyal than the Englishmen." Stratford stood, offering his hand. "I must be off. I've some business to attend to."

He stopped at home to have his horses harnessed, deciding it was a provident moment to visit Ingram. *I will not trouble Miss Daventry this time.* However, when Stratford was being shown to the library, he couldn't resist looking across the hallway to see if the door to the drawing room was open. It was not.

Ingram stood when he entered. "Have a drink?"

"No, I took one at the club. I came with no set purpose, I warn you," Stratford said with a laugh. "Oh, I suppose my time with Braxsen has made me melancholy enough to bring me here. There are soldiers on leave who do not wish to go back," he enunciated with dry humor. "They don't know what restless work it is to be concerned only with one's own affairs." He raised his eyes to his friend. "Do you have plans to go back into the field?"

"I should not mind it, but the work here is too delicate to turn over to someone else." Ingram dusted the letter he had just written and, when he'd closed the envelope, melted some wax and pushed his ring to seal it.

Stratford stared out the window, content to drift off in his reverie, but Ingram broke it. "So you don't wish to be here and settle down. Now this is a side to you I'm surprised to see. No, no—" Ingram held out his hand in a placating gesture. "I do not think you a coward, nor a sluggard. It's just . . . ever since I've known you, you wanted nothing more than to lead a quiet life. Marry, raise a family, and establish yourself. I understand your joining up. No one could blame you. But now you have the chance to start a family, and I'm surprised to see you still fighting it. Not every woman is Judith, you know."

Stratford leaned on the armrest, chin in hand. "My heart's not in it," he said, finally. "Nothing's ever enticing when it's forced."

"Remove the pressure," Ingram advised. "You're no more in need of having to marry now than when you were twenty-one. Go hang it if the estate goes to some distant cousin whom you don't even know. Why should that trouble you? Find yourself someone you like to talk to."

Stratford looked at him strangely. "Is that what you'd do?"

Ingram shrugged. "Well . . . when the question comes up . . ." His voice trailed away as his gaze drifted to a spot out the window.

Stratford thought he would say no more, but Ingram reverted to their former subject. "So Braxsen does not wish to go back. Have you heard any rumblings about people who are discontent with the war? Or who've heard of others who are? In other words, any leads?"

"Nothing unusual. I think Braxsen was upset his brother was killed at Badajoz. He's unhappy with Delacroix's presence in the club, though why he should rail about it now I don't know. Delacroix's been a member nearly as long as I have."

"Unsurprising," Ingram replied. "As my father used to say, the compassion the last generation felt toward escaping Royalists must naturally come to an end when the two countries go to war. Some who've resettled here never lost their heritage."

"No," said Stratford. "But Delacroix is not one of them. He has no ties to the Continent that I know of."

"Did he not go in oh-two?" Ingram picked up the letter he had sealed and tapped it against his palm.

"I was still at Cambridge. Didn't know him then." Stratford, seeing that Ingram was collecting his gloves, stood. "People are apt to be edgy in war," he said. "It will pass as soon as we carry the victory, and the young men go off on their Grand Tour once again."

"Save that sentiment for the women folk," Ingram said. "You know as well as I do this victory is far from being sure."

"Perhaps better, since I was on the field longer," Stratford replied. "But faith is being certain of what you do not see. And where there is no faith, there is no victory." He pressed his hat on his head and turned toward the door.

As soon as they stepped into the corridor, Stratford came flush against Eleanor Daventry so that he had to place his hand on her arm to steady her. Miss Daventry took a step back, but he was unable to tear away his gaze.

"Where are you ladies headed?" Ingram asked.

Lydia answered. "We were on our way to make some purchases—"

"Shocking," Ingram said.

"—it's for the rout tonight, so we have no time to lose," Lydia continued, as if her brother hadn't interrupted.

Ingram took his cloak from the footman. "Then we'll escort you to the carriage."

"We were planning to walk. Would you care to join us? You can tell me if it's true about the bets being laid at Brooke's on whether Mary Wexby will say yes to Mr. Sutherland." Lydia finished tying her hat under her chin and turned her inquisitive gaze to her brother.

"How do you hear about these things?" Ingram shook his head, not entirely pleased, as he held his arm out to escort his sister.

On the street, Stratford took his place beside Eleanor, and after a pause, said, "Please take my arm, Miss Daventry, unless I am again in your black books after promising to pawn you off to the first eligible suitor."

She shot him a surprised glance, then looked down to hide her smile. "No, my lord, why should you be? What have you done other than provide me a service at Almack's by setting me up in the eyes of the ton. It was most generous of you."

That rankled a little, only because she was throwing his own words back at him. He struggled to think of a suitable reply that would convey his actions were not merely from altruism. They walked in silence before he said, "It would only be generous if I were exaggerating your worth. But you, Miss Daventry, are a pearl without price, and it is only befitting it should be known." He glanced at her averted face and saw her lips hovering on a smile. So, it had pleased her what he'd said. All was not lost.

Her next words, however, were dampening. "It's the sort of thing a brother might say, I understand, to bolster a sister with confidence. I thank you, for your words carry more weight coming from a place of disinterest."

Once again, he found himself struggling to reply. Despite his reservations about marriage as an institution, it wasn't disinterest he was feeling where Miss Daventry was concerned. On his left, a maid leaned out the basement window and unrolled a carpet for cleaning. He stared at the bright floral pattern.

As they passed by, the *thwack, thwack, thwack* seemed to give Stratford a jolt, and he blurted out the words before he could censure them. "I admire you, Miss Daventry, in a way a brother does not." He paused in shock, somewhat panicked by his own admission, but he had said it and could not recall the words.

Though she continued to face forward, he was rewarded with glowing eyes and a dimpled smile she tried to hold back, but which only grew broader. His anxiety left him at once, and he felt like shouting in victory.

That had been the right thing to say. And when Ingram turned back to urge them to swap partners so he didn't have to listen to his sister's prattle for the entirety of the walk, Stratford was able to banter.

"Willingly. I think your sister has suffered from your inattention long enough. Come, Lydia, walk with me and we shall agree on the perfidy of brothers."

Chapter Twenty-Two

A week later, the weather promised to be fair when Stratford and his sisters rode in Hyde Park before breakfast. It was a studious decision to go at an unfashionable hour as the goal was actually to ride, not to be seen. At least, this was Stratford's goal. As he turned down Rotten Row, however, he admitted there was one set of sparkling brown eyes he wouldn't mind seeing, and he was contemplating when he might again visit Grosvenor Square.

"What a surprise the park is thin of company." Anna reached down and straightened the bottom of her blue velvet habit. "Whatever possessed you to propose riding at this time of day, Stratford?"

"If we want to ride, we must do it now. Later is for peacocking." He squinted his eyes and, to his surprise and delight, spotted a group he made out to be Miss Daventry with Lydia, Mr. Braxsen, and Major Fitzwilliam. The horse responded to his unconscious gesture and began to trot toward the party.

"I'm wearing a stunning peacock blue, Phoebe's wearing the green . . ." Anna's horse trotted obediently behind the roan. "And you have the beak. How nicely we might have fit."

"It's Lydia," Phoebe said, third in line.

"And your Miss Daventry," Anna added, drily.

Stratford ignored them and came abreast the party of four. "Good day, ladies," he said, and nodded at Mr. Braxsen and the major. His sudden lightened mood lent a disposition to tease. "Braxsen, I'm surprised to see you at such an early hour. Your reputation for dissipation must be false."

"Ha!" Lydia interjected. "Do not be precipitous, for he only just arrived. An hour after our rendezvous." Her horse stretched his neck down and nibbled on a clump of grass.

Mr. Braxsen responded, "I'm terribly sorry, Miss Ingram. As you see, I'm quite a man of leisure. My father had it in mind that a year or two in the military would cure me of any leanings in that direction."

"And did it?" Stratford inquired, a smile lurking on his lips.

Major Fitzwilliam laughed. "He was nearly put on probation for running a gaming ring among the infantrymen. It all came out when he was injured and soldiers came looking for their blunt." He turned to Lydia, his perfect gravity belied by a twitching lip. "You see, Miss Ingram, while I owe myself obliged to Mr. Braxsen for the introduction, I don't think he's at all the sort of gentleman with whom you should be acquainted."

Lydia turned her amused eyes from the major to Mr. Braxsen. "Except that I was barely out of leading strings when he abandoned a coveted spot in the county fox hunt to rescue me from a tree I ambitiously chose to climb. So you see I cannot throw him off."

While Lydia was holding court, Miss Daventry allowed her horse to edge alongside the twins. "Phoebe, are you quite recovered from the pain in your ankle from last week? One of your castoffs—Mr. Puntley—solicited me for a dance when you had to turn away your remaining suitors," she said with a twinkle in her eye.

Anna pulled her horse over to join Lydia's conversation as Phoebe answered. "I did not walk overmuch for two days and am now perfectly healed." She raised an eyebrow. "I'm glad Mr. Puntley was so quickly consoled."

Stratford watched in delight as Miss Daventry gave a peel of laughter. How inviting it sounded. "Oh yes, perfectly consoled," he heard her retort. "He used the entire dance to ply me with questions about Miss Phoebe Tunstall, and I had to disappoint him with my lack of knowledge."

Perhaps that can be remedied, thought Stratford. But Phoebe beat him to it with a prompt reply. "We shall have to spend more time together."

Best of sisters, he thought with a flash of gratitude. Stratford turned to Miss Daventry. "I see the exhaustion of late-night routs does not prevent you from getting your exercise in the morning."

"I need only a few hours' sleep to be restored, and I must always be doing something. I am quite a trial to my aunt." Miss Daventry's gaze darted to Lydia, who had begun to ride again, and the two parties naturally converged into one. "I'm not the only one, however. Lord Ingram was up at an unseasonable hour and had already left before we got to the stables. And of course the three of you are here as well." She glanced around the park. "It appears we are in small company."

Lydia called something to her companions and nudged her horse into a gallop, faster than the rules of the park would allow, but a rule broken by many in the early hours. Eleanor saw Major Fitzwilliam slide as his horse followed suit, but he quickly righted himself and matched her speed, apparently determined to keep pace.

Stratford raised an eyebrow. "Ladies?" That was all that was needed before the trailing party took off. The twins leapt ahead, and although Stratford would have liked to have ridden to the hounds, he was content to trail behind and enjoy the scenery, the fresh air, and Miss Daventry's company.

"You ride well," Stratford called out. "Who taught you?"

"The squire's son. My friend," she added, and he wondered just how close they were.

"Did your father keep horses? Your uncle?" He realized he didn't know what had happened to her father's estate.

"My father lost everything," she said, breathless from riding, her sparkling eyes making him think she had not been made to suffer from the loss. Or perhaps she put aside everything in the pleasure of the moment. He would take her out riding more often if he could see her look this buoyant.

At the end of Rotten Row, the head of the party wheeled about, and Stratford and Miss Daventry followed suit. As they rode the opposite way, his horse shied from a cat darting in front of it, forcing her horse closer to the fence. Startled, Stratford urged his roan forward to catch Miss Daventry's reins, but she already had the horse well in hand.

"Sorry. It was a cat," he said.

She flashed him a smile. "There was no harm done. Stardust is a good girl." She patted the mare's neck as she hugged the edge of the path, the other riders already well in the distance. Stratford was just about to suggest they move closer to the center when Eleanor cried out.

"*Ho!*" She pulled firmly on the reins, slowing her horse to a trot, then inexplicably sped up again.

"What is it?" Stratford followed as Miss Daventry galloped ahead, worried that something had spooked her horse. But she reined in and turned into an opening in the fence that separated the alley from the field and shady copse of beech trees. He followed, nonplussed.

"There's a man in the alleyway," she called out.

Backtracking through the field, she rode faster than he would have liked, weaving around the trees, and arriving at the spot parallel to where they had been moments before in the alley. Miss Daventry leapt off her horse, and he followed, grabbing his reins and hers and tying them around the branch of a nearby tree.

She hurried to one of the side alleys, breathless. "It's a man. I saw his legs as we were riding by." In a few steps she was upon the unconscious figure. "Oh, gracious." She sank to her knees. "It's Lord Ingram." He was perfectly immobile, and she scanned him for visible wounds.

Ripping off his gloves, Stratford felt the head for injury. His fingers came away red, and he sucked in his breath. "He's breathing, but he has a nasty blow to the head. He must have hit this rock here when he fell. Thank goodness it's not very sharp, and most of the impact would have been cushioned by the grass." He continued feeling his friend's limbs and shook his head. "His leg is broken. This is a bad business. Miss Daventry, can you—"

She jumped up and darted forward to grab the reins of her mare. "Yes, I will go fetch them. We must have their help, and Lydia needs to know."

Stratford moved to assist her to mount, but Miss Daventry climbed to a tree stump, leapt onto the horse, and was off. He returned to Ingram and took out his handkerchief to press to the head wound. Considering the matter, it looked as if the blood was still trickling out slowly, but that the injury was beginning to matte. The broken leg should not be difficult to set right, he decided. It was not lying at an odd angle like he'd seen in battle. Though it would be perverse to thank the experience that allowed him to keep his head in the matter, he reflected that he was not at all the green boy who had first gone to war.

Within moments, the others arrived, with Lydia last, pale with shock. She burst into tears as soon as she saw her brother, and a harassed-looking Mr. Braxsen tried to console her. The major was the first to reach the scene, and he immediately took command. "Here. Miss Daventry, Misses Tunstall . . ." He glanced at Braxsen and saw he had his hands full with Lydia. Turning his attention back to the others, he said, "Will you assist me in finding another branch like this?" Striding to a place beyond where the horses were, he picked up a solid branch with no twigs. "It must be straight like this, and no thinner."

The three ladies were quick to search further in the alley where there were more trees. Phoebe held one up. "Like this?"

"The very thing." Major Fitzwilliam had shed his coat. "It's still too cold out for him to remain uncovered. Worthing, can we use your coat to keep him warm? I will use mine to cushion his leg once it's set."

"Certainly." The task was accomplished with speed. When the two branches were ready, the major looked up again. "I need something to tie the branches in place. Have you a leather strap in your saddlebags? Or anything long enough that can be used for the purpose?" Everyone stood waiting for someone else to speak.

"I think . . . perhaps I can . . ." Miss Daventry, eyes on the ground, spoke in a barely audible voice. "I think I can help, but I need a knife or scissors of some sort."

No one came forward, and the spirits of the group were further dampened by the renewal of Lydia's tears. Matters might have remained like that, but relief came in an unlikely form.

"Hallo!" Lord Delacroix pulled up short at the sight of the inanimate body and the group that had congregated around it. "But what is this?" He looked at each face in astonishment.

Stratford thought it strange he would be riding alone at this hour and off the riding path, but he was the first to speak. "We were going for a run when Miss Daventry perceived Lord Ingram lying on the side of the road. He has some broken bones and is unconscious. We're attempting to find a solution to lift him."

Delacroix's horse sidestepped impatiently. "Allow me to ride and fetch a bolt of cloth so we can carry him. There's a cloth-maker not far from the park who will surely have large enough scraps that can be borrowed for the purpose. Or I will purchase them." He turned his horse around.

"I will reimburse your expenses," said Stratford, then called out, "Wait—" Delacroix turned back. "Have you a knife in your possession?"

"*Absolument.*" Le vicomte reached into his saddlebag, pulled out a hunting knife, handed it to Stratford, and rode off.

"So timely," Anna murmured. Stratford handed the knife to Miss Daventry, who went some ways into the wooded area and came back with a large swath of fabric in her hands that she had ripped into four strips. *The girl has sacrificed her shift*, Stratford thought with shock, and not a little admiration.

"This should serve the purpose," she said, and she gave it to Major Fitzwilliam. He made quick work of immobilizing the broken limb, and when Lord Delacroix returned not twenty minutes later, having had the foresight to bring ropes in addition to the textile, they transferred Lord Ingram to the woven cloth. Stratford, Fitz, and Delacroix crafted a hammock so Ingram's inanimate form could be carried, while the ladies led the horses at a sedate pace. Mr. Braxsen accompanied Lydia ahead of the rest to warn her mother, and since the Ingram residence was providentially situated closer than any other, there they went.

Chapter Twenty-Three

The surgeon had arrived at Grosvenor Square before his patient, and he stood by Lady Ingram as the small crowd jostled through the doorway.

"Softly now. Lift the legs higher as we go up the stairs." Major Fitzwilliam's voice rang out with authority.

Lady Ingram peered up the railing. "Stratford, how thankful I am you're here. I've sent Lydia to bed with a draught." She followed the party up the stairs. "Bring Lord Ingram to his bedroom, the first door on the right." Only a slight breathlessness gave hint to deeper emotions.

Miss Daventry was ready. She darted ahead of the group and swung the door wide open so they could carry Lord Ingram through as the doctor unbuttoned his coat and laid it over a chair. Major Fitzwilliam rapped out the orders. "There. Lay him down like this. Remove the cloth from under the shoulders here, and we'll ease it out from where his leg is broken. That's the trick."

The surgeon strode to the bedside with a word over his shoulder. "Everyone should leave the room except those who are most needed." He studied the bandages binding the broken leg and looked at the major. "This your work, sir?" When Major Fitzwilliam nodded, the doctor continued, "Well done. You might've saved his leg. It appears to be fractured in at least two places, and the ride home would have done considerable damage."

Major Fitzwilliam replied, "I've learned a few things on the field." He gave a slight bow to Lady Ingram and withdrew, joining Delacroix and Braxsen, Miss Daventry, and Stratford's sisters in the hallway.

The doctor felt for a pulse and then examined the contusion on the back of Ingram's head. Without taking her eyes off her son, Lady Ingram said, "Stratford, would you stay?"

At this, Stratford, who was at the door, paused. "Of course, my lady." They were both quiet as the doctor listened to Ingram's chest and examined the fracture. "I will not need to reset the leg. That soldier behaved with remarkable aplomb. Lady Ingram, in addition to the hot water, I'll need hot bricks to warm the patient. The timing of the discovery was fortunate. He would not have fared well out there in this cold. It's too early in the spring."

Lady Ingram repressed a shudder as she moved toward the door. When she opened it, the crowd outside dispersed, each with a mumbled excuse. With only the two men remaining, the doctor asked Stratford to recount exactly what had happened. When he'd finished, the doctor said, "Except for the nasty fall, this was a series of fortuitous events, beginning with Miss Daventry spotting something out of the ordinary, and culminating with Lord Delacroix arriving at just the right moment, able to secure the materials that were missing. Most fortuitous," he repeated.

Stratford watched him apply a poultice to the contusion. "Ah, excellent," the doctor said when Lady Ingram returned, trailed by a servant carrying hot bricks. He lifted the covers to place the bricks, and Lord Ingram moaned.

"That's it. We're just getting you more comfortable, my lord," the doctor said. "You'll be awake in a trice, although I don't doubt with a headache of sizable proportions." Turning to Lady Ingram, he said, "Who will be here to nurse the patient?"

"I will," said Lady Ingram. She signaled for the footman to leave.

"It will be too much of a trial for one person alone. I suggest at least one other with whom you might share the vigil." The doctor looked at the earl. "You're close to the family, I presume?"

"Yes, I will make myself available as often as I can," Stratford assured the doctor. He watched him return his tools to his bag, then turned to Lady Ingram. "Might I also suggest Miss Daventry as someone who can assist. She behaved with great presence of mind this morning."

Lady Ingram, distracted, only nodded. She waited for the doctor to put his coat back on and said, "I'll require specific instructions regarding medicine and anything that needs to be done."

Stratford took his leave, inclining his head to the surgeon. "I must see that my sisters are brought home. I will receive my directives from Lady Ingram."

When he went downstairs, Lord Delacroix and Major Fitzwilliam were gone, and Miss Daventry looked slightly less pale. The tea service had been brought, and she was sitting with Anna and Phoebe, each with a cup of hot tea in her hands. Miss Daventry gestured to an empty chair. "Won't you please sit, my lord?"

Stratford was anxious to seek out the major and gain his thoughts on what might have happened to Frederick, and see if he'd had any luck from having Delacroix and Conolly followed. Perhaps Delacroix's presence this morning was not quite so innocent, although it would not do to rush judgment. He was about to decline the offer to stay when he saw his sisters had barely begun their tea. It would be unfair to rush them off like that. "Thank you," he said, and sat opposite Miss Daventry.

"Would you like a cup of tea? Or . . . something stronger?" Miss Daventry seemed uncertain of herself, playing hostess in a home that was not her own. Lady Ingram would be occupied for as long as Ingram was incapacitated, and who knew when Lydia would rouse herself from her fit of vapors. *I should be more charitable*, Stratford thought. Lydia's father had died from a fall while horseback riding.

"Tea suits me fine, thank you." Stratford sat, taking the cup of tea from Miss Daventry's hands that betrayed only the slightest tremor. *Good girl*, he thought. *Lydia cannot appear to advantage beside Miss Daventry's calm competence.* After sipping the tea, he said, "I told Lady Ingram you'd be the best person to share the vigil during Ingram's convalescence."

"I was hoping I might be able to share the burden. I will do so most willingly." Miss Daventry set her cup on the side table and folded her hands on her lap.

Anna turned to her brother. "Did the doctor say when Lord Ingram will wake?"

"Before I left, he showed some signs of consciousness," Stratford said. "Well, enough to elicit a moan when the doctor handled him. I imagine he'll be in a great deal of pain, but the doctor left a heavy sedative for when he's awake enough to drink it. In the meantime, the surgeon is not so worried about his head wound. He thinks it's superficial and that the shock of pain is what's keeping him from waking up."

"Whatever came of Ingram's horse?" Phoebe asked.

"Major Fitzwilliam promised to look into it and see if he can find more clues as to what happened," Stratford replied.

Miss Daventry sighed. "That's a relief. I can't think why he would have been out at such an hour. It's rare for him to leave the house before breakfast. I would ask Lydia, but I'm afraid of causing her more pain by having her relive the incident."

"Ingram will recover from his fall. As soon as Lydia sees it's not the same situation as her father, her frame of mind will be restored," Stratford replied.

Phoebe shuddered. "I remember the funeral. It was the first time any of our friends suffered such a loss, although who knew at the time that Mama would go that very year. I don't envy Lydia for suffering the grief of the same accident twice."

Stratford swallowed his tea. "Lydia was gay enough when she came home from school the following Christmas. She does not have a long memory for troubles, I assure you." This was met with indignant protests on all three sides.

Miss Daventry was the first to defend her friend. "She may seem to move on quickly, but the same forgetfulness applies to remembering her friends' faults, my lord." She pressed her lips together, adding, "I knew her those months at school, and I assure you, her grief was deeply felt. I would not have her suffer this for the world."

Chastised, Stratford shook his head. "Nor I." He remembered the charge laid on Ingram to fill his father's shoes, a task he was only now beginning to understand. Any support Ingram might have gained at his young age, to assist him in stepping into the role, had been stolen by Lydia's rather dramatic outpouring of grief that had seemed to disappear as soon as it came. Stratford took a breath and spoke. "Perhaps I am severe with her as an older brother might be. I've known Lydia her whole life. But I've a great deal of affection for her and wish her no misery." This disclosure was met with silence.

Stratford, sensing that his impatience with Lydia's weakness had put him on shaky ground with Miss Daventry, desisted. "Please inform Lady Ingram I will return after supper to learn how I can be of use."

The three women stood, and as Phoebe and Anna collected their affairs, Stratford bowed over Miss Daventry's hand. He had better done to have kept quiet, but he admired the way she leapt to her friend's defense.

When he lifted his head, he met her steady gaze. It would be something to have such loyalty turned toward him.

Eleanor remained in the drawing room after everyone left. She poured herself a fresh cup of tea and leaned back on the settee. Looking down at her shoes, she realized with a start that she had neither changed her muddy shoes for clean ones, nor had she exchanged her riding habit, now minus a slip, for something more decent. She had given no thought to the fact that she'd paraded around in a dress that was practically see-through.

It gave a different shade of meaning to Lord Delacroix's constant regard on their ride home. He had looked her over like a filly at the market every time he thought her head was turned. She set her teacup down, and it clattered on the saucer. Here was someone she aimed never to cross paths with again, and he had come into the house where she was staying. She hoped he would not consider it his introduction to their society.

Lord Worthing, on the other hand, was more likely to seek out her gaze. She remembered his eyes lifted to hers when he took his leave, apologetic, she thought, for having been impatient with Lydia. He did not always begin by grace, she noticed, and had been hard on Lydia as one he'd known nearly all his life.

But then he is most sincere in his apologies. This brought an unexpected smile to her face.

Lord Worthing had surprised her on their walk to town the other day, all but admitting the words he'd doused her with after their waltz at Almack's had been fickle and indifferent. Another man would have thought it too insignificant to mention. The truth was, he *had* been in her black books, and she'd been ready to put all thoughts of him from her mind forever. Clearly she'd been mistaken in thinking his growing feelings matched her own. But then . . .

I admire you, Miss Daventry . . . the rich timbre of his voice, the warmth of his arm next to hers.

She set her teacup on the table and stood, too jumpy to remain idle. Despite all her worries for Lord Ingram and Lydia, her heart felt like air. She must see what Lady Ingram needed. And for heaven's sake, she must change this dress.

Chapter Twenty-Four

Frederick Ingram woke at his usual time the next morning and, as predicted, with his full mental faculties. He was startled to see Miss Daventry standing at the window of his room and looking out. When he tried to move, he swore under his breath. "Miss Daventry," he said, then cleared his throat and attempted it again. "Miss Daventry, whatever are you doing in my room unchaperoned, and what *in the devil*—Sorry. That is to say, what has happened to me?"

"You had a nasty fall, my lord. Do you remember riding in Hyde Park yesterday morning?" She hurried to his nightstand to pour a glass of water.

"Yes, of course, I . . . I wanted to take Melody for a run. She had not been out. We were about to clear the wooded area and return to the pathway, and that's the last thing I remember." He frowned, then groaned as a fresh wave of pain hit him.

"Here, sir. You must drink this. The doctor has left it behind, and you will feel much more comfortable." Miss Daventry brought the paregoric draught to him, along with the glass of water, and he drank obediently.

"How did I come to fall? Who saw it?" Ingram felt his limbs with his free hand and gave a sharp intake of breath. "My leg. It appears to be broken."

"Yes, my lord. The doctor said Major Fitzwilliam set it beautifully, and it will mend in a trice." She sat at the side of the bed.

"Fitzwilliam. So he was there, was he? A good fellow . . ." Lord Ingram fell silent, lost in rumination.

Miss Daventry ventured, "Would you like me to fetch Lady Ingram for you?"

"No, stay a moment. How came you to be nursing me? Has my family used you shockingly?" He looked at her with amusement, but his brows were furrowed with pain. "And was it Major Fitzwilliam who found me in the park?"

"I'm here because I volunteered." Miss Daventry's gaze fell. "Well, Lord Worthing volunteered my services, but it was the very thing I wished to do."

"Stratford!" Ingram lifted his eyebrows a fraction, then groaned. "I have the devil of a headache. So Stratford is involved too? The mystery deepens."

"Yes, I was with Lord Worthing." She stopped and cleared her throat. "I mean, we were all together. I was with Lydia and Major Fitzwilliam— oh, and Mr. Braxsen. And we met, quite by accident, Lord Worthing and his sisters in the park."

"Mr. Braxsen . . ." Ingram said. "Go on."

"The major galloped ahead of everyone with Lydia—"

"Major Fitzwilliam matching strides with Lydia? That must have been a merry chase." Ingram's lips quivered.

"Lord Ingram, will you please stop funning. I begin to believe your head injury is worse than the doctor feared."

Ingram folded his free arm over the other. "I promise to be a perfect listener."

"The major and Lydia galloped ahead," Miss Daventry repeated, "with Lord Worthing's sisters not far behind. I . . . I did not care to gallop just yet, and Lord Worthing was content to remain at my side." Here Ingram swallowed a laugh, and she glared at him until he stopped. "Finally, we reached the end of the row, and when we turned, something caught my eye—the legs of a man, partly concealed in the bushes. I didn't know who it was, but I rode around the fence with Lord Worthing to find out."

"And it was me," Ingram concluded. "And my horse? What became of her?"

"She hadn't returned to the stables, so after you were brought in, your groom went out to look for her and found her with her reins tangled in a tree branch further in the wooded area. She had no injury, my lord." Miss Daventry studied him, and he suddenly felt weary, all traces of humor gone. "Shall I tell your mother you're awake? She has been most anxious."

"Stay." Ingram took her arm in a weak grasp. "I'm feeling tired. You can fetch my mother, but tell me first. Was there anyone else in the park when this happened?"

"No one, sir. Only . . . Lord Delacroix came down the path moments later." Miss Daventry seemed to struggle within herself. "He was most helpful. He had a knife in his saddlebag that we were able to use to create strips of linen to tie your leg—Major Fitzwilliam did that—and Lord Delacroix offered to procure the bolt of fabric with which to carry you. He even remembered the ropes." She did not meet his gaze.

"And Stratford was there for all this? For Delacroix's arrival?"

"Yes," said Miss Daventry. "Both Lord Worthing and Lord Delacroix assisted in carrying you. Lord Delacroix offered to take charge if Stratford should wish to ride ahead to ready your household, but Lord Worthing said he would on no account leave you, and he sent Mr. Braxsen and your sister to do it."

Ingram nodded. *Trust Stratford to see to everything. He will follow up if there's a lead where Delacroix is concerned. His appearance was too smoky by half.* "My thanks. Tell my mother to come. Although—" he yawned. "I don't promise to be awake when she arrives."

As he had warned Eleanor, Lord Ingram was sound asleep when his mother came into the room. "Asleep," she exclaimed, turning to Eleanor. "Why did you not fetch me the moment he awoke?"

Eleanor responded quietly. "I would have. He did not permit it. He wanted to know exactly what happened to him first, so I gave him all the details in my possession."

Lady Ingram's gaze returned to her son, who emitted a small snore, which seemed to reassure her. "Thank you, Eleanor. That will be all."

Eleanor left the room and paused with her hand on the bannister, wondering if it were too early to wake Lydia. Before she turned to go, Hartsmith, Lord Ingram's butler, called to her from the end of the corridor and started forward. He said, "My lady has informed me that Lord Ingram was awake. Might I ask you to pass a message to him from me?"

Eleanor's brow creased. "Lord Ingram has taken a sedative and is asleep again. Why could you not have spoken to Lady Ingram if you wished to see him?"

Hartsmith ignored the question. "Miss Daventry, I ask that you inform me when he awakens again. If possible, before he has taken his sedative and without Lady Ingram's knowledge."

He saw her confusion and added, "I assure you it's nothing of a dubious nature, but only what he would wish me to do himself. Something has occurred that Lord Ingram foresaw as a possibility, and he expressed his desire for the household to remain unconcerned with the details. As you and Lady Ingram have taken over his nursing, and Lord Ingram was very specific about Lady Ingram remaining in total ignorance on the matter, I ask that you notify me as soon as he is awake again. I believe if you mention I wish to see him on the private matter we discussed, you will find he is eager to receive me."

Eleanor could not find fault with his request if Lord Ingram were indeed willing, although she could not like doing anything without Lady Ingram's knowledge. But surely, if Lord Ingram approved there could be no cause to worry. "I will let you know once he is awake," she promised.

She went into Lydia's room and found her with swollen eyes, lying in near darkness. "I told you to get out," Lydia yelled. Then, with a sniff, she added, "Please."

"Lydia, it is I. You must get up and stop torturing your well-meaning servants." Eleanor strode across the room and opened the curtains. "Your brother is fine. He woke up this morning." She turned and offered her friend a tired smile.

Lydia threw off the covers and sat up. "He woke up? Let me go see him." She scrambled to put on her slippers before Eleanor stopped her.

"No, he awoke, but the draught the doctor had him take has put him out again. There's no sense in rushing to his side. Your mother is there. What I think you need is a good cup of tea and something in your stomach." Eleanor walked over to the bed. "I'm going to call your maid to assist you. Unless you've sent them all packing."

"I couldn't bear to have people talk to me," Lydia said with a sniff. "I was so worried."

Eleanor gave her friend a hug. "I understand. And now you see you have no further cause to be. Come, let us eat something." She reached for the bell.

When Lydia had seen for herself that her brother was sleeping and didn't look so pale as he had yesterday, she was ready to partake of a late breakfast and made a good appetite of it. Ingram had even mumbled in protest when she got too loud to "stop her yammering and let a body sleep." Thus reassured, and at the urging of her mother, she and Eleanor left for the modiste to collect the latest gowns she had ordered. "A return to your routine will do you good, and it will quell any rumors," her mother had said.

They exited the shop into the noonday sun with Lydia carrying three bandboxes. The footman took them from her and stowed them in the waiting carriage. He opened the door, but their departure was stayed by someone calling their names.

"Miss Daventry, Miss Ingram. Just the ones I wished to see. May I inquire how your brother is faring?" Lord Carlton was breathless, having rushed out of Brooke's, where he must have spied them from within.

"So you know about that, do you?" Lydia pressed her lips together.

"I'm afraid it cannot be helped. His . . . he was carried up Park Lane, and it's impossible to dampen people's curiosity—"

"Vulgar!" interjected Lydia with a stamp of her foot. "People only care about the latest on-dit."

"I don't deny it," protested Lord Carlton. "However, Lord Ingram is very well liked, and people in the club want to know how he goes on."

After a pause, Lydia softened. "He was awake this morning. I thank you for your concern."

"Will he make a full recovery, then?" Lord Carlton beamed at them both. "That would be good news indeed."

Eleanor answered on Lydia's behalf. "He seemed to be in good spirits when I spoke with him earlier."

"I don't dare ask if you will attend Mrs. Drewmont's assembly." This was directed at Eleanor. Lydia could barely contain her impatience to be off and took a step toward the waiting conveyance.

"I'm afraid we're not entering society at present," returned Eleanor, with a gentle nod to Lord Carlton. Eleanor followed Lydia into the carriage and watched through the window as Lord Carlton continued down the street with a frown.

Stratford sat at the table at White's that always seemed to be waiting for him when he arrived. He was tired, having volunteered—no, insisted—on taking the night shift with Ingram until Miss Daventry had relieved him at dawn, fresh and welcome in the morning sunlight. The long night had left him alone with his thoughts as he tried to piece the clues together. Yes, Delacroix continued to have a run of bad luck, and though he was mistrusted by some, there were others who took him up. According to Fitz, following Delacroix and Conolly so far had come up with nothing.

Fitz had also gone back to search the area and found nothing by way of clues. He knew what Ingram had been doing that morning but didn't feel at liberty to disclose it without Ingram's specific permission. "Even though," Fitz added, "he told me he'd taken you into complete confidence." Stratford wondered how he would get to the bottom of all this without being able to talk it over with Ingram.

"Worthing." At hearing himself addressed, Stratford looked up, surprised at seeing someone he knew only by half. *The rival.*

"Hallo, Carlton." He saw that the gentleman lingered, so he added, "Will you be seated?"

"I think I will. Thank you." Lord Carlton nodded when Stratford lifted the carafe in front of him, and he pushed the spare glass forward. When he had taken a sip, Carlton settled in more comfortably. "It's a dashed business, Lord Ingram taking a spill the way he did. I understand his father went off in the same way." He looked up with a self-assured smile, which fell when he saw Stratford's implacable expression. "You'll think I'm overly familiar. Forgive me. I've just run into Miss Daventry and Miss Ingram."

Stratford was surprised to hear they had gone out and beat back an impulse to ask where. "No one likes to hear of ill-luck trailing the people we know," he answered instead. "Fortunately in this case, the doctor thinks he'll only have to deal with a broken leg. It could have been much worse. But, of course, we'll only know when he wakes up." Stratford refilled his own glass and crossed one leg over the other.

"Is it possible you don't know?" asked Carlton in, what seemed to Stratford, the most provoking tone.

"Know what?" Stratford's words were as curt as politeness allowed.

"Lord Ingram has already awakened. Miss Daventry and Miss Ingram just told me."

Stratford sighed, feeling the weight of the long night's vigil. He was relieved at the news but impatient to end the interview with the messenger. "That is indeed good news. Is Miss Ingram about town then? When I saw her last, she was taken to her room."

"I think Miss Daventry must have convinced her," Lord Carlton said. "She's a rare gun. It seems like nothing will send her reaching for the smelling salts."

Stratford, remembering her sangfroid in face of discovering her host's inanimate form, and her willingness to sacrifice her own undergarments, nodded silently. She had been nearly blue with cold by the time they reached the townhouse, and though he wished to cover her or rush her home quickly, he couldn't leave Ingram.

"Actually—" Lord Carlton let out a nervous chuckle, "there's a reason I wanted to speak with you today and am glad to find we are quite private." He looked around the room at the few tables, which were occupied in its various corners, none near theirs.

"Oh?" Worthing raised an eyebrow, a silent bid for him to continue. Or desist, for a man of lesser courage.

"You see, I've come to form an attachment for Miss Daventry." Lord Carlton met Stratford's gaze briefly, then looked away. "I have come to see in her the virtues that would exactly suit me in a wife. She shows courage to defend those who are less fortunate. Her intellect is not to be despised, and she shows a fine understanding on every topic on which we converse. And her smile, well . . ." He gave a boyish laugh. "You don't care to hear about all that. I don't think I need to convince you that I can offer her a good name and a comfortable living. But if you'd like to discuss the particulars, I can have my lawyer meet yours—"

Stratford could stand it no longer. "Good God, man. What are you about? Why ever are you telling all this to me?"

Lord Carlton looked up, startled, and for the first time, unsure of himself. "Why, you're her guardian. Lady Jersey said so herself. Naturally I must approach you."

"As Lady Jersey knows full-well I am no such thing, you must have misunderstood. It was my uncle, the *Fourth* Earl of Worthing, who was her guardian. I'm nothing to her." Stratford reached for the carafe, only to realize both glasses were untouched.

Lord Carlton leaned forward and gripped his cane. His ears were red. "Might you know to whom I may address my suit?"

"To the lady herself," Stratford replied with a bitter edge. Then, forcing his voice to be steady, "She is, as you know, under the protection of Lord Ingram for the season. I can't imagine Miss Daventry's aunt will oppose such a suit as yours, and Lady Ingram has undertaken to see her suitably wed."

After a pause, he added quietly, "I imagine your suit will prosper."

Chapter Twenty-Five

Two days had passed since his meeting with Carlton, and each time Stratford had presented himself at the Ingram house to offer his help, he was thanked and told his service was not needed now that Ingram was out of danger. He'd not set eyes on Ingram himself, as Frederick had been sleeping both times. Stratford set out for another attempt, this time on foot, being in no mood to drive in a crowded roadway, which would require a patience and restraint he did not have. His set face was hidden under the low brim of his hat, and soon, the quiet *clip, clip* of his boots drowned out the bustling metropole.

The lack of something concrete to put his mind to, concerning Ingram and his assailant, only meant Stratford had more time on his hands to think. This turned out to be a less-than-happy circumstance since his thoughts these days were increasingly laced with bitterness. So she had caught Carlton's fancy, had she? Of course. Now she'd have exactly what she wanted. A man who would marry her for love. That was what she'd said, wasn't it? Of all the hazy bits of conversation he could drag from the recesses of his alcohol-soaked subconscious, he remembered those words, clear as a bell. "I want to marry for love."

If only Stratford hadn't revealed any of his own feelings for Miss Daventry. He didn't like to be taken for a fool. How could he have mistaken her regard for him? How could he have underestimated her feelings for Carlton? Fuming, he ignored a peer's attempt to greet him. *Well, if you're willing to take a husband who's still wet around the ears, I suppose he's a choice candidate. I wish you happy, Miss Daventry.*

He couldn't blame Carlton for taking a shine to her, though. The way she spoke her mind challenged one to be a better man. She was unflinchingly loyal, generous to those she loved, forgiving . . .

She might not be pretty in the classical sense, but she was comely to him. Her eyes held a certain understanding to them. Then there was the way her nose turned up. And when she smiled at a person, everything came to life. Those laughing eyes, the dimples that would always look like she was plotting mischief. A tidy figure that invited you to steal an arm around her waist—

Stratford's steps faltered as that thought flooded his senses.

I'm thinking about another man's soon-to-be-wife, Stratford chided himself. He walked on, furious with himself for this weakness. She may have wanted to marry for love, but that calf-stage was over for him. He would not be such a fool again. He walked on, plunged in thought, remembering her pert expression and challenging words—*It may not be Christian of me, but I should like to think it over before I decide*—and laughed softly.

He'd been sullen when they dined together. He insulted her when he proposed to her. He mangled his apology. And even at Almack's, he'd bungled it further by comparing her to one of his sisters. Then again . . . there was the pull of attraction when they'd waltzed together, and her glowing reaction when he said he admired her. Maybe he'd misjudged the situation. Maybe she didn't care for Carlton at all.

And if she didn't care for Carlton, it meant he still had a chance.

Stratford felt a sudden need to see for himself and quickened his pace to Grosvenor Square. Perhaps she was at home at that moment. In any case, he must call and find out how Ingram was doing and give him what little news they had. When he ran up the short stairwell and rang the bell, he heard it chime inside, followed by the muted footsteps of the butler coming to answer the door.

"Ah, Lord Worthing," the butler said, as stately as if Stratford had not once been his master's childhood friend of little consequence. There were noises in the stairwell when he entered, and he looked up to see the object of his rumination. Miss Daventry came downstairs in a walking dress the color of her eyes. He caught her gaze, and her steps stilled for a moment, her lips quivering on the edge of a smile. She looked glad to see him.

Lydia was on the bottom step and held out her hand, which he took as he bowed. "Stratford, have you come to see Ingram? He's awake, but he chased us out of the room, so we've decided to go to Hyde Park."

Stratford nodded. "Yes, I've come to see him." Turning to Miss Daventry, he searched for a hint of what she was feeling, wondering if her heart could still be won. "Have you anyone to escort you to the park?" he asked. "I will undertake to do so, willingly."

"Did you not wish to see Fred?" Lydia asked. He had. *Good grief. Where had his wits gone begging?*

The door to the drawing room opened, and Lord Carlton stepped out with Major Fitzwilliam. "Worthing—you, here!" Carlton said, and took his place at Miss Daventry's side. "Came to see Ingram for yourself, did you?"

"I did." Stratford set his lips in a firm line and turned to Lydia. "You said he's awake now?"

"He is, though who knows for how long. He's in pain, and it will soon be time for his sedative. Shall we wait for you then, Stratford?" Lydia pulled her gloves on and peered up at him.

"I see you are both in good hands, and I will only be in the way. Good day, gentlemen. Miss Daventry." He turned quickly and climbed the stairs, not sparing a second glance toward the departing group.

"Miss Daventry, you look a picture," Lord Carlton said. Stratford, gripping the railing, did not hear her reply.

Ingram was lying in bed, a dull look in his eyes as he stared out the window. His valet was at his side, reading out loud from the morning paper. When Stratford came in the room, Ingram sent his valet away and told him to dissuade his mother from entering since he would surely be asleep once his friend had left.

Stratford clasped his hand on Ingram's shoulder. "I'm mighty glad to see you awake. You look much more the thing than you did when I left you three days ago." A fresh wave of pain came over Ingram's features, and Stratford sat. "Easy now. How's the pain?"

"It's fine," Ingram returned, not convincingly. "Tell me if you've discovered anything. What have you been about since we last spoke?"

"Nothing to the purpose. Fitz and I are still looking. No footprints, no forgotten objects, nothing out of the ordinary. Delacroix showed up, just like that."

"So I was told." Ingram met Stratford's gaze. "He's the one to watch, I think. I put Fitz on him." Stratford nodded.

After a minute of silence, Ingram continued. "Hartsmith came to see me when I woke up with news that there had been a break-in in my library the same night I was attacked."

Stratford's brows shot upward. "I should stay here," he started to say, before realizing it was impossible. He could not leave his own sisters unattended.

Ingram smiled and shook his head. "Hartsmith is clever. He left nothing of value in the library and barred the door leading to the rest of the rooms. I suspected my house might one day be a target, and he was cautious after I was attacked. I had him send for Fitz to apprise him of the situation. The net will tighten, and one day our man will grow careless."

Stratford chewed his lip. "Any idea what he was searching for?"

"I know precisely what he was after," Ingram said. "It was the report I was sending to Le Marchant with troop and supply details, although I cannot figure out how anyone could be aware I was carrying it when only two other people knew of its existence."

"Who were those two people?" Stratford asked.

"Le Marchant and Fitz," Ingram replied. "Le Marchant would have no reason to intercept his own courier, and Fitz would draw too much attention to himself by attempting it, besides the fact of it being so very out of his character. I'm convinced of his innocence."

"Strange to say on so little acquaintance, but so am I," Stratford said. "And let us hope it is so because he's currently escorting your sister to Hyde Park."

"He persists with Lydia, does he?" Ingram chuckled. "To each his own folly."

"So someone intercepted the report." Stratford puzzled over this mystery. "Do you think the attacker meant you real harm?"

Ingram thought for a minute. "I don't know. He could have finished the job and chose not to. Or he could have thought the fall enough to do the trick. Or he could have been interrupted. It's anyone's guess. But I must correct your supposition. He does not have the report. I slipped an envelope with a false document in my coat pocket by way of precaution, which is what was stolen. The true report was in the saddlebag, where it was found when Melody was brought back to the stable."

"That makes me think the spy was either interrupted or an amateur. No one takes the first paper one finds without giving further search." Stratford got up when he saw Ingram put his hand to his head.

"I've the devil of a headache," muttered Ingram.

"I'll get you your draught." Stratford went to the table and stirred the medicine into a glass of water and then brought it to him.

"Time will tell." Ingram took the glass and swallowed its contents. "The fact that the man broke into my library last night shows he's close enough to our operations to have suspected the document was a fake. I had Fitz add a watch over our house as well as headquarters in case he tries again. Fitz'll escort my sister to the park, but the watch will be in place before nightfall. He's not a man to be distracted."

Stratford sat back. "It's a good plan." He stayed quiet for only a moment before he could hold back no longer on what else had been occupying his thoughts. "I've just received a request from Lord Carlton to address Miss Daventry. He was here when I arrived, ready to walk out with her." Stratford lifted an eyebrow.

"Ho! What's this? That greenhead? Can he be old enough to wed?" Stratford said nothing, and Ingram continued reflectively. "Our Miss Daventry, hmm? He'll make a fair enough husband for her. No debts that I'm aware of."

"No," Stratford said, shortly.

When he said no more, Ingram eyed him shrewdly. "You sent him about his business, didn't you?"

"Told 'im he had the wrong earl," Stratford said.

Ingram laughed robustly, which then elicited a groan. "You must use me more kindly. I'm forbidden from finding humor in anything."

"And I, it seems," said Stratford, "from finding joy."

His cryptic words were perfectly understood by his friend. "So that's the way of it, is it? She may yet turn him down." Ingram's kind tone caused Stratford to scowl.

He rubbed at the leather on the armchair, alternating between hope that Miss Daventry might have kept her heart for him, though he'd done little to deserve it, and despair that he'd been too slow and had lost her forever. The silence stretched before Ingram broke it.

"I need your help, Stratford." Ingram had the slightest slur to his words, but he waited until Stratford looked at him fully. "I need someone to escort my mother, sister, and Miss Daventry to the social functions until I'm fully recovered. Someone attacked me, and until we find out who it was and what their intention was, I don't want my family to be in any danger. They probably aren't, but I must be certain. I can think of no one better than you. Will you do it?

"I know——" Ingram continued when he saw Stratford's look of alarm. "You have your hands full already. But all they need is one male presence to keep an eye on them as they attend the assemblies. It's well known that you're a close friend to the family, and no one will think twice if you are the one to do it."

Stratford sighed. "Of course. You may count on me."

Ingram chuckled at Stratford's tone, a sleepy laugh. "If you had thought to escape to Worthing, you must surely know by now you won't make good your escape as long as your own sisters are having their Season. You must cut your losses and surrender to your fate."

"I've accepted it, believe me." The two men sat in silence. "Now I presume Carlton will be glued to our party. I don't suppose he can pull the thing off," Stratford said, flickering his eyes to Ingram's face.

"No," Ingram said, eyes closed, the corners of his mouth lifting. "I don't think he will." His words gave Stratford hope.

After a minute, Ingram drifted off. He jerked awake again, and seemed to be struggling to follow a train of thought before saying, "Fitz has access everywhere, but people will say to you what they won't say to him. Though your peerage is recent, your friendships are not. When I go out, I'm listening to conversation as gentlemen play cards and when they gather in the clubs. I hear things that help me piece together my intelligence. Stratford," he yawned and closed his eyes again, murmuring, "I need someone who can do that in my place."

Stratford leaned over and placed a hand on Ingram's shoulder. "You know you may safely rely on me."

Chapter Twenty-Six

*L*ydia placed her hand in Major Fitzwilliam's arm as he directed his steps toward Hyde Park, with Lord Carlton and Eleanor following suit. It was the fashionable hour, and streams of people strolled in the same direction, but there was no one they knew to disturb their peace.

"Miss Ingram," the major began, "I wanted very much to come to you before, but I was detained by military business. You seem to be at peace. Are you reassured regarding your brother's recovery?"

Lydia fixed her eyes on a distant point. "You must have thought me terribly vaporish, but you see, my father died falling from his horse, and all I could think of was that I would lose my brother too. I suppose I also feared we'd be turned out of our home because, at present, the person set to inherit is a third cousin with whom we are not at all acquainted. I feared a drastic reversal of our fortunes."

Major Fitzwilliam hesitated before asking, "Does the thought wear on you so? To be without fortune?"

She followed his lead as he sidestepped a group of women gathering, and she could hear snatches of conversation from Eleanor and Lord Carlton behind them. "No. You might not think it for all I seem to care about balls, routs, and parties. But that's not what matters most."

If she expected Major Fitzwilliam to ask her what *did* matter most, she was disappointed. Although she was not sure she'd know how to answer him if he had. There was some vague longing for safety and security, and a home where there was laughter. This was what she sought. Major Fitzwilliam seemed to pull her closer, though she wasn't sure whether she'd imagined it.

After walking a short distance in silence, Major Fitzwilliam said, "You're a beautiful woman, Miss Ingram."

She felt the sharp knife of disappointment that such predictable words should come from him. "With a fortune," she added. "Quite the catch."

He looked at her in surprise, his brows furrowed. "I had not finished my thought. I've never been a man who flusters easily, but around you . . ." His voice trailed away, and in the ensuing silence, Lydia's heart beat strangely. She thought of how Major Fitzwilliam commanded every room he was in, but around her he faltered?

Major Fitzwilliam continued. "Had I completed my thought more quickly, I would've added that it's your spirit that animates your beauty, and your goodness and loyalty that makes it timeless. I imagine what matters to you most must be that which ignites those qualities in you." He put his warm, gloved hand over hers and caught her gaze until she held her breath in anticipation of his next words. "Miss Ingram, it is my increasing ambition to discover what that is."

Eleanor and Lord Carlton followed in the major's wake, conversing about inconsequential subjects until they reached the park. He seemed to be in high humor and in no hurry either to meet up with acquaintances or to get her alone. The troubling suspicion that he might try and declare himself began to subside as he followed Major Fitzwilliam and Lydia toward the green.

"I'm sorry I won't be able to attend Almack's Wednesday night." Lord Carlton broke off to wave to a gentleman hailing from across the road. "I'd hoped I might ask you to save me a waltz, but my uncle is in town—my former guardian, though he forgets his role has ended—and he requested I attend to him that evening."

"I understand perfectly, Lord Carlton. Of course you must go. Is your mother enjoying improved health?" They stopped behind the major, who had paused to shake hands with Mr. Braxsen and another soldier.

"I fear my mother never enjoys what you might call robust health. Mr. Braxsen—" Lord Carlton broke off to greet him in turn.

When Major Fitzwilliam and Lydia moved forward, Lord Carlton resumed. "My mother desires to meet you and has commissioned me to invite you to dine with us before the theatre on Saturday night. I've even brought you a formal invitation." He slid a white sealed envelope partway out of his coat pocket. "I will keep it for you whilst we are out walking."

"She honors me," Eleanor replied. "When we return to Grosvenor Square, it won't take me but a minute to write her a reply if you'll be so kind as to take it to her from me."

"Most certainly." Lord Carlton beamed. "She'll be delighted by your acceptance. Cecily, too. She quite looks up to you, you know, and relies on your accounts of the balls, which she longs to attend. She must wait a year to make her debut since my aunt is her chaperone, and my cousin won't be brought out until next year."

"It's hard to wait for one's Season when you're too old for the school-room but not yet out. Men don't understand such constraints and cannot know how much it chafes." As she spoke, she took in the green landscape before her, grateful these few weeks afforded her a brief respite from such constraint.

"I would not wish to contradict a lady," Lord Carlton replied, "but men can understand impatience. When one wishes, for instance, to go off and fight or see a bit of the world and cannot, we are forced to accept our lot. My father told me about the Grand Tour, once considered *de rigueur* for all gentlemen, and which is not possible now with the war . . . Then there are sick mothers and younger sisters and responsibilities that fall on a person like a weight." His pace quickened without his seeming aware of it, and Eleanor struggled to keep up.

"This," Lord Carlton concluded, "is the lot of men who cannot do quite what they would wish."

Eleanor felt a pity she'd not thought possible for any gentleman who had enough to live on and the freedom to come and go as he pleased. "If you could do anything you wished, what might it be?" She turned her head and looked him fully in the face, despite the large rim of her poke bonnet.

When their eyes met, Lord Carlton's look changed, and he opened his mouth to speak. Fearing what was coming, Eleanor whipped her head forward again, and at that moment, the major turned back to speak to them. "We are contemplating taking this path and exiting the park on the southern side. What say you?"

Lord Carlton answered in a hearty voice. "That sounds excellent. Lead on." The moment was lost, and Eleanor was relieved to see he did not speak words she was not ready to hear.

"If I cannot go off and fight," he said, instead, "and I think I really cannot leave my mother and sister without someone to fend for them, I should like to go into politics."

"Politics. You'll be the first person of my acquaintance to pursue it. Have you someone to sponsor you? From my limited understanding, this is something necessary." Eleanor was ready to latch on to any safe subject.

"Lady Jersey has been a friend to our family since I was born. She was the one who put the idea in my mind and caused me to turn to this field of study at Oxford. She's spoken of it to me since, but I cannot turn my mother warm to the idea of it."

"That seems constraining, indeed," Eleanor said.

"Perhaps you can convince her of its wisdom when you come for dinner," Lord Carlton said, cheered.

Eleanor turned toward him, eyes wide. "I have no business influencing her ladyship on *any* topic. I wouldn't be so ill-mannered as to attempt it."

Lord Carlton placed his hand over hers and gave it a pat. "I hope you may one day feel that it's your place to do so." His words were laden with significance, and Eleanor's discomposure increased.

"When did you start telling fortunes?" She strove for a light tone, pulling her hand away. "I hardly know what I may be tomorrow, much less 'one day.' I wish you will not say such things."

"Eleanor, you are not so changing—" Lord Carlton stopped short.

He had used her Christian name, which revealed his intentions as clearly as if he had spoken them. Eleanor walked quickly, trying to break the spell before he could speak whilst she knew so little of her own heart. Lord Carlton was handsome and kind, and with him she would gain a sense of family and a stable household. Beyond the comfort of security, however, he elicited no feelings in her. He was just one friendly face among others. Was security, alone, enough?

She veered toward the small lake, forcing a cheerful tone. "Oh, here are the swans. Shall we go and feed them? I've a ha'pence for the bread."

Chapter Twenty-Seven

Lady Ingram poured tea into three cups and directed the footman to bring one to her daughter and the other to Eleanor. She moved with brisk gestures and, when she had taken a sip of tea, launched into her objective without preamble.

"Eleanor, Lord Carlton has asked permission to address you, and I've given it. I must say, I'm surprised you've caught his fancy out of all the other debutantes, but you appear to have done so. I wish you happy."

Eleanor almost choked on her tea. "I . . . I am not at all decided—"

"Of course you will say yes," Lady Ingram dictated. "It's not every girl that can boast of turning the head of an earl. Lydia, for instance." She turned to her daughter. "You are wasting your time with that Major Fitzwilliam instead of making a push to secure one of the titled gentleman. I cannot understand what you mean to accomplish."

"Did it not occur to you, Mama, that I *like* Major Fitzwilliam?" Lydia's jaw set, and two spots of color appeared on her cheeks.

"Oh, he's a very good sort of man, I am sure. Your brother would not associate with him if he were not. But he's a soldier. No income to speak of. It's time you set your sights on someone higher and allow the major to move on as well." Though Eleanor pitied Lydia her mother's attention, she could not but be grateful it was drawn away from her.

"Freddy said he's the very best of men, and I'm inclined to agree—" Lydia stopped the conversation short because Hartsmith opened the door to announce the arrival of the new maid the agency had sent over.

"We will finish this discussion later," Lady Ingram said, and she followed the butler out the door, leaving Lydia and Eleanor alone.

"So . . . Lord Carlton." Lydia raised her eyebrows. "I'm not surprised. Of course he would love you."

Eleanor sighed. "Can we speak of something else?" She met her friend's gaze but could not explain further. She needed time to think. "I'm sorry."

Lydia raised her eyebrows but set her biscuit on the plate, apparently willing to obey. "You'll never guess who I saw on Edwards Street today."

Eleanor, already exhausted from turning over in her mind the subject of Lord Carlton, his intentions, and what she should do about them, could only reply, "I will not even try, so you must tell me." However, Lydia's next words brought her head up in alarm.

"Harriet Price."

Eleanor sighed. Harriet had come after all. "I'd hoped we might escape her presence in London." She patted the smooth cover of the book she'd been reading. "Harriet Price will be up to no good, I'm sure. She treated me dismally at school, never failing to remind me I didn't belong to *your set.*"

Lydia lifted a shoulder. "She was only jealous because everyone liked you. I told her so when I saw her." She looked smug. "I also told her about your inheritance."

"I wish you would not have. What can that have to do with her?"

Raising an eyebrow, Lydia countered, "Set her down a peg, which she sorely needs."

Eleanor crushed a lump of sugar over her saucer, reducing it to dust. "I cannot help but be ill at ease, though. Wherever Harriet Price goes, she leaves a trail of victims behind. And in my case she actually has something to latch on to besides pure spite."

"Even so," said Lydia, "there's nothing she can accuse you of. So she saw you climbing in the window in the middle of the night. You had a ready excuse, and she has no other certain proof of anything amiss."

"Only that I was out of the seminary in the middle of the night, and innocent girls don't do that. Reputations have been destroyed for less." Eleanor glanced up, and seeing Lydia's stricken face, repented immediately.

"I would do it again," she said, coming over to take Lydia's hand. "You mustn't think I regret it. I'd only hoped I might escape having to deal with

Harriet while I was in London." Attempting a smile, Eleanor added, "But who knows. Perhaps she has changed and means no mischief."

Lydia didn't look convinced, and Eleanor did not have the heart to attempt it. She sat back and stared at the black marble ormolu clock on the mantle, lost in the memory of that appalling night. What she had gone through had been trial enough, but to have Harriet, of all people, witness her return? It was the worst of luck.

It'd been after midnight when Harriet had confronted her, and late enough that Eleanor should have been able to creep back into the seminary without being spotted. She had no longer been shaking from nerves but was determined to get into her room and, if she were lucky, to sleep a couple of hours after her dispiriting adventure.

She had only just made it to Lydia's assignation with the Latin teacher at eleven o'clock that night. The instructor, furious to behold a penniless and determined Eleanor rather than his intended prey, grabbed her by the arm with the threat of taking her with him. Eleanor twisted free and having darted away, told him, untruthfully but with broad assurance, that the head teacher had been put into possession of the facts of his seduction, and if the Latin teacher did not want to have the mark on his character follow him to his next post, he had best leave with all haste and not contact Miss Ingram again.

Having effectually sent off the man whom her friend did not yet view as a danger, Eleanor walked the two miles back to school, trembling with both victory and from imagining more sinister outcomes. The moon was overhead as she began to climb the trellis to reach her room, and when a window to her right opened, disrupting her concentration, it frightened her so much she nearly lost her foothold.

"What in heaven's name are you doing out at this hour, Eleanor?" Harriet had whispered, with a glance back into the room. "You woke me out of sound sleep, and if you haven't awakened Mathilda, it's only because she sleeps like a log. Do you want to rouse the entire household?"

Eleanor paused in her ascent only to lean over and whisper back, "I forgot my shawl in the spinney, and I was so worried it would be taken I couldn't sleep and rushed out to get it. If Mrs. Wrightworth sees me without it, she'll give me a thundering scold."

Harriet peered out the window. "But you haven't your shawl. Where is it?"

Eleanor's nimble imagination was taxed, but she replied, "Oh, it wasn't there after all. So all I had for my trouble was some fresh air, and most likely the death of a cold." She gripped on the vine above her head. "Good night, Harriet. I'm sorry to have woken you. I must climb the rest of the way before I lose my strength."

"I won't tell a soul," Harriet whispered loudly.

Somehow your pledge of secrecy does not reassure me, Eleanor had thought.

The present mood in the room, oppressive from the ticking clock and Lydia's uncharacteristic silence as she darted surreptitious glances at her friend, brought Eleanor back to the present. Her tea was growing cold.

A quiet evening at home would have done much to restore her peace of mind, but it was unthinkable to give up their evening at Almack's when they had vouchers. To add to her troubles, she was sure to see Harriet there. It seemed at that moment as though the number of people Eleanor did not wish to encounter in London was beginning to outweigh the number of those she did.

Eleanor looked at Lydia and attempted a smile. "Well . . ." was all she said.

Stratford dressed for Almack's with ponderous movements, eyeing the black knee-breeches with distaste. He had given his word to Ingram that he would keep an eye on Lydia and Miss Daventry, but he had no desire to spend the evening watching Miss Daventry sit in Lord Carlton's pocket. He walked into the sitting room and found his aunt and sisters dressed in the first stare of elegance and waiting impatiently.

"Good lord, and women are to have the honor of being called slow. Whatever did you find to do all this while, Stratford?" Anna stood and adjusted her skirt in a brisk movement.

"Aunt, if you're ready, shall I ring for the footman?" Phoebe walked toward the bell-pull, but her brother checked her movement.

"There's no need. I crossed James on my way in, and I've had the carriage readied." Stratford helped his aunt stand and wrapped her cloak around her. "Aunt, I daresay you'll find the weather agreeable, even at night. The damp has left off."

The line of carriages outside Almack's was long, and it was ten-thirty when they entered. *I haven't begun my discharge faithfully*, thought Stratford. *I should've arrived before the Ingram party.*

He needn't have worried. Lady Ingram appeared with Miss Daventry and Lydia five minutes after Stratford and his sisters. From across the room of twirling couples, he watched them bestow their cloaks before turning to survey the room. He caught Miss Daventry's sweeping gaze and gave a small wave. She smiled back, prompting his feet forward as if of their own accord.

How could he have hesitated to win her heart? He was going to make a push to secure her affections, and if there were a God above, she would not have accepted Carlton. *Has the proposal already occurred? Was he too late?* He had put down Carlton for his youth and inexperience, but if he were being honest with himself, it was not Carlton's youth that made him the wrong choice for Miss Daventry, Stratford realized. It was because he himself had feelings for her.

If only he could convince her he was the right one for her. *Her eyes don't light up when Carlton walks in the room. And unless I'm very much mistaken, when I am near her, they do.*

Stratford strode toward the Ingrams and Miss Daventry, ignoring other greetings, and met the party before they had fully entered the room. "Ingram asked me to serve as chaperone in his place. If there's anything I can procure for you, I hope you will not hesitate to ask."

Lady Ingram answered for everyone. "Good evening, Stratford. Frederick told me of your intentions, and I approve. We shall do much better to have a gentleman escort." She looked around and eyed with misgiving Major Fitzwilliam, who was making his way to their group. "Has he gained access here?" she said under her breath.

Stratford had just the time to reply. "He's a gentleman, even if he must earn his living, and his connection to your son has given him the access he needs. He's here on official business." Lady Ingram nodded, apparently satisfied.

"Good evening." Major Fitzwilliam encompassed everyone with a bow. "Miss Ingram," he said in a clear voice that showed no fear he might not be received, "I believe you've promised me a dance." Lady Ingram's eyes narrowed at his pronouncement.

Stratford used that opportunity to voice his own request. "Miss Daventry, I haven't had a promise, but I hope you will spare a dance for me." He knew there was a pleading quality to his voice, but it couldn't be helped.

"Of course," she said. Their attention was diverted by Mr. Braxsen's entrance just as the doors to the assembly closed to further guests.

"It seems we are all of us tardy this evening," Stratford said, and watched idly as Mr. Braxsen made a beeline for where they stood. He knew he'd have no chance to converse further with Miss Daventry until their dance.

"Braxsen, well met," Stratford said. "I expected you would not be far behind your comrade. But who do you partner with when Major Fitzwilliam is dancing with Miss Ingram?" With a guilty jump, Stratford caught himself and looked around to see if Lady Ingram had heard the reference to her daughter, breathing a sigh of relief when he saw her in conference with Mrs. Brooks.

"I dance with whomever is on the sidelines," Mr. Braxsen returned. "If she's heir to a great fortune, all the better." He gave a roguish smile.

"There are not many of those," Stratford said. "Best to look out for a young lady of character."

"I believe there are even fewer of those," Mr. Braxsen replied. "I shall have better luck pursuing a fortune." Stratford could not tell whether he was serious.

The first set was full, so Stratford staked his claim next to Eleanor while his sisters went into the hands of their waiting partners and Lydia passed from Major Fitzwilliam to the next promised gentleman. He saw the major's frown as he watched her leave and didn't envy the man. Before Stratford and Eleanor could take their places in the set that was forming, the Master of Ceremonies brought two newcomers to the debutantes on the sidelines and encouraged them to fill the set.

With a shrug, Eleanor turned her face to his. "The set is full."

Struck by her nearness, and his hope of triumph after so many days of wrestling to come to a decision, he suddenly felt tongue-tied. "Did you wish to be dancing?"

"I'm content to stand on the sidelines," she replied, her bright gaze following the swish of skirts and click of boots in front of them. She did indeed look content. Had she accepted her suitor already? He wished he could ask.

"Have you—"

"Will you now—"

Each laughed self-consciously, but Stratford bade her continue, and she asked, "Will you now have a chance to go to your estate as you'd wished? I hope the affairs are well in hand."

Stratford was standing as near to her as he dared, and her scent, as fresh as spring flowers, made it hard to concentrate on her words. He took a step back and answered. "Ingram's fall has put off the visit. Most of the affairs I can manage by correspondence, but I must go soon, be it just for a week."

"You have put off your visit for Lord Ingram. You're a good friend to have, my lord."

When she smiled at him like that, it made his heart skip in a queer way. He almost blurted out—*Call me Stratford*—but caught himself in the nick of time. Good heavens! What if she were already betrothed?

He pretended to move further back from the dancing couples as an excuse to pull her close. "I have noticed, Miss Daventry, the same can be said about you."

The first dance finished, and Eleanor put her hand on Lord Worthing's arm and followed him onto the floor. Just as well they'd missed the other set because this one was a waltz, and there was no one she would rather dance it with. He placed his hand on her back, waiting for the music to begin, and her knees felt weak from that light pressure.

If only she might know how he felt. Lord Carlton did not hold back from expressing his admiration, to the point where it overwhelmed her. Sometimes she suspected Lord Worthing admired her as he had once confessed, but then he would say something that seemed indifferent, or he would shutter his expression so she had no idea what he was thinking.

Tonight, however, something had changed. *He* had changed. She was prompted then to search his face to see if she had not imagined it.

When their eyes met, she received a shock. The look he gave her was purposeful. Resolute. At that moment, the music started and he moved, pulling her into the steps. It took a full turn around the room before she could recover her composure enough for conversation. After the first look, his expression went back to being indecipherable, and she wondered if he had been affected.

Perhaps not, for he smiled down at her and raised his eyebrows. "Not once have you stepped on my toes."

She had tamed her wildly beating heart and was ready with a reply. "You are surprised, my lord. Are the other ladies you dance with so heavy-footed?"

"No, I am only admiring the lightness of yours," he teased back.

Eleanor liked this side to him and suspected he did not show it to many people outside his family and closest friends. "Well, I must own myself to be agreeably surprised in you, my lord," she returned with a glimmer of a smile. "You have a sure way about you when you dance that I would not at all have guessed upon first making your acquaintance."

"Ah." Lord Worthing nodded sagely. "Are you referring to my lack of conversational arts or my ineptitude at making a decent proposal?"

A bubble of laughter escaped her. "So you're willing to concede that there were some manners lacking in your address. Never fear, my lord. You've more than made up for it in these last weeks." Eleanor paused and then added, reflectively, "I suppose you can't but avoid learning diplomacy living with two sisters."

"I'd spent too long in the Peninsula to remember my manners," Lord Worthing said. "But, as you say, my sisters have not been slow in reminding me of them." He leaned down to murmur, "Nor, I might add, have you."

Her heart lifted at the intimate way in which he spoke those words, though the words themselves were nothing special. Her feet barely touched the ground as they spun, and when the waltz ended, he held her close for a minute longer, releasing her only long enough to lean in and say, "I've never had so much pleasure in dancing as I have with you, Miss Daventry. I hope I will have many more occasions to do so." The smile he gave her cracked her last defense, and she could barely feel her legs as he led her to the sidelines.

Eleanor knew her face was expressive, and that the pleasure she felt was patent to all, and she thought she did not care. But when she looked to her right, it was clear her sentiment was not universally shared, for just then she caught a set of sharp eyes turned in her direction. It was Harriet Price, and the look of speculation in them brought a chill to Eleanor's spine. This did not bode well.

Eleanor was still wondering how she might handle meeting Harriet that evening when Lord Worthing led her toward the other side of the room, where her gaze clashed with Judith Broadmore's. Eleanor was taken aback by the hatred brimming in the other woman's eyes, and her steps nearly faltered.

Then she grew indignant. Why should she cower? She had nothing to be ashamed of. It was Miss Broadmore who had thrown off Lord Worthing, not the other way around. It was Miss Broadmore's loss, and she must face it and move on.

As Eleanor bolstered her confidence through this reasoning, they stopped so Lord Worthing could exchange a few words with Mr. Braxsen, and she glanced at the other side of the room, where she discovered Harriet still staring at her. *Agh! Hemmed in on both sides!* she thought with a sudden, panicky bubble of mirth. Where was Lydia so she could share this with her?

Her humor and confidence fled, however, when Lord Worthing stiffened and pulled away from her. As she felt the physical loss of his presence, understanding dawned. *He has perceived Miss Broadmore and wishes not to be seen walking so closely with me.*

When Lord Worthing turned to her, his eyes were full of concern. "Miss Daventry, I had intended to bring you to the refreshment table, and now I find I cannot. Pray, forgive me." He looked as if he regretted having to abandon her, and the thought gave her some small comfort, but it was small indeed.

Then he glanced toward Miss Broadmore again, and Eleanor's gaze followed his. She must keep her feelings in check because Lord Worthing's heart did not belong to her. And she must seriously consider Lord Carlton, whose heart, it appeared, did. No matter how she might feel, she would be a fool to hold out for one who had no serious intentions of marriage. *Or who has those intentions only when he is drunk.* She forced herself to give a light shrug.

"It is of no matter, my lord," Eleanor replied. "Look. Lydia is sitting this one out. Will you bring me to her?"

No sooner had Stratford brought Eleanor to Lydia's side than he left. Lydia was immediately claimed by her next dance partner, leaving Eleanor alone, and Harriet Price lost no time in coming her way, a sequence of events that felt most unjust.

"Eleanor," Harriet said, with an arched brow. "What a surprise to find you here. I've heard about your inheritance, and I suppose that must surely open any door. How lucky for you. First you have a guardian who can smooth over your"—she leaned in—"less-than-desirable past, and then he leaves you with an inexplicable fortune that begs one to understand the cause behind it."

Eleanor smiled sweetly, though it cost her. "Most people are not as motivated by jealousy as you are to search for cause."

Harriet's eyes narrowed. It was war. "I do not know how you were able to hoodwink the patronesses to secure you vouchers, but you have not fooled me. What have I to be jealous of? *I* am the daughter of a baroness, and as such will always be better than you."

"Then let me not detain you any longer," Eleanor said, her cheeks stiff from smiling. Harriet turned on her heel and marched to the nearest group, where Miss Broadmore was holding court.

They deserve each other, Eleanor thought. Then—*good!* No false pretense needed. Still, never before had she felt the want of partners more acutely.

Stratford regretted leaving Eleanor so abruptly, but he couldn't ignore the urgency in Fitz's signal. He made his way to the entrance of the card room to meet him. Inside, they took the last free table in the corner, where the level of noise precluded any threat of someone eavesdropping. "You have news?"

Fitz nodded. "I've instructed my man to send any urgent message to me, no matter where I am, and he's a resourceful fellow." He leaned in, voice low. "Headquarters was broken into. It was Ingram's office. I don't want to leave the investigation at this critical point, so I'm hoping you can pass on the information for me. I'll be looking for any clues that connect the break-in at headquarters to the one in Ingram's library. And," he shook his head, looking weary, "following up on some possible leads at Boodle's."

"I'll go see Ingram first thing tomorrow," Stratford said, "but perhaps not so early as to arouse suspicion from his household. He doesn't want anyone to suspect something's amiss."

"No, no need," said Fitz. "In any case, there's nothing he can do. I'll report as soon as I'm able. But first let me tell you what I know."

Fitz left immediately after their talk, and Stratford returned to the ballroom, feeling at a loss. Miss Daventry was dancing, of course. He didn't have it in him to play the gallant to another young lady and could not order his sisters—and, he must not forget, the Ingram party—to leave without provoking questions he was unable to answer. Stratford felt every bit as weary as Fitz had looked and wished the evening might end quickly.

Chapter Twenty-Eight

The morning after Almack's, Eleanor accompanied Lydia to Lord Ingram's chambers since he was now well enough and indeed appreciated the visits, even if it meant a detailed recount of last night's adventures. Still vaguely dissatisfied with how her evening had ended, Eleanor forced herself to add her mite to Lydia's enthusiastic description, teasing Lord Ingram at the end with, "I was certain you'd not wish to hear a word about Almack's."

"When you're stuck in bed, any entertainment is better than none at all," Ingram said. "Now." He folded his hands on his lap. "Had you chose the silk accents or the satin?"

Eleanor was obliged to laugh, but Lydia answered in all sincerity. "The blue dress with satin bows. I danced nearly every dance, and I swear I'm worn to the bone. So many people asked after you, you would have been most gratified. All the usual people, but there was also a Miss Georgiana Audley who'd just arrived in town. When we were introduced, she mentioned having made your acquaintance."

Lord Ingram looked up at this. "Miss Audley is returned?"

"Yes. She was shockingly brown, but I daresay the London air will do her good. Her mother has passed away, and her father brought her home to settle affairs."

Ingram frowned. "When did her mother die? Did she say?"

"No, but I imagine it to be of recent date. She's still in half-mourning and refused to dance with anyone."

Lord Ingram digested this but made no further comment except to say he hoped Lydia would pass his regards the next time they met. With effort, it seemed, he turned the conversation back to the ball. "And you, Eleanor, had you all your dances claimed?"

"Nearly," she said. "I was not disgraced at any event." Her mind involuntarily went to her encounter with Harriet Price who, by the look of it, was eager to bring about Eleanor's downfall. Her joy at dancing with Lord Worthing could not stand under the combined forces of his having abandoned her for Judith Broadmore and Harriet's assault immediately following the dance.

Lydia pulled Eleanor out of her brief reverie with the words, "Stratford said he would come visit you today." After a wild flash of hope, Eleanor realized, of course, Lydia had been talking to her brother.

"I do hope he will be so obliging. It's an intolerable bore just lying about like this." Perhaps regretting his frustration, Ingram flashed them a smile that Eleanor thought must make some young lady's heart flutter somewhere.

"Fred, are we not company enough?" Lydia glared at him.

"I apologize for this black humor of mine. You are, of course." Ingram pulled on the pillow behind his head so he was more upright. "The truth is, I'm itching to get up and do something, but I know I can't. I'm fixed in this position until the bone has set, or so the doctor says."

"Well, let us hope Lord Worthing does come to relieve your boredom," Eleanor said. "However, we can amuse you between the two of us, can we not, Lydia? Where is the backgammon game?"

"So you mean to stay and indulge an invalid," Ingram said. "By all means, bring out the game. If you'll just pull the bell, Hartsmith will know where to find it. Oh, speak of the devil. Hartsmith, do you know where a set of backgammon can be found?"

The butler, his hand still on the doorknob, waited for Lord Ingram to finish. "I will bring the set straight away, my lord. But here is Lord Worthing wishing to see you, and the cook is waiting only for your summons to send up a luncheon." Eleanor looked up as Lord Worthing entered the room, but her gaze dropped as soon as he looked her way.

"Ah, Stratford, you're here," Lord Ingram said. "We were just speaking of you, and you're in time to sit for lunch."

Lord Worthing shook his head. "I hadn't meant to inconvenience you all. Ingram, I came to have a word with you today, but I can come back later."

"No, Stratford," Lydia insisted. "You must join us for lunch."

Ingram brooked no argument. "Hartsmith, set another plate at the table, would you?" Turning to Stratford, he added, "No sense in watching me try to balance a plate on my lap. Go join the ladies for a civilized lunch, then come up afterward and we can talk then."

Lord Worthing allowed himself to be persuaded and followed the ladies downstairs, where Lady Ingram moved to sit at the head of the table. After greeting Stratford and ordering the fruit and sandwiches to be passed around, she called to Lydia to explain what's this she'd heard about Mrs. Dartmouth's informal party to hear Mrs. Bannings sing. Lydia launched into what she knew of the affair, and Lord Worthing addressed Eleanor at his side.

"I'm hoping we might see you Saturday evening at the theatre if you care to join us in our box. Anna and Phoebe will both be there. Are you and Lydia free?"

"No, my lord. I'm afraid I've already accepted an invitation to dine at Lord Carlton's house and attend the theatre with him and his sister." She looked up and caught the disappointed look in his eyes before he averted them. Reaching for a small cake from the plate in front of her, she strove for a normal tone. "Lydia declined the invitation, and I'm not sure what she's planning."

Lord Worthing did not reply right away. At last he said, "I see I've come too late, then. Never mind. I was honoring Frederick's charge to escort you, and though I know you're perfectly well taken care of, I didn't want to neglect my duty."

That was a daunting speech. *He thinks only of his duty. Do not hope*, she scolded herself. However when she compared his words of duty with the disappointed look in his eyes, she couldn't help but think the words were just a mask. Hope took root and sprang up anew. Eleanor darted a glance at Lydia, but Lady Ingram kept her attention. She must carry this end of the conversation on her own.

"Are your sisters enjoying the Season?" Eleanor asked, after a space.

"Yes, I believe so." Lord Worthing took a sip of water, then after a quick glance at Lady Ingram, turned to her and said in a quiet voice, "Miss Daventry, I apologize for leaving you so abruptly after our dance last night."

"Yes, of course," she said, her eyes on her plate. "You had other obligations to attend to."

"I did have other obligations. It was only that I've been trying to discover what I can after Ingram was hurt, and I saw . . . someone signal to me urgently so I had to leave you." He caught her eye. "I assure you, little else would have torn me from such delightful company."

"I see." Her eyes darting to his, Eleanor had only time to respond as much before Lady Ingram asked Lord Worthing about his likelihood of attending the soirée where the soprano was to sing. He responded that he had not yet received an invitation, and the topic drifted to upcoming performances at Covent Garden. There was no time for more private conversation between them, but when he passed her a plate, his fingers grazed her hand and, startled, her eyes met his. He risked a fleeting smile before turning his attention back to Lady Ingram.

As he climbed the stairs after lunch, Lord Worthing thought about their too brief conversation at lunch. He wished he'd been able to talk more with Miss Daventry and to hear her say she'd understood. When he had first arrived, she had not held his gaze. No wonder. He had left her so quickly last night it was on the point of being rude. But after he explained the reason, the warmth in her regard returned. He would settle for that—for now.

An evening at the theatre in the same box would have afforded him plenty of opportunity for further conversation. He reached the landing and exhaled through clenched teeth. *Plenty of opportunity to lay further claim to her heart.* It cut that she'd already accepted to go with Carlton. Was she already engaged then? Surely Ingram would have said something.

When he entered Ingram's bedchamber, his friend shooed his valet out of the room. "Finished, are you?" Stratford asked.

Ingram waved him to the chair. "I assume you have some news for me?"

"Fitz asked me to relay this information to you and promised to come with a report as soon as possible. Your office was broken into at headquarters last night."

"Did they catch the man?" Ingram shifted restlessly. "Fitz had someone watching headquarters, so they should have seen the break-in."

Stratford shook his head. "It happened at the close of workday while there was still staff present. There were too many people entering and exiting the building for the trail to distinguish any unusual activity. As per your request, your secretary is letting Fitz investigate fully, and the break-in is not widely known. Your secretary said there was a partial list of inventory he had forgotten to take with him, and the thief stole that. It will not be too damaging, he said, but it's still useful information for the enemy, and he blames himself. He said his resignation will arrive by courier tomorrow."

Ingram made a dismissive gesture. "It must be urgent for the thief to attempt it at such a high risk. I wonder if the enemy is planning a broad-scale attack for them to be so intent on getting this document." Ingram let out a short expletive. "I loathe being bed-bound this way. I'm completely useless."

Stratford nodded, not adding insult to injury by attempting to console. After a minute, he said, "There was an announcement in the paper of Conolly's betrothal to a widow of no small fortune, and he's selling out. You can have Fitz continue to follow him, but I don't think he's your man. Delacroix's run of bad luck, on the other hand, has continued."

"Very well. We'll drop the trail on Conolly," Ingram replied, vaguely. "Delacroix might just be desperate enough to sell information to stay ahead of the dun. *And* he's French."

Stratford leaned forward. "Now, that's the piece that makes me think it's not him. I *know* these French who came over during the Reign of Terror. They worked with my father in Spitalfields. They've no ties to the emperor and are eager to distance themselves from everything on the Continent."

He met Ingram's gaze. "However, in full disclosure, I must add that Delacroix was expected last night at Almack's and did not show. I overheard his cronies expressing their surprise at his absence. Said it was most unlike him to miss out on advancing his interests with a particular lady of fortune when there were so many other suitors vying for his place."

Ingram stared at Stratford shrewdly. "That is a useful piece of information and is worth looking into. These clues make him suspect, but there's too little proof to bring him in. Since he's our only solid lead and it costs nothing to follow him, let's keep doing it. Despite the confidence you may have in him, evading creditors can lower a man's morals, no matter how lofty he starts out."

"Yes, of course," Stratford said.

Chapter Twenty-Nine

Lord Carlton arrived at six o'clock, along with his sister Cecily, to escort Eleanor for the evening. Lydia, still on an extended riding excursion, would miss their departure and be in time only for her own family dinner. Eleanor was glad for the Ingrams to have dinner just among themselves. Though Lady Ingram was unfailingly cordial, it must be a strain always to have another person about who was not a member of the family.

They were to follow dinner with the theatre, and the plan was for Eleanor to meet Lydia there and return with her to Grosvenor Square. Eleanor wore a gown in claret red that came to a slight *V* in the back, lower than she was accustomed, with tiny pearls sewn into the enclosure. There were garnets around her neck, and matching pendants in her ears, and her cheeks were unusually bright.

Eleanor felt—feared, actually—that Lord Carlton would propose tonight. The thought made her nervous because, while he was everything she could wish for when imagining an ideal, it was not love she felt for him. His beautiful face did not swim before her eyes when she was falling asleep. His kindness was appreciated, but it did not thrum an inner cord.

Even without Lady Ingram's warning, Eleanor couldn't ignore Lord Carlton's partiality for her when he had been so open about his feelings at their last meeting. Too open. She wondered whether feelings that came so quickly could disappear as fast. His social standing meant nothing where there was no love, and it did not add to the temptation. Yet there was some part of her that wondered whether love would ever come, and if it were not better to seize what was offered and learn to be content.

As soon as the thought entered her consciousness, she shook her head. The attention Lord Worthing showed in increasing measure each time they met made her say *no*. It was not enough to learn to be content.

Lady Carlton received Eleanor in her drawing room and made to rise, but her son assured her it wasn't necessary. Eleanor came and made her reverence before his mother, taking a seat on the settee with Cecily when she was bid.

"May I offer you some cordial water, Mother?" The frail woman shook her head but signaled that he should bring some to Eleanor. He did so and then sat across the room watching her. Although Eleanor returned the look, his expression didn't change, and she turned to face his mother feeling like a bug under a glass.

"You're to attend the theatre tonight," said Lady Carlton. "Who will join your party?"

"I had understood Cecily . . ." Eleanor looked in confusion to Lord Carlton.

"Cecily will not be attending. We will be joined by Mr. Braxsen and a Miss Redgrave." Eleanor felt a flash of annoyance that he'd not shared this information with her earlier, even if she was glad it was Mr. Braxsen, whom she knew. He asked, "Do you know Miss Emmeline Redgrave?"

Eleanor shook her head, shoving down her displeasure. Perhaps Miss Redgrave would be a comfortable replacement for Cecily. "But I shall be delighted to make her acquaintance."

When the butler opened the door to announce that dinner would be served, Lady Carlton stood. "We are quite informal here, but you must excuse me if Lord Carlton takes my hand. I find I'm not as stout as I would wish."

"Of course," said Eleanor. She stepped alongside Cecily. "I hope you mean to tell me where you found that ribbon threaded through your hair. It suits you becomingly. I've been on the lookout for furbelows to dress up one of my plain muslins, and this would suit quite nicely. Never fear," she added with a laugh. "I shall not put you out by choosing something identical."

"I would not dream . . ." Cecily said, eyes downcast. "In any case, I'm not yet out, and no one will see what I'm wearing."

Eleanor squeezed her arm. "You will be next year, will you not? Which will come before you know it—although I had hoped you would be able to accompany us to the theatre. I thought this was a treat even for those who have not yet made their debut."

"Matthew said he preferred I not go. He said it would be inconvenient . . ." Cecily's voice trailed away when her brother glared at her, causing her to turn crimson.

Oh dear, thought Eleanor, suddenly nervous. Was it too much to hope Lord Carlton would not try to press his suit tonight? If she knew nothing else, she knew she was not ready to promise anything.

When the first dish came out, Lord Carlton continued to stare at Eleanor, and she accepted the bowl of soup with a pang of dismay. She'd be unequal to the task of eating anything with her nerves jangling so.

"Where will you spend the summer months, Miss Daventry?" Lady Carlton asked. "They are almost upon us. I own to being ready to seek the fresh air such as we get in the country house."

"I will stay with my aunt, Mrs. Daventry, and her sister, Mrs. Renly, in Bath. They are there now, and Mrs. Renly's poor health will be keeping them there through the summer."

"I wondered why Lady Ingram might be sponsoring you this Season. She must quite dote on you." Lady Carlton took one sip of her soup, but lifting the spoon to her mouth a second time seemed beyond her.

"Lady Ingram has been most generous," Eleanor said. "She offered to sponsor me because she thought it would be more pleasant for her daughter to have a companion for her come-out. But she didn't know me beforehand. I think she trusted in my guardian's sponsorship as credit enough. Lydia—Miss Ingram—and I are very close, and I'm thankful we're able to have our come-out together."

"As am I," Lord Carlton said. "I might not otherwise have met you." He smiled warmly, causing Eleanor to freeze with alarm. Though his mother and sister seemed to take nothing amiss, Eleanor felt his was too public a declaration when she had never given him cause to believe his feelings were returned. It might speak of a pleasing boldness in him, but she would prefer a gentleman to be sure of her feelings before he wore his heart on his sleeve.

Over dinner, Eleanor taxed her brain to find ways of engaging in conversation a widow, a gentleman, and a girl not quite out of the schoolroom. Lord Carlton was not much help, alternating between a state of rumination and fixing his regard on her in the most discomfiting way. All together, it was not the most delightful of evenings spent.

Finally, Lord Carlton announced it was time to leave for the theatre as the others would arrive any minute. No sooner had the words been spoken than a muffled knocking was heard with the sounds of the front door being opened.

Outside, the sky had darkened, and one or two stars were visible. Mr. Braxsen alighted from the carriage to help Eleanor into it, all apologies for having kept them waiting. He gave a perfunctory smile at Lord Carlton's suggestion that the delay might be explained by his complex cravat, and the number of discarded neckcloths required in order to achieve the perfect mathematical. Miss Redgrave greeted Lord Carlton warmly, but gave only the stiffest bow to Eleanor. *Hmm. I wonder if Miss Redgrave has her sights set on Lord Carl*ton! *She may have him*, thought Eleanor, still uncomfortable from his marked attention.

At the theatre, Emmeline Redgrave took her place next to Lord Carlton in their box and engaged him in chatter, while Mr. Braxsen sat at Eleanor's side. Eleanor scanned the seats, searching for Lord Worthing, whose eyes, she discovered, were on her. When their gazes met, he jerked upright and looked away.

Mr. Braxsen finally woke to his duty to Eleanor. "Miss Daventry, how is Lord Ingram faring? Have the doctors said when he will get up?"

"Not for several weeks, unfortunately." Eleanor wrenched her gaze from Lord Worthing's box. "He is not a compliant patient." She smiled up at him. "I had not realized you were so closely acquainted with Lord Carlton."

"He was friends with my younger brother and would join us at the clubs in London over the holidays. I gave him his first black eye at Jackson's. A round of boxing," he explained.

Eleanor laughed. "I can see the friendship was deeply forged then." She shot a glance at the subject in question, adding, "But Lord Carlton? I cannot imagine him engaging in the sport." *Nor can I imagine your exerting yourself in such a way.*

"It's only because he's caught your fancy that you think him so nice . . ." began Mr. Braxsen with an arch look.

Her expression must have been forbidding because he pulled back slightly as the curtain opened, and the footmen snuffed the candles. He leaned over to whisper, "I taught him a salutary lesson, and he did not try that again." Eleanor smiled but was relieved by the ensuing darkness.

At intermission, Miss Redgrave stated her wish to get some air and have a glass of refreshment. Mr. Braxsen stood, saying, "Why so do I." Turning to the occupants in the box, he added, "Shall you join us?"

"None for me," answered Lord Carlton, "I thank you. Miss Daventry, you do not wish to endure the crush, do you?"

She looked across the theatre and saw Lord Worthing's box fully occupied with more people pouring into it. Without the hope of meeting the earl in the gallery, she felt she may as well stay where she was. And surely Lord Carlton wouldn't be so improvident as to choose the theatre to propose. "No, I'm content to remain." She smiled at Mr. Braxsen.

When the two left the box, Lord Carlton switched seats to the one next to her. "Have you enjoyed the first part of the play?"

"Immensely," Eleanor replied. "This is my third time to the theatre, and I've not yet found it boring. I wonder if I ever shall." She looked up, studying the gilded moulding on the ceiling.

"Some people are able to find joy in everything," Lord Carlton said, in a breathless voice that brought her gaze straight ahead in alarm. She did not dare look at him but could feel the heat emanating off him.

"Miss Daventry, I must have a word with you. It will not wait, and since I will not be accompanying you home . . . It's a nuisance, but I can't seem to get you alone long enough, and this will have to do." Eleanor glanced at Lord Carlton's red face and felt her stomach drop.

I've been naive. I'm not ready for this. It was too late, and Eleanor could not stop him from proceeding.

"From the moment I met you, I have held you in high esteem. I dare not enumerate all the ways, for the situation we find ourselves in may not permit it." Lord Carlton looked behind him. "I don't know when Braxsen and Miss Redgrave will return. Miss Daventry—" He took a discreet hold of her hand. "Eleanor. I love you, and lately I have dared hope that you have some feelings toward me. Will you make me the happiest man alive and become my wife?"

Until the words were out, Eleanor still hadn't known how she would respond. Lord Carlton was everything she should want. He was pleasing to look at, considerate of her comfort, and he seemed to love her, if his words and attention could be believed. She didn't love him, of that she was almost sure. But she didn't dare refuse him. *What if I'm wrong?* At the last minute, she found she could not, without further reflection, turn away the security of belonging to someone even if it were based only on esteem. Just as quickly, she despised herself for such weakness.

"It's sudden for me," Eleanor said. "You have always been so kind. I don't think . . . I ask only that you give me time to consider. I don't know my heart." *I should have said no*, she thought in a rush. *I'm getting his hopes up. But what if saying no is a mistake?*

Lord Carlton's face had fallen. "I confess my disappointment. I'd hoped you would be led to . . . perhaps I was not wise in choosing my setting. If we had been more private, I could have convinced you . . ."

"I don't think," Eleanor said before he could follow that train of thought, "the location would have changed my answer. I will not pretend ignorance that your feelings have developed for me over the last two months. I've known this, but I have not been sure of my own. Your proposal today throws me in confusion, and I must have time to search my heart."

Eleanor reached out and touched his hand. "Will you give me this time?"

Lord Carlton was looking down, but at her gesture he met her gaze fleetingly and answered, "I will not yet despair."

No sooner had he said these words than Mr. Braxsen and Miss Redgrave rejoined their box, and Lord Carlton's demeanor changed. He began to quiz them on being unable to endure the crowds just as he had warned them. Eleanor wondered at Lord Carlton's ability to change on an instant and questioned if the current of his feelings did not run deep. *He will indeed be a good politician.*

She looked across the theatre. Phoebe was standing in conversation with Lydia and Major Fitzwilliam, and Anna stood in their box scanning the crowd. Lord Worthing was still seated with no one at his side, his eyes fixed on her. And this time he did not look away.

Chapter Thirty

All the next morning, Stratford kept remembering Lord Carlton's face across the theatre, animated and smiling as he talked to Miss Daventry. The visions taunted him.

However, if he were not very much mistaken, Carlton had chosen to declare himself to Miss Daventry right during intermission and had been met with a rebuff. If not refusal, at least not an immediate acceptance. His was not the face of a man who was *aux anges*. As a gentleman, Stratford did not wish such unhappiness on anyone, but he could only be happy that Miss Daventry hadn't thrown herself away at the first offer she got.

Not that she had done that, Stratford recalled. She had not said yes to Amesbury, and she had not said yes to him.

Stratford hated to leave while Miss Daventry's heart was not secured, but his trip to the estate could wait no longer, and he had promised the bailiff he would come. Setting out the next day, he accomplished the voyage in short order, entering the stables and handing the reins to Jesse, who greeted him as if he'd just returned from an afternoon ride as opposed to two months' absence. "See that you give her a good rub-down," Stratford said. "I didn't change her at the last stage as I ought to have." He patted the horse's side and turned toward the house.

The butler greeted Stratford with a stately bow. "Welcome home, my lord. I've already ordered a hot bath to be drawn, and Cook has begun to prepare your dinner. Have you your trunks?"

"Benchly is one day behind me. I have a change of clothes that will serve until then. I've written to the bailiff to expect me. Have you had word from him?" Stratford started up the stairs.

"He came today thinking you might have reached the estate, though your appointment was not until tomorrow. There's a matter of urgency he wished to discuss with you if you happened to be here, but he assured me it could wait." Billings signaled to the footman to take Stratford's port-manteau and began to climb the stairs behind him.

"As eager as I am to go over the accounts, if it can wait until tomorrow, I am glad." Stratford entered his room, and Billings followed, preparing to help him off with his coat.

"I won't need help, except for my boots." Stratford sat and allowed the footman to pull off one boot, then the other. "There is something I wish to discuss with you, Billings. Come see me in the library following dinner."

Later that evening, when Billings knocked softly at the library door, Stratford bid him come in and then walked around the desk and sat on the corner of it. He stared at the painting over the mantelpiece of hounds nipping and snarling before the fox hunt, then turned to the butler. "What do you know about the Munroe hamlet that was bequeathed to Miss Daventry? You knew my uncle well. Did he bring you into his confidence? I'm struggling to understand his intentions and am hoping you can shed some light on the matter."

Billings took his time answering. He had been in the Worthing employ almost his entire life, beginning as a stable boy when the young and newly titled fourth earl took him off the parish. Stratford knew the confidence the earl had entrusted to him was not easily shared.

Billings raised his rheumy eyes to Stratford. "The fourth earl hadn't yet been sick—or, perhaps he knew he was sick but had not disclosed the fact to anyone; that would be just like him—when he announced that the solicitor was coming to adjust the will. The fourth earl had known by then that Nicholas would not be his inheritor, so there was nothing unusual in the request. I made arrangements to set one more place for lunch, and the earl and his solicitor were closeted in the library for a good part of the morning before the doors finally opened. They ended the meeting with lunch.

"When the solicitor had his carriage readied and had driven off, the fourth earl called me into the library and was sitting on the edge of the desk, precisely in the way you are now. He said, 'Do you remember the girl who is my ward—Eleanor Daventry? She stayed at the estate once, and I believe you troubled yourself on her behalf when she dropped her doll on the other side of the bull pasture.' He waited, and I gave a nod. Yes, I remembered her.

" 'Well,' he said, 'I've seen to her schooling and have set aside a sum for her to make an appearance in London, called in a favor from a lady friend of mine . . .' At that point the earl fell into a period of reflection before picking up his train of thought. He said, 'The girl has not returned to Worthing, but I've seen to her education and comfort. I wanted nothing lacking in her upbringing. I'm confident her aunt has her education well in hand, and although Mrs. Daventry seems to be a soft creature, she won't allow for impertinence. The gel will be brought up well.'

"I said nothing, of course. It was not my place. So the earl continued. 'I'm about to make a scandal with this will of mine, and I tell you now so you may know I was of sound mind when I did it. Of course, the solicitor can attest to that . . .' At this point he seemed winded, and that's when he circled his desk and sat down. It was the excitement, I believe, or perhaps the old earl had indeed known he was not long for this world.

" 'I will be leaving the most lucrative part of the estate to the chit,' he said, 'and *oh ho* if that won't make someone grind his teeth.' "

Billings shot a glance at Stratford now and clasped his hands behind his back. "Then he said, 'If Stratford doesn't take it in stride, he's not the man I thought him to be. Keyes, however . . .' The earl had chuckled softly to himself, saying, 'He always cared so much about his association to the estate and what he could get out of it, although the answer to that was always *nothing*.'

"Then the earl looked at me again, saying, 'Miss Daventry will inherit only upon her marriage. And why, you may ask, did I do such a thing that must seem bacon-brained?'—I didn't ask, of course—and the earl went on to say, 'Why, I may not be able to do much, but I can right a wrong, by God.'

"He folded his hands, then, and leaned back in his chair and said, 'M'father did not win that piece of land squarely. What must he do but cheat at cards and risk bringing shame on the Worthing name? No one found out, of course, or he would have been driven from the ton. He told me in his final confessions.'

Billings glanced at Stratford to see how he took the news, but Stratford revealed none of the surprise he felt in knowing the land had not been fairly acquired.

"The old earl looked at me then, and said, 'Billings, perhaps I will predecease you, and I feel it incumbent upon me to share these bad dealings with someone I know I can trust—' "

Billings broke off his recital to clarify to Stratford, "He didn't say 'someone I know who will keep it to himself,' mind you!" before continuing with his discourse.

"He went on to tell me his father had died when your uncle was but thirty. That's when he followed the impulse to befriend Daventry's son. He thought to make amends without telling him what had happened. Whatever else, he couldn't bring shame on his father's name that way. Young Daventry was good-natured and just as anxious to put aside their fathers' differences, but he inherited the estate with his pockets to let because of his father's foolish gaming. When Daventry came into possession of the title, he was forced to marry a Cit who brought a fair amount of money into the marriage, but not a heart. When she ran off, she took it all with her—the remaining money and the heart—and gave no thought for her daughter, who was only seven."

"Young Daventry and Lord Worthing became so thick," Billings continued, "when my master was asked to serve as her guardian, he agreed without hesitation. I believe he truly mourned his friend's death and was determined to save Miss Daventry from an impoverished life with an indifferent education."

"And have you a guess as to why my uncle specified she would only inherit this upon marriage?" Stratford asked, a shiver of trepidation creeping up his spine.

"I can only think of two reasons, my lord." Billings seemed reluctant to offer them up, and Stratford was forced to prompt.

"And they are . . ."

"They are that the earl wanted to see Miss Daventry comfortably settled in matrimony because her only example was one of flight and brokenness. Perhaps he feared she would make an ill-judged decision without his forcing her hand. He thought marriage would be the best thing for her." Billings paused. "Or—"

Stratford waited but was again forced to prompt the butler. "Or . . ."

"Or my master thought it would be the best thing for *you*."

The words hung in the air. *Based on that one meeting?* Stratford thought. He was only twelve at the time and hadn't even made an effort to be more than civil. *Why would my uncle think about me at all?*

As if Billings could read his thoughts, he said, "He did follow your career, even before he knew you would inherit. He knew—" Billings stopped so short, Stratford wondered if he was going to say his uncle had known Stratford had run off to Portugal because he had been disappointed in love. Instead, Billings said, "He knew you were distinguished in Portugal and Spain. He boasted of you."

Stratford exhaled. Even with his uncle's high-handedness concerning the inheritance, he was touched that the old earl, in whose footsteps he was following, had not been opposed to his inheriting the title. That his uncle had tied Miss Daventry's name to his own did not threaten him as he might have expected. Instead, he was left with a longing he could not identify. If he let himself think about it for too long, he might admit that he longed for her.

"Thank you Billings. That will be all."

That week, Stratford threw himself into the decisions that needed to be made over the estate, returning to London as soon as he could get away. He refused to believe Carlton's suit could be successful. Nevertheless, his nerves were taut as soon as he entered the crowded streets of the metropolis, and he was hard-pressed to wait until the next day to visit Ingram. He might meet Miss Daventry there, if luck were in his favor. It was.

Upon arriving at Grosvenor Square, he asked first for the ladies of the house and was shown into the drawing room. Lydia sat listlessly and did not look up when he entered. Miss Daventry, however, sat up straight and gave him a smile of welcome that shot a bolt of hope through his heart. He bowed and took the seat opposite.

"You're back, are you?" Lydia said in a dull voice.

"You look rather pulled," Stratford replied. "Is it from all your flirting at the Hampton's last night? Phoebe told me about it this morning. I hope you don't mean to make a long night of it tonight." It was easier to fall back into teasing Lydia, whom he'd known from childhood, than it was to find measured words that would not reveal too much of his heart toward Miss Daventry when Lydia might comment on it.

"Stratford, it's not kind of you to comment on my appearance," Lydia said, "Unless it's to say you are in slavish adoration."

"You know very well I won't do that. You are too much like my sisters, and I don't mollycoddle *them*. Besides," Stratford said kindly, "you do look pulled. Well, I won't be overly familiar with Miss Daventry and say *she* looks tired. Of course that would be a falsehood."

Her gaze shot up, and he tried to hold it, but she looked at her embroidery again, her cheeks pink.

"Are you here to see Ingram?" Lydia asked pointedly. "You seem to have come for no other reason than to cause mischief and poke at one like you used to when we were children."

Stratford didn't answer right away but continued to observe Miss Daventry, whose head was bent over her work. *If only she would look up.*

Eventually she did raise her head, and he noticed her strange look. *Oh!* He hadn't answered.

"I didn't poke at you," he said. "You were forever pestering us, and it was all I could do to keep you from trailing along behind us where you might have got hurt."

"*Hmm!*" Lydia said. "Well, as you see I'm not trailing behind now. If you have such bad memories, why do you not seek your company elsewhere?"

"I see you are provokingly cross for no reason." Stratford put out his legs and leaned back. Miss Daventry had her head buried in her stitches again, and he thought she was hiding a smile. He wished he could take her out driving without Lydia, but of course he could not ask. It was unbearable, not being able to pursue her without Lydia scrutinizing his every move. That—and not knowing whether she were betrothed to that greenhorn.

Stratford stood. "I'll go visit Fred if he'll see me. Is he awake, d'you think?"

Lydia nodded. "I left him not five minutes ago."

When Lord Worthing exited, Eleanor wished she had thought of something clever to say. Her heart had leapt when he came into the room after a week's absence, but all she could do was stare at her stitches like a simpleton. Really. How could she ever hope to capture his heart if she couldn't put two words together?

Eleanor folded the embroidery. "Lord Worthing knows how to pull your strings." Twinkling, she added, "Especially when you are indeed pulled. Perhaps we should sit out tonight's gala."

Lydia rounded on Eleanor. "And you! You were so quiet just now. Did you and Stratford quarrel?"

"Whatever have we to quarrel about? And when would we have found time? He's been gone this past week," Eleanor said, trying to pass off her comment with a laugh. When Lydia didn't respond, she looked up at her. "What?"

"You've been quiet this entire week, now I think of it." Lydia peered at her. "You're not in love, are you? Is it Carlton?"

"Put that notion aside, I beg of you. I do not mean to marry."

"Eleanor," cried her friend. "I know you too well to believe that balderdash. You hope very much to marry. You're meant to have a snug home and children toddling about, and . . . and, what's this? Why are you crying?" Lydia rushed over and put her arms around Eleanor. "Tell me, what is it?"

"Nothing, nothing," gasped Eleanor. "And I'm not crying."

"Eleanor. In our entire friendship, I have never seen you shed even one tear, and you *are* crying. So out with it. What is it?"

Eleanor exhaled and met Lydia's gaze. Her lips trembled, and she dug her fingernails into her palms in an effort to keep her voice even. "It's just that I don't think something like this can ever come true for me."

Lydia drew her brows together. "Nonsense. Did Lord Carlton propose?" But that only provoked another bout of tears. "Eleanor, I do not understand you. You want someone who loves you, and Lord Carlton is that man."

Eleanor shook her head and raised brimming eyes to her friend. "But I do not love him."

Lydia was nonplussed for a moment. "But he is . . . is there someone else?"

"No." Eleanor shook her head. "I don't know."

Neither spoke while Eleanor wiped her tears. Lydia looked at her shrewdly and opened her mouth to speak, then clamped it shut. Finally, she took Eleanor's hands in hers. "I know there's someone for you. Someone who will not be blind to your charms, and who in turn will win your heart. You must not give up hope."

Stratford had not meant to overhear, but he couldn't tear himself away when his name was mentioned. Now, if he didn't move quickly, he was in danger of being spotted. He moved stealthily toward the stairs, praying Hartsmith wouldn't appear and call out his name, revealing that he was not upstairs where he should be.

Once he was out of danger, he stood outside Ingram's door to marshal his thoughts. Miss Daventry didn't believe that marriage to someone who loved her could happen to her? Stratford shook his head in disbelief. He allowed himself one more thought before he entered Ingram's room.

*She would not marry Carl*ton. As if of their own accord, his lips lifted into a smile before Stratford stepped through the door.

Chapter Thirty-One

With such heavy matters to weigh Eleanor down as being proposed to by one man she meant to refuse, barely exchanging words with another to whom she could not deny her attachment, and the vague fear that seeking employment would not bring about the freedom Eleanor had so desired, she was willing enough to put them aside in favor of finding a Vandyke lace trim to match her yellow gown. At least the excursion would allay Lydia's questions.

To Lydia, the outing was unalloyed by weightier considerations, but both threw themselves into arguing the merit of a white sunshade with the yellow ribbon versus a poke bonnet dear enough to exclude other purchases, but which would protect a fair complexion equally as well. If Eleanor were to add the white silk gloves that were still sitting at the bottom of her trunk, the outfit would be nothing short of fetching.

"We must also see if the Pantheon Bazaar doesn't have a wider selection." Lydia turned one piece of lace over to see how it wore on the other side. "You don't mind the crush, do you?"

"You know very well I don't," Eleanor said. "But if we go there, we will have to abandon the promenade in Hyde Park, and I believe—" here she leaned in to avoid being overheard, "Major Fitzwilliam will be hoping for a sight of you."

"I don't care for that," Lydia said, with a shrug that, to the sharp eyes of a friend, seemed affected.

Eleanor had observed how Lydia softened whenever the major was near. Seeing that in the bustle there was no one near to overhear their conversation, she replied in a low voice. "Lydia, I don't believe you. Unless your mother has influenced you not to care for him? He is clearly smitten with you, and he's not one to trifle." Lydia shrugged and offered no reply.

Eleanor, certain her friend could not be so fickle, pushed the matter. "Does Lord Ingram approve his suit?"

"I'm surprised to say he does but not enough to influence Mama. Major Fitzwilliam must earn his living. And I . . ." Lydia fell silent, either unwilling or unable to articulate her reticence.

Eleanor furrowed her brows. Lydia had been showing a preference for Major Fitzwilliam, but her mother's disapproval must weigh more than she had realized. Surely it couldn't be his lack of wealth, for Lydia had never cared for that before. In a flash of insight, she recognized that it was merely a case of jitters. It was not an easy thing to surrender one's heart. "For all that, his strength of character—" Eleanor began.

She was interrupted by a shrill voice. "Lydia, I see that chance has thrown us together again." Both turned to see Harriet Price approaching them from the store entrance. She ignored Eleanor completely.

"This is only my second week in London, and I simply must find time to call. We were held up from coming early, and now I shall have to make my debut late in the season. But then, there's no fear of London being thin of company in May, so perhaps it was the best time after all. Lydia, what a charming hat you're wearing. I could positively swear your complexion has lightened."

"Hallo, Harriet," said Lydia with a marked lack of enthusiasm. Eleanor refused to cower by looking away.

"Yes, I've had invitations every day since we arrived." Harriet Price turned her glittering smile on Eleanor. "Where are *you* staying? I didn't think your family had a residence in London."

"You know perfectly well I'm spending these months with the Ingram family. Oh—" Eleanor turned as the shopkeeper called out, "Here, miss." She took the package wrapped in brown paper but didn't miss Harriet's reply.

"I suppose there's no surprise there. You always were *such* friends." Harriet's tone voiced an unspoken retort that seemed to say, *I have no idea what Lydia finds in you to amuse her.*

"Well," Harriet continued, her glance flickering at Eleanor. "I will have invitations sent to your house for my coming-out ball. You may tell your brother his name will be on the card."

"My brother is laid up with a broken leg," Lydia said, shortly. "He will not be able to attend,"

"Pity," Harriet exclaimed in a voice agog with curiosity. "Was this an injury of some date? How long will it take to mend?"

"The doctor said we won't know for a couple of weeks." Lydia reached out her hand for her own package and said, "Good day, Harriet."

As Harriet opened her mouth to reply, the bell over the door rang, and Judith Broadmore walked in. "Are you ready?" Eleanor asked Lydia, turning toward the door. As the shop did not permit three people to walk abreast, there was no escaping Miss Broadmore, and they came face to face.

"How do you do?" Judith said with a nod that encompassed Lydia and Eleanor and a greeting that was mystifyingly cordial. Eleanor couldn't imagine why Miss Broadmore would address her at all.

Judith continued, eyes on Lydia. "Is your brother on the mend? I imagine that's why Stratford must escort you everywhere. Your families are on such dear terms."

"Although my brother asked Stratford to perform this duty for him while he was laid up, and Stratford was gracious enough to comply, I believe he does it because he enjoys our company. I've known him since I was in leading strings." Lydia tucked her package under her arm. "Stratford is like a brother to me."

"Ah, yes." Judith shot a look at Eleanor. "I suppose Stratford feels this request almost as an obligation. He was otherwise intending to leave London as soon as his sisters and aunt were comfortably settled. He told me when we met, right after his return from the Peninsula, before he had even left for Worthing. He felt at ease confiding in me, you see. We've been friends for so many years." She gave a nod to the shopkeeper, who had appeared at the counter again.

Lydia arched an eyebrow. "Why yes, so I've heard. I'm sure you've had all the latest news about our prospective families directly from him, and your asking about my brother was a mere formality." The jab afforded Eleanor some private amusement, but Miss Broadmore didn't seem affected by it. She was a woman impervious to insult, it appeared.

"Well." Judith shrugged and gave a light sigh. "As I've come on the same errand as you, I shan't keep you. I'm certain we will meet at one of the upcoming assemblies."

"Undoubtedly," said Lydia. Eleanor caught the beginning of Miss Broadmore and Harriet's greeting but could not judge from it how well they knew each other.

She and Lydia exited into the bright sunshine, made cheerful by balmy weather that was not overly hot. "Good lord, what a cat," Lydia said. "I was more than tempted to tell her the real reason Stratford was escorting us everywhere."

Eleanor, having a vague dread of where this was headed, said nothing until Lydia stopped and looked at her. "I finally figured out why Stratford kept looking at you in our salon, and why you could not bear to meet his gaze."

Eleanor shot a sideways glance at Lydia, heat stealing into her cheeks. Lydia gasped. "I knew it. He has developed a *tendre* for you, confess it! It's not Lord Carlton you care for, it's Stratford. And he feels the same for you," she finished in triumph.

Eleanor, trying to regain her ground, countered with, "You mustn't say that, Lydia. He has never declared himself." As soon as the words left her lips, she faltered, remembering he *had* declared himself, but not in a way that did either of them any credit. "Believe that he has no such thought in his head."

"You may believe it, but I certainly don't, and I know him best," Lydia insisted smugly. She grabbed Eleanor's elbow and forged a path through the throngs of afternoon shoppers clustering around the milliner's. "Oh heavens. Who needs to go to Pantheon Bazaar? We've found the circus right here at McAllister's."

Eleanor sent up a whisper of thanks that the crowd had diverted the direction of Lydia's thoughts, and she was granted a reprieve to think how she might deny it.

Lord Carlton had given Eleanor a week, and she knew the confrontation must come soon. Some of that time was devoted to his mother, which she knew about because he had sent a note informing her of it, tucked into a bouquet of flowers. Once they had met at the opera, but he was not improvident enough to attempt a second proposal under such circumstances. And the last time they met was at a dance to which he arrived late, only to find her dance card was full.

Eleanor was still no closer to understanding how she was going to refuse Lord Carlton, only that she must. This much was clear as soon as she'd laid eyes on Stratford after a week's absence and felt her heart turn over. If only she could guarantee that by refusing Lord Carlton, she was not only freeing him to find a young woman who would cherish him in return, but was also ensuring her own life would not end in drudgery.

She could not guarantee it, however. The more she contemplated this, the more nervous she was to make the wrong choice. Her resolve was only strengthened by the knowledge that in her heart of hearts, she did not love him.

The opportunity came rather simply. Eleanor was in the drawing room during the hours for morning calls, and Lydia had not yet come down. A maid entered Lydia's chambers the moment Eleanor came out of hers, and she knew her friend would not be ready straight away.

Lord Carlton was announced ten minutes later, and when he found her alone, his face lit with pleasure. "Miss Daventry!" And with words that made her heart leap into her throat, "Or—dare I call you Eleanor?" He came and sat beside her, taking her hands in his. "Please put me out of suspense and tell me you'll become Lady Carlton. I want to send the announcement to the *Morning Gazette*. I want to tell the whole world of my fortune." He lifted her hands and laid his lips to them.

"*Shh*. Please, Lord Carlton—"

"Matthew, I insist."

"No, I dare not. Lord Carlton . . ." Pausing, Eleanor almost lost her resolve when his expression turned desperate, then hardened. He wrenched his hands from hers and faced front, but her pleading gaze remained on his face. "Please, believe me grateful of the honor you've given me by offering for me. I am sensible of it—"

"Don't talk to me about gratitude," he ground out. "Do you mean to refuse me?"

"Yet I must be grateful," she replied. "I will never think of your proposal without recognizing the honor you've bestowed upon me. But I must refuse—"

"Eleanor, don't! You simply need more time." Lord Carlton leapt to his feet and began to pace in front of her.

Eleanor shook her head. "I don't. I know I won't change my mind. It is nothing you've done. It's simply that I don't return your feelings. I'm grateful for your friendship—"

"Friendship," he spat out. "I don't desire friendship." He walked to the chimney and laid his hand on the mantelpiece, his back to her.

"Nevertheless, it's of great value to me, and I hope you will see it that way too. My lord, you deserve a woman who returns your feelings. You deserve . . ."

Through sheer will, she adopted an encouraging tone. "You deserve a woman who will enjoy hosting great political parties and who can debate on the topics that inspire you. I want a quiet life—in the country, and not in London, if at all possible. I'm convinced, my lord, that you will see the wisdom in my refusal with time, and that you will be thankful I was steadfast."

Lord Carlton's expression was wretched when he turned to face her. Dismayed, angry even. Eleanor's mouth went dry at the prospect of remaining unmarried and without a living to fall back on. What if this were her only chance? *But it's the right thing to do. I know it is.*

Lord Carlton's arms dropped to his side. "I will not force my attentions upon you any longer, ma'am." He gave a short bow. "Your obedient servant."

With those words, he stalked across the room and yanked open the door, shutting it firmly behind him. Eleanor calculated she had only ten minutes for which she might indulge in a good cry and allow the red blotches to fade before Lydia appeared. She released the flood.

Chapter Thirty-Two

Early in the morning, Stratford pored over the accounts in his library. His attention kept wandering to the column where the Munroe hamlet income was recorded. Now the money went directly into a trust for Miss Daventry's future husband, and he refused to think more about whom that might be until he was in possession of the facts. He'd asked Ingram if she had accepted a proposal from Lord Carlton, but Ingram had just shrugged. Said it wasn't his affair. In any case nothing had been announced.

When the figures started to blur together on the page, Stratford stood. Phoebe should be down to breakfast by now and could help him with the mission he had in mind. He wanted to see if he still had a chance with Eleanor Daventry, and for that, he needed enough time to have a proper conversation with her.

Stratford found Phoebe alone at the table and was relieved he would not have to ask under Anna's piercing gaze. Pouring himself a cup of coffee, he sat. "I was thinking we might get up a picnic in Mary-le-Bone. You said there was an old fortress there you wished to see."

Smiling, Phoebe replied, "That was four years ago, Stratford, and I've since gone twice." Perhaps there was something in his expression because she assessed him shrewdly for a minute before adding, "But why not again? It's beautiful out, and it's supposed to remain so for the whole of this week after a rather chilly spring. I'll see if we can get something up with Anna. Who else would you like to invite?"

He scratched his head. "Well, why not get a bigger group organized? I've been wanting to talk more to Braxsen about his time in the Peninsula, and wherever he goes, Major Fitzwilliam goes too. So whatever ladies might be a good fit for our party besides you and Anna . . .”

Phoebe replied with perfect gravity. “I do believe Lydia might be keen on just such an outing. That would give us an even number.” She took a sip of her coffee and dotted her lip with the cloth napkin.

Stratford drummed his fingers on the table. “Well, I’ve noticed Mr. Richards quite a bit in Major Fitzwilliam’s company. I believe they will be going back to Spain at the same time this summer. We might have room for one more lady if he comes along.”

Phoebe did not disappoint. “I suppose it’s only natural we invite Eleanor Daventry. She’s staying with the Ingrams, and that will keep our numbers even.”

“Why, yes it will,” Stratford said, pleased to have organized the party so simply without having revealed his intentions. Phoebe would be the one to discuss it with Anna and the invitation would come from his sisters, with none the wiser. “Shall we say Saturday next?”

Stratford went out with a light step. It was only natural that he propose the outing to the ladies at the Ingrams’ straight away before they made other plans. As expected, he found them in the sitting room, as it was the peak hour for morning calls. He needed only find a moment to ask when no one else was around. When he was shown in, however, the drawing room was packed with people. *I’m never going to have a chance to speak to her at this rate.*

“Morning, Lydia.” He bowed over her hand. Without wasting words over someone who was crowded with suitors, he went to Miss Daventry and did the same. Her face was peaked, and he thought he detected a pleading look in her eyes when he touched her hand. Then he glanced at the gentleman with whom she was conversing. No wonder. It was Monty Smith, who had a reputation for being a dead bore.

“Worthing!” Monty cried out. “I was just explaining to Miss Daventry here the intricacies of the gas lighting. She has never heard it explained in quite such an in-depth manner, have you, Miss Daventry. *Eh?* Worthing, pull up a chair. I can back up to the part where I was describing the burners and valves and how they fit together. I don’t think Miss Daventry understood it the first time through—” He looked around for a chair. “There doesn’t seem to be a seat available at the moment, but if you’ll just stand right there—”

"Sorry, Monty." Stratford gave an apologetic shrug. "I'm on my way to see Ingram, and he requested I bring Miss Daventry for some domestic service he did not trouble to explain."

"Certainly, Lord Worthing." Miss Daventry's eyes were brimming with gratitude as she stood and nodded to Monty. "A pleasure, sir," she said, and placed her hand on Stratford's arm.

"Lydia," Miss Daventry called out as they passed by. "Your brother needs me. I will not be long." Surrounded by suitors, Lydia barely glanced at them.

He brought Miss Daventry into the hallway, where he accompanied her as far as the stairwell before turning to face her. "Miss Daventry," he said, solemnly. "I have told a Canterbury tale. Lord Ingram did not ask for you."

Miss Daventry's laughter rang out, though she tried to stifle it, and Stratford was so delighted, he couldn't help but laugh as well and lean his head toward hers. Though her amusement died down, the smile did not quit her eyes. "You have saved me, then," she said, her dimples deepening.

"With no one to listen to him, Monty Smith will not stay above ten minutes, and you may safely return to your suitors."

She rolled her eyes. "My suitors. Of course." Miss Daventry grinned and pulled her arm away. "Thank you, my lord."

"I am on my way up to see Ingram, but there is something I wish to discuss with you and Lydia when I return, so don't leave," he said.

She inclined her head and entered the library. "I will not leave."

In direct contrast to Stratford's sense of exhilaration was Ingram, who was sitting up in bed, crumpling one piece of parchment paper after another and aiming for the fire. "Stratford," he said. "Come in. Would you do me a service and pick up the papers I missed and toss them into the fire? Confidential, you know."

"Are you sure this is wise?" Stratford asked. "You need only one fiery ball to roll right back out of the grate and where will you be? You can't move from here."

"Oh, I suppose someone will come and drag me out in time," Ingram replied in a listless voice. "Or not. It's all the same."

"Blue-deviled, are you?" Stratford picked up the few balls of paper that had missed the fire and tossed them in. "How many more weeks are you bed-ridden?"

"The doctor said another four weeks. I need something to occupy me. I cannot bear the inactivity."

"Take up needlework," Stratford recommended. When that didn't elicit a smile, he continued, "I'm sure Fitz will tell you the whole when he comes, but he's still having Delacroix followed. The fellow is all over the place. Fitz had his trail take it a step further and rummage through his room when he knew Delacroix to be out. He found nothing in his possession. Nothing to make him suspect."

"He could already have sent it over . . ." Ingram stopped short. "No. I'm sure Delacroix would not entrust it to someone else. He must still have it in his possession. I'm almost certain he will take it to the French himself if he's worth his salt. Which means it's hidden somewhere else or he keeps it on his person."

"Or it's someone else entirely," Stratford said.

"Or that," conceded Ingram. "Listen. Have Fitz continue following Delacroix, but we're going to have to extend our search to idealists. Those who don't need the money, but who will sell the information on principle." He added, "Which is almost worse."

Stratford nodded. "We may have more information soon. Fitz is hearing rumblings—said one of his men might have a lead on when the next attempt will take place, as well as a description of the fellow. Don't ask me how, for he did not entrust *me* with the intelligence. Said he'd come today or tomorrow to give you a full report. That'll keep you occupied."

Ingram sighed loudly. "Yes, if we get a real lead. But I want to be doing it myself. Not passing it on to other people. Even competent ones like yourself." He looked Stratford over. "You seem in good spirits. Unusual for you to be so jolly. What gives?"

Stratford shrugged. "Nothing. My sisters are planning a picnic for Saturday, and I've been charged to invite Lydia and Eleanor—Miss Daventry."

"*Eleanor*, is it now?" Ingram replied with the ghost of a smile. "So you're taking my sister out? Or you're taking Eleanor?"

"Both," Stratford replied. "Or rather, my sisters are. It will complete our party. We'll have Fitzwilliam and Braxsen too."

"Your sisters don't even know Fitz." Ingram tried to puzzle it out. "This doesn't have to do with my project, does it?"

"Not in the least." And before Ingram could ask another question, Stratford said, "Well that jaw-me-dead must be gone by now. Let me go tell them about the outing. I'll stop by before Saturday." He escaped and headed back to the drawing room.

Miss Daventry had returned, and the room was empty but for her and Lydia, who was tying her bonnet. "I was just telling Lydia you wished to speak with us, but I had trouble convincing her to wait." Miss Daventry held her own bonnet in her hands.

"Yes, Stratford, what is it?" Lydia said. "I must spend some time outdoors or I shall go mad. This is the warmest day yet this spring."

"I shan't keep you," Stratford assured her. "I wished only to invite both of you to go riding with my sisters and me Saturday next. We want to make a day of it and bring a picnic. I believe Major Fitzwilliam will join us, as well as Mr. Braxsen and his friend Mr. Richards. His gaze sought out Miss Daventry's. "We would be delighted if you'd come."

Miss Daventry, eyes alight, looked to Lydia, who answered for them both. "That sounds delightful."

Chapter Thirty-Three

On Saturday, the party set out for Mary-le-Bone at a bright hour. Not even Lydia had tarried over breakfast when faced with the prospect of a good gallop. Stratford, leading his sisters to the Ingram household, converged upon Mr. Braxsen who was just arriving. They found Miss Daventry and Lydia with the horses saddled as they waited for John Richards, the new recruit Major Fitzwilliam had taken under his wing.

However, to Stratford's surprise, it was not Mr. Richards who headed toward them, but Mr. Amesbury. He directed a quizzing glance at Major Fitzwilliam.

"It was Richard's idea," the major said. "He was called away on urgent business, and when he met Mr. Amesbury at the club, who'd just returned to London, and discovered Amesbury was—" Fitz paused, trying, it seemed, to keep a straight face, "a great favorite with the ladies of the party, he thought it a perfect way to make up for his absence without skewing our numbers."

Stratford directed his gaze to Miss Daventry, and she returned it with a long-suffering look that had him choking back a laugh. She could say plenty with one look. Well, he would not have chosen Miss Daventry's past suitor as an ideal companion for their outing, but it would not hinder him from spending the day with her.

Amesbury rode up. "I believe I have beat my own record by a full two hours in having left my premises at such an ungodly hour. Worthing." He nodded and seemed about to greet the rest of the party, but caught himself when he came to Miss Daventry and settled instead for an all-encompassing nod.

Phoebe was delighted with the day ahead of them, and not even Mr. Amesbury's dour face could mar her enjoyment. Having redistributed the supplies for their picnic, Stratford gave the order to move forward, and they set off. The London streets were sparsely populated this early in the morning, and it was not long before they'd left town and rode down the country lanes that led to their destination.

"Who's got the picnic basket?" Anna asked her sister.

"Stratford has provided it, and he's given a portion to Major Fitzwilliam to carry and another to Mr. Braxsen," Phoebe responded. "Lydia was in charge of bringing the blankets we are meant to sit on, although I don't see if she's got them. Never mind. We shall contrive somehow."

"If Lydia remembered, I shall own myself astonished. You know she'll be the first to cry out when she realizes it. She can't bear to be seated in the dirt and ruin her dress." Anna's face showed what she thought of such paltry behavior.

"Lydia will have to learn to get accustomed to dirt if the major's suit prospers, as I expect it will," Phoebe said. She sat up in the saddle and breathed in the smell of freshly turned earth.

"The major's suit." Anna looked at her askance. "She will never accept him. I don't see how he dares pursue her. Ingram won't stand for it."

"Anna," Phoebe returned with a rare smile of smug complacence. "How little you pay attention. Next you will say our brother does not mean to add to our sisterhood by taking a wife." She looked pointedly at Eleanor, who was riding ahead with Stratford.

Anna's face took on a belligerent look. "Although I prefer her to Judith, I cannot see why he must needs get married now. What can he possibly see in her, apart from a bit of land that will add value to his own? I grant you, some men will marry for such a thing, but not our Stratford."

Phoebe looked at her in surprise. "Are you so opposed to the match? They will suit very well." Anna looked unconvinced, and Phoebe continued. "She's not a flirt, she's not a scandal-monger, she's not bracket-faced . . ."

"I agree with you. She is none of those things," Anna said, with no trace of her usual teasing. "But what *is* she? She's not vivacious, she's not

225

taking, she's not witty. She is nothing. I can't picture our brother hitching himself to her."

"She is one who will love our brother back," Phoebe said, simply.

Anna's jaw was set and her eyes were unusually somber. However, she had no time to reply as the group heard voices calling out to them.

"Hallo! What's this? Have you had the same notion as us to get up a picnic in the country to enjoy the fresh air?" Phoebe and Anna turned to see a party of four, led by Judith Broadmore and Lord Delacroix, with a redheaded woman and a dandy of a gentleman trailing behind. The party pulled up short to greet them, and Phoebe saw shock register on her brother's face.

"Shall we join parties?" Judith asked.

"Of course we shall," Mr. Amesbury said, his eyes on the other woman riding with Judith. "The greater the number, the more entertaining the party."

Stratford looked at Mr. Amesbury for a long moment. Then, after glancing at Miss Broadmore, he clicked his tongue and his horse shot ahead.

Eleanor watched the earl gallop to the head of the party and sought comfort in the fact that he had barely afforded Miss Broadmore a glance. Eleanor rode alone, as the only available gentleman was Mr. Amesbury, and he studiously avoided her, preferring to attach himself to Miss Redgrave, never mind that the gentleman she had come with was shooting daggers at Mr. Amesbury with his eyes.

Lord Worthing slowed his horse's steps and eventually came to a halt while he waited for the others to catch up. Lydia rode past with Mr. Braxsen, and Major Fitzwilliam followed, entertaining both Anna and Phoebe Tunstall. When Eleanor came abreast, the earl matched her pace.

"For a moment, I forgot that this was a day for company," he said, "and that I was fortunate enough to have yours."

"It is of no matter." Eleanor turned to face him with a bright smile. "We have the day ahead of us."

Lord Worthing returned her smile and then called out, "Look ahead," and pointed to the open countryside in front of them. "Now we shall have a good run." Eleanor had been waiting for only that, and though the earl had had a head start, she quickly matched his pace.

The party reached the fortress just before noon, and when they set up the picnic, Lydia discovered she had indeed forgotten the blankets. "Never mind," she said equitably, "although I'm sorry to have inconvenienced you all." She darted forward to take the portion of the picnic lunch, handed to her by Major Fitzwilliam. "A simple fare," she exclaimed, "It is just as I would wish."

Since Lydia appeared to be on excellent terms with the major, Eleanor could only surmise her earlier indifference had indeed been due to jitters that had now passed, and she was glad for Major Fitzwilliam's sake. She was glad for Lydia's too. He would be good for her.

"How did they find an imposter who so resembles our Lydia," Anna muttered just loud enough for those around her to hear. Lord Worthing laughed out loud.

Stratford was content watching Miss Daventry fill her plate and then lean back to take in the scenery around her. She presented a charming picture. Lunch was simple with cold meats and hard-boiled eggs, cut tomatoes, and wedges of country bread. However, they did manage to bring some dishes of jelly that had been carefully packed so as not to spill.

Mr. Amesbury and Mr. Braxsen's attention to Miss Broadmore and her friends was so thorough, Stratford had managed to avoid all notice of the interlopers. He did spare a moment to find humor in the gentlemen's rivalry for Miss Redgrave's attention that had caused even Braxsen to put aside his distaste of the "foreigner" and mingle with Delacroix. Now, Lord Delacroix's foppish friend offered to entertain them all with a game of charades, and his proposal was met with resounding enthusiasm.

Stratford stood. "You will not miss two from the party, I hope." He looked at Miss Daventry. "There is a patch of tulips that are growing wild near the ruined farmhouse over there. Would you care to come help me gather them?"

Miss Daventry glanced at the others in the group, then grasped his outstretched hand and stood. "I believe it would please Lady Ingram if we did not come back empty-handed." As they walked past the others, Stratford noticed the calculating look in Judith's eyes, but he ignored it. Nothing would distract him from today's pleasure, and now, walking with Miss Daventry, he felt as free as the open field before them.

"It's a fine day," Miss Daventry said, taking brisk steps, as one accustomed to walking. She sounded as happy as he felt.

"It's fine company I keep," he responded. "May I?" He held out his arm, and she put her hand in it so that he was able to pull her close. When they approached the swath of color, part of which had been hidden from view by the dip in the land, he took pleasure in her gasp of surprise. At one point, these tulips had been planted, but over the last century, they had spread into a riot of colors of all sizes.

"Where shall we begin?" she asked, wide-eyed.

"Here," Stratford said, and he bent down to snap the stem of a white tulip, the tops of whose petals were tinged with pink. "We will start here, and I will gather a bouquet so enormous that when I present it to you, you will be hard-pressed to see over your horse's head to ride home."

"How thoughtful," Miss Daventry murmured, and with a mischievous grin, added, "You do like enormous bouquets, my lord."

He had to laugh. She had not forgotten the apology bouquet he'd sent to the Ingram drawing room. "For that trick, ma'am, we shall have a competition. I propose that for one quarter of an hour, we go our separate ways. I will attend to the patch of tulips on the other side of that hedgerow, and you gather safely here in full view of our party. When I return, whomever has gathered the most . . . unique bouquet wins."

"And what is to be the reward, my lord?" she asked, her face turned up in earnest.

Stratford's gaze flicked to her lips, then to her eyes again, the corner of his mouth lifting. "That remains to be seen."

Miss Daventry's eyes widened in surprise, but Stratford turned before he could see more of a reaction. He did not want to tempt fate. Beyond the hedgerow, there was a patch of black tulips, purple ones, and yellow so deep as to be gold. He would create for her a bouquet made of these three varieties.

Eleanor had finished gathering a large bundle of tulips in a multitude of colors. She stood and looked around, her arms as full as she could carry, but didn't see Lord Worthing on the other side of the hedge. She had gathered so many tulips, it was nearly impossible to carry them all, but she was determined to leave not one behind.

Looking down at her awkward bundle, she laughed at her folly in having tried to win their little contest. *Reward, my lord? Or punishment.* The smile died on her lips when she saw Miss Broadmore heading her way carrying a basket.

"Miss Daventry," Judith said. "I noticed you'd gone off without bringing anything to carry your flowers. I've brought you a basket. You may put your tulips in here to carry them back to our picnic."

Eleanor mistrusted the gesture coming from someone who had never been kind to her, but with her hands full of cut blossoms, the green stems threatening to stain her riding habit, she had no choice but to accept the offering. "Thank you. You are right. We did not come prepared."

"I aim to be of service," Miss Broadmore replied. Darting a glance toward the hedgerow, she added, "You'd best return with your flowers and find a method of transporting them so Lord Worthing may use the basket in his turn."

Eleanor held the handle with one hand and carefully placed the tulips in the basket by twos and threes. It allowed her the moment's reflection she needed to decide how to respond. Insisting she stay behind to wait for Lord Worthing would be equal to declaring her regard for him in front of his former fiancée. She could not do it.

"Very well," Eleanor said. Turning, she walked toward their group.

Stratford had gotten his tulips arranged in just the way he wanted them, with the blacks interspersed with purples encircling the golden ones in the middle. He rounded the hedgerow, eager to see Miss Daventry's reaction to his offering, but instead nearly ran into Miss Broadmore. Impatient, he searched the field beyond her, already having an inkling she had scared away Miss Daventry.

"I brought her a basket to carry her tulips," Miss Broadmore said. "Have no fear. She will empty the contents into something suitable and will walk back to meet you. In the meantime, would you allow me to put my hand in your arm, my lord? The ground is uneven, and I'm afraid of twisting my ankle."

Stratford couldn't refuse. He shifted the tulips to one arm and held out his other arm. Having performed this service, he walked as quickly as he could with Judith hobbling alongside him.

"Wait, Stratford," she said in a sharp voice. "*You* will be the one to cause me to fall if you force me to gallop about at this pace. Only think how tiresomely slow it will take us all to get home then. You won't be able to attend to your *Miss Daventry*." Her last words came out in a sneer.

"You knew it was over between us," Stratford said. "The nature of my current interest is none of your concern." He could see Eleanor ahead, her back to him as she searched through her saddlebag. *For something to hold the flowers,* he thought. *What a stupid thing not to have brought spare baskets with me.* Beyond her, the party was still caught up in the game of charades.

Judith's voice brought him back to his surroundings. "You didn't even give us a chance," she said, her voice low and angry. "I've changed, and it didn't occur to you to notice. To think I turned down Lord Garrett for you."

Startled, he faced her and pulled her hand out of his arm. "That was foolish. I would not have had you do that after three years with no contact between us. How could you know whether I still had any feelings for you or whether I'd moved on?" He strode forward while she struggled to keep up.

"You could not have," she hissed. "You were at war, and there was no time for a betrothal."

They were almost upon the party, and Stratford shook his head. "Still. It was most foolish of you, Judith."

The game of charades was at its peak with Phoebe making the most ridiculous gestures by twisting her fingers to make spectacles around her eyes and then pointing to her legs.

"A monkey."

"A rabbit."

"I'm sure this is not decent," Phoebe protested.

"My great-aunt Helen!"

There was a round of laughter, and Phoebe stood with her hands on her hips. "Bluestocking," she said in exasperation. "It was bluestocking."

"You're not supposed to tell us," Lydia said. "You're ruining the game."

"Stratford has returned with his treasure, and I'd enough of making a fool of myself," Phoebe replied, glancing at his tulips.

Stratford, his mood spoiled, was anxious to start back. "Come. Let us saddle up our horses. We'd better get a start if we are to return before tea."

When everyone had begun gathering their belongings, he sought out Miss Daventry, glad that no one had made a comment about his bouquet. She was giving a lump of sugar to her horse, but she turned as he approached.

"Miss Daventry," he said in a low voice. "This is your bouquet, but I will not make you carry it, of course. Can you guess what it is?"

She looked at his artfully arranged bouquet in blacks and purples, with the deliberate point of gold in the center, and shook her head.

Stratford raised an eyebrow. "Think on it, and hazard a guess. And only then I will tell you," he said.

Eleanor could only wonder what had transpired between Lord Worthing and Miss Broadmore, but whatever it was, it gave her cause for hope. Upon his return, Lord Worthing had sought her out immediately while Miss Broadmore, eyes glinting, marched over to Lord Delacroix and leaned over to whisper something to him.

On their ride home, Lord Worthing spoke little to Eleanor, but neither did he leave her side. The two groups parted ways at the street where they had chanced upon Miss Broadmore earlier, and their own party reached the Ingram house in time for tea. Fatigued by emotions as much as exertion, Eleanor put her reins to the side, preparing to dismount, but Lord Worthing jumped down from his horse to assist her. His gaze held hers as he reached his hand up to help her alight.

Retaining Eleanor's hand in his, he passed the reins to the stable boy and led her to the shaded awning. She could hear the major asking Lydia about the Skeffington ball, but they were shielded from view by the edge of the mews.

"Have you divined the meaning of my bouquet?" Lord Worthing asked.

"You expect your answer so soon?" she asked. "No, my lord, I cannot hazard a guess."

His eyes searched hers, and under his scrutiny, her chest rose with quick breaths. The earl seemed to accept her answer because he asked, instead, "Lady Ingram said you will attend the Skeffington ball?"

Eleanor nodded, breathless.

Lord Worthing took a step closer. "I would like to escort you into dinner there," he said. "I find that I'm increasingly desirous of your company and have little enough chance to enjoy it." Before she could respond to his words, or even register them, he reached up and touched his gloved fingers to her cheek. "Will you save the dance before dinner for me?"

"Yes," Eleanor whispered. Her cheek tingled, and she could feel a coursing joy sweep through her, tugging at the corners of her mouth.

Then Lord Worthing leaned down, his cheek close to hers, to whisper, "The bouquet is a metaphor."

He stepped away. "Till Thursday then, Miss Daventry." Tipping his hat, he strode to his horse and called out to the footman standing by. "You there. Take these flowers and bring them to Miss Daventry's room. Provide some water for them."

Eleanor stood, rooted to the spot. She was not sure she could move, even if she tried. Five days. She must wait five days.

Chapter Thirty-Four

$\mathcal{E}$leanor dressed for Mrs. Skeffington's ball in a state of dreamy anticipation. She had hoped to catch a glimpse of Lord Worthing in the
days before the party, particularly at Mrs. Penniwraith's assembly, but he
did not make an appearance. At least, he didn't come before they took an
early leave, the crush proving too much for Lady Ingram.

Her selection of new dresses had dwindled to nearly nothing, but she
chose with an eye to looking her best and settled on a sage green gown,
cut in a low square neckline with lace extending from the cap sleeves. Lady
Ingram's maid curled her hair and attached a necklace very like emeralds,
but in paste, to match the dress.

She knew the minute he walked in. He sought her gaze and raised his
hand in a half-salute, eyes sparkling. Eleanor trembled with anticipation.
Gone was the agony of indecision, of not knowing how he felt. She fought
to keep her mouth demure, though she felt like grinning.

When Eleanor turned, she was glad she hadn't worn her heart on her
sleeve. Harriet Price had caught the exchange and fairly bared her teeth
in animosity. Eleanor was dreading the day when Harriet's mean-spirited
jealousy would cause her harm, but she decided not to worry about what
Harriet Price was thinking tonight. This evening contained too much to
enjoy.

Eleanor turned her attention to Lydia. "Who are you looking for? Although, if it's who I think it is, he's over there." She gestured with her chin.

"I don't know that I'm looking for anyone in particular," Lydia said,
raising an eyebrow, but she peeked at Major Fitzwilliam. As if drawn by a
cord, the major strode toward them.

"Miss Ingram, how glad I am to see you this evening. I spoke with your brother before coming, and he invited me to a family dinner next week. He has promised to be seated at the dinner table for the occasion." Major Fitzwilliam bowed and spoke and smiled all at once, so clearly smitten to be in Lydia's presence. As an afterthought, he added, "Good evening, Miss Daventry."

"Well, if my brother has promised to be at the table, he will surely accomplish it. He has always done whatever he set his mind to." Lydia opened her fan and shielded her profile, ignoring a gentleman who was trying to catch her attention.

Major Fitzwilliam stepped between the gentleman and Lydia, cutting her off from the man's line of sight. "In the meantime, do say you'll dance with me for the next waltz? Save the country dances for some other poor fellow." Eleanor suppressed a smile. Lydia would not stand a chance. One accustomed to commanding men on the battlefield would know the way to conquer a woman's heart.

"Very well," Lydia said. "This next one. Before supper."

Major Fitzwilliam gave a slight bow, eyes gleaming. "To which I hope you'll allow me to escort you."

Eleanor had been witness to this conversation, but the major had included her in his address in the way of co-conspirator so she wouldn't feel left out. Now she looked around and caught sight of Judith Broadmore and Harriet Price deep in conversation, and she noticed them look her way more than once.

She frowned. As Lydia went to dance with the major, Eleanor was left alone, and she took a seat on the sidelines, searching for a glimpse of Lord Worthing. *Where was he? He had specifically requested this dance.*

On the other side of the room, Judith was now in conversation with another woman, whose eyes widened, her hand at her mouth. Eleanor hated to think who might be the object of their gossip and shoved down a feeling of apprehension she was sure was misplaced.

"I wanted to come sooner, but I was detained. Please accept my apology, Miss Daventry. It could not be helped." Lord Worthing's face was haloed by the light of the chandelier, and the creases in his jaw were set in shadowed relief. "Though to leave you alone is unpardonable."

The relief she felt on his arrival nearly took Eleanor's breath away. She had not seen him approach. "You are forgiven, my lord."

He helped her to stand and placed her hand on his arm. "A pardon granted so rapidly? We've come a long way," he quizzed. "We have missed the waltz, but I see it's nearly supper. I've come to hold you to your promise. Shall we go in?"

Throngs of people were already making their way toward the dining room, where large tables were set up with chattering groups around each one. Eleanor was too nervous for speech, but the noisy bustle of conversation swirling around them made words superfluous. Lord Worthing led them to a table with two empty seats.

"I don't know where the others are, but let them find their own way," he said, giving Eleanor a private smile. "May I leave you here for a few moments while I search out some refreshments?"

She nodded. Lord Worthing went to the sideboard and returned, balancing a plate with sandwiches and a couple slices of ham, as well as two glasses of capillaire syrup and water. "I think Mrs. Skeffington is trying to rival Almack's in her choice of banquet," he murmured in Eleanor's ear, giving her a tingle of delight. Despite the crowd, she felt as if there were only the two of them.

"Oh-*ho*! You've saved no seats for us, have you?" Major Fitzwilliam teased, stopping with Lydia on his arm. "And have you given any thought for your sisters?"

"How trying it is to be burdened with sisters," Lord Worthing bantered, his eyes on Eleanor. To the major, he said, "They're well taken care of. Anna's with Harris and Phoebe's with Mr. Drake. They're friends, so I can count on the men to toe the line. See? They're seated over there."

Lydia touched Eleanor's shoulder. "I believe we will leave you to your supper," she said, giving her a squeeze.

Eleanor watched them go as Lord Worthing took a sip of his drink. He set it down and focused on her. "Your first Season is coming to a close, Miss Daventry. Did it play out as you had envisioned it?"

"Nearly," she said. "I hadn't expected to be solicited to dance quite as much, or to make so many friends. It was more delightful than I could have imagined." She placed her hand on the tablecloth, unable to take even one bite of her supper.

Lord Worthing seemed to take in her words. "I cannot say this Season turned out at all as I had expected."

"Did it not?" Eleanor asked, her voice faint. What did he mean? Did he regret their connection?

"No, I—" He stopped short, then with a change in subject she was not prepared for, asked, "Have you at last guessed at the meaning of my arrangement?"

The bouquet had sat on the small table in her bedroom since he had given it and was blooming still. He had found straw-like grass to secure the bundle when he gathered the flowers, and she left it exactly as he had given it. It looked like a black-eyed Susan, only inverted. The black on the outside, the yellow in the middle.

"I have not been able to guess, my lord."

Lord Worthing leaned in and murmured, "The black and purple tulips are the stormy sky. The storms that hit when your life twists in a way you do not expect. The yellow in the middle is the bright ray of sun. The hope amidst the storm."

He paused until she met his gaze. "*You*, Miss Daventry, are the sun."

The last thing Stratford had planned on doing tonight was to declare himself in public—having witnessed Carlton's rejected suit and humiliation. However, when he saw the joy his words had produced in Eleanor, infusing her eyes with a happy light, he could not help himself. "Miss Daventry—"

Stratford was interrupted by the lady of the house, who came and tapped him on the shoulder, asking if she might have a word with him. Mrs. Skeffington looked at Miss Daventry with hard eyes, adding, "Alone."

With an apologetic glance at Miss Daventry, he followed Mrs. Skeffington out of the dining room, and they wound their way along the edge of the ballroom until they reached the corridor leading to the private wing. There she stopped and turned to face him.

"Lord Worthing, I feel compelled to inform you that you have been mistaken in the reading of Miss Daventry's character." Mrs. Skeffington was laboring under some strong emotion, and she forced calm into her words. "Miss Daventry's mother is a well-known lady of easy virtue on the Continent."

Stratford lifted his brows, anger rising. "I know her mother had the most unusual marriage. She ran away with a French count before she had put off her blacks. But she *is* married. And all this happened when Miss Daventry was but seven years old. Her mother has not returned to England since."

"I have it on good authority that there is a taint on that family, and she is not worthy to be received by society. At least not by any household that wishes to retain its reputation." Mrs. Skeffington peered into the rapidly filling ballroom and fanned herself.

Annoyed, Stratford protested. "What does any of this have to do with Miss Daventry? Her father was a gentleman, and she was good enough for my uncle to have taken her guardianship upon himself. Good enough for Lady Ingram to have sponsored her—"

"I'm afraid that's not all," Mrs. Skeffington continued. "I've spoken to one of her schoolmates, and Miss Daventry was seen climbing into her window *after midnight* on the very night the Latin teacher mysteriously fled his post. She had displayed quite an aptitude for the language and had been taking private lessons. When Miss Price questioned her about where she'd been, she refused to answer. Miss Daventry," Mrs. Skeffington concluded in awful triumph, "was having a liaison."

The room spun. Stratford's gaze remained fixed on Mrs. Skeffington as his mind went through the implications. If Miss Daventry was being accused of this by the host of tonight's ball, her reputation was in imminent danger. He must do something. He opened his mouth to speak, but Mrs. Skeffington was not finished.

"Lord Delacroix told me everything. If Miss Daventry's mother is of such easy virtue, it is no surprise that her daughter—" She would have gone on, but Stratford cut her off.

"Lord Delacroix is here?"

"Yes, he arrived not long ago—" Mrs. Skeffington was not destined to finish her thought because Stratford left abruptly, depriving her the satisfaction of the earl's outrage.

"Well!" she huffed from behind him.

Eleanor, alone, began to feel ill-at-ease. More than one pair of eyes looked her way, and she saw women whispering behind their fans, staring above them at her with various expressions of horror and glee. She began to feel hot and looked around for her friends but saw none of them. Lydia was nowhere in sight. Phoebe had her back to her. Eleanor took one hesitant step toward Phoebe, but the sight of Anna staring at her with a strange expression made her stop.

The whispers and giggles grew louder as Eleanor forced herself to walk around the edge of the ballroom. Even the men leered at her in the most uncomfortable way. The stairwell leading to the exit was only a few steps farther.

Mrs. Skeffington met her at the bottom step and in a loud voice announced, "Miss Daventry, you are no longer welcome in my house. I request that you leave immediately."

Eleanor gulped, and managed, "But why? I didn't—" She looked around and saw only unfriendly faces. Lydia had turned by now, her expression a mix of shock and dismay. Phoebe was staring at her in horror, and Lord Worthing was nowhere to be found.

Mrs. Skeffington blocked her view of the crowd and any source of support she might receive. "Please leave," was the implacable reply.

Chapter Thirty-Five

*C*leanor held her expression in a mask until she had given the voucher for her coat and rushed through the front door. Only then did the tears fall, and she turned her face aside to avoid looking at the merry group making its way up the steps. She was vaguely aware of the pungent odors produced by a London street in June, and she walked a half-block before realizing she had nowhere to go. Even Lydia had been stunned, and Lydia's mother—oh, Lady Ingram had looked thunderous. Lord Worthing . . . Hot tears poured down her cheeks when she thought about the shock and disgust he must feel when he'd heard everything. It was surely Harriet's false tale that had led to her condemnation.

Eleanor went blindly for another block before slowing her pace and forcing herself to focus on her next move. It would be impossible to impose upon the Ingrams any longer. That much was sure. She considered the small amount left in her possession. There would be no time to request money from her aunt or to draw a draft on her bank. She would need to leave Lady Ingram's house immediately and with only the bare necessities, if possible before they returned from the party.

It would be a simple matter of packing a small portmanteau with only a change of dress, take a room in a hotel . . . *but I have no maid! They will never receive me* . . . There was no chance to think over this quandary further when Eleanor heard a voice calling her, a man stepping out of the shadows of a closed carriage. It was Lord Delacroix.

She drew back with a feeling of revulsion. "Lord Delacroix, I'm sorry, I cannot . . . I'm unable to stay and speak with you just now. I must reach Lady Ingram's house without delay."

"Ma'am, you are unattended. I cannot allow you—my honor as a gentleman will not permit me to let you continue without seeing you safely escorted."

Eleanor paused but was borne away by his insistence. "Miss Daventry, the Ingram house is some ways from here, and it would not do to walk there alone." When he saw she still hesitated, he added, "You need not fear I will press my advantage. I quite see I was mistaken in the reading of your character."

The sight of two gentlemen, heavily intoxicated, leering after a woman of questionable morals decided the affair. She allowed Lord Delacroix to assist her into the carriage. Once inside, she shrank to the edge of the seat, hoping he would take the other side and keep a proper distance. To her relief, he did.

"Shall we not open the windows?" she asked. "So that we are not quite private in the carriage?"

"And allow it to be seen you are driving alone with a gentleman?" Lord Delacroix shook his head. "*Je ne peux pas le permettre*. It would threaten your reputation. I've instructed the driver to bring the carriage around the corner of Lady Ingram's house so you can alight without being seen."

"That is kind of you . . . I hadn't thought clearly . . ." Eleanor reached into her reticule for a handkerchief and pressed it to her eyes, hands trembling from suppressed emotion.

"I'm sorry you suffered under the eyes of the ton. They can be cruel." There was bitterness in Lord Delacroix's voice, and Eleanor looked at him in surprise.

"Had you been there, then? How did you know what transpired?"

Lord Delacroix looked momentarily nonplussed. "I heard only the rumblings before I left. I was already on my way out."

"So did you know to find me here? Were you waiting for me?" Suspicion knotted her forehead, and Eleanor had difficulty drawing a breath.

"How could I possibly know which direction you would turn? I left because I had a rendezvous to keep, *mademoiselle*." His eyes narrowed, and he stared at a spot above the squabs of the carriage. "My interests lay in another direction."

Eleanor bit her lip, wondering to what poor creature he was referring. "Am I taking you out of your way, sir?"

"Only the slightest *détour*. It's nothing to speak of." With that, silence reigned.

Eleanor worried at one of the lower buttons on her spencer. Now she was well and truly in a fix. She would not find a husband, and although she had renounced the idea before her London Season, she had begun to hope and now felt its absence acutely. *You are the sun . . .*

Lord Worthing's face, from when he spoke those words, hovered in her vision, and Eleanor drew a sharp breath from pain so acute it stole her senses. There would be no stern husband to cajole, no children tugging at her skirts, no hearth to sit before and embroider as she presided over a merry family. A blissful fantasy she had only recently dared dream was dashed, and its loss was more painful than if she'd never hoped at all.

There would be no comfortable income from the property she inherited. She would likely have to serve as a school teacher—if even that position were not to be denied her—and an occupation that had once seemed a natural choice for one who refused to settle for anything less than love or independence now appeared stark. The property would revert back to the earl, or his descendent, on her eventual death. Eleanor shook her head bitterly at these reflections, though she was of too prosaic a disposition to consider throwing herself into the Thames. Perhaps if she were lucky, a virulent strain of influenza might carry her away.

The carriage rumbled over cobblestones, which made their way to a smoother path. The noises from the streets ceased to penetrate to where Eleanor sat, and she darted forward to slide open the shade of the carriage window. Her efforts were blocked by the gloved hand grasping hers, which Lord Delacroix shot out from his otherwise lazy posture. "I told you it would not be seemly to be spied in a carriage alone with a man."

Eleanor's voice held the barest tremor. "Surely we would have reached Lady Ingram's by now. I did not know it to be so far."

"We have reached it, *ma chérie*, and we've left it behind on our way to Dover. I have other plans, which will not entail your needing to collect your belongings." His hand still gripping hers, Lord Delacroix opened the window shade closest to his side and peered out.

Eleanor forced the fear from her voice and spoke calmly. "The other rendezvous . . . your other interest . . ."

". . . *n'est pas venue.*" Grief was replaced by terror as his chilling words settled into her marrow. "The gentleman in Paris, who holds my future in his hands, requested I bring a pretty, young Englishwoman when I come. Fate smiled upon me when she placed you in my path. My lady friend did not come, but I find in her absence, you'll do."

Chapter Thirty-Six

Stratford, witnessing the scene of Eleanor's departure on the heels of what he had just heard, pushed through the crowd to reach her. The hostess's voice rang out in sharp accents, *Miss Daventry, you are no longer welcome in my house,* and he saw Eleanor's face, pale but dignified, as she turned toward the cloak room.

The music had stopped, and silence filled the room only for a minute before the crowd burst into speech with gasps and muffled laughter. Skirts bustled from one group to another to exchange their speculation over the event, and Stratford saw Lydia, frozen next to Lady Ingram, who wore a forbidding expression.

He could not get to the door. The crowd was thick, everyone delighted with the scene, straining so as not to miss anything and closing gaps so they could be the first to comment on what had happened. Stratford shoved through to his left where a group of gentlemen stood, and one grabbed his arm.

"Leave her," came Amesbury's bored voice. "I warned you. You are well out of that fix."

Stratford yanked his hand free and continued to push forward, nearly through to the other side of the crowd when he was held back again, this time by Mr. Braxsen. Braxsen's eyes held sorrow, and he shook his head, the most emotion Stratford had seen in him.

"Nay. Leave her for the moment. You have your sisters to think about too, and Lady Ingram is demanding to see you. Miss Daventry is innocent of these accusations, I am sure. But there is a smarter way to go about clearing her name than giving more food for gossip by running after her."

Stratford's shoulders slumped. Braxsen was right. If he ran after her, the ton would think she was his courtesan. The damage might already be done. He looked for his sisters and saw Phoebe weaving her way to his side, unhurried and stately.

"Stratford, you know this is not true," she said. "I don't know Harriet Price all that well, but she has the worst reputation for a gossip-monger—a known trouble-maker. Her source cannot be trusted."

Before Stratford could reply, Carlton appeared at his side, his words nearly drowned out by the gossip flowing freely around them.

Carlton had heard Phoebe's words, and he bit out, "*She* is the source. Miss Price saw it herself. Gossip occurs for a reason. It may be puffed out of proportion, but a grain of truth lies at the heart of it."

Stratford looked at Carlton in disgust. "You were never worthy of her."

Phoebe left Stratford and went to Lydia, whose mother had sent for the carriage, stopping mid route in the ballroom to confer with another dowager. Phoebe stayed with Lydia in quiet conference, and when it looked as if Lydia would get upset, brought her to a more intimate spot behind the column.

Turning his back on Carlton, Stratford watched as the major went over to interrupt the *tête à tête* Lydia was sharing with Phoebe. Then there was a voice at his elbow.

"Stratford, I'm sorry to see there was an unpleasant report about someone who is so nearly connected to you. I know you hate scandal." Judith rested her hand on his sleeve, her expression haughty.

When he said nothing, she went on. "I knew her mother was in some disgrace, but I was willing to give her the benefit of the doubt. There's no reason to think she'd go in her mother's footsteps. Yet . . . after what we've just heard, it seems I was wrong to have acknowledged her. I was trying to be kind, for your benefit, though I admit I had my doubts."

Judith inched closer to Stratford, looking over the crowd. "Harriet said she saw her with her own eyes climbing up the trellis in the middle of the night. If you were thinking of aligning yourself with Miss Daventry, you may wish to reconsider."

Stratford turned to Judith savagely. "Who told you about her mother? Where do you have this piece of fact?" He spat out the last word in irony.

"Why, I had it from François Delacroix. He used to meet her mother when visiting friends on the Continent. 'She was not at all the thing,' he told me. And it's no surprise, considering her mother's upbringing. Who can predict the outcome when a gentleman marries a Cit?" Judith gave a shrug. "This is why it's so important to consider all facets when making an alliance."

You made clear your revulsion for my mother's upbringing when you turned down my offer. Why are you now here? This wild thought flashed through Stratford's mind, but instead he asked, "When did you hear this from Delacroix?"

"Just this evening." Turning an innocent face to his, Judith added, "I'm sorry, Stratford. I thought you would want to form your own opinion."

"And so I still do." Stratford stalked across the room to where his sisters and friends were gathered in a group. Crooking his fingers with an imperious summon, he said, "Anna, Phoebe, let's go."

"But what are you going to *do*, Stratford?" Anna said, following in his wake. Phoebe stayed behind whispering furiously in Lydia's ear.

"I must go as quickly as I can," Stratford replied.

Major Fitzwilliam, his eyes fixed on Lydia, laid his hand on Stratford's arm. "Worthing, wait," he said. Resisting an impulse to shake the major's hand off, Stratford stood in silence.

"Stratford, may I have a word with you in private?" Lydia asked.

He moved to follow, with barely concealed patience, but Lydia stopped short. "Major Fitzwilliam, if you will be so good as to come, I'd like you to hear what I have to say."

There was an unoccupied room off the corridor on the first floor, and Stratford went in, followed by the major. "Phoebe already knows," Lydia said, "and Anna you may as well come."

When the entire party was assembled in the room, Stratford said, "Make it quick, Lydia, I beg of you. I must not delay."

"Stratford, *you* know how I was when my father died. I felt I had lost everything. My father always made me feel special and never foisted me off on the nurse if he had time to spend with me. After he died, I had no one. Of course, I don't blame Freddy now, for I can see he had quite his share of burdens that come from being the heir. But I held it against him at the time."

Stratford made an impatient gesture, and Major Fitzwilliam glared at him.

"I was difficult," Lydia continued, "and when my governess could no longer manage me, my mother dismissed her and sent me to school, where

I met Eleanor. She was good to me. She never complained about her situation, though I know it was difficult to have lost her father and then have her mother run off and marry someone, leaving her behind as if she were of no importance. But Eleanor was unfailingly cheerful and courageous, and I became determined to imitate her spirit. I began to pay attention in my studies and participate in school activities. Only . . ."

"Go on," Fitzwilliam encouraged, and Lydia continued with difficulty.

"The Latin teacher was most attentive, and I fear he saw in me an easy prey. He convinced me to run away with him, and he was charming, and older, and I . . . I was weak and agreed to it. I confided in Eleanor, and she dissuaded me most earnestly to turn from what she said would be a ruinous path. When I didn't listen to her, she locked us both in the room and pocketed the key. I threatened to scream or grab it from her, but she only told me to go ahead and try. Then she put one foot over the windowsill and began to climb down. She knew I was terrified of heights and would not follow.

"I was mad enough that I could have screamed just to make sure she got caught. Except I thought it would all come out that I was the one who was going to elope. I have an inheritance, and they would have no trouble believing it was me."

"Why didn't she stay in the room with you? Why did she climb out the window at night to meet that devil?" Stratford paced the room, angry at Lydia for being selfish, angry at the Latin teacher for seducing innocent girls, even angry at Eleanor for having taken a risk. She was probably too innocent to know how great a risk it had been.

"Because the Latin teacher said he would wait for me at the same place and same time every night until I came. He knew it was not easy to get away when one wished, and he was sure I would eventually come. He was determined to ruin me. Eleanor went and threatened him."

"And spared you from ruin," the major finished.

"Yes." Lydia looked at him for the first time, her cheeks crimson, but refusing to look away. "I was so angry I didn't speak to her for the entire week before we left on Christmas break. And by the time school was back in session, I had realized the extent of my folly and begged Eleanor's forgiveness. She forgave me instantly."

Anna, darting a look at Lydia, said, "Was she able to escape with her virtue intact?"

"Anna, I have never been closer to strangling you," Stratford said.

"It's a fair question," Anna protested. "Perhaps, through no fault of her own, there is some substance to the rumors."

Stratford's jaw worked furiously. He spun around and strode to the fireplace. When he turned back, he was just in time to hear Lydia say in a succinct voice, "Eleanor has no cause to blush."

"How do you know?" Anna insisted.

"No one can play act that well," returned Lydia. "She tried to cajole me to good humor the very next day. She was natural. No one could have been like that after being harmed in such a way, least of all Eleanor. She hasn't a deceitful bone in her body."

"Enough." Stratford had been pacing back and forth, and he strode to the door. "Major, can you see to it my sisters get home? I don't want to spare another minute."

"Count on me," Fitz replied. "However, I came on horseback. May I take your carriage and lend you my horse?"

"Do whatever you need," Stratford said. "You'll find your horse in my stables when you arrive. I'll take my bays from there. Good night." He gave an all-encompassing nod and left.

Phoebe was the first to speak. "Please, Lord, Let him reach her in time." Lydia nodded vigorously, and Anna said nothing. "Anna," Phoebe continued, "shall we get our wraps? Lydia, if you give me your voucher, I can get yours as well."

"I must search for my mother," Lydia said vaguely, her eyes still locked with Major Fitzwilliam's. "She will have mine." Anna seemed perfectly ready to stay where she was, but Phoebe crooked her arm through her sister's and pulled her off.

Fitz took a step toward Lydia. "We must not stay here alone," he said. "If anyone were to find us . . ." Taking her by the elbow, he looked out the door that had not yet closed and saw there was no one in the corridor. He pulled Lydia after him and stepped behind a pillar on the edge of the ballroom. "Come with me here where we can talk privately without risking a scandal." Lydia stood with her back to the pillar, unable to meet his gaze.

"Miss Ingram," he said, but she did not lift her eyes to his. The major pressed on. "I owe a great debt to Miss Daventry."

When Lydia raised her eyes, she saw a faint smile on his face. "How can you look at me so, Major Fitzwilliam? How have you not taken the greatest dislike to me after learning of my folly?"

"You were a schoolgirl; you were grieving for your father . . ."

Lydia shook her head, "I don't see how you haven't thrown me over after witnessing my behavior this season. I've been nothing but weak-willed, foolish, and shockingly shallow. I can't fathom how you can still stand my friend after knowing everything you do about me."

Fitz took a step closer and, grasping her hand, he placed it on his chest, covering it with his own. "You see yourself as shrinking in fear, and I see someone who loves her brother desperately. You see yourself as volatile, and I see someone who is lively. You see yourself as shallow. I see to the heart beyond that. Of course I stand your friend. I hope I may become more dear to you than that."

When her gaze darted to his, he said, "Lydia, may I speak to your brother to request his permission to ask your hand in marriage?" Lydia was unable to reply and dropped her eyes to the medal pinned to his chest, so Fitz pushed on. "I cannot provide for you more than the simplest of life's elegances, and there will be periods where you'll need to choose between following the drum and taking up residence in London without me at your side."

When she still didn't answer or even look at him, he refused to falter. "But, my sweet, I promise you that no one will love you as I do, and if I have but one ambition for the rest of my life, it will be to secure your happiness."

"Why did you choose me?" Lydia asked, looking up at last. "Did you suspect I could handle the rigors of a soldier's life better than I let on? For I know I did not lead anyone else to think that." She gave the ghost of a smile.

"I *do* think that," Fitz replied. "I think you have a great deal more gumption than you let on. But I chose you, my sweet Lydia, because once I laid my eyes on you, I couldn't take them off again. It was all arms down—a complete capitulation. Do you think you can find it in you to love me back?" He waited, stoic, and when she lowered her eyes, he raised his fingers and lifted her chin, refusing to break her gaze.

"You may talk to my brother," Lydia whispered. It was all she had time for before Lady Ingram bore down upon them, her expression livid. She refused to acknowledge Major Fitzwilliam. Lydia gave one lingering look before following her mother to the front doors. When the major turned, Anna and Phoebe were nearly at his side.

"We have our coats and are ready to set out," Phoebe said. Major Fitzwilliam nodded, his gaze fixed on Lydia's retreating form.

Later, as she and Anna prepared to wait for Stratford's return, Phoebe remarked how very bright the major's eyes seemed that night.

Chapter Thirty-Seven

The coach rumbled on, and the swaying motion did little to lull Eleanor's nearly overwhelming despair. Lord Delacroix, thankfully, attempted no conversation, and she was allowed her own private reflections. After two hours on the road, the carriage lurched to a stop, and private reflections were of little consolation. Terror rose up within her as she contemplated what he might be willing to do.

Lord Delacroix's demeanor was inoffensive. He got down and spoke a word to the driver, then held his hand up to help her alight. She ignored it, and they stepped into the courtyard, which was still bustling with people, as the hour was not yet advanced. Lanterns were placed on the bench outside the door, and there were lights in the sconces set at odd angles in the yard. Eleanor followed him into the inn, her eyes searching for possible opportunities of escape—but so far she saw nothing, no one she could apply to.

"A private parlor for my sister and me," Lord Delacroix said to the innkeeper, who led the way through the crowded taproom toward the back.

"You're in luck, milord," the innkeeper said, bowing deferentially. "The gentleman who has reserved this room did not come. My wife is just roasting the fowl, and we have a suckling pig left over from lunch if that'll suit. Shall I bring you a meal and some drink?"

"That will be excellent," Lord Delacroix replied, "and a glass of lemonade for my sister. The landlord looked sideways at Eleanor and bowed himself out, closing the door behind him.

"Sit," Lord Delacroix said. "There's no point in hovering near the doorway. For one thing, you will allay suspicion if you act naturally. I did you a service by saying you were my sister. You'll not be compromised until we are well away from England, and by the time I bring you to France, my host will give you a different type of consequence. In any case, whether or not I had come along, your reputation would have been ruined."

"My reputation will *not* be ruined because I have done nothing to deserve it. I will find a way to clear my name," Eleanor said, regally. But she sat as he directed, knowing her words would have no substance the minute he forced his attentions on her.

After his directive, Lord Delacroix didn't seem aware of her existence, and she wasn't sure if she should find it reassuring or worrisome. The landlord came with the promised fare, and when he bowed himself out again, Eleanor noted the knife that lay next to her plate, as Lord Delacroix served her boiled potatoes and a cut of meat.

Eleanor sat, ramrod straight, and as Lord Delacroix bent down to take a bite, she slid the knife into the sleeve of her dress and used her other hand to drink her lemonade. He polished off the contents of his glass and set it down with a clunk. "Remove the knife from your sleeve and put it back on the table. It will do you no good, and it will only make me angry."

Lips pinched, she lay the knife on the table with dignity.

Major Fitzwilliam's horse was waiting at the door as soon as Stratford exited the Skeffington manor. He swung into the saddle and turned toward Ingram's, hoping he'd find Eleanor there. Before he could ride off, a man in dull colors and a low-brimmed hat sidled up and took hold of the horse's reins. Alarmed, Stratford raised his whip to strike.

"Easy, guv. I see you wid the major's rum prancer, and I must 'ave words wid him." The man lifted his eyes, and Stratford could see him clearly in the lamplight.

"How do you know the major?" Stratford asked, lowering his whip. The man didn't appear to be a source of danger.

"He 'ad me follow Dela-craw. That's right, milord. I see you're a sharp cull that don't miss a thing. This is 'bout that furriner, and the major bade me find you if he warrn't 'vailable."

"What is it?" Stratford demanded, impatient to be off. "What is it about Delacroix?"

"Cove's took a conweyance bound fer Dover with a trunk strapped to, if I'm not mistook. I followed him to 'Aymarket, and 'e took up a flash mort who dunnit look right pleased."

"A woman," exclaimed Stratford. What did she look like?

"Green dress, yaller coat . . ." *Eleanor.*

"I must be off," Stratford said. "Major Fitzwilliam will be out soon, accompanying two women. Please do not frighten them, but try and get word to him where I've gone."

"I'll do, cap'n." Before the man could say any more, Stratford was off.

Stratford urged the major's horse in the direction of Cavendish Square and, in short order, his bays were harnessed to the phaeton. *Delacroix is run off his legs*, he thought as he urged his horses forward as quickly as London traffic would allow. Therefore, the man had nothing to lose. They must have had more than an hour's head start, and although that was reassuring odds with his bays, he could not be sure of catching them without stopping at each posting house on the way, and he must not miss. The boat would set out when the tide was full, and if he could not overtake them before Delacroix left for France, all would be lost.

Stratford's phaeton was far lighter than whatever carriage Delacroix rumbled in, which gave him hope. After an hour of hard riding, he came to the first posting inn and stopped only long enough to be sure no carriage was hidden from view. There was none, and one glance was all it took to see that no one of quality was inside.

Stratford didn't think they would have stopped so soon on the road. Delacroix must be as anxious to get to the coast as Stratford was to find him. But he couldn't take a chance that he had missed them, and he knew Miss Daventry was a resourceful young woman. No, he must stop at every posting inn on the way.

As he rode on, it dawned on him that his thoughts had only been for Eleanor. Why was Delacroix leaving *now*? Fitz's intelligence had warned them something was afoot and that it would occur this evening or next. And here was Delacroix in dun territory and leaving for France. It had to be him. But what role did Eleanor have in all this? Stratford spotted another posting house just ahead, and though he almost passed it by, he pulled his reins in and dismounted.

His caution was well-served. There was a carriage off to the side with Delacroix's crest, horses unharnessed and dipping their heads into a bucket of feed. He had not even tried to hide them. The villain must not have thought anyone would go after Eleanor.

The hostler rushed over as soon as he pulled in, and Stratford tossed him the reins, slipping a coin into the man's outstretched hand. "Give them some water and a rub-down, but don't unharness them. I shall not stay."

Entering the crowded taproom, he spotted the door to the private parlor and advanced toward it. The landlord darted to his side to intercept. "Milord, the room is occupied at present. You were not here when your letter said you'd arrive."

Stratford pushed him aside and flung the door open. It clattered against the wall, revealing Miss Daventry seated across from Lord Delacroix. She stood, and he had only time to glance at her pale face, her frightened eyes, before he turned his gaze to Delacroix.

"The devil," he said, furiously.

Miss Daventry moved to the side of the room, and he could hear the fear and uncertainty in her voice. "I'm glad you are come, my lord. I was taken against my will." *Why is she afraid? I'm here now.*

He spared her only the briefest of looks, not wanting to take his eyes off the scoundrel still seated at the table. He did not trust him.

Lord Delacroix stood and began clapping his hands, "Bravo," he said. "You've come all this way only to interrupt what was a nice little *tête à tête*. Now that you see where things stand, why don't you turn back to London?"

"Oh *ho!*" Stratford could not contain his fury or his words. "I imagine you'd find that mighty convenient, but you'll pay for your ill-usage of Miss Daventry. And while I'm teaching you a lesson, *sir*, you'll answer for the packet of information stolen from the war offices, which you're planning to drop into enemy's hands. Don't bother to deny it."

"So that's to be laid at my door, is it?" Delacroix rolled his eyes and sat down. "Good lord."

Stratford paused. His certainty that Delacroix was the spy had only come about after the man had abducted Eleanor. Until then, he hadn't been fully convinced of Delacroix's guilt, despite rather strong evidence to the contrary. Maybe his attachment to Eleanor had blinded his impartiality in this case, and he was seized with feelings of doubt. Still, he must see this completely through.

"All evidence points to you," Stratford said. "Your leaving London coincides with the information drop to the enemy. You were not at Almack's the night the document was stolen from headquarters. And our intelligence tells us the spy in question is likely to be of French descent." He jabbed his finger at Delacroix. "You were there when Lord Ingram fell, and I'm sure if you came back, it was to finish the job. Except you were too late!"

Lord Delacroix threw up his hands. "Whatever will you throw at me next? Had you considered I would *not* make an appearance that morning if I were guilty of what you accuse me? That I wouldn't be so paper-skulled as to be caught in the vicinity?"

"Your appearance was to throw off suspicion. A case of double dealing. You come back on the scene, show yourself as an angel of mercy, and all suspicion of your actions is cast aside." Stratford untied his cape and threw it off, then pulled at his neck cloth. "Tell me. If you are innocent, why flee the country with Miss Daventry? Why not stay where you were?"

"The heat was getting too strong, and no—" Delacroix raised his hand. "It was not that I feared being thought a spy, although I did have a suspicion when Ingram began to take an interest in my affairs. Yes, of course I knew he was having me followed. I have my sources too. The heat was on because I dug in too deep. I'm all rolled up, Worthing. And with the unforgiving eyes of the ton already on me as someone who is of French ancestry, as you so graciously pointed out—never mind that I went to school with the rest of you and spent my entire life here, doing all but bleeding for this country—the debts were more than I could bear. I had to flee."

"If you're not spying . . . It's too much to believe." Stratford shook his head and eyed the leather satchel by Delacroix's plate. "The description, the motives."

"Motives!" Delacroix shot back. "When have my actions ever called into question my love for England? It's only my blood that calls it into question. But I was raised on English soil, studied in English schools, found a peerage in English clubs. There is no motive. When was this night you speak of where someone stole a paper from headquarters, to which I have no access, might I remind you?"

"It was May thirteenth when the rest of the ton was at Almack's. Everyone was there, except you. All the clues fit together."

"Ha. Almack's," Delacroix rejoined bitterly. "My voucher was revoked to that illustrious assembly. I went to play cards instead, and you can ask anyone at Boodle's whether I was there."

Stratford remained unconvinced, but he had enough doubt to pause again. "Everything points to you. Who else fits the description so well?"

Lord Delacroix sighed. "I do not like to embroil myself in the affairs of others, unless it's to save my own skin. But have you considered Mr. Braxsen?"

"Braxsen," Stratford said, puzzled, "but he would have no reason."

"No? Born the son of a French revolutionary who has sympathetic ties to Napoleon? Of course it's not well known. His mother's parents chose an English royalist for a husband, and Braxsen's father tried to direct the boy's thoughts into more proper English channels. But a mother's whispers go a long way in forming a boy's ideology."

"But he fought in the war," Stratford said. "He fought for us . . ." He stopped, remembering the details of his conversation with Braxsen. He wasn't keen to return to the Peninsula; he questioned his brother's death, even alluding to the fact that it came under suspicious circumstances. "Braxsen is of your height and coloring," he said slowly. "And he appeared at Almack's just before the doors closed." Suddenly, everything became clear.

Chapter Thirty-Eight

*S*tratford was now convinced Braxsen was his man, and he couldn't believe he'd missed it. Braxsen, always negative about his military career, had even tried to throw dust in Stratford's eyes by hinting that Delacroix was unsavory, simply for being French. He had been thoroughly taken in. He needed to let Ingram and Fitz know as soon as possible and get to Braxsen before he could pass on the information or disappear.

At the moment, he had more immediate matters at hand. Stratford took a step toward Delacroix. "Why Miss Daventry? Why bring her life into ruin?" He looked in Eleanor's direction, pained by what she'd had to suffer. "After this night's work, she may not have had the easiest future before her, but she's not a straw damsel."

Behind him, Eleanor made what sounded like a half-sob, and Delacroix gave a harsh laugh. "So you say. But as you can see, Worthing, she was eating her dinner as calmly as you please before you walked in here. So I'd say you're *de trop*, sir."

Stratford upended the table, sending it crashing into Lord Delacroix. He grabbed the *vicomte* by the neck, pulled him up, and punched him in the eye. Delacroix fell backward with a loud crash.

With Delacroix on the ground, Stratford rushed to Eleanor. "Have you suffered any ill?" Grabbing her arms with both hands, he urged, "Let me take you from here."

Shaking, she fell into his arms, and the sensation of holding her whole body against his nearly blindsided him. "I have suffered from no permanent harm. *Oh*—" she shrieked. "Behind you!"

Stratford whirled to see Delacroix standing with a sword in hand. The *vicomte* wasted no time before rushing toward Stratford, who had his own sword out of the scabbard in a matter of seconds. There was a mighty clash as the two came against each other, and Eleanor inched to the door, her wide eyes transfixed on the scene before her.

"Now we shall have it out," Stratford shouted, and he thrust his sword forward but was met with a parry. He removed himself out of the way before Delacroix could counter-attack. *Think*, he scolded himself viciously. *Don't react, think. Plan your moves ahead.* He now saw his opponent more clearly and scanned the room for things that could help or hinder his battle. There was the broken container with gravy on the floor next to the table. There was his drink that had spilled and formed a puddle. One chair down, one chair still upright. A sideboard that could be tilted . . .

Stratford began to fight in earnest. Swords clashed, again and again, without either opponent showing weakness. He blocked one thrust, but ineffectually, and felt a sting on his left arm. Eleanor covered her mouth with a gasp.

Knowing he would tire easily because of the wound, Stratford had to put a quick end to the fight. He drove his opponent backward with short, relentless thrusts of the blade until Delacroix was at the edge of the spilled gravy near the table. Just as he'd hoped, Delacroix stepped backward and slipped, causing his sword arm to drop instead of blocking the thrust. Stratford curled his blade around Delacroix's sword, sending it clattering across the floor, and he put the tip of his own sword to Lord Delacroix's neck.

"You are vanquished," Stratford said, his chest rising and falling as he caught his breath. Lord Delacroix had his hands half-raised in surrender, and he acknowledged this with a nod.

Stratford lowered his blade. He walked over to the table, eyes trained on Delacroix, and looked inside the leather satchel. There was nothing in it apart from a few bills and some jewelry. "I suggest you leave. Whether you go to France or back to London is one and the same to me. Just don't bandy about Miss Daventry's name, and I will stay out of your affairs."

Delacroix reached for his fallen sword as he stood, picked it up, and slid it back in the scabbard. He looked down and clucked in annoyance. "The gravy has stained my stockings, and I will not be able to change before the harbor. I present a shocking appearance." Stratford continued to hold him steadily in his gaze as the man came before Miss Daventry.

"*Je vous souhaite une bonne soirée, mademoiselle.*" Delacroix bowed in irony, and with a nod to Stratford, he was gone.

When the door from the private parlor opened to the taproom and Lord Delacroix made his exit, the noises of people drinking and talking resumed and the landlord rushed in. "Milord. Oh! . . . and broken crockery. Ours is a correct establishment, sir, and you've turned it on its end with your fight. Who will restore my reputation?"

Stratford was not in the humor for theatrics. "I will pay you for the damages. Now leave," he said, propelling the landlord to the door. When he had closed it behind him, he strode to where Eleanor was and pulled her hands in his.

She allowed him to hold them for only a moment before she noticed the blood. "Your arm," she said, and turning to the sideboard, she found a clean napkin to tie a bandage around it. "This will do until it can be looked at." Then she reached her hand up to his face, and her fingers feathered lightly on his cheek.

Stunned by the gentleness of her touch, Stratford was lulled by the spell she had cast over him. He wanted to speak—was loathe to leave her in any doubt of his feelings for her—but they must go. He did not want his proposal to come when she was in such a vulnerable position. She might one day doubt whether it was motivated by anything other than charity. And the longer they remained, alone and unmarried, the more risk of scandal attached to her name.

"I need to bring you back to London," he said. "I know not how to do this without exposing you to unnecessary criticism, but the safest bet is for me to take you to my house, where my sisters can see to your needs. And I'll speak with Lady Ingram in the morning."

Eleanor was shaking from head to foot and hoped it could not be seen. The turmoil of emotions she'd experienced—elation and relief when Lord Worthing walked into the room, fright from her near escape—all proved too much for her composure. Although the earl had reacted when she touched his face, leaning into her hand and closing his eyes, his emotions were now hidden, and she wondered if she had imagined them.

He helped Eleanor into the phaeton, her hand trembling in his, then climbed in on the other side before tossing a coin to the waiting postboy. He took the reins, and they were off. The carriage was so well-sprung, she was slowly able to relax and settle her thoughts as they sped over the country lane.

Neither spoke for some time, and Eleanor began to wonder if they would not exchange a single word on their entire trip to London. Was he angry with her for the scandal? No sooner had she had this unhappy reflection than he found his voice.

"I know you must be feeling some shock over the events of this evening, but these feelings will pass." Lord Worthing looked at her in the dark, and she met his gaze.

He turned to face forward again. "For the rest of my days, I will remember this evening. I will remember—" Lord Worthing stopped short. He swallowed, and when he continued, his voice caught. "—that I was on time to save you. I will remember that God granted me the answer to my prayer." He went silent and urged his horses to pick up their pace.

Eleanor looked forward too, a weight lifted. Never could she have imagined the evening would finish this way, that Lord Worthing would not hold the scandal against her, but instead would come rushing to save her from it. She felt the warmth emanating from his side, and she leaned into it.

They continued like that, the emotions seeming too weighted for words, and in what felt like a short time, they arrived in London proper and then his house in Cavendish Square. There was a lamp burning in the sitting room, its light visible through the shutters. He pulled on the reins, and the tired horses came to an obedient stop.

"Eleanor," he said, taking possession of her hand. "I will make everything right for you with Lady Ingram, and . . . with everyone."

Tears sprang to Eleanor's eyes. She had not expected them to come so long after the danger had been removed. It must have been the shock, but she thought that it might also come from this sprig of hope that refused to be dampened. Why hope should make one cry, she did not know.

"If Lady Ingram will receive me," she said, "I must thank her for her hospitality and beg her to overlook the events that occurred tonight. That is, if she believes you that I'm not at fault."

"She will believe me," Lord Worthing said grimly.

When they reached the front entrance, the butler was already there. Anna and Phoebe opened the door to the corridor and sprang out of the drawing room, Phoebe coming forward immediately. "Eleanor," she said, taking her in her arms. Eleanor's tears threatened again.

"Come," said Phoebe, "I will have Cook bring you a warm glass of milk. I've had the room made up for you next to mine, and there's a bath just waiting for the rest of the hot water to be brought."

Anna was rooted to her spot, but as Phoebe and Eleanor walked by, she said, "I'm glad Stratford was in time."

Eleanor turned to face her. "Thank you."

Stratford undressed slowly, conscious that Eleanor was just down the hall. He was dead with fatigue, and as such, his thoughts jumbled together. *I reached her in time. I reached her in time.* But he had been wrong about Delacroix's involvement. It wasn't like him to be wrong.

Still, Delacroix wasn't innocent. Stratford remembered how Eleanor had started out of her chair, relief written all over her face. And Delacroix, the scoundrel, thought to catch him unaware and put an end to him. He must have been desperate indeed. Did Delacroix think Stratford would try to stop his flight if it were just over debt? Or was his main intent to carry off his victim?

He put Delacroix from his mind. It was too late to ruminate over all this, and he needed to see Ingram first thing in the morning before going after Braxsen. Come to think of it, he'd better bring Major Fitzwilliam along as well. Fitz was fully involved and knew what he was about, though he had not seen through Braxsen either.

Stratford fell asleep, not thinking of Braxsen and Delacroix, but of amber-colored eyes that he hoped—once he had taken care of the urgent business—would be lifted to his, as she said the one word that mattered. *Yes.*

The next morning, Stratford woke too early to accomplish his mission directly. He would never be received at Ingram's house at this hour and might as well have breakfast first. He dressed carefully, wondering when he would see Eleanor that day and how she might be faring after her terrifying ordeal.

He had just sat down to breakfast when Anna walked in. Surveying him in silence, she chose a seat opposite him as the footman entered and set a pot of coffee by her side. She reached for a scone.

"You were successful," she observed. He nodded. She waited for him to say something, and when he didn't, she cut her scone in two and covered it with cream. "Is your Miss Daventry recovered from the shock, do you think?"

"She was unharmed when I found her in Delacroix's company, and I . . . convinced Lord Delacroix to continue to Dover without her. But no, I'm not certain she's fully recovered from the shock."

"So she's respectable then?" Anna asked, her face unusually grave.

He nodded, his throat tightening. "She was always respectable, Anna."

She took the implied rebuke in stride. "Stratford, I did a little investigating last night before we left the Skeffington house, and I believe it was Lord Delacroix who started the rumor."

Stratford nodded again. "With Judith."

"So you know," she said. "He was in conference with Judith, and from there she went from group to group until the entire room was abuzz with the news. But the damage was not done until she had conferred with Harriet Price, who gave *her* bit of information. I can only suppose that Harriet—who everyone knows missed the beginning of the Season because she broke out in *spots!*—has been holding on to this news for a particular occasion where, I suspect, she could do the most damage. She really is a spiteful cat."

Stratford looked at his sister curiously. "Anna, if I didn't know better, I might think you are in support of Eleanor, which would be a most peculiar thing inasmuch that you don't bestow your affection on anyone without a hard-won battle."

Anna smiled at this, but replied, "It's just not fair that society can ruin the reputation of a perfectly decent young lady on the whim of two or three who have no attributes to their name but their own spite. It so happens I have proof Harriet Price is not the innocent maiden she lets on because she was foolish enough to carry on in the shrubbery with John Fortescue at Vauxhall Gardens—and no, dear brother, I was not there, nor will I tell you from whom I had my information.

"Until now I never thought to be so cruel as to expose her. But she has thrown down the gauntlet, and I will eat my hat if, after a little chat with her, she does not publicly acknowledge her mistake about what she thought she saw that night. And once Harriet capitulates, Judith must do so as well or look stupid. So yes, I'm willing to champion your Eleanor."

She looked smug. "We both know it's *your* Eleanor, you know. You'll just have to convince her to overlook your shortcomings."

"Spoken like a sister," Stratford said, standing. He went over and kissed her on the cheek. "But you are perfectly right. I will beg her hand as many times as is necessary."

"Beg her forbearance first," advised Anna.

Stratford gave a tired smile. "I'll try my luck with Lady Ingram to see if she'll come around once she knows the facts."

"Don't betray Lydia!" his sister broke in to say.

"What kind of fellow do you take me for? If I can get her to come around, I'm sure we can scotch the scandal." Stratford had his hand on the doorknob when Anna spoke.

"If I know Lady Ingram, she will not come around. However, I am not without my own influence. You laugh," Anna said, "but it's true! See if I don't turn this thing to good account. Phoebe has Eleanor well in hand here. Leave the rest to me."

Chapter Thirty-Nine

Upon arriving at Grosvenor Square, Stratford announced he had pressing news for Lord Ingram and ran up the steps to his room. Ingram, lying on a chaise lounge by the window, turned his head when Stratford burst through the door.

"You're back," Ingram said. "Fitz sent word. Did you retrieve Miss Daventry? What did you do with Delacroix? I hope he's in custody."

"Delacroix's not our man." Stratford walked to the window. "Braxsen is."

"What?" Ingram moved as if to rise from his chair and made an impatient gesture when he realized his handicap. His gaze didn't quit Stratford's face. "Impossible. I've known him nearly all my life. What has he to gain?"

"Apparently, he sympathizes with the emperor. His mother is French, did you know? But more than that we cannot comprehend until we bring him in." Stratford shrugged. "The purposes of a man's heart are deep."

"I remember hearing something about his mother, but it was never a thing that mattered." Ingram scowled. "It's enough for him to turn, is it? Where's Fitz? We must not waste a moment."

Stratford paced to the window and looked out. "I'll go after him. It's still early, and I imagine he's at Steven's. But I must have an interview with your mother first."

Ingram blew out his breath. "I'm sorry, Stratford. I don't think she will change her mind about Miss Daventry. But I will stand by the girl no matter what happens."

"Thank you." Stratford walked toward the door and put his hand on the knob. "I'll keep you apprised as soon as we have Braxsen in hand."

Lady Ingram received Stratford alone in the morning room, preempting anything he was going to say with, "Stratford, my dear, I know why you've come. Lydia has confessed the whole, and I see that I have grossly misjudged Miss Daventry."

"I'm glad to hear you say it, ma'am. I was hoping she might find a home with you here to finish her Season and quiet the scandalmongers. She's with my sisters now."

"Bring her here?" Lady Ingram exclaimed. "Eleanor cannot come here. She's in disgrace with the ton—never mind that it's through no fault of her own—she will not be received anywhere."

"I was hoping she might be received here," Stratford insisted. "You know Miss Daventry is not to blame. Surely if you take her in, the others will have no choice but to accept her back into society."

"Then you know nothing of the ton, Stratford. They do not forget so easily, I assure you. I can do nothing of the kind. Conjecture may be aimed at my Lydia—" She looked up as the damsel herself walked in, saving Stratford from uttering an ill-timed remark.

"Stratford!" Lydia's face had the suspicion of tears, but all obvious traces were removed. She looked from Stratford's controlled expression to her mother's implacable one. "Have you found Eleanor?"

"Yes, she's with Anna and Phoebe now, but I had hoped she might stay here . . ."

"Oh yes, please, Mama. You know she must have a home with us to be reestablished in society. We must show that *we* don't believe everything the rumors say. Especially since we know they are not true." Lydia crossed the room to her mother and sat, leaning forward with pleading eyes.

"It's too late for that, my dear, as I was telling Stratford. If we take her in, we will be scorned as well. I'll not take that risk with you not yet married."

"Never mind that, Mama. You *know* I'm going to marry Major Fitzwilliam. And if my brother has given his approval, there is no reason to think it will not happen."

"Anything can happen in a six-month engagement. You might find you change your mind." Lady Ingram shot a look at Stratford as if she hoped he would be the one to do it.

Not wishing to get further embroiled in what he foresaw would be a dispute between mother and daughter, Stratford made one last attempt. "Surely I can persuade you to reconsider. We present a united front, spreading it about that she went off to visit her aunt for a week or two until things die down, but insist the accusations against her are groundless. The best way to prove this is by accepting her into your home."

"That is something I cannot do." Lady Ingram pinched her lips together. "I'm sorry. The girl will have to find her own way in life. She's resourceful. I'm sure she'll go on very well with her own sort. She was never meant to be more than a companion for Lydia."

"Ma*ma*!" cried Lydia, leaping to her feet. "She is a gentleman's daughter."

At this Stratford stood. "If you will not help me, I'll not waste any more of your time. I must take care of urgent business, and then I will go to Eleanor."

"Mind, she will not stay here," exclaimed Lady Ingram. "Where do you plan to put her?"

"I'll retire to Grillon's, and my sisters will welcome her in Cavendish Square until the wedding. If I'm able to win her hand, as I hope to do, she'll have a rightful place in our household as my affianced wife!" With these words, Stratford took his leave.

Major Fitzwilliam was just leaving the hotel when Stratford pulled up in his phaeton. "Fitz," he called out. "If you have a moment . . ."

The major darted to the carriage and put his hand on the horse's bridle. "Were you successful?"

"Yes," Stratford said, in a curt tone, still angry from his interview with Lady Ingram. "Please, climb up. We have pressing business, and I'll need your help."

After putting Fitz in possession of the facts, they agreed to pick up a hack and one of the hired men. Stratford would proceed alone to Braxsen's rooms, and Fitz would stay downstairs in case Braxsen decided to bolt. When they arrived at Braxsen's place, his man tried to keep Stratford out, but he pushed his way into the dining room, where he found Braxsen seated at the breakfast table, a stack of corded trunks against the wall.

Mr. Braxsen stood. "What's this, Worthing? I told Griggs I wasn't receiving anyone."

"I'm afraid this isn't a social call, Braxsen." Stratford stood at the entrance, his two hands resting on the cane that held his sword. Mr. Braxsen fidgeted with the napkin and then dropped to his chair.

"You may as well sit," Mr. Braxsen said, minus his usual urbane tone. "Griggs, please bring another tankard for Lord Worthing." Turning to the earl, he said, "Unless you'd rather have coffee."

"I've come from Longfield," Stratford said.

There was a pause before Mr. Braxsen attempted a jovial tone. "Why, whatever were you doing there? Fleeing London? I've seen you at Boodle's. Are you swimming in the River Tick?" He took a sip and set the tankard down with a barely perceptible tremor in his hand.

"I've been chasing Lord Delacroix," Stratford replied. He tapped his cane on the ground. This was the part he had to handle delicately. There must be no mention of Miss Daventry.

Mr. Braxsen raised an eyebrow. "Lord Delacroix, indeed! Longfield, you say? Whatever was he doing on his way to Dover?"

"I believed him to be spying for France," Stratford said. He watched Braxsen under hooded eyelids to see how he would respond.

"That would not surprise me in the least." Mr. Braxsen gave a weak laugh. "I've always thought he was too smoky by half." He watched the earl with wary eyes. "But what this all has to do with me that you would barge in here at this ungodly hour is beyond my ability to fathom."

"I was mistaken in Delacroix." Stratford pierced Mr. Braxsen with his gaze. "He's not spying for France. You are."

Mr. Braxsen remained motionless at the accusation. Only his fidgeting with the salt cellar betrayed his agitation. Without warning, he leapt to his feet, grabbing the knife by the side of his plate, and lunged at the earl's chest. Stratford, who had been anticipating such a move, darted to the side as Mr. Braxsen plunged forward into empty air. Stratford swiveled and grabbed him by the forearm, forcing Braxsen's arm that held the knife downward. He rammed the arm with the knife against the table until Mr. Braxsen released the weapon, and it clattered to the floor.

"Fitz," Stratford shot out. In mere seconds, the major rushed into the room to find Stratford holding Braxsen face down on the table with his arm behind his back.

"What took you so long?" Stratford said, between his teeth.

"Looks like you have it all well under control," the major answered, his face grim as he surveyed the culprit. He grabbed Mr. Braxsen's other arm. "Let's go, Braxsen. I'm as sorry as can be to see you're the author of this. The carriage awaits to take you to Newgate."

When Mr. Braxsen was hauled to his feet, he said, "I demand you release me and allow me to walk to the carriage like a gentleman, without being restrained."

Stratford replied, "You lost that privilege when you began spying. A gentleman is not a traitor."

"What is this spying I'm to have done? What is the proof you have against me? Tell me that, at least." Mr. Braxsen's face was livid, nothing like his usual look of indolence.

"The leaks on the campaign trail always came from your regiment. And it's only since you've returned to London that there has been a spike in stolen intelligence going back to the Peninsula. You were late meeting the riding party the morning Ingram was attacked, and you showed up late to Almack's the night of headquarters' break-in."

Fitz had begun the charge, but Stratford finished it for him. "We thought it was Delacroix. You've been clever in hiding your tracks and throwing the scent his way. But I've spoken to the man and can vouch for his innocence. You, however, cannot prove yours. What's more to the point—" Stratford reached into the front pocket of Braxsen's coat and pulled out an envelope containing the half-page inventory stolen from headquarters. He waved it in his face. "*That's* all the proof we need to bring you in."

Mr. Braxsen looked sullen and somewhat fearful. "Allow me to . . ." He yanked an arm away and arranged his neckcloth so it was straight. He tugged on his shirt collars to pull the coat back in place and examined himself in the glass to verify that his hairstyle was not overly disordered. "You may proceed," he said when all these operations were performed.

They walked past the stunned servant, down the stairs to where the carriage was waiting, each man holding one of Braxsen's arms. Major Fitzwilliam got in the hack first, and Stratford shoved Braxsen next before climbing in himself. He tapped on the roof of the carriage, and they began to ramble down the street.

"Tell me this," demanded Stratford. "Why? Your situation and mine were the same when we went into war. We both came from gentlemen's families with the same education. What caused you to turn against your country like that?"

Stratford almost thought he wouldn't answer until Mr. Braxsen said, "My mother spoke of the noble Bonaparte from the cradle, and my profligate father did nothing to alter my views. We were particularly close, my mother and I, and when I went to Eton, I was prepared to hate everyone but found I liked it, enough even to get swept up in the call to arms a year after my younger brother. *He* was passionately devoted to the cause, not having the same training my mother gave me. I followed him to war, aiming to keep an eye on him, but he was such a devoted fool. He obeyed the officers' every whim and went wherever they said to go. And, you see, it eventually led to his death.

"After I found him far from the scene of battle, I sought out one of his fellow soldiers. He said Robert had been ordered to bring a message from the officer to one of the demi-monde whose house bordered the field of battle on one side. That was what he died for. Not for his country. For an officer's mistress. What kind of country is this?" Mr. Braxsen spat on the floor of the carriage.

"But you will die for your betrayal," Stratford said, disbelief and sadness fighting for dominance. "You need only turn what you see to good account. We're all faced with things in society we find intolerable. As citizens we must take action against injustice and leave behind greater order. That is our mark in the world."

Braxsen looked out the window. "I do not care if I die. I don't belong here. I don't belong in France. There is no place for me in this world, and I may as well quit it sooner rather than later."

Stratford shared a look with Major Fitzwilliam, then turned and watched the dark clouds roll in what promised to be a big summer storm. It looked as bleak as he felt.

Chapter Forty

*E*leanor woke in a strange bed, well after the breakfast hour. It took her a minute to remember what had happened and where she was. She was clean from her bath the night before, and hungry. From her vantage point, she could see a dress hanging on the back of the door that was not hers. Perhaps Phoebe had left it for her.

Despite the goodness of the gesture and their welcome last night, Eleanor was conscious of her precarious place in the household. As one who was not a relation, and who had been thrown out of the home where she'd expected to stay for the entirety of the Season, and all because of scandal, it was best to remain transient.

Until Eleanor knew Lord Worthing's intentions, she could not accept her place in the home and dared not even accept the dress. Instead, she slipped on her gown from the night before and with it, a film of dirt that had more to do with association than real filth.

There was a knock on the door, and a maid entered, carrying a cup of hot chocolate and two pieces of buttered bread. "Good day, miss. Cook asked me to bring this to you, saying as you might not be bold enough to ring." She set the platter on the small table and rushed over to help Eleanor button her dress in the back.

"Thank you." Eleanor sat on the chair near the small table, grateful for the cook's thoughtfulness. "Where is Lord Worthing? And his sisters?"

"My lord left early this morning and has not come back," the maid said. "Miss Anna has gone on a visit, and Miss Phoebe has set out for the market." The maid bobbed a curtsy. "Will that be all, miss?"

Eleanor nodded, a thread of worry marring any joy she might otherwise take in a much-needed breakfast and the cozy surroundings. Everyone had gone on with their lives, and she? Her life was not here. Eleanor forced herself to eat the bread and drink the chocolate, but it settled poorly in her stomach.

Two hours passed with no sounds coming from outside her bedroom, and Eleanor began to doubt her welcome. It started with only a seed—a seed that was nurtured by silence and no contact from the outside world. If she had been important to Lord Worthing, he would be here this morning to make her feel welcome. Or he would send his sisters if he had important business to attend to. He must have rescued her as a gentleman only—on the basis of her connection to his uncle—and not as a lover.

Sighing, Eleanor reflected that the room would feel like a prison before long, as her lack of a rightful place in it began to take on increasing proportion. Whatever could she do? She had no trunk, little money . . . It took only a moment's reflection.

Gathering her shawl and reticule, Eleanor opened the door to the hallway. Lydia would surely help her if only Eleanor could get word to her. Not a soul was in sight as she descended the stairs, and at the landing, she looked at the row of wooden doors that stretched down the hallway behind her. Dare she open them without knowing where they led or whether someone was behind them?

To her relief, the butler exited a room, and upon spotting her, came quickly. "Miss, how may I help?"

Eleanor smiled at him. "If you would bring me to the morning room and provide me with a pen and ink, I should be grateful to send word to Lord Ingram's house."

"Of course, miss. If you'll follow me." The morning room was a cheerful shade of yellow with one large window overlooking the wet street. She noted the warm colors, but the empty room was made bleak by the thundering rain outside that had yet to show signs of letting up. Collins opened the drawer in the escritoire and pulled out a paper and pen. The inkpot was full. "I will have your letter sent as soon as you're finished, miss."

"Thank you." Eleanor took a seat at the desk and dipped the perfectly trimmed pen into the inkwell.

Lydia,

I must go to my aunt in Bath. I have enough money for the stagecoach to take me there, but I will need to have my trunk sent. Will you have the goodness to send it under the care of Mrs. Renly on Abbey Street?

I remain most affectionately yours,

Eleanor

The next letter was more difficult, and she paused to think before attempting it.

Lord Worthing,

You have been kind and generous throughout my stay in London, and I'm most grateful for your friendship, and for the rescue you performed last night. I'm afraid I cannot trespass upon your goodness, or that of your sisters, any longer. I have taken the coach to Bath to join my aunt.

She dipped the pen and blotted the ink before continuing.

Please convey my deepest respect and gratitude to your sisters, and know that I am, hereafter,

Yours,

Eleanor Daventry

Sealing both letters, Eleanor left the drawing room and handed them to the butler, who waited outside the door. "This one is for Miss Lydia Ingram, and the other . . . Would you kindly give it to Lord Worthing?"

She tied the bonnet under her chin, feeling at once overdressed and shabby in last night's apparel, and held the reticule in her arm. As she reached the door, Collins stopped before opening it. "Shall I not call a conveyance for you, miss? I believe Lord Worthing would prefer it."

Eleanor was about to refuse but decided it would be better to swallow her pride. It would do her reputation no good to be seen, unescorted, walking through town in the rain, and especially after last night's scandal. *Was it only last night?* "I would be most grateful. I must go to the stagecoach," she said.

"Very well, miss. I will have the carriage brought around and have a maid accompany you there." Eleanor nodded her approval and waited by the door, not knowing whether she wished her flight to be intercepted or not.

Stratford arrived late afternoon, as the worst of the rainstorm settled into a drizzle. He contemplated how soon he might propose to Eleanor, imagined various scenarios, the best of which was her throwing herself into his arms. He was anxious to see her in the flesh after what seemed like an interminable day. What could he say to get her to accept his suit this time? He was nearly certain she returned his regard, but he could not know for sure until the words were out and he had his response.

It was not as if his record were flawless. Never in the history of proposals had anyone bungled one so badly as he had the first time, of that he was sure. The minute he walked through the door, Anna and Phoebe pounced on him.

"Finally!"

"Stratford, you must go at once. Collins says Eleanor has gone to the stagecoach. Here is her letter."

With an oath, Stratford grabbed it at once and perused its contents. "I may yet have time before it leaves London," he said. "Collins, have my other team brought around. No, never mind. I will go myself."

His horses were harnessed in no time, and he swung up on the seat, leading them toward the stagecoach. Cursing under his breath at the delay, he threaded his way through the streets as quickly as the other carriages would allow, arriving at the station just as people were piling into the lumbering equipage. He handed his reins to a boy and leapt down. *I'm just in time!*

When he looked inside the coach, then on top, and even inside the taproom, Eleanor was nowhere to be found. "When did the last one leave for Bath?" he asked the man at the tap.

"An hour ago, sir."

Reining in his frustration, he tossed a coin to the man and strode to the phaeton, climbed up and clicked to spur his horses. If he were lucky, he would overtake them not far outside London.

As soon as Stratford quit the teeming London streets, the incessant rain stopped, and the fresh air allowed him time to think. What had possessed her to leave without waiting to see him? Whatever he did, he must win her heart. He must convince her it was not too late, that there was hope for them. Eyes narrowed and jaw clenched, he picked his way across the mud, going through, over and over again, what he must say.

A short distance ahead there was a bend in the road, and as soon as he rounded it, he stopped short. There, in front of him, was the stagecoach, all its passengers on the side of the road and the strongest men attempting to push the coach from where the wheel had gotten stuck in one of the deep ruts.

Eleanor, drenched from head to toe, turned her head at the sound of Stratford's carriage, and her eyes widened. "My lord," she said, shock evident on her features when he pulled up, and he thought he saw a flash of hope.

"Please, get in, Miss Daventry." Without waiting for a response, Stratford climbed down and assisted her to alight. Her hand sent a shock through him as helped her climb into the phaeton. *I must not lose her.*

He steered the horses to the side and turned his vehicle in the grass that bordered the road, then took off at a clipping pace, leaving the coach and crowd of people behind. Neither said a word as he drove, but when he rounded the bend and saw the empty road stretch before him, he reined in slowly and steered the phaeton into a clearing off to the side. Alighting, he looped the reins around the branch of the nearest tree and walked to her side of the carriage, holding his hand up. "Miss Daventry, we must talk."

Eleanor was swirling with emotions. She'd been focused only on remaining strong until she reached Bath, where she would have all the time she required to sift through her thoughts. That is, once she had found a way to explain to her aunt how she came to be in such a predicament. The thought made her ill.

Privately, she'd need to acknowledge the hopes she'd had of a life with Lord Worthing and grieve its loss. She must come to terms with whatever place she'd have in society and surrender to repercussions she had perhaps not yet thought of. She would have to decide how to proceed in earning her living and discover what could be done about an inheritance in the case where there was no husband. What she didn't expect was to have Lord Worthing come after her. He had *come*.

Placing her hand in his, Eleanor stepped down, her soaked dress clinging to her legs. Her knees were so weak, she nearly stumbled, but Lord Worthing caught her and held her, slow to remove his hand from around her waist. Finally, he released her, placed her hand on his arm, and indicated ahead. "Let us follow the path to those trees."

They began walking, and he cleared his throat. "You left."

She darted a glance his way before answering. "I needed to leave, my lord. I couldn't be a charge upon you and your sisters any longer."

He stopped and turned to her, his expression bordering on anger. "Why, in heaven's name, did you think you were a *charge* upon us, Eleanor?"

She did not know how it could be that, in face of his anger, what she'd feel was elation. But the joy and hope at hearing her name on his lips nearly suffocated her. Her voice was faint as she answered. "You did not come this morning. Your sisters did not come."

Lord Worthing started walking again, and she followed. "I was bringing Jonathon Braxsen to justice, the only thing that could have kept me from your side. My sisters were busy making calls at every residence in London in an effort to clear your name. We were not there because we could not be."

Oh. She had not been forgotten then. But perhaps . . . perhaps his was simply an exaggerated sense of chivalry. Eleanor had to reassure him that she would be fine, so that he would feel under no obligation. "You needn't have feared for me," she said. "My aunt will take me in. And I've sent a letter to Lydia asking for her to send my trunk."

At the mention of Lydia, Lord Worthing exhaled, his voice tight with frustration. "Lady Ingram will not welcome you back."

It was just as she'd dreaded. "I did not expect it," Eleanor said. Then, her heart frozen with fear, "And Lydia?"

"Lydia, I'm happy to say, is not of the same mind, but she cannot thwart her mother while living in her brother's house." Lord Worthing sought her gaze. "I believe she will make every effort to keep the connection. That is," he said, "if you wish it."

"Oh, I most certainly do. Lydia is my best friend." *Indeed,* Eleanor thought, *except for you, my only friend.*

"If I know Lydia," he continued, "she means to do more than correspond. She means to visit you. Her mother may dictate who stays in her household, but Lydia will dictate whom she befriends."

"Of this I'm sure." Eleanor sighed. "But I haven't decided where I'll go next. I own that I'd been hoping for Lady Ingram to acknowledge me because it will be easier to find a position if she sponsors me. Now I have no one to recommend—"

Lord Worthing did not let her finish. "Will you not consider marriage?"

Eleanor was amazed she could continue to put one foot in front of the other with such trembling. *How am I supposed to respond to such a question when he has not made me a proper offer?* With a shaky breath, she answered, "No one has asked me, sir."

Lord Worthing looked startled and gave a strangled laugh. "No? I have it on good authority that you've received *no less* than three proposals, ma'am."

Shocked, Eleanor could feel heat stealing up her cheeks. That he would know about the other proposals . . . that he would reference his own at such a time!

"My lord . . ."

"Please. Let us be done with 'my lord.' " Lord Worthing turned suddenly, her hand still tucked in the crook of his arm. "Will you not call me Stratford?"

She stopped short, her heart beating so loudly she was sure he could hear it.

"Eleanor." When she lifted her eyes to his, Stratford took a deep breath. "You once said you wanted to marry for love. I . . . I have an unfortunate way with speech, but I promise you I do love you." Stratford shook his head then, displaying an apologetic smile. "My words may be inadequate—in fact, I know I've made a wretched botch of it. But if you'll have me, I promise I'll spend the rest of my life *showing* you just how much I love you."

When she didn't respond, he took hold of her hands, his voice pleading. "Miss Eleanor Daventry," he began, formally, with eyes that refused to let hers look away, "I, Stratford Joseph Tunstall, the Fifth Earl of Worthing, hereby present myself—*sober*—that I might beg you to accept my hand in marriage."

The earnest look on his face was unbearable, and Eleanor's mouth tugged upward as joy ballooned in her chest. Vague awareness teased her consciousness, that though theirs had not been an instant or easy connection, the ties were no less strong. From the beginning, these inexplicable bonds had drawn them together—this, despite their own resolution to the contrary. Those same bonds would let them weather any storm.

Unable to keep him on pins and needles any longer—not that she needed any time to decide—Eleanor raised her eyes to his. And with words that were whispered more than spoken, she answered: "Yes, Stratford. I think I shall."

The earl let out a *whoop*! He picked her up by her waist, swinging her around once, laughing, until he set her down, and her wet skirts clung once again to her legs. The only sound around them was the raindrops that fell as the wind whispered through the birch leaves. Stratford reached up to take her face in both hands, holding her captive in his gaze.

"This, my love, is one of the ways in which I will show you." He leaned down and kissed her as Eleanor's mind whirled, and her knees went weak. Only his hands on her arms kept her upright. *This!* she thought, *This is what love feels like.*

As Eleanor melted into him, Stratford wrapped one arm around her waist and his other around her shoulders to pull her as close as possible in his embrace. Just as he was about to get lost in the kiss, he broke away, breathing hard. *I must not forget my surroundings. I have time enough to make her my wife.* He settled for pushing back her bonnet so he might lean his forehead against hers, his fingers caressing her cheeks.

And because that was not enough to tame these lofty feelings that were swirling around him and threatening to make him do some very great thing, he whispered, "*I love you, I love you, I love you . . .*"

About the Author

Photo by Caroline Aoustin

Jennie Goutet is an American-born Anglophile who lives with her French husband and their three children in a small town outside Paris. Her imagination resides in Regency England, where her regency romances are set. Jennie is author of the award-winning memoir *Stars Upside Down* and the modern romances *A Sweetheart in Paris* and *A Noble Affair*. A Christian, a cook, and an inveterate klutz, Jennie writes about faith, food, and life—even the clumsy moments—on her blog, aladyinfrance.com. You can learn more about Jennie and her books on her author website, jenniegoutet.com.

Scan to visit

jenniegoutet.com   aladyinfrance.com

What the best-selling second book in this series has to offer . . .

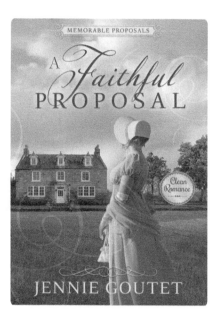

Despite his worry that Miss Tunstall may have sustained serious harm, Harry strove to resist the urge to smile at her headstrong, albeit misjudged, determination. The urge proved too strong for him, however, what with the giddiness of his wildly beating heart and his head swimming from an attraction that felt about as pleasant as being hit by lightning. The corners of his mouth crept into a grin. *I might faint dead away myself.*

"How fortunate that my situation affords you some amusement," Miss Tunstall said with a quizzical look.

Harry instantly sobered. "I assure you, I find no humor in your situation. Well," he added, conscientiously, "only a very little, and it is more at myself. My only concern is that you might be made comfortable. And I could see you were a trifle pale to allow for sitting on the bench beside me. However, let me adjust the coat to provide more cushion while you are seated." He did so, adding, "I would remove my neckcloth too, if I thought it could provide enough padding to protect your head to make up for the lack of delicacy. But I'm afraid it won't, so we will ride slowly."

Miss Tunstall allowed herself to be seated with her back to the driver's seat, his coat behind her to provide some support. When she was thus positioned, she adjusted her skirt to cover her ankles.

"If only you were sporting the toggery of a London gentleman, we might have fabricated even a hammock from the cravat. I now see the disadvantages of country life, for you are wearing only a paltry neckcloth."

Harry had as yet to move from her side, and he threw back his head and laughed. When she raised her clear eyes to his and he saw the answering gleam of fun, Harry knew the end to his bachelor days had come. He was done for.